SWEET SACRIFICE

King's Trace Antiheroes Book Three

SAV R. MILLER

To the fear of the unknown.

May we one day conquer you.

"You can sacrifice and not love. But you cannot love and not sacrifice."
– Kris Vallotton

Sweet Sacrifice is the third and final book in the King's Trace Antiheroes series. It can be read as a standalone, however, reading the first two books in the series may enhance the reading experience.

As always, this book contains triggers and dark themes that may not be suitable for all audiences. I'm going to go out on a limb here and say that if you **have any triggers at all,** this book probably isn't for you.

Reader discretion advised.

CHAPTER ONE

Fiona

The Montaltos are a staple in King's Trace, a fixture achieved through force and intimidation.

They run our little town in Maine, although if you asked random passersby on the cobblestone streets downtown, the unspoken truth would somehow bleed out—that, while the Montalto family *seems* to run this place, the Ivers are the historical and financial backbone of the community.

We have fingers in every pie, from organized crime to generational wealth, with the added benefit of being reclusive

My family lives in a gothic mansion, more haunted castle than home, on an isolated stretch of land away from prying eyes and outstretched hands, though that hardly keeps the evil at bay.

Our ghosts roam the narrow halls and embed themselves into the rare hardwood flooring, holding each of us hostage as we continue our communal living. My older brother Kieran stays because he's afraid, too paranoid for his own good that our late brother's watching him from the afterlife, waiting for the perfect moment to strike.

Considering their history and how things went down between them, I suppose it's not entirely out of the question, although he's certainly adopted more than a few of our ailing mother's oddities.

It's honestly a wonder that either of them leave the house at all. Especially for such a public function; one hosted by my parents, where we're seated at the front of the ballroom, privy to every single prolonged stare and whispered conversation across the circular tables.

And even though I know they're not really talking about *me* — because on the scale of interesting Ivers family members, I rank fantastically low — it's hard not to wither beneath the weight of the scrutiny.

Especially when Kieran and our mother excuse themselves from the table, leaving me to leer at Elia Montalto as he spins his pregnant wife around the dance floor, while I try my best not to drool over my brother's best friend seated next to me.

Reaching into my pink Valentino clutch, I dig out a piece of *Hubba Bubba* and unwrap the gum, popping it into my mouth as I continue my perusal, desperately trying to ignore the cologne wafting from my side. It's rich, something clean and bold and *sweet*, intoxicating like the first drag of a menthol cigarette, and I squeeze my legs together in an attempt to relieve my core of its pulse.

Elia, the capo of the Montalto outfit and owner of the arts center where we're having the fundraiser, dips his wife back; she stretches in his arms, her golden hair falling from her slim shoulders in a delicate waterfall, her navy blue gown pulling tight against the swell of her belly.

Longing pools in my gut, twisting with envy, though it's not particularly directed at either of them—more so the complete adoration in Elia's eyes as he swings Caroline back into a standing position, like she makes up every single piece of his heart.

It's the kind of look my father gives my mother, even after almost thirty years of marriage, three kids, and a whole lot of evil deeds in between. The kind she returns, in spite of everything my father's done and who he is, although sometimes I wonder if she even remembers the majority of his crimes.

Tearing my gaze away from the newlyweds, I chew the gum lodged between my teeth, trying to ignore the itch to fix the floral centerpiece at the middle of our table; one of the white roses has drooped, pulling away from the rest of the flowers as if it simply can't withstand the pressure.

I reach out anyway, the tightness in my chest winning over the logic in my head that says fixing the flower will bear no real consequence in the grand scheme of things. But damn, if it doesn't send a flood of relief through me when it's erect and back in line with the others.

"Thank God, that was bugging the shit out of me."

Freezing at the first words to come from our table in half an hour, I shift, sneaking a glance from the corner of my eye at Boyd Kelly, unsure if the sentence was my imagination or not.

My brother's best friend rarely speaks, and certainly never to me—in fact, after seven years of him being a quiet, mysterious fixture in our lives, I'd decided to comfort myself with the fact that I'm very likely invisible to the twenty-seven-year-old.

Though he's never been anything *but* to me.

"You know, I can see you looking at me," he says, his voice low and raspy, like he's been quiet for so long, his vocal cords have forgotten how to work properly. "Peripheral glances are not at *all* discreet."

Anxiety washes over me, and I place my gum between my teeth, blowing through the hole I make with my tongue. The bubble pops against my lips as I turn slightly, meeting his deep hazel gaze, somehow seeming to glow beneath the gold material of his Colombina mask.

My own mask, also a gold Colombina since my parents insisted we all match at the masquerade fundraiser, sits on the table beside my clutch, collecting dust.

I lick my lips, searching for gum residue, my heart in my throat. If having strangers' eyes on me was nerve-racking, having Boyd Kelly's undivided attention is panic inducing.

My nerves pull tight, my stomach flip-flopping when his stare momentarily drops to my lips, then further, swallowing the sight of my cleavage pressed against the emerald gown I'm wearing.

His throat bobs, the tattoos lining his skin dancing with the motion, and his eyes snap back to mine, pupils dilated slightly.

Probably not enough for the average person to notice, but I've spent an ungodly amount of time studying everything about this man, from pictures online to stolen glances at family dinners, that I'd be blind not to notice the change.

I just can't quite place the *why*. Boyd's practically a god in his own right—tragically handsome, with honey blond hair he keeps slicked back with some kind of product, a jawline you could commit suicide on, and ink etched into every visible inch of his skin—maybe even the not visible parts.

He's mysterious, keeping the details of his past under wraps and preferring his own company to that of others'.

Not to mention, as one of the top cyber security engineers at my father's firm, he's got to be at least moderately wealthy.

The perfect specimen, by all surface-level accounts, and way out of my league. Especially given the busty date pounding champagne flutes next to him, with her long black hair and massive tits. That he's even giving me an ounce of attention when he brought her here confuses me.

"Um," I say, pinching my eyes closed as the filler word leaves my mouth. When I open them again, I aim for nonchalance. "That's... awkward. I didn't know you could tell when someone side-eyes you."

Nerves tangle in my chest as I consider how many times I've thought I was watching him discreetly, when really he's probably known all along. *Kill me now.*

Boyd smirks, his pink lips curving up at the corners. "Learn something new every day."

I steal a glance around the table, watching his date, Melanie, as she continues plying herself with alcohol, as if that might distract from the fact that she's higher than a kite.

The rest of the seats are empty, my father across the room speaking to the older patriarch of the Montalto family. Kieran and our mother appear at the far end of the ballroom where the hall leads to the restrooms and other various areas of the arts center.

My brother stays close to her side as they weave through the crowd, his tall frame towering over hers.

Other than their electric green eyes, you'd hardly be able to guess that they're related; his dark brown hair curls at the ends, his limbs long and lined with lean muscles, where her hair is the same dark red as mine, her body petite and frail.

She no longer really looks like any of us, the twitch beneath her eye symbolizing a disease that's been ravaging her body for the last few years.

But the harsh stare, the one that's a little *too* focused, designed to hide our suffering—that's our family trait.

Heat sears my bare shoulder, and I turn my head to see Boyd leaning across Kieran's empty seat into me, his dark gray suit setting my skin on fire where it brushes my flesh.

God, he looks *sinful* in a suit.

"How much do you want to bet that Mel passes out before your brother steals her away from me tonight?"

Looking at her as she swipes her hand across her mouth, I refrain from making a face. "You think he'll take your *date*?"

Reaching for the glass tumbler on the table in front of him, he shrugs. "Probably. She's here for him, anyway, and I'm only here because Murphy was supposed to take her."

At the mention of my late older brother, my stomach deflates, a balloon of acid souring the elation caused by Boyd's proximity.

"She couldn't have gone with Kieran?"

"I don't know if you've noticed, but your brother's been a little preoccupied lately."

One long, inked finger points across the room, a direct line to a blonde girl I wouldn't recognize if not for the amount of times I've seen her get blackout drunk on social media or the shit storm that came out about her senator father a year ago.

Juliet Harrison stands against the white wall in a silky black dress that clings to her curves, the material making her skin glow as her blue eyes stay trained on her sister and brother-in-law.

She looks immeasurably sad, like the entire weight of the universe somehow rests on her shoulders, and I can't help wondering what the sister-in-law of a capo has to worry about.

Guilt flares in my stomach as that thought flashes across my mind, a reminder that anyone could think the exact same thing about me if they didn't care to look hard enough.

As Kieran and our mother approach the table, I watch my brother cast a quick glance over his shoulder, as if ensuring the object of his affection is in the same spot he left her; he slides into the seat on my other side as Boyd retreats, cold air filling the space where his body was.

I blow another bubble, letting it smack loud enough to startle my mother, who sends me a *look*. Ignoring her, I glare at Kieran. "I knew you'd try to sneak off before the night was over."

He adjusts the lapels of his black suit, reaching to take a sip from his wine glass. "You smell like smoke. Seems all the Ivers kids are prone to breaking promises."

My eyes widen, sliding frantically to our mother to see if she heard that quip. Luckily, she's lost in the soft jazz music coming from the band on stage and not paying us any mind. "I'm sorry we can't all exercise the utmost control over our addictions."

"You just lack adequate willpower."

The temptation to scream at him that he doesn't know what he's talking about is strong as it thrums through me, singing in my blood, but I'm not supposed to cause a scene. *Daddy's orders,* I remind myself, praying Boyd has suddenly lost his ability to hear and isn't witnessing this conversation.

"Okay, dick. Maybe I have reason to be stressed. Ever think about that?"

Kieran glances my way, boredom dulling his gaze, and sets his glass on the table. I can tell he just thinks I'm being dramatic, and the realization drags rage into my throat.

My hands curl into fists in my lap, the urge to reach out and be violent causing a low hum in my fingertips.

With my hands balled up, I can't tap out of the intrusive thoughts, so instead I focus my gaze on the centerpiece, reminding myself of how I fixed it moments ago and the relief it gave me.

"Maybe you shouldn't have taken up smoking in the first place."

Poof. Just like that, my relief vanishes, leaving me a time bomb, slowly ticking its way to explosion.

I scoff, unfolding my hand and flipping him off with one manicured finger, the pink nail pointing outward. "Hindsight is twenty-twenty, you know. If all of us could go back and *not* make mistakes, we'd be in much better shape. But we don't exactly get that option."

Still, my words ring hollow as his mind travels elsewhere, landing on Juliet as she sits at her table. I huff, crossing my arms and slumping in my seat, feeling scorned for no reason by a psychopath with more mistakes in his past than good decisions.

My cheeks heat as I sneak a glance at Boyd, who watches me with a thoughtful expression despite Mel practically sitting in his lap.

He doesn't drop my stare, even as she tries to cajole him into making Kieran jealous, and the intensity in his gaze makes me uncomfortable.

Stretching my fingers, I tap the tip of one on the outside of my bicep, the rhythm slightly soothing.

Tap, tap, tap.

Without another word, I push back from the table and excuse myself, on the hunt for my second cigarette of the night.

CHAPTER TWO

Boyd

Long, dark red hair swishes against her back, bright against Fiona's creamy, freckled skin, as she flounces from the room.

Until tonight, I've managed to ignore her existence, downplaying her role in my life as my best—and only—friend's baby sister, far too young for me to pay any mind in the first place.

But Christ, I've seen her now—she's the kind of train wreck you can't look away from. The wistful expression as she stared out onto the dance floor, longing for someone to twirl her in their strong arms, had mesmerized me.

I watched her doe eyes soften at the edges as she gazed at the couples, saw how the look on her face melted into something almost sinister, as if she'd do anything she could to get someone to acknowledge her that way.

I should've known all the Ivers would be bloodthirsty. It's not as if that gene falls very far from the tree.

My phone vibrates in my suit pocket as she disappears from the ballroom, the sound of her heels clicking against the tiled floor obscured by the band onstage and the low chatter all around us.

Pulling it out, I glance at the screen and groan internally, my thumb hovering over the "clear" button.

Riley: will you stop by tonight?

Kieran left the table long before his sister did, my date in tow, so I'm stuck here watching their mother, Mona, alternate between picking at a house salad and trying to hide her twitches as she moves with the music.

If anyone paid even a modicum of attention to the woman, they'd see the way the vein beneath her eye pulses, or how when she smiles, half of her facial muscles refuse to play along.

That's the thing with the people in this town, though; they really only see what they want to.

It's why the mafia is able to exist so seamlessly, why things like poverty and drug addiction go unchecked, why a thirteen-year-old boy was abandoned so his mother could spend her days bouncing from drug deal to drug deal.

Pulling up the keyboard on my phone, I type out a quick reply.

Me: I'll see what I can do.

Truth be told, I don't want to step foot in that house, but the kid rarely texts me unless she needs something.

Just like her mother.

Pocketing my phone, I glance back to the hall leading to the front of the colonial building, contemplating if I should stay still or head out. The desire to get away from the crowd wins out, propelling me forward.

Scooping Fiona's mask off the table and tucking it under my arm, I get up from the table, tilting my chin toward Mona even though she's looking at the table and doesn't seem to notice my presence one way or the other.

Staying on the outskirts of the dance floor, I avoid eye contact with anyone, not really sure where I'm going or what I'm hoping to accomplish as I head in the direction I just saw the redhead go.

Exiting through one of two doorways leading out of the event space, I stop at the bottom of the winding staircase, trying to decide whether or not she'd have gone up there.

No, when she left she'd been agitated, and considering the conversation she'd had with her brother, the most likely place would be outside.

14

Pushing open one of the large wooden doors, I scan the driveway, ignoring some of the odd looks I get from people standing around, waiting on their rides or gossiping in their little groups.

I hook right, following laughter as it bounces off the white sides of the building; when I round the corner, grass sinking beneath my steps, I spot her plastered against the wall, some guy in a Stonemore Community athletic jacket glued to the front of her body. His arm is propped above her head on the wall, his clean-shaven face angled toward hers.

Something curdles in my gut, knots twisting the muscles until they ache, but I don't really understand the reaction. I'm not fucking jealous of this little prick, and certainly not because he's fucking around with Fiona.

It must be that she's Kieran's sister—a natural protectiveness evolving from prolonged association. Still, that doesn't explain the way my cock stiffens behind my dress slacks at the flush on her pretty cheeks, or the way my chest feels tight when he dips his head to kiss her jaw.

My fingers squeeze the material of her golden mask, and I lean against the wall, interested to see how far she's willing to take things. Reaching into the pocket without my phone, I pull out a pre-rolled joint and light up, hoping the bud calms my nerves before I make my presence known.

The desire to squash the freshman rears its ugly head, violence pumping through my veins the longer I watch them. His fingers edge toward the ends of her hair, tangling gently in the strands, and I roll my eyes at him thinking she needs to be handled like glass.

Like her very namesake doesn't suggest otherwise.

Taking a drag off the end of my joint, I inhale the substance deep into my chest, blowing a plume of smoke out above my head as he pushes off the wall, holding his hand out for her. She takes it, brushing her hair off her shoulder, and my eyebrows shoot into my hairline.

I start forward before I can stop myself, my feet ten steps ahead of my brain, stepping from the shadows as her heels touch the sidewalk.

"Going somewhere, Fi?" I ask, tossing her family nickname into the air like I've said it a million times. It feels sour on my tongue, too intimate and dishonest, but I ignore the taste, focusing instead on the small gasp that falls from her pouty red lips when she hears my voice.

Whipping her head in my direction, I don't miss the way her eyes hungrily scale down my body, snapping back to my face when she notices what she's doing.

"Butting in where you're neither wanted, nor needed, Boyd?" she snaps, a hand cradling the soft flare of her hip, one perfectly shaped brow arching.

Taking a step closer, I suck on my joint again, casually sizing her little toy up. "Just trying to keep you from making a colossal mistake, is all." I point at the kid with my joint. "What's your name, anyway?"

Fiona puts her free hand on his bicep, and he runs a hand over his blond crew cut, eyes darting between the two of us. "You don't have to answer that," she says, giving me a dirty look that shoots a jolt of electricity straight to my balls.

I clear my throat, trying to dispel the arousal and subsequent guilt clawing through me. "If you want to leave this place alive, I suggest answering the question. And I don't repeat myself."

The frat boy pulls his arm out of her grip. "My dad's a lawyer, and I doubt you're a cop if you're getting high at a public function."

"Weed's legal."

"Not federally. And besides, you've been sitting with the Ivers family all night, and we all know they aren't cops."

Noting the way Fiona's face falls at his words, I take another step forward, flicking my ashes toward the guy's Sperry shoes. *Christ.* Frat boy, for sure. "*You're* hanging with an Ivers, so what does that tell me about you? What was your plan with her, hm?"

He holds up his hands, moving away from Fiona. "Look, she wanted to ride *my* dick. Said she'd pay for a cigarette."

"I meant with cash, you asshole." Crossing her arms over her tits, Fiona huffs. "God, what is wrong with you?"

The guy laughs woodenly. "Whatever, I don't fuck virgins anyway, and I don't need any of your petty drama."

A virgin. Inappropriate images of pushing into her sweet, untouched cunt flash across my vision, blasting me with a rush of arousal I immediately tamper, cursing myself. Like I need the added complications.

Bumping my shoulder as he pushes past me, *Ethan* stalks off, leaving me alone with a fuming Fiona. She glares at me, her eyes turning into little slits, anger ebbing off her in waves that have me inching closer, seeing if the heat from her flames is potent enough to burn me without touching.

Of course, I touch anyway, apparently unable to stop myself.

I reach out and tuck some hair behind her ear, reveling in the blush staining her chest; the light from inside spills through the large windows, illuminating her curves, and for the first time I can remember, I'm realizing she *has* them. My throat constricts, and I busy myself with my joint, fitting it between my lips and inhaling.

She frowns, moving her head back. "What's going on? Did my brother send you out here to check on me or something?"

"No."

Her eyes fixate on my lips as they curl around a cloud of smoke, pushing it upward. Up close, I see the smattering of freckles dousing her nose and cheekbones, the tiny white zigzag scar at the corner of her mouth, the flecks of orange in her irises.

18

Bits and pieces that might not work on their own, but on her come together to create God's magnum opus.

"Then why are you suddenly acting like you care about me?" She tilts her head, studying my face, and I don't like the way it feels like she can split me open with her penetrative gaze and see right inside. "You've barely spoken a single sentence to me in the seven years I've known you."

I lift my shoulder in a half shrug, unable to pull my eyes from hers. "People change."

"No, they don't."

It's the definitive way she says it, like she's been proven wrong on that count, that tugs at something inside me, startling me out of the haze of lust my dick is pulling me into. I clear my throat and step back, putting distance between us and the weird magnetism cropping up, trying to glue me to her.

Think about who this is, Boyd.

She swallows, breaking free of the trance too, and then holds out her hand. I raise an eyebrow, and she rolls her eyes, reaching into her mouth and plucking her pink bubblegum from it, tossing the wad over her shoulder.

"I feel like I deserve your joint, since you ruined my night."

"Sounds like I saved you from being sexually assaulted."

"Show me where I asked for your help, Boyd." Her hand drops. "I'm not some helpless princess incapable of taking care of herself."

Princess. My tongue rolls the word around silently, fitting itself into the syllables and loving the way it feels. Far more natural and neutral than Fi, and a hell of a lot more truthful.

She might not see herself as a princess, but the rest of King's Trace certainly does—a fallen one, at least. Her family lives in an isolated mansion with their demons, ruling things from behind the curtain of their wealth and prestige, untouchable because of the number of criminals they have dirt on.

"I'm not really understanding all the animosity I'm getting from you right now," I say. "A simple thank you would suffice."

Smiling sweetly, she shoves at my chest, catching me off guard as her anger seems to expand, a wildfire spreading without an end in sight. "How about a nice big fuck you, instead? That work?"

Moving past me, she rips the mask out from under my arm and heads back for the front of the building, the sway of her hips mesmerizing as I keep my distance, trying not to bite the bait she's throwing in my face, clearly aware of how her fire singes me in all the important places.

It's a long time before I think about the messages on my phone, unread pleas for my presence, too wrapped up in a game I've only just begun to think about the other people who need me.

CHAPTER THREE

Fiona

y the time I get back inside, my skin is crawling with the need for relief, annoyance falling down my spine like rain, the drizzle stealing my focus. I glance into the ballroom and see my father gathering his things from our table, bending to kiss my mother's forehead and probably telling her he'll be right back to walk her to the car.

The tightness in my chest expands to my throat, a cautious fire igniting with each breath, anxiety swimming through my veins and absorbing all of my conscious energy

Even the anger and confusing arousal I'd been feeling when I fled the yard dissipates, lost in my brain's struggle to maintain control over itself. To not give in to the overwhelming need to fix *something* — anything, really — when nothing's broken in the first place.

Cigarettes dull the sensation, providing an immediate balm to the sharp edges of consumption, of the need for control inside a body incapable of releasing it without feeling like the entire world is crumbling.

But I made a promise to my mother when she was diagnosed and began relying on me to assist her with everyday life; she'd never shamed me for the disgusting habit, possibly because she was aware of my internal battle, but she did ask me to stop. To *control* myself when it came to my addictions, as if wars can actually be won by sheer willpower.

'*Ninety-nine percent of your reality is perception,*' she says, spouting off what I'm pretty sure has to be a made-up statistic. And while I get the sentiment, it feels like an oversimplification.

Still, I agreed, because I'm willing to try anything once, especially if it might make my life easier. Being an Ivers is difficult enough when you're not adding problems into the mix.

Sweat beads along my hairline as panic seizes my esophagus, crushing it beneath its greedy little palm, and I can feel myself slipping into a spiral once I reach the bathroom off the foyer of the arts center. It's not an attack so much as an eruption, like when a volcano has been dormant for so long and finally lets go.

Locking myself in the cramped space, I grip the porcelain sink and let the cold water run, cupping my hands under the stream and splashing my face with it. The act is more ritual than anything, something an ex-therapist suggested as a way to shock my system out of its self-destruction, but that has never once actually worked.

Standing up straight, I use a paper towel to dry my skin, put my mask back on, and toss the towel into the metal garbage bin hanging on the wall. My hands drop to my sides, the index finger on one curling as it begins tapping in sets of three against my thigh, the gesture pushing a shudder of calm through me.

My mind fixates on the *tap, tap, tap* instead of its desire or the embarrassment of having Boyd butt in where he wasn't concerned. I'm not stupid — I knew what I was getting into when I agreed to even speak to Ethan Shultz, a quarterback from King's Trace Prep attending community college in Stonemore, our neighboring town.

Truth is, I just wanted a cigarette, and sometimes you have to be willing to get your hands dirty to get what you want.

I was also curious to know what on-campus life is like; after graduating last year from KTP, the only private K-12 school in town, I started classes at Stonemore Community. Only, I'm stuck attending online, drowning in psych textbooks and cursing the universe for making my mother need me.

As the weight crushing my chest lightens with each tap of my finger, I turn and lean against the sink, crossing my arms, swishing the skirt of my gown with the movement.

The bathroom door swings open, and Boyd strides in with a bored expression on his face, as if joining me in an occupied restroom is a totally normal, everyday occurrence.

"Can I help you?" I ask, trying to melt into the sink behind me, wondering what I've done to suddenly earn his presence multiple times in the same night, after years of him ignoring my existence.

He walks to the single stall, shoving the door with his shoulder. "That depends—got any more fuck boys hidden in here?"

Ignoring the implication that I was hiding one before, I roll my eyes. "Sorry, you just missed him. After a raucous round of lovemaking, he was parched and set off to find a drink."

Boyd's eyes sear into mine, an unreadable glint in them making my face heat. I clear my throat, shifting on my feet when he doesn't respond. "I could've been using the bathroom, you know."

"Without locking the door?" He cocks his head, letting his gaze travel slowly down my form. I clench my thighs together, trying to ward off the pulse beating between them.

Tilting my chin up, I meet his stare head-on, my body doused by the heat reflected back. "Maybe I like to live dangerously."

He smirks. "Is that right?"

"*Maybe*. You don't know me, Boyd."

A humming sound comes from somewhere in his throat, deep and delicious, sending a shiver down my spine. The panic from before is replaced with a new discomfort entirely, one that says I'm nowhere experienced enough to take on a man like the one before me.

"Don't I?" He comes closer, running a hand through his dirty blond hair, disheveling it *just so*, giving it that sexy bedhead look. My toes curl inside my silver Jimmy Choo pumps, my brain melting as his scent assaults my senses. Clean and crisp, the essence of his persona, although the way his eyes darken with molten lust makes me think there's a beast hidden beneath his sculpted body and trademark suspenders.

Something *dark*. Something I want to get lost in.

"I *know* you would've been in a shitload of trouble tonight had I not come to your rescue, princess." His smirk turns malicious, the corners of his mouth sharpening as it morphs, and again I press myself into the sink, equal parts intimidated and intrigued.

"I didn't ask for a knight in shining armor," I whisper, my resolve liquefying as he shifts closer, the fabric of his suit jacket brushing against the sequins on my dress.

"I never claimed to be one." His breath ghosts over my face, warm and somehow minty, despite the joint he'd been smoking just minutes ago. A knock sounds on the door, breaking the odd spell weaving between our souls, and I shimmy away, remembering that I'm supposed to be annoyed with him.

"Well, whatever it is you're doing, stop. I don't need another brother."

Pushing open the door, I narrowly miss smacking into an elderly man with a bright blue mask, skating around him and heading for the front of the building. Boyd's hot on my heels, his fingers grasping at me as I increase my speed.

Shoving through the front doors, I rip the mask from my face and toss it to the ground, just as Boyd's palm curls around my shoulder, the heat from his touch scorching against my bare skin. I whirl around, irritation coming back full force, and shake him off.

"Don't touch me."

"Fiona, I'm just trying to explain—"

"I'm not interested."

Whipping my hair over my shoulder, I turn back around and start down the steps, heading toward my father's silver Aston Martin. Kieran stands at the back passenger door, and I push him aside, yanking it open to reveal his unconscious conquest. I note the smeared lipstick around her mouth and the fingerprints on her neck, but I don't ask because I truly don't want to know.

Climbing in over her, I settle onto the seat beside her body, holding up a hand when Kieran glances at me quizzically.

"No, I don't want to talk about it. But you'd better tell your friend he needs to respect that he's not *my brother* and back the hell off."

Boyd stops at Kieran's side, rolling his eyes. "Those theater lessons are really paying off, Fi. Dramatic as ever."

My chest caves slightly at the insult—not because it's untrue, but because he thinks he knows me well enough that he can toss it around the way my family does. As if proximity makes up for his emotional distance, and you can know someone just by being in the same room as them.

Kieran's eyebrows furrow. "What happened?"

But I shake my head, unwilling to answer. Not wanting to relive any of the embarrassment, and because I'm not sure what he'd do if he knew his best friend was meddling in my romantic affairs.

Kieran doesn't care about much, but something tells me he wouldn't necessarily appreciate that.

I can feel Boyd's gaze on me as I stare out the front windshield, Mel's soft snores the sound I try to anchor myself to, and then my brother slams the door shut, barring me from the rest of the conversation.

CHAPTER FOUR

Boyd

The soft contour of Fiona's profile is what brands itself onto my brain hours after I've left the arts center, the mask she pulled over her features startling in contrast to the sunshine usually found there.

It's not even that she looked away, completely over me, but that she didn't seem to spare a cursory thought before making the decision. Her pointed turn made my gut sour for absolutely no reason when, before tonight, her response to me had no bearing on my soul whatsoever.

Her face is all I see as I weave through the desolate streets of the "bad" side of town on my bike—a vintage, forest green

Harley that I bought at an auction not long after getting my first real paycheck with Ivers International. Gripping the handlebars harder than necessary, I try to steel my thoughts away from the redheaded vixen, aware of the destruction leading that way.

Instead, I focus on the likely mess awaiting me at Carson Pointe, the unanswered text messages and voicemails on my phone burning a hole in my pocket as I pull into the trailer park. It's a small conglomerate of rent-to-own single wides, all with the same beige siding and slabs of concrete serving as carports beside their plots of land.

My old one is situated at the back, smushed between two newer models—if not for the fact that I've dragged my mother's overdosing ass up the same plastic stairs and shoved her into a cold shower more times than I care to admit, I wouldn't be able to find it at all.

Parking my bike beside the empty concrete slab, I kick down the stand and yank the key from the ignition, staring at the home for a few beats before getting off. Yellow light bleeds from the window above the kitchen sink, indicating *someone's* awake, despite it being well past midnight.

Not that I expect *her* to have a normal sleep schedule, especially considering the odd hours she keeps as a line cook at the Waffle House on the edge of town. I guess it'd be too much to ask Riley to at least pretend she lives a normal life.

Hauling my leg over the bike seat, I take off my helmet, hooking it over the handlebar, and head to the front door. My hand trembles slightly as I raise it, curling into a fist around the nerves trying to poke holes in my resolve. I swallow as my knuckles connect with the wooden door, rapping twice, leaning in to listen for footsteps.

Shoving my hands into my suit pockets, I roll back on my heels, waiting.

Always fucking waiting.

I check the Rolex on my wrist after a stretch of silence passes, noting that it's been approximately half an hour since I left the Montalto Arts Center. Five more minutes pass before I knock again, louder this time, unwilling to let either of them ignore me after practically begging me to show up in the first place.

The door swings open finally, just as my shoulders slump and give in to the defeat of being too weak for them. An almost malnourished frame stands in the doorway, dye job platinum hair matted to a slightly wrinkled forehead, eyes unsurprisingly bloodshot.

She looks me over, pausing when she sees the expensive crest on my decorative handkerchief, and pulls the door wider, stepping aside to let me in.

"LeeAnn," I say in lieu of a formal greeting, knowing neither of us expects much else anyway. Anger surges like an unchecked wave inside my stomach, slapping against the shore of my sanity when I enter, noting the pile of dirty dishes in the sink and the rotten smell coming from them, the clusters of dog hair brushed against the white baseboards from a pet that's been dead for months.

Christ, when was my last visit?

I try to calculate the time away in my head, turning in the small alcove to face my mother as she tries to finger brush her hair, knowing it's been too long.

Biologically speaking, we look a lot alike, although when I was a kid she still tried to pass me off as her sister Dottie's spawn. Her dark blonde roots are coming in, spreading like a disease against her scalp, her hazel eyes harsh and uninviting. There's nothing about the woman that screams "maternal" or "warm," which makes how Riley turned out a true phenomenon.

"Boyd." LeeAnn sizes me up again, a frown spreading across her haggard face—even though she's only forty-two, the way her skin hangs from her bones, as if God began plastering it onto her body and quit halfway through, makes her look decades older. "Finally step away from your fancy party long enough to stop by and see the common folk?"

Cocking my head, I stare into her eyes, noting the minuscule dilation in her pupils, the way they can't quite seem to focus. Tension builds in my shoulders, coagulating like cement, sending a spike of apprehension through me.

"Are the common folk high right now?" I ask, raising my eyebrows.

She rolls her eyes, shuffling toward the kitchen, catching her hip on the white fridge as she passes it. Yanking the door open, she reaches in for a jug of orange juice, unscrewing the cap and taking a swig from the container. "Just getting over a cold. Which you'd know, if you ever bothered to answer my calls or texts."

Disbelief threads into my vision, but I ignore it. Her words feel like dull knives; not quite sharp enough to slice through on the first swipe, so she keeps sawing until she breaks through the skin. Rolling my shoulders, I try to dislodge the feel of their blade, ignoring the pang sluicing through my chest.

"I'd be more likely to answer your calls and texts if they weren't always requests for cash."

"Oh, right, like the *small* amounts I ask for would break your fucking bank. You're wearing a five-*thousand*-dollar suit, for Christ's sake, but your mother needs a little help making ends meet and suddenly she's the goddamn Devil."

She slams the orange juice back on its shelf and kicks the refrigerator door closed, the sound bouncing off the cream-colored walls, then walks around me to flop down in the navy suede recliner at the other side of the room.

Kicking the footrest up, she lays back in the chair, flipping on the small flat screen television mounted on the wall, then scoops up a pack of cigarettes from the end table at her side and shakes one out, lighting up without another word.

I don't bother mentioning how it's not her needing money that makes her the Devil—she's been that in my book for as long as I can remember. Maybe since the day she left me on Dottie's front porch and told me to figure shit out for myself at thirteen.

Maybe even before then.

But I never mention it.

If someone doesn't know they've hurt you, doesn't know how they affect you, then they don't hold any real power over you.

So I don't give LeeAnn that power — at least, that's what I tell myself. The ache as I ignore her and head toward the back end of the trailer spins a different story, though, one I'm never in the mood to hear.

Riley's room is the size of a shoebox, complete with a twin bed, a small desk, and a chest of drawers. She's sprawled out on her mattress, bobbing her head to whatever she's got playing in her headphones as she scrolls through her phone absently.

Her honey-blonde hair hangs off the side of the bed, bright against the yellow quilt beneath her, one leg propped up on the opposite knee.

She doesn't notice when I walk in, too engrossed in her phone; as I bend, peeking over her head, I notice she's scrolling through some guy's feed.

His page is primarily professional shots of himself or him playing the drums or guitar on various stages, wearing leather jackets and half-buttoned Hawaiian shirts, some of him drinking from brown bottles, some of him floating in alarmingly blue water.

"Aren't you a little young to be stalking people?" I ask, startling her; she jumps at my words, one headphone falling from her ear onto the floor.

A wide smile, fixed by braces I paid for when she was twelve, breaks out on her face, and she scrambles into a sitting position, a light blush staining her cheeks. "Statistics show that most people with stalking tendencies actually begin around the age of thirteen. Might even be younger now, thanks to social media."

I grunt. "I think you're listening to too many true crime podcasts."

Shrugging at my words, she turns her phone toward me, a picture of the guy posing with a ukulele in front of the Parthenon pulled up. "But just *look* at this face. Aiden James is totally stalkable, right? Not to mention, he's *wicked* talented. The Rolling Stones did a spread on him at Christmas that literally called him the next Dave Grohl."

Excitement drips from her words as she widens her eyes, staring at me with an expression drenched in longing.

I hate it.

Hate that I can practically feel the expectations swimming in her blood. Hate that my coming here only ever seems to let her down.

Clearing my throat, I perch on the end of her desk, crossing my arms over my chest. "Tell me this isn't what you called me over for. I don't do celebrity gossip."

Her face falters, and she sits back on her heels, letting the phone fall to the bed. "Of course not," Riley mutters, tucking her hair behind her ears. "You don't *do* anything. I have to beg you for days before you finally stop by, even though I'm your only real responsibility outside of work."

"Riley, come on."

Sighing, she shakes her head, waving me off. "Okay, you're right. Sorry. I'm not your kid, not your responsibility."

My head throbs at her words, but I don't take the bait. *Like mother, like daughter.* "So what *did* you call me here for?" I glance around, looking for something to anchor myself to and coming up short.

Her room is small, but for the most part it looks like a typical teenager's room — not that I have any recent experience in that department. But between the pop star posters on the wall above her bed and the glass dog figurines on her dresser, I assume this must be what they're into.

"Well, I was *hoping* I could talk you into maybe... sponsoring me so I can afford to go on our class trip?" Leaning back on the bed, she reaches beneath her pillow and pulls out a King's Trace High brochure, handing it to me.

I take it, unfolding the sleek paper to scan it. "New York City?"

She nods, her chin rising and falling rapidly. "We voted at the end of last year, and that's what won the majority. If you think it's too much, I don't have to go, but..."

Looking up, I tilt my head to the side and meet her wide eyes. "But?"

"I've never left King's Trace. Ever. I think it'd be good for me."

Something painful twists in my gut, an angry storm churning at her words. It's the kind of trip I only could've dreamed of going on as a kid — then again, I didn't have an older brother so uncomfortable with my existence that he threw money at me any time I asked in lieu of an apology, either.

"You said sponsor?" I ask, flipping to the back of the brochure, admiring the picture of Times Square on New Year's. "Does that mean you're providing some kind of service?"

Again, she nods, now casting her gaze down as if nervous. "Yeah, I... I don't know what I'm gonna do yet, but I wanted to make it worth it. You already pay for so much, and I'm—"

Tossing the pamphlet at her, I hold my palm up, waving her off. As if any amount of money I ever spend on the kid could touch the resentment I try to bury. "You don't need to explain, and you don't need to give me something in return. I'll cut you a blank check and let you fill in the amount."

Before she says another word — especially a thank you — I turn on my heel and exit the bedroom, stalking past an unconscious LeeAnn and slipping out the front of the trailer. Once situated back on my bike, I ignore the curdling inside my bones, the way the marrow aches for forgiveness and acceptance, to go back inside and take my sister with me.

Save her from the Hell I was kicked out of.

But I don't, because the hurt that existed before Riley burns too bright for me to see anything else. Like amnesia, the barbed wire erected around my heart tries to keep me safe, to protect me from those with the utmost power to destroy me.

Slipping my helmet on, I start my bike and pull out my phone, clicking on Kieran's contact as pent-up rage swells inside me like the sails of a ship lost at sea. I'm pulled along, propelled by the unruly winds and unable to steer.

It's the anger I focus on as I type out my message, hoping he's working. That he has something I can exorcise my demons on.

When he replies with an address, relief floods my chest, and I lower the kickstand, pulling away from the trailer without a single glance back. But the anger doesn't dissipate, not even much later when I'm covered in another man's blood, sweat, and tears, his desperation coating my skin.

I can't help wondering if this is the kind of rage that makes a home in your body. The kind that roots itself in your soul, wrapping like ivy around the only good pieces of you until they're no longer recognizable.

CHAPTER FIVE

Fiona

Standing at the glass doors leading into Ivers International, one of the only buildings downtown with more than two stories, I groan into the crisp air for the millionth time, my feet glued in place. I've tried moving them, but they're stuck, physically incapable of taking me inside.

"Fiona, honestly." My mother's shoulder bumps into mine as she tries to push me forward, growing more and more agitated by the second. "Sometimes you're too stubborn for your own good."

"I'm a Scorpio," I mutter, my fingers curling around the lip of the Tupperware container in my hands. The red lid creases with the pressure, wrinkling the plastic until I relax. "It's in my blood."

"You're the one who wanted to do this." She clicks her tongue, palms gripping my shoulders and giving a harsh shove; this time it dislodges me, and I catch the door handle just to keep from falling. "So, go do it. I've got to get to brunch with the girls from the gardening club."

Nerves slosh around in my stomach as I enter the building and cross the lobby. The so-shiny-I-can-see-myself-in-them tiled floor and glass cubicles give the illusion of transparency, despite the nature of the company.

I glance at myself in the elevator doors as I wait for them to open, smoothing my hand over the part separating my French braids, shame spiraling like a tidal wave when I realize how painfully young the hairstyle makes me look.

But I'd been aiming for innocence and subtlety, going against the advice of my two best friends, who'd FaceTimed me before I left the house. Heidi didn't want me coming here at all, saying it mixed the feminist message of being a strong, unapologetic woman, and Bea had simply suggested I show up naked beneath a trench coat, even after being reminded that my mother was tagging along.

Instead, I paired a burgundy tartan pleated skirt with a black knit sweater and called it a day, figuring that even if I embarrassed myself by coming to the office, I'd at least look good doing so. The braids, though, I'm now realizing, make me look like a slutty schoolgirl, and my palms grow clammy against the plastic container.

When the elevator stops, I step inside, noting that the lobby is pretty much desolate — I wonder if anyone actually even works down here other than the two custodians chatting by the emergency stairwell, or if my father's penchant for facades extends to the structural integrity of his office as well.

The doors close as I push the button for the top floor, leaning against the wall and trying my best not to focus on the impossibly small quarters, or the fact that the death trap is only being moved by sheer cables and gears.

Technically speaking, they could snap at any moment.

I reach up and pull the hair ties from my braids, letting them fall out, shaking the strands in an effort to alleviate some of the anxiety coursing through me. I'm nervous enough about seeing Boyd Kelly after last weekend, I definitely don't need the added apprehension.

Jolting to a stop on my floor, the doors slide open, and I try not to scramble from the death trap. My father's executive level of the building looks a lot like the lobby, except the glass cubicles are replaced by actual offices with blinds barring what's inside. The whole north wall is closed office doors and expensive, imported artwork from artists my father's never even heard of, while reception sits out front, separated by another glass wall.

Inhaling a deep breath and ignoring the way my stomach quivers, I suck on my tongue as I approach the blonde behind the desk. I don't recognize her—last I was here, my father's receptionist-slash-assistant was a gray-haired woman named Valerie who smelled like roses and motor oil and always wore tights with runs along the sides.

This receptionist is brand new, and the delicate shape of her pretty face, her clear ocean eyes, and tan skin makes my stomach twist in an entirely new way.

Setting the container on the desk, I prop my arms on the ledge and lean over, looking down as she tilts her head toward me. The red silk blouse she has on hangs open on its fourth button, revealing perky, round cleavage that feels inappropriate for the workplace, and I don't see a ring on her left finger.

"Can I help you?" she asks, flipping her long hair over one shoulder. The name tag pinned to her chest says CHELSEA, and suddenly I loathe everything about her.

I offer an overly sweet smile. "I'd like to see Boyd, please."

"*Mr.* Kelly?" She glances at the container, then at me, scanning my face for some sign that I belong here—never mind the family portrait hanging beside my father's office door, where I'm situated between my brothers and the spitting image of my mother. "I'm sorry, he's in a meeting. You can wait, though, if you'd like, or I can take a message?"

My eyes narrow. The likelihood of him getting that message is slim, I can tell by the snarky glint in her gaze. "If you'd just tell him I'm here to see him, I guarantee he'll let me through."

"I'm afraid that's against protocol, and Mr. Kelly would likely have my head if I allowed you to interrupt."

Tension seizes my shoulders, and my hands curl into fists on the top of the cookies. An image of serving Chelsea's head to Boyd on a platter flashes across my vision unbidden, macabre in nature and completely startling, sending a shiver of unease through my chest.

Clearing my throat, I try again. "Look, Craig Ivers is my dad. Call him and tell him I'm out here, I'm sure he'll say it's fine if I go in."

Her head cocks, a small smirk playing at her mouth. "Unfortunately, Mr. Ivers is at lunch."

Sure, he is. Sighing heavily, I sag against the tall wooden desk, reaching into my pocket for a piece of bubble gum. Unwrapping the candy, I pop it in my mouth and chew, glancing around the upstairs lobby, noting Boyd's closed office two doors down.

At least ten feet away, it's a stretch, especially given the thigh-high boots I'm wearing with their stiletto heels. Still, it's probably the only chance I'm going to get.

My mother's words from earlier ring in my head. *Go do it.*

Extending my hand on an exhale, I pinch the gum wrapper between my fingers. "Do you care to throw this away for me?"

Scoffing, Chelsea grabs a tissue and catches the trash when I drop it, swiveling in her chair to open the wicker basket behind the desk. As she's turned, I snatch the cookie container, clutching it to my chest, and bolt.

Her shouts of irritation barely register as my feet sprint across the tiled floor, aching with each exuberant step. I reach Boyd's office door before she reaches me and drag the handle down, pushing inside and slamming it shut, plastering my body against the wood and scrambling to lock it.

Chelsea's fists beat against the door as I lean my back into it, panting, the lid of the container lopsided from being squished. I push on the opposite end, insecurity ebbing through me, and exhale as it pops out, correcting itself.

As my lungs decompress, I lift my chin and see Boyd sitting behind his desk for the first time ever. The image is so disgustingly erotic and powerful, him regarding me with a bland expression and a corded phone held to his ear, that my knees weaken and my core quakes.

My mouth parts on an explanation, but he holds his index finger up, and I clamp it shut. "If that's the case, Antonio, I suggest figuring out whether you've got a fucking mole in your midst, because I damn well know you're not suggesting a program I designed myself would be privy to a privacy breach. We're a fucking cybersecurity firm, for God's sake."

Oh, my God. The grip I have on the cookies weakens at the deep, authoritative tone; paired with the navy suit vest he has on, the dress shirt with its sleeves rolled mid-forearm to reveal some of the tattoos inked into his skin, and I'm practically drooling. I can feel my pulse between my thighs, and I shift, pressing them together to try and relieve myself of the ache.

It doesn't do any good; the pressure just heightens my arousal, and I think I might actually come just from standing here, watching this man.

The muscles in his forearms bulge against his skin as his fingers flex around the phone, nostrils flaring. "I'm not asking, and if I have to make my way down to your shithole casino just to figure out what the problem is myself, I can guarantee you won't like the resolution. Get it the fuck together or I'm shutting you down."

Yanking the phone from his ear, Boyd slams it down on the receiver, tugging at the knot in his tie. He stares out the large windows that overlook downtown for several beats—so long, I start to wonder if he's forgotten my presence entirely.

Clearing my throat, I take a half step forward, using the cookies as a shield. As if he's some kind of wild animal and I'm potential prey, walking right into a trap. "Boyd?"

He doesn't turn, doesn't even flinch. Just keeps staring, hand resting on his giant oak desk. The leather desk chair he's sitting in hides half his body from me, but I can still see the broad slope of his shoulders and the weight he holds there.

It's all in the posture — people who carry their stress in the rotator cuff muscles always sit too straight, holding their necks slightly forward. Boyd's strains so far away from his body, it's almost as if they're two different entities traveling in separate directions.

"Fiona," he says finally, turning so he's situated properly behind his desk. "Did Chelsea not say I was in a meeting?"

"No, she did." I walk over to the two gray suede armchairs angled across from him and stand between them.

"And you came in anyway?"

I swallow, my tongue swelling. "Well, I drove Mom here and didn't want to take too long. Her garden brunches are only half an hour long."

"Ah, yes. Don't you usually join her for those?"

"Usually, but today I needed to do this." Taking a deep breath, I pinch my eyes closed, drop the container on his desk, and shove the cookies in his direction.

He studies them for a few seconds, eyebrows furrowing. "You had to... bring me cookies?"

"Yep." Relief washes over me at the deed being over, my nerves loosening with the removal of that obstacle. "They're an apology, of sorts."

"An apology."

The way he says it, so unfeeling and monotone, makes me second-guess myself, and my face flushes, heat staining my cheeks as I drop my gaze to the black rug beneath my feet. "For this past weekend, at the gala. I wasn't exactly myself, and I felt bad that you got the brunt of that experience. So, I wanted to apologize, because—"

He cuts me off before I can launch into a full ramble. "Right. That was a bit out of character for you, no? You're usually so..."

"Responsible?" I offer.

"*Light.*"

What in the world does that mean?

I can feel him staring holes into my forehead, but I don't dare look until I hear the lid of the container pop open. When I raise my eyes, he's still watching me, holding a cookie in one hand. The missing cookie makes the remaining stash uneven; they'd been stacked in careful towers of four, and now one stack only has three. My eyes glue to the imperfection, my finger tapping out its natural rhythm before I even consciously have to.

Tap, tap, tap.

"Do you realize I'm allergic to chocolate?" he asks, turning the cookie in his hand.

My eyes almost bug out of my head. "Um, no... I wasn't aware of that."

Is it possible to die of humiliation? Because holy *hell* am I on a roll. Anxiety practically vibrates my entire body, and I shiver as I reach for the container, spewing apologies.

Boyd shuffles the Tupperware into his arms, rolling back in his chair so he's just out of reach. "What are you doing?"

I blink, my mind spinning just trying to keep up. "I... you're allergic. Shouldn't I get these away from you?"

"You should get away from me, yes." Bringing the cookie to his pillowy lips, he bites off a piece, holding my gaze while he chews slowly. Tingles dance across my skin as I take in his jaw as it works, and I feel the bob of his throat in my pussy when he swallows, a dull ache spreading through me like an asteroid hurtling through space. "But only because I have a terrible habit of indulging in the things that are bad for me. I like the pain, princess. Is that someone you think is worthy of an apology? A coward?"

My mind swims through a million different shallow waters, struggling to keep afloat even though I could probably stand if I really wanted to. I also have no idea what he's talking about, or why I'd need to have an opinion on his personal preferences—but the hungry look in his caramel eyes makes every logical thought flee my brain, short-circuiting even the bad wiring.

I think Boyd Kelly would eat me alive, truth be told. Not that I necessarily think he wants to, even as his gaze drops to my legs, lingering on the exposed skin between the hem of my skirt and my boots. And while he's a different kind of dark than most other men in town, I think his is the kind you don't ever find your way out of.

It's that all-consuming, no-moon-in-the-sky darkness that permeates your soul until it's all you know.

The kind born from sadness, a violence wrought from pain and not the other way around.

A scoff pulls me from my thoughts, and I refocus, watching him spit the cookie out into a handkerchief from his breast pocket and slide the Tupperware back in my direction. "Keep your cookies, and keep your apologies, Fiona. Save them for some bastard who gives a shit. I am not that guy."

There's a clicking sound as he reaches beneath his desk, and the office door cracks open, Chelsea's blue eyes shining through the space. "Mr. Kelly, I'm *so* sorry, she—"

"I don't give a fuck. Please escort Ms. Ivers from the premises and get me Finn Hanson on the phone."

Snatching the cookies off his desk, unsure of what the fuck just happened, I stalk from the office before that bitch can try to say she told me so, power walking so I don't have to see her smug little face before I hop into the elevator. My heart pounds in my ears, embarrassment coursing through every nerve ending in my body, and when I get downstairs and outside, I collapse onto a nearby bench just outside the brick building, a confused sob tearing from my chest.

But no tears come. They rarely do—sunshine and rain exist in a mutually exclusive agreement inside my body, never overlapping to create rainbows. It's always one or the other, which means I've gotten used to keeping the rain on the inside.

No one wants to see that, anyway.

Everyone wants to bask in the sun.

Correcting the lid on the container, I reach in and grab the uneven stack of cookies, tossing one to the pigeons collecting near my feet and sighing at the uniformity inside, taking solace in the calmness it provides.

CHAPTER SIX

Boyd

I don't have time to think about my actions with Fiona at the office, because the second she leaves, my throat constricts so painfully that I have to page the assistant and have her drop me off at King's Trace Medical; I don't miss the way the blonde's eyes continually flicker from the road to my form, reminding myself to put a disciplinary note in her file when we get back that somehow punishes her for being easily distracted.

After the day I've had, I'm certainly not fucking interested in Craig Ivers' sloppy seconds. Not when I could have his virginal little princess eating out of the palm of my hand by sundown.

Maybe that's why, when the patient access rep hands me a clipboard with a packet hooked to it, I write Fiona's information under the emergency contact section. Chelsea sits in the seat beside me even though I told her she could leave, watching over my shoulder.

"You could put me down, if you wanted," I snort silently. *God, I'd fucking love to.* "Here, let me just write my number —" She reaches into my lap for the board, intentionally brushing her fingers against my dick, letting out a giggle when she does. "Oh, God, I'm so sorry! I swear, I'm just so clumsy sometimes. Let me help."

Batting her hands away and giving her a dirty look, because it still feels like there's a concrete balloon lodged in my esophagus, I finish the form just as a nurse calls my name, gesturing for me to enter the closed-off emergency wing. She's a short, heavyset woman with a bandana wrapped around her head, and she glances behind me as I walk through the door, observing Chelsea.

"You can bring your girlfriend back, if you want."

I just stare at her, flames sliding down my throat.

She stares back.

My eyebrows raise.

Finally, she sighs and lets the door fall shut behind us, barring Chelsea from following. Once we get to the private room and the nurse administers the EpiPen, she leaves me to relax on the exam chair and allow my body to return to its pre-panic state.

It was stupid to eat that chocolate chip cookie, even though the allergy is fairly mild. Even more stupid not to keep my own EpiPen in my desk at work, but since getting promoted a while back and cleaning out the stuff from my downstairs office, I haven't restocked.

Worse yet, I wanted it to mean something to Fiona — wanted to see her pretty brown eyes flare with lust as she drank in my words and soaked in my depravity, wanted that sunshine demeanor she wears as a mask to falter in my shadows.

From the second she stepped in, I'd seen how her body responded to me; noticed the blush staining her cheeks, the slight indentation in her sweater when her nipples puckered against the material. I don't think she even noticed them hardening beneath my perusal, but fuck me. I did. It was all I could do not to throw her down on my desk and ravage her right then.

And Christ, the way her thighs clenched tightly together, as if her strength would ever be enough to keep me from between them if I really wanted to be there. The sudden onslaught of uncontrollable lust I have for the redhead is intoxicating and confusing, and the fact that she's completely forbidden seems to make the temptation so much sweeter.

I'm Adam in the Garden of Eden, powerless against the whims of humanity.

Not that I'm ever going to act on those desires; I'd destroy Fiona, absorb her innocence, and spit out something tainted instead if I ever got my hands on her.

But that doesn't mean I can't imagine how she'd feel, crumbling at my feet, begging for my mercy. When the door to the exam room flies open and she's standing there in her short, plaid skirt, hair askew, it's all I can do to think of anything else.

I grab the Dixie cup of water the nurse left on the metal stand beside me and take a sip, watching as her eyes dart around the room, a deer trapped in headlights. She pulls her purse strap tight against her shoulder, closing the door with a soft click.

"Um, Boyd?" she says, a slight wobble in her voice sending a bolt of arousal down my spine. *I like the fear.* It's the most honest, real thing about her. "Where's Kieran? Reception called my cell phone and said my brother had been checked in and might need a ride home."

"You got here quick."

"Yeah, I was shopping at Green Apple Grocery, the little food store downtown?" She tucks a stray hair behind her ear, shifting on her feet. "I know they're kind of small, but Mom likes the salmon they carry because it's all caught locally, and the Walmart in Stonemore just doesn't—"

"Fiona."

She sucks in a breath, her sentence deflating. "You keep interrupting me."

"Because you keep going off on tangents." I tilt my head, setting the cup back on the table. "Do I make you nervous, princess? Is that why you try to fill the space between us with nonsense?"

Her eyebrows furrow. "It's not nonsense, I was explaining where I was and why I came so quickly. I didn't want you to think I was, like, sitting around and pining over our earlier conversation."

I smirk; the blush that spreads from her cheeks to the slender slope of her neck says otherwise.

"Anyway," she continues, crossing her arms over the tight little sweater she has on, making me wonder if her nipples are responding to me again. "You're not my brother, and we aren't friends. I don't really understand why you called me here."

Sitting up, I swing my legs over the side of the table, swiping my suit jacket from the plastic chair against the wall and slipping into it. "To be fair, I didn't call you. I put your name down, just in case."

"But... why?"

Walking over to her, I reach out, hooking my index finger beneath her chin and forcing her to meet my gaze. Her brown eyes are so warm and inviting, I find myself wanting to get lost in their depths, wishing I could swim in the chocolate seas and drown there.

Truth be told, I don't have a good reason for putting her name down, and she's right. We aren't friends. We *barely* know each other. But for some inexplicable reason, the gala last weekend put her on my fucking radar, and I can't seem to erase her from it. Thoughts of her fire consume me, singeing my flesh.

It's that trademark Fiona Ivers fire, the one everyone around town whispers about.

A fire she seems completely oblivious to that lives in her soul, expressing itself through her sharp tongue and inherent backbone.

The kind that burns from the inside and leaves absolutely nothing in its wake.

"You wanted to apologize to me for your behavior before," I say, so close that her breath caresses my lips. "I don't typically accept apologies. I like an exchange, something concrete that wipes the slate clean."

"Okay..." She trails off, her gaze dropping to my mouth; her pink tongue darts out to wet her ruby red lips, and a hunger ignites in my bones. "I don't understand what you mean."

"We're even. See to it that the receptionist gets back to the office, and I won't tell anyone your dirty little secret."

"My *secret*?" Fiona frowns. "It was a bad evening. I didn't murder anyone."

Bending down, I move my lips to her ear, reveling in the shiver that shudders through her when they brush against the sensitive flesh. "You have more bad evenings like that than you care to admit, don't you? You're not always sunshine. In fact, given your bloodline, I'd wager you're a rainstorm more often than not."

Shoving me away, she glares. "Stop talking about me like you know me. You *don't*."

"Not yet." Chuckling at the dumbfounded expression on her face and unsure as to why I'm pursuing this when I know it can't work, I grip the doorknob in my hand and exit the room, tossing another *not yet* over my shoulder for good measure.

CHAPTER SEVEN

Fiona

"I'm not saying you should fire him. Just, I don't know, send him to have a psych evaluation done, or something."

Slurping my chocolate milkshake through its paper straw, I glance at my father as he adjusts the newspaper in his lap, pushing his reading glasses up onto the bridge of his nose. He's in the living room at the front of our house, a mere thirty feet away from where I'm seated at the kitchen island, but in this haunted mansion a little distance can often feel like an insurmountable canyon.

This used to be a tradition I shared with my mother, but the chocolate milkshakes make her sick now. Everything makes her sick.

As my father regards me with boredom, the way he always looks when I talk about things he's not interested in, the distance turns into miles, and I feel small in his presence.

Stupid and naive.

Dramatic.

I don't think it's his intention to make me feel that way, but when you've spent your entire life trying to prove a fundamental difference between you and the people you share DNA with, a rift forms. The more you work at separating yourself, the wider it becomes, until one day there's no way to cross it.

"Fiona, if I gave all of my employees psych evaluations and kept them on the payroll based on the results, do you honestly think I'd have anyone left?" He licks his finger, turning a page. "It's an international web security firm that does a lot — a *lot* — of under the table dealings. No one would even apply if they weren't at least a *little* messed up."

"That sounds like good business."

"It is what it is, sweetheart. I've got loyal men beneath me, and some of the most powerful ones in the country owe me favors. I'm just playing the hand I was dealt."

Being born into a wealthy family with an ancestry dating back to the colonies hardly seems like such a *trial* someone would have to come to terms with, but leave it to my father to figure out a way.

His father was a dirty lawyer that Finn Hanson, the leader of the Irish Stonemore gang's grandfather kept on retainer, but for the most part, he kept his name fairly clean.

When my father turned eighteen, he fell in with one of the Stonemore pups and started running drugs for them, steering clear of the more inhumane business dealings they're involved in — namely, trafficking. His father didn't like the direct involvement, but there was really nothing he could do to stop it.

Once you're in bed with the mafia, there's no turning back. Even the people who retire or buy themselves out don't ever really lose the demons they earn during their time inside the different families.

Love, though. That's the kind of power that changes a man. Makes him shift things around so it fits in his world.

Not so he bends to it, but still powerful all the same, I suppose.

And when my dad fell for my mom, his entire life changed forever. Irrevocably.

When my brother Murphy was killed, my mother was diagnosed, and Kieran left the family company to pursue a career in the darkness, things shifted again, and I watched him take all the punches standing up.

My father isn't the kind of man who wavers or cowers; he adjusts, adapts, and makes life his bitch.

But for some reason, it often rings hollow, as if there are secrets he keeps hidden. Evil doings lurking in his shadows, sheltered by the facade of normalcy he presents to the rest of the world.

I've been trying to emulate the practice for as long as I can remember, which is how I recognize that it's a veil. One I don't ever see him shedding.

I sigh, glaring at my straw. "I just think it's weird he ate the cookie, is all. Why would you do that if you're allergic to chocolate?"

"Maybe he was trying to prove a point." My father shrugs. "He did say you burst in while he was on an important phone call."

"He *told* on me?"

"Well, no. Chelsea did, and then I asked Boyd about it, because Chelsea can sometimes be a little..."

"Bitchy?"

He shoots me a look. "*Dramatic.*"

And there it is. A rock sinks low into my stomach, the weight unsettling, and I feel the tears spring to my eyes before I have a chance to stop them.

I take a long drag of my shake, swishing the icy chocolate around my teeth, and swallow, flipping my hair over my shoulder. "Maybe I should befriend her, then. Sounds like we'd get along; maybe we can share horror stories of how uptight you and Boyd are, or maybe — "

My mother comes in from the greenhouse, stopping in the mudroom to wash her hands, and my train of thought derails as I wait for her to call for me. I get to the bottom of my milkshake, the slurping sound drowning out the initial vibrations coming from my father's phone across the island counter.

"Could you bring that to me, Fi?" he says absentmindedly, and I reach over, scooping it into my palm, stealing a glance at the screen as it lights up.

An unknown number flashes — not totally unusual, given the secretive nature of his profession. As I walk over and place the phone in his hand, though, numerous text messages from the same number appear below the missed call. The actual message previews are hidden, and while it shouldn't immediately give me pause, something about the urgency makes me uneasy, though I can't quite pinpoint why.

As the CEO of the company, my father doesn't usually deal with daily operations or trivial matters. He's typically consulted on emergencies and big accounts, and if someone is trying to get a hold of him now, that must mean something is wrong.

At least, that's what my gut is screaming. It sends ripples of anxiety through me, a foreboding sensation settling over me the way it did when my brother Murphy dove off the deep end and wound up dead.

'Trust your gut,' my mother always says. But as I watch my father check the screen and slip the phone into his shirt pocket, I realize trusting your gut is one thing, but learning what to do with the information is another entirely.

Knots twist in my stomach, vomit teasing the base of my throat as my body begins to reject all my food from today, and I swallow over the panic, trying to ignore it.

Tossing my milkshake in the garbage beneath the kitchen sink, I stop by the mudroom to make sure my mother doesn't need any assistance. The questions now are almost part of my daily routine, as is her constant refusal for anything around the house outside of showering and occasionally getting her ready for bed.

She waves me off, wiping the inside of a ceramic pot clean. The vein in her forearm pulses visibly as she works slowly, struggling to maintain her energy. Unease threads into the very fiber of my being, and I grip the doorframe with one hand, tapping the pad of my finger against the paint.

Turning off the water and leaving the pot in the plastic sink, she dries her hands on a nearby dish towel and sighs. "Did you need something, darling?"

I chew on the corner of my lip, wishing I had a piece of gum right now that would distract from the unease bubbling up inside me. Or a cigarette.

Part of me wants to mention the weird feeling I have about my father, but the other part knows she'll only launch into a lecture about fine tuning the understanding of my body or she'll share in my concerns and worry herself to death.

A tremor rolls through the left side of her body, causing her arms to lock at the elbows and her hands to shake slightly, and I can't bring myself to add to the load.

"You need any help?"

Smiling, she leans against the hutch at her side for support. "If I do, your father is home. I'll just ring for him." When I hesitate, she raises an eyebrow. "Unless... you'd *rather* help me?"

I scratch at my arm absently, the itch beneath my skin a welcome distraction from the volcanic eruption threatening inside me. "Just let me know if you need me."

She nods, a curious expression on her delicate, aged face, and I turn on my heel, using the back staircase hidden behind a sliding door in the hall to head up to my bedroom.

Once inside, I slam my back against the closed door and exhale slowly, some of the tension fleeing my body with the familiarity of the room. I curl my toes against the pink braided rug on the floor and walk over to the four-poster king-size bed, smoothing my palm over the plush pink comforter. One corner is slightly askew, telling me that Giselle, the housekeeper we have who keeps weird hours, must've been sweeping the rooms for laundry.

My gaze homes in on the corner, the urge to adjust it accordingly blaring like a car horn in my mind. Collapsing onto the mattress, I stare up at the vaulted ceiling and pull my phone from my pocket, responding to a text from Heidi and Bea about drama club tomorrow afternoon, saying I'll try to be there.

Making circles with my eyes on the wall, I unlock my phone and pull up the Ivers International website, clicking on the employee database and scrolling through the lower level employees until I hit the executives. Boyd isn't *technically* a higher-up, but I know my father wants to hand the company over to him one day, and I know he has the salary and responsibility to match.

But given that everyone in town already believes Boyd stole his spot and didn't earn it, I think he keeps the lower-ranking title to avoid further speculation from the gossip rags.

I click on the hyperlink with his name, and a small, circular picture of him heading a meeting in a maroon button-down and black dress pants appears. Someone in HR must've snapped it when they realized Boyd would never willingly give them a photo of himself.

God, it's ridiculous how good he looks.

White-hot frissons of electricity coil in my stomach, my heart beating between my thighs, and I scoot back on the bed, studying the picture more closely as one hand slides down my stomach. My fingers slip beneath the waistband of my shorts as my eyes travel the delicious contours of his face, the smooth outline of his neck and shoulders, down to his tapered waist, the ink on his knuckles, and the slightest hint of a bulge behind his slacks.

My chest tightens as the pad of my index finger reaches my center, a gentle exploration I rarely allow. There's something so vulnerable in the act, something that almost takes me out of it when I try with other online paraphernalia.

It's almost too intimate for my brain to fully relax into, but now, lying here staring at the god I've been drooling over for years, I can't help wondering why I haven't tried using him as a muse before.

Drawing my hand lower, I use some of the moisture pooling at my entrance and circle my clit, shuddering as I stroke the sensitive flesh. The heat from Boyd's gaze yesterday flares in my vision, the memory of his deep, husky voice and the way he'd raked his eyes over my form, like a man who'd never tasted dessert, has pressure winding in my stomach, constricting my breaths as they try to escape my lungs.

I swirl my finger faster, applying more pressure to the right until liquid fire zaps through me, shooting down to my toes and up my spine. My pulse beats harder, faster, in time with the direction of my finger, and when I come, it's Boyd's name that causes stars to burst behind my eyelids.

I'm panting when I take my hand out of my shorts, my breathing labored and skin slicked with sweat. Smiling to myself, it doesn't even occur to me to feel ashamed or guilty over what I've just done, even though I know no one would approve.

Even though I know Boyd would never do something like this. Would never lose control this way.

The blood rushing through my veins makes me feel alive, though. It feels *real*.

I slide off the bed, getting up to wash my hands before dinner, when I notice there's a short bio section beneath his picture.

Boyd Kelly: Master's in Cybersecurity Engineering, Camden native, King's Trace High Alumni.

Three facts, displayed exactly how I imagine he gave them. Bullet points, the only things he's willing to divulge to strangers.

But it's the last line that gets me. That feels too personal, too poignant not to have been a recent update, probably from himself.

Allergic to chocolate.

CHAPTER EIGHT

Wiping my cheek with the handkerchief I wrench from the waistband of my athletic shorts, I clean the blood off my skin, increasing the pressure of my forearms against my opponent's throat.

Once upon a time, I liked to believe I was better than this. Better than biology and above circumstance. That not being born in King's Trace gave me a leg up when it comes to the evil that rains in the streets, exists behind every closed door, and whispers in the wind.

I should've known better.

The first time I beat a man's face to a bloody pulp, there should've been shock. Remorse. Fear. But when his skull cracked against the lip of the tub in LeeAnn's tiny bathroom, splitting his skin where it connected, and leaked blood when he settled on the floor, I didn't feel anything.

A kid shouldn't be so comfortable with that level of violence. With death. By that time, though, I'd already pulled LeeAnn from the brink countless times, shielded her body with my own when her drug dealing one-nighters or the thieves she kept as boyfriends decided they wanted to take some of their anger out on her.

I let them use me instead.

That was my normal. Black and blue skin, busted lips, broken bones. The will to live wasn't present in me for a long time outside of the need to make other people hurt the way I did.

It wasn't until I moved in with my aunt Dottie and her husband, William, that I realized violence isn't supposed to be inherent. You're not supposed to crave it or chase the release you get from partaking in it.

At that point, it was too late, a carnal need that burrowed into my bones, replacing the marrow with its filth.

For Dottie and William's sake, I buried it. Kept the tendencies a secret, only hit people I knew would fight fair, didn't actively go searching for trouble.

In college, I happened upon the Crystal Knuckle, an underground—and completely illegal—MMA fight club that exists in the interconnected basements of several downtown businesses, beginning at the King's Trace Courthouse.

Owned by the Bianchi family, a small organized crime unit that came to town a few years ago trying to encroach on Montalto and Stonemore territory, it's an elite club whose members pay exorbitant fees and undergo extensive background searches just to beat the shit out of each other, or watch other people get the shit beat out of them.

Angelo Bianchi, a middle-aged man with a sleek ponytail and biceps bigger than my thighs, steps up through the ropes around the ring, kicking at my bruised ribs. He's the head of the crime family and is extremely strict when it comes to the things he allows down here.

"Where are your fucking gloves, Kelly?"

Proper gear is a must. There are posters detailing the things to be worn inside the ring plastered against every cement wall down here, from the lobby to the locker rooms, but I rarely pay them any mind. It's not like my opponents get many hits in, anyway.

I unwrap myself from the Rhode Island tourist who'd picked my ticket tonight, apparently unaware that my showing up in an expensive, five-piece suit didn't mean I was clean. He spits in my direction, this time just missing my face as he scrambles away, cursing in a foreign language.

Rolling over, I smirk at the molar stranded on the mat, the bloody root still in place, and reach for it before Angelo has a chance to realize what I did.

I don't fight clean at all. What's the point when everything you're doing is illegal, regardless?

Plus, there's no thrill in following the rules that the Bianchis set. No excitement to be had with simple leg kicks and elbow strikes. If you want the gratification of the violence, you have to dig deep, or else you'll never be satisfied.

Angelo shakes his head, shoving his hands into his maroon tracksuit pockets. "I tell you time and time again, 'no gloves, no fights,' but you never fucking listen. You deaf or somethin', kid?"

As if on some sort of cue, the ache in my ear intensifies, and I sit up slowly, trying to gather my bearings, curling my fist around the tooth. That fucker knew what he was doing, I'll give him that; before I could even blink once the timer sounded, he'd launched into an attack, elbowing my ribs as I climbed inside, taking out my feet, and ramming his knee into the side of my head until all noise grew distant for me.

When I rounded on him, slamming his body into the soft padding of the ring floor, I'd shoved my fist into his mouth, found a loose tooth toward the back, and yanked it out before pulling him into a guillotine, reveling in the different shades of red and purple his face turned before Angelo interrupted.

I wipe my mouth with the back of my free hand, taking the one he outstretches and getting to my feet. "I don't need you to worry about me, Angelo. I'm a big boy, I can take a few blows."

He rolls his eyes, muttering something in Italian, and smooths a hand over his ponytail. "Be that as it may, rules are rules for a reason. I don't want anyone dying while they're down here. I got enough shit above ground to clean up without having to worry about this gig, too."

"I'll try to remember," I lie, waving as we part ways and I head for the locker room showers.

Once inside, I drop the tooth with the others in the cloth knapsack I keep tucked in the back of my locker. *Evidence.*

Stripping down, I hang a towel on the shower divider and step beneath the scalding spray, rinsing myself of the blood and sweat. Pain flares through every nerve ending in my body, and I'm focused on the way it caresses my skin, a hot blade dipped in ecstasy.

I almost don't notice the shadow in the corner of the room or hear the throat when it clears.

My head whips to the side, meeting eyes so dark and evil they're almost black, completely devoid of any emotion whatsoever. His black trench coat is buttoned to his sharp chin, even though it's a million degrees in this basement and incredibly humid, his inky hair matted down beneath a knit cap.

Kal Anderson, dubbed Doctor Death around town, though no one knows *exactly* why. He's more of a fucking

71

mystery than I am, with the only certainties being that he's downright terrifying and has a medical degree, occasionally moonlighting at different hospitals around the country and doing in-house work for Stonemore, the Montaltos, and their parent family in Boston.

Other than that, his past and present are an abyss of nothingness, secrets so protected by the vile man that no one ever dares question them.

He's Kieran's mentor for all things fixer and hitman, but he's never really bothered with me, so I can't quite understand what he's doing here now.

"Not into peep shows," I mutter, shutting off the water and drying myself. I wrap the towel around my waist and step out of the stall, keeping a wide berth between us as I walk to my locker and take out a pair of sweats and a hoodie.

"Not interested in peeping," Kal replies, following with a dark chuckle. "Didn't know you frequented this club."

"Didn't know it was pertinent."

He nods. "Fair enough. I was just surprised to see you, I suppose. You don't exactly look the type."

"Isn't that the whole point?"

Again, he nods, holding his palms up in mock surrender. "I'm not going to out you or anything, if that's what you're worried about. I know how difficult it is to keep a certain... persona, in towns like this."

Pulling my hoodie on over my head and yanking my sweats up, I toss the towel into my locker and cross my arms over my chest. "Cool. Was there something else you needed?"

Scratching at his chin, he shrugs. "I'm assuming you know who I am."

"Hard not to know anyone in this town."

"Right." He shoves his hands into his pockets, and backs up, watching me. I can't help wondering what he's doing down here in the first place—I've never seen Kal around these parts, and he's certainly not dressed for the occasion. "I'd appreciate the same sentiment extended to me, in that case. Don't really want a lot of people knowing I'm back in town, and certainly not that I was here. Image to protect, and all that."

"No problem." Pocketing my keys and wallet, I give him a curt nod and fake salute. "Great chat, then."

As I walk off, pushing open the locker room door, he doesn't respond. Just watches me. Even as I turn the corner and head up the emergency exit, coming out at the back of the courthouse, I can feel his eyes on me, burning holes into my flesh.

I'm curious to know what *he* was doing there, but not interested enough to ask. The reason is probably similar to mine, and anything else isn't worth my time.

Stopping by the Green Apple Grocery, I purchase two Dasani waters from the gray-haired owner, Gladys, and a bag of sunflower seeds, then head down the sidewalk toward my bike, swinging my leg over the seat as I stuff the bottles into the cooler strapped to the back.

Tearing open the packet of seeds, I pop a handful into my mouth and reach for the keys in my pocket, pausing when I hear a familiar laugh.

Like a magnetic force field, I'm drawn to the sound — my eyes scan the dark street, searching for the source and immediately spotting red hair a ways down. Fiona's seated at a patio table outside the only Starbucks in town, sipping from a plastic cup, her long legs illuminated by the glow of the sign above the overhang on the building. She laughs again, the sound tapping into a direct line to my cock, and reaches across the table, squeezing the bicep of someone whose head I can't quite make out.

Getting off my bike, I walk closer to where they're situated, careful to stay in the shadows until I can make out her companion.

A lead weight plummets in my stomach, apprehension mixing with something inappropriate until red flares behind my vision.

Nico. Fucking. Bianchi.

CHAPTER NINE

Fiona

"You can't be serious." I laugh, squeezing Nico's arm as his brown eyes crinkle at the corners. "He *paid* a *prostitute* to be your prom date? That's insane."

Nico laughs too, tipping his head back to take a sip of his Americano. A thin layer of the drink appears on his upper lip, and his tongue darts out, erasing it. "I know, and he had the gall to explain it as some sort of Bianchi tradition. Said his father and his grandfather all took escorts to their formal dances, and that it made me a man in the eyes of '*The Family*.'" He raises his hands making air quotes around that last bit, and I giggle at the absurdity of the mafia putting anything other than murder on that kind of pedestal.

"And I thought my mom making us spend birthdays at the cemetery as kids was crazy." I shake my head, retracting my hand and slipping it around my frozen caramel latte. Even though it's still March, the air tonight is exceptionally warm, and the icy drink under my fingers is a nice contrast, giving my nerves something to settle on.

"The cemetery? That sounds..."

"Depressing?" I smile, shrugging. "It was definitely not a favorite pastime of ours, to the point that eventually we all started not looking forward to our birthdays. But I think that was kind of her point."

"Kind of like facing your mortality, no?"

"*Exactly.* She wanted us to be aware that every new year we're blessed with on this earth increases our chances of having everything ripped away."

'And eventually, it will be. Death is our only guarantee in life.'

I can still hear her whispering those words, clutching Murphy to her side as we stared at the family plots, as if she knew all along he'd be the first of us to go.

"How *is* your mom?" Nico asks, and I'm slightly surprised—not that he knows, considering that's just how things work in towns like this, but that he's asking at all. I've known Nico since his family moved into town a few years back; we

76

worked on the King's Trace Prep yearbook together with Heidi and Bea, and ran a food drive one winter, using his dad's vans to transport the donated goods and bonding over shared complaints about our older brothers.

When we graduated high school, Nico came out to me, desperate to get his sexuality off his chest and unable to confide in his father or brother, Romeo, whose Catholic backgrounds run much deeper than the Ivers'. And ever since, we'd formed a tentative friendship, one held together by random coffee dates.

"She's okay," I say, my fingers flexing around my cup, the cold spreading to my palms and traveling up my arms. My tongue feels thick inside my mouth, too big to form more dialogue about her declining health. "But enough about me, you're on spring break, right? Is California everything they say it is?"

A shadow passes over his face for a brief moment, like Helios dragging the sun against the sky to create night. When he blinks, removing his hands from his coffee and placing them against his cheeks, it's gone, replaced with a smile that looks painful.

"California is great, and campus is beautiful. Berkeley is such a different atmosphere from the one I grew up in, and I'm —
"

"Fiona, what the fuck are you doing?"

Jumping at the sound of my name attached to a deep, *angry* voice, I swivel my head just as Boyd jaywalks across the

77

street, arms crossed over his broad chest, gray sweatpants slung low on his hips.

Oh, my good God.

My gaze falls involuntarily, noting a very distinct outline, and I quickly look away as he approaches our table, eyes wild and blazing.

Nico's eyes slide to mine, one dark brow raising, as he takes another drink. I suck in a breath, prepared to fend off Boyd's overprotective nature the same way I would with Kieran. "This is Nico—"

Boyd scoffs. "I know who it fucking is. What are you doing here with him?"

"Um... having coffee?" I gesture at our cups on the table, confusion washing over me. Kieran usually settles after an introduction, using it to remind people of who he is, but Boyd doesn't seem to relax in the slightest.

Warmth rises to my cheeks when I realize this must look like a date, and since the Bianchi boys have a notorious reputation for whoring around town (even if, in Nico's case, it's untrue), I'm sure Boyd's assumption is that I'm one cup of coffee away from jumping into bed with him.

Not that it should *matter*. I'm an adult, and really nothing to Boyd. He made that pretty clear the other day when he called me to the hospital and left me there with Chelsea, so I don't really know what his problem is right now.

"Are you asking or telling me?"

Scrunching my eyebrows together, I frown at Boyd. "I was answering your question?"

His nostrils flare, and I tear myself from the intensity swimming in his cappuccino eyes to steal a glance at Nico, who's watching us with an amused expression. I tuck my hair behind my ears, tension collecting in my spine because I can't place where Boyd's hostility is coming from.

Ignoring him and focusing on the cold in my hands, I sigh, smiling gently at Nico. "Sorry, you were saying? Berkeley is different?"

He opens his mouth to answer, but Boyd's hand clamps down on my bicep, cutting him off. I'm yanked from my chair and into Boyd's hard body, knocking my latte over in the shuffle. "What are you —"

"Coffee's bad for the baby," Boyd snaps, clenching his jaw. Casting Nico a side glance, Boyd jerks his thumb in my direction. "Only ten weeks along, but the doctors always say it's never too early to start changing your habits."

Nico snickers, and my chin drops in shock. "What are you *talking* about?"

"Fiona, there's no point in keeping it a secret. Everyone else is going to find out at some point, anyway. Don't be shy, princess."

"They'll only know because you're shouting it!"

My blood boils beneath the surface of my skin, and I feel eyes on me as I try to twist out of his grip. Sure enough, when I look over my shoulder, Erica Moore, a Starbucks barista who was a year ahead of me in school, is plastered against the window, a phone pressed to her ear as she watches us like we're part of a daytime soap opera.

The store window is cracked, probably so she can hear enough to sell to some tabloid, although our small town spreads never pay enough to make the leak worth it.

I force a laugh, anxiety pooling in my chest. "He's just kidding, there's no baby."

Boyd yanks again, pulling me flush against him, and when I look up, his face is mere centimeters from mine. I can smell his soap, feel his breath mixing with my own, and it makes me dizzy for a moment.

Blinking from the spell and trying to ignore the way my core grasps at air, I lower my voice to a whisper. "Have you completely lost your mind?"

Moving his hand from my bicep to my elbow, his fingers dig into my skin, a bite of pain bursting beneath his touch. There's a desperation coloring his tone, something hungry and needy that makes my womb flutter. "Yes, I have. Help me find it."

"I'm not—"

But I don't get to finish my sentence, because in the next second he's slipping his hand into mine and dragging me away from the patio. My body feels like it's on fire with each step we take, my brain only capable of processing the fact that our fingers are interlocked, sparks flaring where our skin connects, so I don't notice at first when he turns down a dark, narrow alleyway behind the Green Apple Grocery.

I barely notice when he shoves me against the wall, chest heaving as he glares at me.

Don't notice the way his body practically vibrates, violence throbbing inside of his skeleton as if begging to be set free. It's not something I've ever seen in him before.

"Are you okay?" I ask, my voice barely a whisper, afraid to shatter whatever control he seems intent on exercising.

"No," he breathes, dropping his gaze to my lips. "Not even a little bit."

My heart pounds behind my ribcage, a thunderous sound that I'm pretty sure he'd be able to see behind my shirt if he glanced down.

"Were you on a date with that kid?"

Pressing my lips together to resist the urge to laugh in his face, I shake my head. "No, I already said we—"

"You know what he does with girls when he brings them home, right? How he and his brother share?" Raking his eyes down my form, lingering on the exposed skin where my black leather skirt stops and my boots begin, Boyd shakes his head. "They'd eat you alive."

"Not that it's any of your business, but I wasn't going home with him," I snap, scowling, hating the way his gaze seems to slip right under my skin.

It penetrates deep, on a search and rescue mission to find something I'm not even sure exists. A desire that seems to really only flare up in his presence, making my body hum with potential.

Except, there *is* no potential, because this is my brother's best friend. His *only* friend, not counting the people he works for. This is all wrong, and Boyd's moral compass is too strong to give in to that temptation, if it's even there for him.

Right?

Still, the look he's giving me reminds me a lot of the way he stared me down in his office, and I'm flooded with the memory of touching myself to his picture, finding my release in the idea of him, and my knees suddenly feel like jelly.

His arms come up as he shifts forward, bracing against the brick wall behind me. Caging me in. "I don't believe you."

Dropping his hooded gaze to my lips, he brings one hand up, smoothing his knuckles over my cheekbone; the touch is so gentle, so sudden, that it steals my breath even though I can just barely feel it. The oxygen evaporates from my lungs, captivated by the feel of his skin on mine, and my body practically melts into a puddle right there.

My voice is scratchy, raw, when I speak. "You don't have to."

I don't have a fucking *clue* what I'm expecting him to say, but lust contracts in my center when he steps even closer, his hip bones brushing against my stomach, humming low in his throat.

I'm pretty sure I stop breathing altogether.

Maybe his moral compass is skewed after all.

His hand glides from my face to my neck, his index finger making a slow trek down to the dip between my collarbones, exposed by the V-neck camisole I'm wearing. "I changed my mind," he says finally, slowly toying with the hem of my top.

"About what?"

"We're not even. Not by a long shot."

"Okay," I pant, confusion worming into my sex-fogged brain like a parasite, making me tense up for all the wrong reasons. My mind automatically defaults to the worry sector of my brain, searching for something to focus on that I didn't fix, like the comforter on my bed. "What do you want, then?"

God, why didn't I fix the bed?

Panic swells inside me, a sail taking on wind, and I tap out the soothing rhythm in my head over and over, waiting for it to subside.

Boyd's fingers pinch my chin, tilting my head so I'm forced to either close my eyes or look directly at him. His smoldering gaze burns like a wildfire, eyes glowing in the reflection of the moonlight, making my body turn to liquid and, momentarily, forget about the comforter being messed up.

"I want to try something," he says softly — so softly, I can't tell if I imagined it.

We stare at each other for several beats, neither of us breathing, our hearts beating out of control.

And then, mere feet from the coffee I spilled and the friend I was meeting with, hidden between two dingy buildings beside a rotting dumpster, while I struggle to maintain my sanity, Boyd fucking Kelly kisses me.

CHAPTER TEN

Boyd

Fiona *moans* into my mouth, my lips a decadent chocolate she's feasting on after a month long fast, and I can't help but swallow the sound, wishing I could consume her soul the same way. My body moves of its own accord, erasing the distance between us, my cock stiff as it grinds into her hip.

Christ, this is a horrible idea. A mistake, even.

But as I stood in front of her seconds ago, the scent of coffee and bubblegum and *need* stuck to her delicate skin, I couldn't think of doing anything *except* kissing her. My mind went blank, my vision blurred, and for a moment in time, my being was entirely engulfed in the flames of her passion.

Of being on the receiving end of them.

So, I acted, and now I'm not sure how I'm supposed to ever stop.

Her lips are soft, tentative, exactly the way you'd expect; I slip my tongue between them, flicking lightly before diving back in and sliding against hers. I explore the ridges, lapping at the sensitive underside while our mouths participate in a battle of wills, applying pressure and then chasing it, the kind of war that only ends one way.

In surrender.

Dropping my arms from where they're planted on the side of the building, I wrap one around her tiny waist, holding her against me, while the other reaches up and palms the back of her head. My fingers twist in her hair, reveling in the contrast of its smoothness under my calloused prints, while supernovas explode inside my chest.

She steals the breath from my lungs, reaching in and dragging it from my throat until all I can think to do in order to stay alive is keep kissing her.

Desire flares from my toes to the top of my head, making me a little dizzy and throwing me off. I've kissed enough women in my life to know this isn't normal. That something profound is happening here, a universe either collapsing or creating, I can't quite tell.

But fuck if I don't want to figure it out.

Sucking gently on her bottom lip, my hand slides from her waist around to the tight curve of her ass; it's the wrong move, though, because she wrenches her face from mine and shifts so my hand is trapped between her and the brick.

"You're kissing me," she says, completely out of breath. Her pupils are dilated twice their normal size, and her lips are swollen red, ripe and alluring. Such sweet innocence. "Why are you kissing me?"

"Because I couldn't stand not to."

Her eyes widen as her tongue darts out to wet the corner of her mouth, and I can't help imagining what her tongue would feel like licking my cock. How angelic she'd look as she slurped me to the back of her throat, gagging around my length, letting me own her.

And even though this insatiable need I seem to have for her has only been alive for a short time, I want it all.

Everything she can possibly give me.

"Oh." Glancing down at my lips, she nods slightly, almost to herself. "Okay, then."

Hooking her hand behind my neck, she raises up on her tiptoes to meet me, plastering herself against my body as our lips rejoin in a succulent symphony of stroking, sucking, and nipping. My dick throbs painfully behind my sweats, barely contained by the flimsy fabric; I roll my hips slowly, testing the waters, and almost choke on my saliva when I feel her lean into the movement.

Tearing myself from her mouth, I shove her back into the wall and drop my head to her neck, teasing her flushed skin with my breath. I reach the base and dip my tongue in the hollow point there, dragging it upward, tasting.

Savoring.

Pressing open-mouthed kisses beneath her chin, I bite down on one spot until her hands reach up and fist in my hair, another moan spilling from her lips. She tugs me back, her tits brushing against me with each labored breath she takes, and I can't remember a time I ever fucking missed someone else's presence around me.

But the second we disconnect, air filling the space between us, it feels like something inside my chest shatters into a thousand little pieces. The kind of breakage that can't be repaired.

"I don't understand what's happening," Fiona says, blinking up at me.

Straightening to my full height, I bring one hand to her jaw, tracing the curve with my knuckles. The dim light from above the grocery exit barely provides enough illumination for me to make out the explosions of color in her irises, but I can feel the added heat they provide, like molten lava scorching my flesh.

"Didn't we already establish that I was kissing you?"

"Well, yeah, but I still don't get *why*." Bending, she ducks under me, crossing her arms against her chest. "Before a week ago, you'd barely said three words to me in *seven years*, and now we've suddenly progressed to back-alley make-out sessions?"

I smirk. "Are you trying to say you don't *want* to kiss me, Fiona?"

Her fingers tap against the outside of her forearm. "Do you think Kieran would approve of what just happened?"

"I'm not really sure why I need to consider your brother's feelings at all," I say, irritation clotting my veins where euphoria has fled. A hollowness settles over me, the weight of needing to be in everyone's good graces reforming like an inflated balloon. "We're both adults, we can kiss who we want."

"But you don't really think that, considering you just pulled me away from a coffee date to keep me from kissing Nico." I open my mouth to point out her admission, and she rolls her eyes. "Which I *wasn't* going to."

"Why else would you have been out with him?"

She blinks, her brows knitting together above her nose. "What do you mean? I know you have friends, Boyd. Surely you don't want to sleep with all of them?"

Not bothering to correct her, to let her know my only friend is her brother, I stuff my hands in my pockets and shrug. "That's not the same issue."

"Why isn't it?"

"Because I'm not a naive eighteen-year-old girl who'd let just anyone kiss them."

I regret the words as soon as they leave my mouth, my tongue moving faster than my brain and cock, but there's nothing I can do to retrieve them. That's the thing about remorse; it only comes when it's too late for you to change the outcome. It's an afterthought, something our consciences drum up to try and make you feel guilty for being human, but it doesn't really make a difference when it counts.

Now her eyebrows shoot into her hairline, her lips folding in, an indecipherable expression morphing her facial features.

"So, that's why you kissed me." Her voice is small, fragile, and it eats away at something inside my chest, making me nauseous. "Because you could."

When I don't immediately deny it — *can't* deny it, because I've already given away too much of myself tonight — she huffs out an incredulous laugh. Reality comes crashing down around us, our differences in age and life experience smacking me in the face as she stares at me, as if she's never once been used like this before. As if I'm the first person to ever hurt her.

What a luxury that must be.

Annoyance wins out over fleeting regret, my defenses clicking into place once again, imaginary barbed wire fences keeping her separate. Away from me, where the only one who can hurt her is herself.

Knowing her family's history of self-destruction, I have no doubt that she will.

"Well, thanks for ruining my evening, I guess." She takes a step away from me, the heels of her black boots creating a dull thud on the pavement. "See you around, Boyd."

I spring forward, my fingers fisting the material of her shirt, pulling her back into me. "How're you getting home?"

Struggling against me, she tries to elbow me in the stomach, but I flex so it barely registers. "Nico drove me here."

"Then I'm taking you back."

"Jesus, can you drop the macho-possessive-alpha act? It's very tiring trying to keep up with that and you ignoring me."

"Did you prefer it when I didn't acknowledge your existence?"

She doesn't say anything, and a sharp pain stabs at my heart at the crestfallen look that shadows her pretty face. *Why do I seem to only say the wrong things with her?*

"Yes," she murmurs finally. I twist her in my arms and hold her a few inches away, studying the soft lines of her face. Her skin is still flushed—though from the kiss or her embarrassment after, I don't know—and she keeps her eyes locked on the collar of my shirt, deliberately ignoring me.

"Okay, then." Wrapping my hand around her bicep, I drag her out of the alley and back up the street toward my bike, sliding on before she has a chance to. She just stands to the side, silent, arms crossed over her chest, and I sigh. "Would you get on?"

Biting her lip, she shakes her head. "I don't want to ride this."

"I don't really care." Pulling my helmet off the back of the seat, I hold it out to her. She frowns, the gesture creating deep crevices at the corners of her mouth, and only takes it after I threaten to drop the thing.

Gripping the black helmet in both hands, she brings it over her head, flipping the tinted window down even though the sun's set and we aren't moving yet. Almost as if she doesn't want me to be able to see her anymore. Hoisting her leg over the seat, she slowly climbs on, and I can feel her hands in her lap at the base of my spine.

The heat from her cunt sears into me through my clothing, and I grip the handlebars tightly to stave off the chemical reaction happening behind my sweats. Even though there's nothing I'd like more than to bend her over this bike, lap at her until she forgets her name, and fuck her on the seat until it's coated in both of us, I *can't*.

I shouldn't have fucking kissed her tonight, but I meant what I said. It's like there was this overwhelming outside force propelling me toward her, and once the kiss was set in motion there was nothing I could do to stop it.

It was a need, carnal and forbidden and just plain *wrong*, but there'd also been a certain sense of rightness while it happened. As if kissing Fiona Ivers was the missing link in my life, and nothing else would ever compare to the act.

But it can't happen again. I like my dick attached to my body, and there's no telling what Kieran would do if he found out what'd happened.

Not to mention, her naivete is astounding. Perhaps growing up stuffing your emotions into a drawer all while being handed life on a silver fucking platter doesn't do you any favors, if she's any indication.

I have enough complications in my life with Riley and LeeAnn and work. I certainly don't need anything else stealing my attention.

Still, as I bark at Fiona that she needs to hold on to me, taking off when her tiny arms wind around my midsection, I can't quite clear my mind of the dirty thoughts or the sense of impending doom.

Adjusting the lapels of my suit jacket as the office door swings closed behind me, I follow the back of Kieran's head through the packed club floor, weaving between the sweaty bodies of various college kids and the drunken mistakes they'll make tonight.

He pushes through the front doors, nodding at Seamus, one of the Stonemore gang's bouncers, as we take a turn and head down the busy sidewalk.

Even before he stops at the head of the alleyway, I know he's looking for her.

Juliet Harrison, the blonde-haired, blue-eyed reformed party girl that seems to have occupied his every thought since the fundraising gala. Similar to the way Fiona occupies mine, but significantly less forbidden.

If he fucks Juliet, the worst risk he runs is contracting an STD. Or maybe getting shot by her mafia boss brother-in-law.

If I fuck his sister, I run the risk of being skinned alive.

Literally.

Gore is Kieran's MO, and even though I take part in the same kind of side work when I deem it necessary, my friend seems to get a deep satisfaction from ending lives in the sickest ways possible.

That's why I can't admit I kissed his sister, or that I want to do it again.

That I want to do so much more than kiss her.

Evidently, the gala let loose a hunger in both of us, gripping us by the balls and refusing to let go.

Pulling a joint from my suit pocket and lighting up, I watch Kieran's jaw clench as he exhales loudly, spotting Juliet exactly where I'd expected her to be.

We'd been in a meeting with Finn Hanson, leader of the Stonemore gang and owner of The Bar—the premier club in Stonemore for horny young adults to hang out, if the people plastered to the sticky booths and multi-colored dance floor were any indication—explaining the findings of the routine audit we'd run for him, when Kieran noticed Juliet inside and took off, clinging to the walls as he watched her dance and drink merrily with her friends.

Eventually, she slunk off with some hunky firefighter, and Kieran prowled out after her, apparently determined to keep an eye on the flighty bird.

Now, his obsession is kicking him in the dick, and I'm just watching the destruction.

I laugh as he turns to me. "Unclench. You're the most tightly wound guy I know," I say, adding *besides me* as an afterthought in my head, noting that few people ever seem to be as tense as I am. "And you don't have a claim on this girl. Regardless of what she owes you."

His hand travels absently to the heart-shaped locket around his neck—*Juliet's* locket, which seems to have mysteriously appeared in his possession. Their interactions at the gala had included her demand for its return and his immediate denial, lest she *give him something in return*, but evidently, she hadn't wanted the jewelry back bad enough, since he's still wearing it.

Shaking his head, he drops his arm. "I just wasn't expecting her to go off and fuck some guy before I've even had my turn."

I glance over his shoulder, noting the way the firefighter fumbles against her, obviously unsure of himself around the woman. *God, she looks bored.*

Pointing my joint in their direction, I shrug. "I don't think she'll even remember this dude after tonight."

Kieran grunts, turning back to see the finale; I avert my gaze when the man groans, rutting against Juliet a few more times before slipping from her body and adjusting his clothing. She slumps against the wall as they have a short conversation, and then the firefighter heads back inside, leaving her out here. Alone.

The perfect prey for the hunter beside me.

Flicking some ash from the butt of my joint, I grip the end between my teeth and raise an eyebrow, recognizing the ferocity marring Kieran's face. It matches the intensity I feel around his sister, the unparalleled magnetism that draws him to Juliet the way I'm drawn to Fiona, an electrical force we can't deny.

I'm reminded of mine and Fiona's kiss, how her soft, supple lips seemed to melt for mine, how good it felt to hold her body against me, and I'm met with a flashing pang of guilt when Kieran gives me a weird look.

What would he really do if he found out?

"Need me to leave?" I ask, trying to redirect my thoughts.

He tilts his head, seemingly lost in his head, and I hold my hands up, backing up off the curb and relenting, not wanting to stick around to watch round two. My bike sits up the street, my helmet hooked on the back, and when I climb on, the only thing I can think about is Fiona's arms wrapped around me as I drove her home earlier, how her warmth seemed to reach something inside of me that's previously only known the cold darkness.

Remorse floods through me, and I try to focus on the feeling, try to siphon the guilt I *should* have, but I find myself met only with the desire to kiss again, consequences be damned.

CHAPTER ELEVEN

Fiona

"Describe it again, I still don't think I'm getting the full picture."

Rolling my eyes, I toss my gum wrapper at Bea, watching it bounce off her brown skin and float to the ground by her white Converse. "I've replayed the scene like ten times since I got here."

"I know, but where's the emotion? You *finally* kissed the guy you've been pining after since middle school, but I can't even celebrate because I don't feel like you're portraying it accurately."

"It was just a kiss, Bea," I say, flicking a piece of lint off my pink raincoat as I shuck it off my shoulders, letting it droop to the auditorium seat.

She scoffs, twirling a lock of straight black hair around her index finger. "It's *never* just a kiss, Fi-Fi. Don't act like we didn't learn that from every single blockbuster romance growing up."

"Those are *movies*," I say. "They don't matter."

"They don't matter?" She waves her hands around, gesturing toward the stage, the people milling about before practice begins. "Then what are we even doing here? What's the point of all of this?"

Groaning internally, I lean back and rest my head against the back of my chair, strapping in for a lecture on the importance of acting and how the profession dates back to ancient Greece and is the very basis for the foundation of humanity.

It's been Bea's dream to get to Los Angeles since she was a kid, and she's been dragging us to drama club at the community theater in Stonemore for as long as I can remember. Heidi and I come when we can, but every instructor we've had in the club has always been able to point out the differences in our attitude toward participating; Bea's eager and ready before they ever call her name for exercises or auditions, and Heidi and I always seem to be three steps behind.

Now, though, I'm kind of grateful for the club's distraction; just as Bea launches into her bullet points on the history of acting, Olga, our instructor this semester, waves her arms onstage and asks us to divide into pairs and practice our diaphragm breathing exercises.

A teacher's pet at heart, Bea scrambles to her feet and skips to partner with Olga, leaving me with Heidi, who hasn't spoken a word since I mentioned what happened between Boyd and me the other night.

Tightening her blonde ponytail, Heidi stands up, staring at me blankly. "Ready?"

I shrug, pushing out of the seat. "Sure."

We move to a corner of the auditorium, facing each other and focusing on harnessing our pelvic muscles to push air into our chests. Or something like that. I don't think I'm doing it right, but I don't really care to, either.

Heidi sucks in a deep breath, then releases it slowly, her jaw relaxing on the exhale. "So, are you in love with him?"

My eyebrows raise and I sputter, some of the saliva in my mouth getting sucked down my throat. "What?"

"Boyd. Are you guys dating or something?"

"Did you miss the ending of the story?" I ask, pressing my palms flat together. "He basically called me a dumb whore and drove me home in silence. Didn't even have the decency to drop me off at the doorstep; no, he stopped *outside* our gate, and I had to walk up the driveway."

"Maybe he was afraid someone would hear his bike and question his presence."

Not liking how she's defending him, I shrug again, pretending it doesn't matter. Doing what I'm best at. "Maybe. I don't care, either way, though. It was a stupid kiss that never should've happened, and never will again. Just... a consequence of heightened emotions and two passionate people."

She hums, her blue eyes narrowing, and anxiety weaves through my body like a river rushing to empty into the ocean. My heart beats hard against my ribs, and I dig my nails into my thighs until I can feel the indents forming on my skin, trying to focus on the sharp pain instead of the need to placate my friend.

Clearly, she has an issue with my kissing Boyd, but I can't quite tell if it's concern for the status of my heart, or something worse. Still, I do my best not to dwell on it right now—I know it'll be there waiting to torture me when I'm alone later.

Changing the subject to school, I ask about how she's enjoying her second semester—she's on campus at Unity studying environmental science, just visiting for the weekend, and I can tell by the way she dives into the new conversation that she's definitely jealous.

When I get home later that night, Kieran's sitting at the table with Boyd and my father, and I roll my eyes at Boyd's fucking audacity, coming here for family dinner when he sucked the soul from my body mere days ago.

I pass by the table anyway, glancing over my father's shoulder at the documents spread out as I bend to kiss his cheek.

"This is the first time I've ever seen you bring work home, Daddy."

He chuckles, adjusting his glasses. "First time for everything, sweetheart. I've not been able to get much work done at the office lately."

A throat clears pointedly, drawing my attention, but when I look up, Boyd's not paying me any mind, studiously scanning the packet in front of him. I roll my eyes and walk to the kitchen, setting my purse on the island and move to wash my hands in the sink. "Why's Kieran here?"

"Uh, I live here."

Barely. My brother splits his time between this house and Murphy's old cottage in the woods by Lake Koselomal, and truly, when he's here, he's never *really* here. Checks out worse than our mother during one of her episodes.

"It's *unofficial* business." My mother's voice floats into the room, light and airy as she follows the same path I just took, wrapping her arms around my father's neck and kissing his cheek. She smiles at me above his head. "Which means we're ordering from Opulence. How would you feel about going with me to pick it up?"

"Anything to get away from him," I mutter, drying my hands on a dishtowel. When I look back over at the dining table, they're all watching me, and I frown. "What?"

"Him who?" my mother asks, standing up straight to hold her left elbow in her right palm, as if to quiet the storm raging inside her muscles.

"Um..." My eyes dart to Boyd, who's staring back with a dark, dangerous expression, like he's daring me to say something about what happened between us. It makes my fingers curl at my sides as I drop the hand towel, the familiar itch to *fix* trying to claw its way to my brain so it can make my body obey.

I reach out and grip the edge of the island counter, squeezing until the tips of my fingers bloom white and go numb.

"Him being Kieran, obviously." I force a laugh, hoping it doesn't sound as hollow as it feels. "His cooking skills, I meant. If we go pick up food from Opulence, we avoid having to taste anything he makes, which means I won't spend the night vomiting after eating uncooked chicken."

Kieran rolls his eyes. "That was *one* time, and it was pork, thank you."

"Right." Nodding to my mother, I plaster a wide smile on my face. "I'm just gonna change real quick and we can go. Did you order lasagna?"

Her hand flies to her chest in mock offense. "As if I'd order anything else."

Sprinting up to my bedroom, I strip quickly and walk into my en suite, brushing a few of the tangles from my hair and reapplying a thin layer of concealer beneath my eyes. Anything to hide a bad night's sleep.

Pulling my hair into a bun, I head back into my bedroom, gasping when I notice the large figure standing at my desk, holding a framed picture from Christmas 2006.

"I'm not really sure you should be in here."

Turning slowly, Boyd cocks an eyebrow, dragging his hungry gaze over my body. It takes a second to remember I'm standing in a lace bra and matching pink thong, and a hot blush crawls up my skin.

I can tell he expects me to be embarrassed and probably duck into my walk-in closet by the way one corner of his mouth quirks and humor dances in his eyes.

But I don't. Instead, I drop my hands to my hips and straighten my spine, refusing to back down. My eyes burn with the effort it takes to avoid glancing down at the dark suit he has on, my brain imagining all the ways I'd like to shred it off his body, but I don't want to lose this battle, stupid as it may be.

Sometimes, you just need a win.

He takes a step forward, lust flaring behind his eyes as they fixate on my breasts; the bra isn't padded, my nipples are visibly puckered beneath the material, and I feel his desire between my thighs. It swirls, a reckless tsunami of conflict and passion, causing the blush in my cheeks to spread down my neck, staining my chest with its fury.

"I should definitely not be in here," he whispers, taking another step in my direction. We're silent as he continues to move toward me; my breathing grows shallow as our chests brush, hips mere centimeters apart.

"What's happening *now*?" I blurt, trying to resurface after the caramel depths of his irises threaten to pull me under.

"You ask too many questions."

Gritting my teeth, I frown. "It's just that, when you freaked out and got rude after kissing me the other day, I kind of got the impression you didn't want to do that again."

His hand reaches out, knuckles dusting against my jaw. "I don't."

"That's not what your eyes are saying."

As if my words snap him out of some kind of spell, Boyd yanks back suddenly, putting immediate distance between us by leaning against one of my white bedposts. Pulling at the collar of his black dress shirt, he lets his gaze drift lazily around the room.

His prolonged, quiet perusal makes anxiety climb up my neck, its fingers gripping my throat in a chokehold.

I scratch absently at my collarbone, needing to put more distance between us. Moving to the closet, I pull out a pair of distressed jeans and a red Stonemore Community sweatshirt, yanking them on before returning to the room.

When I get back, Boyd's lounging in my desk chair, his feet propped up beside my textbooks.

A book in the middle is slightly askew, farther to the right than the rest of the stack, and I just *know* he knocked it off balance.

I don't leave my things out of place—not when the fucking bedspread having a kink in it will keep me up for days.

An itch grows under my cheeks, and I scrape my nails over the spot, trying to find relief. I think he's talking to me, but the harder I scratch, the longer I stare at the lopsided stack, the farther I fall into an abyss of despair.

The one that has no rationale for *why* that stack needs to be straight, all the spines aligned and in ascending order of biggest to smallest covers, but that if I don't fix it immediately, *something* bad will happen.

What, exactly? I can never be sure. I don't let it get that far.

My fingers move of their own accord, slipping from my cheek to the tickle beneath my scalp, scraping and digging without conscious thought being in control. All the while, the need to fix the stack takes on a pulse inside me, an entity all its own, until I can't focus on anything but.

Tap, tap, tap.

Scratch, scratch, scratch.

I can taste my heartbeat in my throat as it jumps to epic proportions, its thunder deafening, and sweat beads along my hairline. Swallowing, I remember the words my mother used to utter when I was having a particularly bad episode.

Focus on something you can change. Imagine taking control until you've regained it.

"Are you okay?"

Boyd's voice finally penetrates the fog collecting in my head, and I shake my thoughts free but can't seem to tear my eyes from the atrocity across the room. He turns his head, following my line of sight, and after a few beats, reaches out and pushes the wonky book back in.

I heave a breath of relief, serotonin rushing to my extremities, and nearly collapse on my bed from the satisfaction. Wrapping one arm around the bedpost, I clear my throat. "I'm fine. Did you need something?"

He gives me a funny look but doesn't press further. "I just came to make sure you didn't tell anyone about what happened with us."

"You mean when you walked into my bedroom unbidden and ogled me in my underwear?"

His expression flattens. "No, the other night downtown."

"Oh, when you *kissed* me," I half shout, still a little high from everything that's just occurred.

"Christ," he snaps, pushing to his feet. "Say it fucking louder, Fiona."

"I would love to," I say, giving him a sugary-sweet smile. "Boyd kissed—"

The palm slapping over my mouth catches me off guard, even though I watch as it all unfolds. What's worse, it really turns me on—there's something delicious in the way he throws me around, how he's backed me into my own bedpost, the way he glares at me like I get under his skin.

I don't know what's happened in the last couple of weeks since the gala, but Boyd Kelly can't seem to stay away from me.

And *that's* the kind of control I want to have.

CHAPTER TWELVE

Boyd

I should let her go.

Step the fuck away.

Stop staring into her goddamn mesmerizing eyes.

At this rate, it's already going to take months to scrub her floral scent out from where I think it's embedded under my fingernails. To erase the feel of her silky, smooth porcelain skin from my fingertips and palms. To forget how perfectly her curves fit against the hard planes of my body, as if melting just for me.

My throat constricts as I stare down at her, my hand still plastered against her plump lips, our bodies damn near sewn together with how close I'm standing. I can't imagine having her spine pressed into the wood of her bed frame feels particularly good, but she doesn't move to push me away or try to squirm out from my touch.

That concerns me. In fact, instead of the nerves or confusion I associate with her in my presence, she seems to relax into me, as if my proximity and violent nature somehow bring her comfort.

I scan the contours of her face, trying my damnedest to memorize the delicate angle of her nose and count the freckles dusting her cheeks.

Forty-seven. She has forty-seven visible freckles, each one a unique size and shape compared to the one before, but none present enough to hide the pale skin underneath.

A pang rips across my gut, twisting the organ in knots as I press my hand harder against her, trying to imprint the feel of her saliva on my skin so I can beat off to it later. She mumbles something, and I smirk, shaking my head.

Regardless of how badly I want to be noble, to continue flying under the radar of everyday suspicion, I can't stop myself. The cruel beast inside of me loves to dole out pain as much as he's a glutton for it, which is the only reasonable explanation for why I'm fucking touching her again.

In her house, while her brother and father—my best friend and boss—sit downstairs, waiting for me to come back from the bathroom.

The beast is to blame for why I force her to look me in the eyes, my palm moving her head backward, and think about what she'd look like with my spit dripping down her face. It's why my mind goes from zero to one hundred in seconds, why I'm imagining her sucking my cock one minute and fantasizing about drowning her in my cum the next.

My hand shakes as I drag it away, my tongue thick inside my mouth as I distance myself from her. She blinks, confusion sparkling in her eyes, and it chips away at something pulled taut inside my chest, threatening to unravel me.

"I-I'm... fuck, Fiona." Expelling a harsh breath, I back up until my knees hit her bed frame and drop to the mattress.

"Are you going through a midlife crisis?"

A short laugh puffs past my lips. "Not quite old enough for that, I'm afraid."

"Quarter-life crisis, then." Smoothing her hand over where her sweatshirt's ridden up, she walks over and plops down on the bed beside me, swinging her legs over the edge of the frame. "You're the perfect age, give a couple years, for that. Perfect temperament, too."

"What's that supposed to mean?"

She shrugs. "People who have crises tend to be the ones who can't just accept life as it comes to them, yeah? You're not exactly known for being easygoing."

"And you are?"

"God, no." She giggles, the sound ridiculously soft and feminine and something I feel in my cock. "Which is how I can see it in other people. It's like we carry the weight of the entire universe on our shoulders."

I glance around her room, my eyes glazing over all the pink—the walls, the glass perfume bottles on her dresser, the corkboard above her desk covered in pictures and concert tickets and award ribbons. It's all so youthful and *pink*, reminding me of the bubblegum she's always chewing, and not at all reminiscent of the kind of responsibility she claims.

Although, perhaps that's the point.

There's a comfort in the innocence, the ability to shed your worries and just exist. Maybe her bedroom is that haven, and maybe I'm just an asshole.

"I shouldn't have kissed you," I say after a few beats of silence, trying to fill the awkwardness that's settled in around us.

Nodding, she raises an eyebrow, as if waiting for more. "Is there an apology buried in there somewhere?"

"No." I swallow, gripping my thighs. "I don't make a habit of apologizing, Fiona. Especially not for things I don't feel bad about."

"So... you don't think you should've kissed me, but you're also not sorry you did?" One manicured finger presses into the shallow dimple in her chin. "Yeah, definitely *some* kind of crisis."

"You're young, so I don't expect you to get it."

Scoffing, she rolls her eyes and shakes her head. Her fingers dance on top of her knees, and I see her glance at me from the corner of her eye. "Did you like kissing me?"

Turmoil swirls in my stomach, looking for something to glom on to. "It doesn't matter. I shouldn't have done it."

"But that doesn't answer the question."

Sucking in a deep breath, I open my mouth to answer when she whirls to face me, pulling her legs up on the bed and propping herself up on her knees. They brush my thigh as she sits back on her heels, blowing a tuft of hair from her face.

My gaze falls to her mouth—that classic ruby red stains her pouty, heart-shaped lips, and I want absolutely nothing more than to reach out and see if it smears.

And therein lies the entire problem. I don't want just a taste of her, however sudden this attraction may be. I want *all* of her, everything she could possibly give, and I don't want to keep it safe.

I want to destroy it.

Because deep down, no matter the expensive suits or the tattoos or the respect I demand inside a goddamn boardroom, I know that everything I ever love is destined for ruin, anyway.

Fiona clicks her tongue, reaching out and cupping my jaw; her hand is cold, sending a chill through my body that I try not to read into, her touch gentle. As though *she's* afraid *I* might shatter.

"I liked kissing you," she whispers, sliding her hand inward, tracing the dip of my bottom lip with her thumbnail. Goose bumps pop up along my skin, and my dick kicks behind my slacks, desperate for attention. "I wouldn't mind doing it again... minus all the crap you spewed after."

Pushing up from her position, she lets her hand fall to her side and gets off the bed, picking her leather purse off a wall hanger and slinging it over her shoulder.

"I've got to go grab my mom before she tries to drive herself. But, uh, yeah. Close the door on your way out."

When she passes the threshold of her room, she pauses, glancing at me over her shoulder. "You should also know, I'm great at keeping secrets."

Turning the flash drive in my hand, I scan the monitor, pushing my reading glasses farther up my nose while the time stamp reels forward. The other drive sits beside my mouse pad, overturned from where I slammed it down on the desk after reviewing its data.

Backing up the security footage another forty-eight hours, I stare at the basement mailroom as people file in and out, locking up at the end of the workday. No one suspicious appears to come through, according to the facial-recognition software I've paired with the employee roster, which makes the presence of these drives much more unnerving.

When I got back from lunch with Riley, who showed up unannounced to tell me she's donating her time to cleaning up Lake Koselomal since I wouldn't take her services, there'd been a manila envelope at the bottom of a stack of mail. Inside were two flash drives with a Post-it taped around them, Kieran's name written on one in thick black Sharpie.

Mine on the other.

The one with Kieran's name has some content I recognize—stuff he had me download and send in an encrypted folder back when he was working on getting his brother out of the drug and sex trafficking world he'd fallen into. It didn't work, and Kieran instead switched to collecting the dirty secrets of every person in town.

Someone evidently got a hold of that information and is now attempting to blackmail him with it, since it also has his family's deepest secrets.

On the other drive is the stuff I'm more concerned with, though. My birth records, LeeAnn's address, what might be a sex tape, but I can't be sure because once the dingy hotel room came into view I clicked out of the window.

Footage of me walking into the courthouse past hours, of me dragging known drug dealers behind dive bars in Stonemore, of me bloodying my knuckles and carving the skin of the seemingly innocuous. I don't fuck with people who typically don't deserve it, but this drive doesn't tell *that* story.

It paints me as a low-life criminal. As if I'm no better than LeeAnn or the deadbeat who ditched us.

It showcases my violent nature, the beast inside I try so fucking hard to repress.

Makes me look weak. Unstable.

Deranged.

But I'm not. I've worked way too fucking hard to prove that, and so as I download the data in the drive to my cloud server, ensuring I've got at least two copies, I print off the list of things on both of them, tucking them into a folder behind the audits I was asked to run.

Picking up the folder as tension threads its way across my shoulders, I crush my drive with a stapler, smashing it into pieces, and resolve to figure out who the fuck dropped it off after my meeting.

CHAPTER THIRTEEN

Fiona

Gripping the shower nozzle in my hand, I adjust the water pressure and turn down the temperature, running my fingers through my mother's hair as I rinse it. She sits in the middle of the tub with her arms wrapped tight around her ankles, knees to her chest, telling me about how Francis Crump, the treasurer of the garden club, was diagnosed with stage four breast cancer.

"She looked terrible." Shaking her head, my mother folds her lips together. "And I realized that I don't ever want to get to that point."

My hand pauses over her scalp, water raining down over my skin. "What do you mean?"

"This isn't a pretty disease, Fiona. I can feel it taking over my body with every passing day. It's clogging my brain, preventing my mobility."

"But you've been doing really well, I thought. Isn't that what Dr. Anderson said last week?"

She nods slightly, wincing as if it pains her. "I am doing well, but at what cost? My memory's only improved so much. Yesterday, I forgot Murphy was dead." Tears well in her eyes, shining beneath the vanity lighting. "It gets harder to remember what he looks like every day. Harder to move, harder to pretend that I'm not in constant agony."

Swallowing over the burn in my throat, I rinse the last bit of conditioner from her hair and return the nozzle to its hook, switching off the water and wringing her hair with my hands.

"I don't say anything because I'm supposed to be strong. My family needs me, and not being able to help them is a very difficult reality to come to terms with."

"Why are you telling me?"

Squeezing the lip of the tub with her hands, she pushes up to a standing position — it's slow, stilted, as if her body's made of plastic wrap and has to be unraveled instead of unfolded.

118

I help her step over, wrapping her in a blue terry cloth robe and getting her settled in the wheelchair she's been using around the house when it's just the two of us.

"Your father and Kieran aren't going to be the ones who need to know," she says after a moment. Her words come out rushed, like she senses some kind of bodily shutdown looming and wants to get them out before they disappear. "And I need someone to be prepared for the inevitable."

Exhaling shakily, I step back and cross my arms as she applies night cream beneath her eyes. Her hands tremble almost violently, making it near impossible to complete the task. "I don't want to talk about this."

Her jade green gaze meets mine in the mirror and fear mixed with blinding pain ripples through me. A hurricane hellbent on destruction. Tears prick my eyes, and I bite down on the inside of my cheek until I taste blood, tapping my index finger in soft strokes against my bare thigh, trying not to let my mind wander.

Because when I imagine my future, when I think about graduating college, getting married, and doing other adult things, my mother isn't present. There's this hole in the picture, a chasm of sadness where she *should* be, and instead I'm floating aimlessly in a sea of violence and despair while all these good things happen to me.

She's not there, and I'm angry with the universe for taking her.

Even now, I'm angry with it for sucking away both of our lives over the last few years. Angry that I don't know what exactly to expect, don't know how to prepare.

How the fuck does anyone prepare for death? No matter what we seem to do, no one is ever ready for it. It's like grief is this rite of passage and our souls are bound to it, forced to experience it no matter how long we spend accepting that all our lives end the same way.

I'm not stupid. I know the plateau in her symptoms won't last. I know she's lucky she's gotten this many years after her diagnosis, that she's a miracle among patients with Lewy Body.

I also know miracles have expiration dates.

The unknown is what scares me. I don't know how to protect myself against it.

A week later, I'm still trying to grapple with our conversation. We've seen each other countless times, but she hasn't brought up "preparing for the inevitable" again, which really only amplifies my anxiety. It felt calculated and purposeful that day, and now she's going on as if she never mentioned it in the first place.

Maybe she forgot, my brain nags as I leave drama club one afternoon, tossing my tote bag into the passenger seat of my Jeep and climbing behind the wheel. It's not like that'd be out of the ordinary.

My father and Kieran don't seem to be concerned — when I visited Kieran at Murphy's old cabin in the woods, he'd been flighty and weird, but I'm starting to think that has more to do with Juliet Harrison, considering the number of times I've caught him scrolling through her social media in the last month.

And my father, well, nothing ever fazes him, so I'm not sure he'd notice something wrong with my mother in the first place.

I just can't shake the feeling that something isn't right.

Waving to Bea and Heidi as I pull out of the parking lot, I head down the highway back to King's Trace, wondering how different life might be if we hadn't grown roots in the soil there.

If our curse doesn't extend from proximity to the sins of our neighbors, the deeds of our ancestors, and could be reversed by fleeing.

When I get home that night, everyone else is gone. My parents are likely out celebrating my father's birthday, and Kieran's probably off harassing Juliet or torturing people and acting like it's not obvious what he does for a living.

After finishing my homework at the dining room table, I stick a bag of popcorn in the microwave and take it up to my room, glancing around at all the pink.

It suddenly feels suffocating, and the housekeeper hasn't been here in days. There are clothes piled in the corner, outfits I tried on and hated, papers and books cluttering my desk, shoes strewn about the room.

Evidence of an attempt at alleviating stress by reorganizing, and then getting tired of doing it halfway through.

The chaos should disorient me, given that I haven't taken any medication in months, but I suck in a deep breath and find it infinitesimal compared to the chaos reigning in my world as it is.

Instead of succumbing to the urge to *fix*, I lock onto the one thing in the room that's as it should be; the pink comforter on the bed is squared on the mattress, tucked in at the end and beneath the pillows.

The image is almost erotic in its perfection, and I crawl under the covers, tear open my bag of popcorn, and pull up YouTube on my phone, searching for heart-wrenching compilations as something close to pure euphoria washes through me.

I don't hear the doorbell downstairs, nor do I hear the footsteps as they ascend toward my room. By the time the dark figure's lurking in my doorway, I'm too engrossed in the world of people saying goodbye to their pets to truly care.

"Are you crying?"

Boyd's voice yanks me from the land of tears, dousing me in reality. I jump at the closeness of his words, how their heat almost caresses my skin, and drop my phone on the bed, shrouding us in darkness. I can make out his shadow, just at the edge of the bed, and it sends a tingle between my thighs.

"This is my bedroom," I say, clearing the mucus from my throat and wiping my eyes with my sleeve. "I can cry if I want to."

"Why would you want to?"

"My mom says it's good for the soul." I sigh, feeling around on the bed for my phone and turning its flashlight on. He's standing there, looking haggard; his gray vest is unbuttoned, hanging loosely from his chest as if he'd gotten dressed in a hurry, and there's a purple ring around his left eye that gives me pause.

"What happened to your eye?" I ask, momentarily forgetting that he told me just last week that he didn't want anything to do with me, or at least can't bring himself to, and yet I chase his affection like a lost puppy.

God, I'm pathetic.

But I can't help it—in the midst of everything else going on, the innate brokenness inside of Boyd Kelly calls out to me. Begs to be repaired. Something isn't quite right with him, in a different way from the other men in my life.

He doesn't quite ooze violence. His is buried, hidden beneath the cold, polished exterior he puts on display for everyone else to see.

Except me.

I've seen the fire burning behind his eyes when he lets his guard down. Seen it extinguished, too, and what started as a schoolgirl crush feels like it's developing more into a morbid curiosity. I want to know why Boyd is the way that he is, and then I want to help him.

And if I can fix him, then I won't need to harp on the things I can't.

Ignoring me, Boyd sinks to the mattress at my side, kicking the expensive, shiny shoes off his feet and stretching out beside me. "You know, for such a wealthy, shady family, your security here sucks. All I did was jiggle the lock on your front door, and it popped open."

"It's an old house."

"It's unsafe. Your dad should know better."

I don't say anything, the sharp tone of his voice leaving little room to comment. He stares up at the ceiling, moonlight from the balcony window across the room spilling in and illuminating his body in slivers. I roll onto my side and tuck my hands under my head, studying him like I've done from afar a million times.

His shoulders are stiff, even pressed against the wooden headboard, his mouth set in a firm line, hands clasped in his lap so tight I can see his knuckles shift from beige to white. For a few moments, neither of us speaks, a serenity sweeping over us I can't quite explain.

My body should be racked with nerves, lying in bed beside the god of my dreams, but my heart beats at its normal pace, as if this is a regular occurrence. As if I don't want to climb inside his skeleton and die there.

As if I wouldn't surrender my virginity to this man right this second, no questions asked.

No regrets. No anxiety.

Just *us*.

"How come you're here?" I ask eventually, my eyelids growing heavy in the silence.

"I thought we were celebrating your dad's birthday."

"Oh." My eyelids drift closed, lashes soft against my cheeks. "I think he decided just to take my mom out, instead."

Boyd doesn't reply. I'm starting to realize how he's remained Kieran's best friend for so long—neither of them are keen on conversing if it doesn't serve a specific purpose.

Peeling one lid back, I peek at him as he slumps down on the bed, pulling the plush throw at the end of the mattress up over his legs. *Settling in.* My stomach flips, the nerves that were absent moments ago finally surfacing, twisting in my gut.

"What are you doing?"

He sighs, adjusting his head on the pillow beneath him. It takes so long for him to answer; by the time he does, I'm half asleep and only partially processing his words. "Trying to sleep, if you're done with the questions."

My eyebrows furrow, confusion taking the place of my nerves, absorbing the arousal throbbing between my legs. "*What?* Why are you sleeping in my bed? Don't you have your own, in your *house?*"

"If I leave here tonight, I'll end up murdering someone." His head turns, his warm hazel eyes immediately finding mine in the dark. "You want their blood on your hands, princess?"

Blinking, I just stare back, trying to grapple with what's happening. I haven't seen him since last week in my room when

125

he freaked out about kissing me, and frankly, I've been avoiding him while he sorted out his issues.

Part of me feels like this isn't the consequence of a solution, but rather the result of him looking for a distraction.

Maybe Boyd and I aren't as different as we appear.

Maybe he needs something—someone—to focus on as much as I do. Someone to keep the darkness inside us at bay.

A kingdom we can call home when ours gets too burdensome.

It's the first time that anyone's ever so brazenly spoken about the evil inherent in all King's Trace residents. Over the years, it didn't take much to figure out what rumors about my brothers and my family were true, nor did it take long to realize I was expected to carry on as if I didn't understand our reality. As if I'm not a part of it.

And even though I don't know what the fuck is going on right now, don't know why Boyd's *here* in a practical stranger's room seeking solace instead of anywhere else, the warmth that seeps from his presence into my skin makes me refrain from questioning it again.

Besides, I don't have any doubt he'll be gone by the time I wake up.

CHAPTER FOURTEEN

Boyd

There's still blood on my cracked knuckles when Fiona finally drifts off to sleep, her breathing evening out for the first time since I started paying attention at the gala.

It's one of those things you don't really notice until it's suddenly missing from your life; as her body goes limp beside me, her chest seems to deflate slowly, as if expelling all the worry she keeps pinned there so she can rest. I keep waiting for the pre-hyperventilation, holding my own breath just to see if hers still comes out rushed and panicked.

Holding my finger beneath her nose to make sure she's at least still alive, I make a mental note to research anxiety and control issues, then slip from the bed and pad to the bathroom across the hall to avoid waking her up. Flipping on the light, I wince at the brightness, and then again at my reflection.

My eye is swollen, the surrounding skin bruised and mangled. There's a tear at the corner where the candlestick LeeAnn swung at my face broke through, sending a flare of rage through my chest all over again.

I curl my battered hands into fists on top of the counter, then turn on the sink faucet and cup them beneath its spray. The sting somehow dampens the anger, stealing it from my body as I pump soap into my palm.

Drying my hands on the red decorative towel, I pull my phone out as it buzzes against my thigh for the billionth time, Riley's name flashing across the screen. I drag a hand through my hair, not in the fucking mood, but answer the call anyway.

"What the heck happened tonight?" her whisper-shout greets me, sawing at the thread of sanity barely holding me together.

What *happened* was LeeAnn fucking around with big-time drug dealers like Romeo Bianchi, who'd been in the trailer when I'd shown up tonight, concerned that I hadn't heard from her in a few days. As soon as my foot crossed the threshold, my eyes finding Romeo's as he sat fastening a rubber tourniquet around

LeeAnn's bicep, I regretted being so goddamn soft for the woman.

Soft for someone who doesn't deserve it.

Will never return the favor.

I hadn't been expecting her to attack—she hasn't laid a hand on me since I outgrew her, which is why she got such a good hit on me, catching me off guard as she swung, letting Romeo escape.

When I shoved her back and fled the trailer, yelling at Riley to lock her bedroom door and not leave until the morning, I'd been hellbent on tracking the elder Bianchi son down and tearing his intestines out through his asshole, but a reminder on my phone about Craig's birthday dinner popped up, drawing me from the haze of fury clouding my judgment.

My plan was to come and get lost in the general din of Ivers company—for a family with such dark roots, they're so painstakingly *normal* around each other that it's easy to pretend I'm a part of their little tribe.

Craig certainly considers me part of it, though I'm not sure what he'd say if he knew about the recurring thoughts I have about his daughter. How badly I want to strip her bare and ride her raw, how I want to steal her soul and make it mine.

The thoughts consume me at random; I'll be sitting in my office at work and her petite, freckled face will pop up, sudden and all-encompassing in its presence.

When I got to the mansion, abandoning my thoughts of revenge, I knocked on the door for a good fifteen minutes before picking the lock and letting myself inside, not seeing Craig's Aston Martin in the driveway and assuming he'd already taken off.

No one was supposed to be home. Certainly not Fiona.

Soft music and sniffles drifted quietly from upstairs, though, and like a moth to a flame, I'd followed their sound.

As soon as I saw her puffy eyes and stepped into the room, I was stuck. Glued in place when I sat on her bed, unable to leave even though my brain screamed at me that I should. That she's my best friend's sister, my boss's daughter, and so young and seemingly innocent.

But it's that forced goodness that draws me in, despite whatever it is she's hiding. I can't seem to drag myself away, the desire to steal some for my own soul too tempting to refuse.

Now, I sit down on the closed toilet and squeeze the phone against my ear, Riley's voice calling out and pulling me from my thoughts.

"What happened tonight doesn't matter. Are you still in your room?" I ask, running a hand through my hair and glaring down at the shiny tiled floor.

"Yeah, but I'm kind of freaked out. Mom left an hour ago and I haven't been able to get a hold of her."

I scoff. "That's not surprising. She'll turn up, though, don't worry. Can't harass me if she's not around."

She stays quiet for a moment, and there's some kind of shuffling over the line. It sounds like blankets, and I hope she's getting into bed rather than out. "Did... did she hit you?"

"Again, doesn't matter."

"That's guy for yes, you know."

Gritting my teeth, I can feel my patience waning, violence pumping through my blood at the mere mention of LeeAnn putting her hands on me *again*. At myself, for letting it happen—for ever thinking it was over.

The first time you let someone take a punch at you, it sets the precedent for how badly you'll let them treat you. And I've been letting that bitch abuse me my entire life, apparently incapable of making it stop or keeping away.

"Riley, I don't want to talk about this." My eye aches as I say the words, pain spreading from the site into my forehead, a sharp stabbing sensation cropping up behind my temple.

"Of course, you don't. Boyd Kelly prefers to avoid the spectrum of emotion, right?"

"Are you quoting *The Proposal* to me right now?"

Despite the palpable tension flowing between us, she laughs. "Paraphrasing, and I'm impressed you got the reference."

"I'm not a monster."

"Right." Her laughter dies off, an abrupt shift I'm having a hard time keeping up with. A wave of nausea racks through me, and I grip my knee as she sighs into the speaker. "Anyway, are you—?"

"I need to go," I say quickly, cutting her off and ending the call just as bile burns the length of my esophagus; I barely make it to the sink in time, spewing vomit as soon as my mouth hovers over the porcelain bowl. Acid sets fire to my throat, dragging its nails through the sensitive flesh and making me dizzy as my lunch empties from my body.

Coughing on the last dry heave, I wipe my mouth and rifle beneath the sink, finding a bottle of Listerine at the back and swishing it around, the throbbing in my head intensifying with the movement.

Spitting out the wash, I exit the bathroom, stuffing my phone in my pocket and closing the door slowly, unsure if anyone's returned since I holed up in Fiona's room and not particularly wanting to run into them if they have.

My hand grips the doorknob of Fiona's bedroom when I smell it—the familiar scent of extremely cheap perfume. The kind that's been imprinted into my nostrils from my childhood. I only know one other person who wears it.

Turning my head, I meet Chelsea's wide eyes as she adjusts her blonde ponytail, pulling down the hem of her velvet dress. The hall light doesn't offer a ton of visibility, but I'd recognize that smell anywhere.

Craig rounds the corner, slipping his arm around Chelsea's waist and bending to say something in her ear; she elbows him, jerking her chin in my direction, and he stills, slowly straightening to look at me.

For a moment, pure disbelief ebbs between us; I'd already known, of course, that he was fucking her, but a pang of guilt and disgust worms its way into my gut at the realization that he's doing it under his roof, where his *wife* lives.

"Boyd?" he stammers quietly, his eyes darting to where my hand is frozen on his daughter's bedroom door. "What the hell is going on?"

The spike in volume throws me at first, because Craig Ivers isn't the kind of guy who does a lot of yelling. He's always annoyingly unruffled, able to switch from hardened criminal to asshole CEO to doting husband in a matter of minutes.

Guess this is the asshole.

"You want to answer that first?" I challenge, quirking an eyebrow.

"*Excuse* me?"

I nod at Chelsea, who shrinks at his side, trying to step back behind his body. "Just saying. Last time I checked, *that* wasn't your wife."

He sputters, crossing his arms over his chest. "What I'm doing, and who I'm doing it with, is none of your concern, boy. What the fuck you're doing in my daughter's room well-past midnight in my house, however, certainly is."

"All due respect, sir," I say, twisting the knob and pushing the door open. "I'm not sure you have the upper hand here, unless you want to explain to Fiona what you're doing with a girl she could have gone to high school with while her mother is, presumably, asleep down the hall."

"Uh, I'm actually twenty-five," Chelsea says, earning a dirty look from Craig. She mimes zipping her lips, stepping backward.

Craig stares at me for a long time. I see his jaw working, flexing as he clenches and unclenches his teeth before finally letting out a low exhale. Contemplating how loud a physical fight would be, or whether he genuinely cares what I do with his daughter, I can't be sure.

Part of me doesn't want that knowledge; doesn't want to know which option weighs more.

Without another word, he grabs Chelsea's hand and pulls her toward the stairs, dragging her behind him. She trips over her heels, almost toppling down over him, but catches herself at the last second, tossing me a strained glance over her shoulder.

It almost looks like regret, though the fact that I hear a door deeper in the house slam minutes later says she must not feel *that* bad. Probably just that she got caught.

Not my secret to tell.

My hand cramps as my hold on the doorknob tightens, and pain radiates through my temple, down my neck, settling in my shoulders where all my troubles seem to live. They must have some kind of timeshare.

I should leave, especially now that I've been caught in a taboo situation myself. But that goddamn magnetic force pulls me back in, something I don't understand and still somehow feel powerless against.

It's elemental, completely carnal, the universe itself imploring me to continue whatever the fuck this is with this woman.

Creeping inside, I shut Fiona's door gently and make my way back to her bed, discarding my slacks and dress shirt before climbing under the pink comforter. The sheets are cool against my broken body, and when my head hits the pillow, I'm overcome with the sudden urge to just sleep.

The tension in my shoulders uncoils slightly as I situate my head on the mattress, dropping the pillow on my face and doing my best to regulate my breathing. Fiona's body heat surges toward me as she rolls over, mumbling something in her sleep.

I've just started to fall under when the bed dips, her shuffling bringing her closer until she throws a leg around my waist and shimmies forward. Her cunt, separated from me by only a thin pair of cotton shorts and maybe panties, feels like an open flame to my skin, torching the area of my hip it's pressed up against.

My hands grip the pillow over my face, applying pressure until I can't breathe at all, and then I toss it off the side, guilt and arousal declaring war inside my chest as I stare up at the ceiling.

She's asleep, so I shouldn't engage, even though my dick is pleading otherwise.

Her dad's downstairs, her mother and brother likely asleep in this very hall.

She's *eighteen*.

But even as my brain tries to talk me out of it, one of my hands inches toward her calf, desperate to know if the skin is as soft as it looks. A small gasp falls unbidden from my lips as my fingers curl around the defined muscle, squeezing gently. She lets out a little moan, her breath caressing the side of my face.

My dick jerks in my boxers, and I reach down to adjust myself so she doesn't wake up and feel how hard she makes me.

Heart racing, I move her leg up so she's flush against me, sweat beading along my hairline at our proximity. Like I'm some virginal, prepubescent child with a crush.

A blinding flash of pain ripples through my head, exploding behind my eyes, and I succumb to the darkness before I have a proper chance to revel in how fucking right it feels to have Fiona in my arms.

CHAPTER FIFTEEN

Fiona

I'm not asleep when Boyd comes back to bed; even *less* so when he pulls my leg closer to his body, pressing me firmly into his hip. Granted, moving toward him while he *thought* I was asleep probably wasn't the best move, but I couldn't resist the electric pull his soul seems to have on mine.

Now, my body feels like it's on fire, my core throbbing so hard and fast I can taste it in my throat. It's not an unwelcome sensation, death by combustion, but the unfamiliarity of it is what has my gut churning like an unstable bomb seconds from exploding.

Anxiety threads through my nerve endings, igniting each one with a different worry — I'm too inexperienced to be lying in bed with someone like Boyd Kelly, too trusting, too optimistic.

Too *everything*.

Isn't that what people really mean when they assign you qualifiers like "dramatic" and "princess," that you're a catastrophe of emotion and experiences coagulating to create a single high-maintenance soul?

Clearly, he came here for some kind of comfort, maybe even expecting to fuck out his frustrations, and I'm reading too far into things. The fact that he's here right now probably has more to do with availability than anything else.

He thinks you're easy.

Remembering how he suggested as much that night he yanked me away from Nico, I start to pull out of his embrace, a sinking feeling filling my chest. It settles like an anchor in the pit of my soul, weighing me instead of steadying.

Boyd's arm tightens around my shoulders, holding me captive, as the lamp on my nightstand flickers on. "What are you doing?"

I freeze; my body feels like it's being slowly split in half, one side content to stay within the warmth he provides, the other racked with shame to the point of paralysis. "Isn't that supposed to be my line?"

Chuckling, he wiggles around a bit, trying to get me to relax back into him. His hands are warm against my skin as he attempts to coax the stiffness from my bones, but my brain continues to replay the scene of him calling me a whore over and over, blotting out the ability for anything else.

"Are... you having some kind of panic attack?"

"No," I snap, though the palpitations stuttering through my heart say otherwise. "I don't have those."

He slides my leg off his waist slowly, disentangling from me as though I'm a wild animal that needs to be handled delicately. I sit up, curling into myself with my knees against my chest, refusing to look his way.

The heat from his gaze burns, more unnerving than anything else because it feels like he sees right through me. Like he's used to unmasking people and unearthing their true selves, and I can't think of anything more terrifying than Boyd Kelly knowing my secrets.

I didn't spend my life trying to bury them just so he could come in and dig them up.

"Okay," he says, nodding slightly as he pulls his own knees up and drapes his forearms over them. I notice for the first time that he's shirtless, ink stretched across every smooth plane of his skin save for his face, disappearing beneath the comforter.

Intricate designs I feel myself getting lost in, skulls and abstract shapes that don't let any sunlight into the surface underneath.

His eye is still swollen and purple, his knuckles cracked raw — evidence of the beast within, proof that one day it'll claw its way out. Even if that means destroying him in the process.

As I sit there, struggling to grab a hold of the tether barely keeping my sanity together, I blurt out the first thing that comes to mind. "I think my mom wants to kill herself."

Heavy silence stirs in the air around us, bloated with a confession that really isn't mine to speak. One I'm not even sure holds a shred of truth.

Guilt slams into me like a freight train, making my heart accelerate and my fingers shake. I stuff them between my knees, trying to hide the tremor, my brain searching in overdrive for something to focus on other than the sense that my world as I know it is imploding.

That's the only way to fully describe the sensation that ripples through my body when I have one of these... episodes. An irrational fear wraps around my body, sucking out the energy to fight and replacing it with the need to crumble.

Boyd's eyebrows raise, wrinkling his forehead. "I beg your pardon?"

"You speak English, don't you?"

He cocks his head, giving me a look. "Christ, Fiona, yeah but I'm... that just came out of nowhere, don't you think?"

My skull throbs, thundering between my ears in an orchestral grand finale. Propping my hands on my knees, I drop my face into my palms, letting out a loud groan that scrapes the inside of my throat. "How do you think *I* feel?"

"Are you sure I'm the person you should be talking to about this?" he asks, his voice soft and hesitant. Completely out of character. I turn my head, peeking at him over the edge of my hand; there's concern welling in his irises, softening the sharp contours of his face.

Like my issues are siphoning the malice from his soul.

"I don't know who else to tell," I admit, fiddling with a worn spot in the comforter. "If I tell my dad, he'll either deny it or side with her. If I tell Kieran, he'll freak out and demand she's put in a home."

"Don't you think maybe she should be, though?"

My eyes narrow into slits, offense spreading through me. "Are you suggesting I abandon the woman who brought me into this world? The one who used to make me lemon squares when I was too sick to go to school, who attended every one of my cheer competitions even though the other moms tended to ostracize her because of her name? You want me to pretend she never did anything for me and stick her in a *nursing home*?"

"Hey." Boyd's hand reaches out, brushing against my cheek — his touch is so soft and gentle that a chasm splits open in my soul, like he's reaching inside and trying to grip the seam where sunshine meets darkness. Like he's trying to hold me together. "I didn't mean anything by it. But you're eighteen, Fiona. It's not really fair that you have to take care of her."

"I don't *have* to." I try to pull away, but his hand slides down my face and grips my jaw, keeping me in place. "She isn't a burden, and it's not like she asked me to do it." *Not outright, anyway.* She didn't have to because I was always offering.

"Kids shouldn't have to take care of their parents."

"But sometimes they do." Tears sting my eyes, burning with the effort it takes to keep them at bay.

His mouth opens as if he's about to say something else, but then seems to think better of it. My anxiety melts into distant sadness, and when he pulls away, I don't make a move to bolt or escape his presence. I sink into it, missing the warmth of his skin on mine.

Needing the distraction.

"I'm sorry," I say when he settles back against the headboard, propping his arms up behind his head. The veins in his arms bulge against his tattooed skin, and I trace them with my gaze, trying to immortalize their existence in my mind. "I shouldn't have even brought any of this up. Kieran and my dad always say I talk too much or say the wrong thing when I'm nervous, and you make me the most nervous out of anyone I've ever met, so..."

I trail off, picking at my fingernails. Boyd just stares, watching me with an unreadable expression, before he sits back up, leaning in. "What can I do to help alleviate your nerves, princess?"

Gulping, I lift my chin to meet his; heat ebbs between us like the start of a chemical explosion, frissons of desire spreading like tree branches throughout my body.

It should make me more anxious, having his undivided attention. But for some reason, if only to pretend there's nothing else going on in my life, I feel emboldened. Like I could ask Boyd Kelly for anything right this second, and he'd give it to me, no question.

"Tell me a secret."

His eyebrows raise. "That's a big ask."

"Do it anyway."

Humming low in his throat, he reaches out, slipping his hands around my hips and pulling me into his lap. We're separated by the comforter as it falls around my legs, but the unmistakable evidence of his arousal prods at my ass, sending a delicious shiver over my skin.

My core throbs as I hook my knees on either side of his waist, his large palms cradling my hips through the thin T-shirt I'm wearing.

Our breaths spill from half-parted lips, heady and full of promise, and when I smooth my hand up his chest, resting over his heart, I can feel its rapid beat in time with my own.

Leaning forward, Boyd trails one hand up my side, ghosting along my ribs and brushing the curve of my breast. He runs just the pads of his fingers above my breasts, nostrils flaring when a second shiver racks through me.

"A secret, you say." His thumb snares in the neckline of my shirt, pulling it down to expose my collarbone, and then he dips his head, tracing the ridge with the tip of his tongue. As his mouth travels across my skin, his right hand releases my shirt and comes up to grasp my neck.

With his fingers splayed against my throat, I arch into his touch, recognizing that my inexperience might be driving the excessive flames erupting in my pussy right now, but embracing it anyway.

When he touches me, the rest of the world melts away — my mom, the fact that his best friend is my brother and would not approve, the secrets he keeps inside. Nothing else but the feel of his skin against mine matters, and that's not a sensation I'm used to.

"What if I told you," he breathes into me, the vibration of his lips bringing heat to my cheeks, "that I read historical romance novels?"

It takes a second for his words to register, but when they do, I rear back, pressing my hands against his chest to keep him away. "Seriously?"

"Would I joke about that?"

"Maybe to make me feel better?" A laugh tumbles from my lips. "Historical *romance*? Like, viscounts and rakes, that kind of thing?"

"I prefer bodice rippers, but yes, there are a wide variety of titles the characters may hold."

Shaking my head, I try to grapple with the information, then burst out into a full round of giggles. Covering my mouth with my hands, I can't stop the tremors that rack my body with each laugh, my stomach cramping alongside them.

"I don't really see what's funny. It's a perfectly normal hobby to have."

"Sure, if you're a girl not getting any."

Shifting, Boyd pulls me so I'm sitting farther up on his lap, the length of his cock pulling me from my fit as it presses into me. His eyes hood as my laughs die out, his fingers slipping beneath the hem of my shirt and digging into my hips, moving me in a slow grind on top of him.

I gasp at the friction of his movements against my clit, the slow, circular rotation sending sparks of pleasure between my thighs.

"Barring the sexist notion of what you just said, I can *assure* you I'm not a girl." His grip on my hips tightens, pulling me down more firmly onto him as he rolls beneath me, his erection hot as it pokes against my ass. A moan tumbles from my mouth, and he grins. "Feel that?"

"Y-yes," I rasp, sure that if he reached down and cupped me, he'd be able to feel the arousal pooling in my panties, soaking my sensitive flesh with each thrust of my hips.

He palms my jaw and rubs his thumb across my lips, smearing my saliva. The gesture is rough yet erotic, the kind of pain that catapults into pleasure. His free hand slides from my hip, pulling the elastic of my shorts away from my body, slipping beneath the flimsy material.

"Anyone ever touch you here before?"

I shake my head frantically, my throat dry.

He smirks, tilting my head back slightly, twisting to ghost his fingertips through my slick folds, my clit pulsing so hard I'm sure he can feel it. My fingers tingle in anticipation, thrill coiling tight in my stomach as release draws near.

I'm on the precipice, seconds from falling, not fully understanding the shift happening between us but also not willing to think too hard about it.

"Fuck, you're wet," he growls, the pad of one finger circling my clit, the pressure making me move even faster against him. I shift so he presses more fully where I need him, supernovas dancing behind my vision when he hits the spot I've never cared to help anyone else find. But right now, I want this release. "Take what you need from me."

As he pinches his eyes closed, I swear I feel the thread of his control popping loose, abandoned with me here on top of him.

Goose bumps sprout along my skin at the desperation in his voice, the hunger igniting a fire in my belly that consumes my soul. My mind is reeling, trying to keep up with what's happening and failing as I succumb to the unreached heights of euphoria he's bringing me to.

And for the first time in as long as I can remember, there are no intrusive thoughts barreling their way into my brain.

Nothing pulling me from the moment as I throw my head back, losing myself in the pleasure as it cascades through my body in waves.

"Here's my real secret: I really, really want to kiss you again," Boyd whispers, not giving me a second to protest or acquiesce, craning his neck to capture my mouth in a kiss that sends me over the edge, shattering my reality into a million jagged pieces incapable of ever being put back together.

CHAPTER SIXTEEN

Boyd

My knuckles rap against the trailer door, unease spreading like poison ivy through my gut when I'm met with deafening silence, no sign of movement coming from the other side. I knock again, checking my watch to make sure I'm not going over on my break.

School's out for Riley today because of some kind of teachers-only gig, and since I haven't been back in a week, I figured I'd pop over on my lunch and make sure things hadn't gotten progressively worse. There's only so much I can do for my sister from afar, and the knowledge that she might be in danger any other time tends to keep me up at night.

I'd be lying, too, if I said part of me isn't at least a *little* curious to see how LeeAnn is. Especially after the shitstorm with Craig Ivers getting shot after our rendezvous at his house — he'd *supposedly* been minding his business when the tires of his car were shot out, and when he stopped to assess the damage and call for a tow, someone attacked him.

I've been slightly more on edge ever since. Clearly, someone has it out for the Ivers, and those flash drives turning up the day before Craig was shot wasn't a coincidence.

So now, here I am, checking on my deadbeat mother. To see if she's okay, but also to see if she's apologetic or if she's been riding a perpetual high since our fight, pretending nothing happened so she doesn't have to live with her mistakes or their consequences.

Pathetic. I shouldn't give a single fuck about the woman, especially considering what happened last week, but for whatever fucking reason, she's stuck on my permanent list of things to obsess over.

I've added sneaking around with Fiona to that list, though, stealing kisses from her ruby red lips and copping a feel every chance I get — between courses at weekly family dinners and in the elevator when she brings her mother in for lunch dates with Craig.

It wasn't supposed to turn into anything, that night I spent at her house. But when you go looking for comfort, sometimes you get attached to the things that bring it, and

149

watching Fiona let go of her troubles and that carefully curated bubblegum personality for just a few moments as she came against me was too fucking addicting.

When I went home the next morning, I could still smell her on me.

Roses. Candy. Anxiety.

She may try to deny it, but I recognize the signs. Researched the possibilities.

Know how the worry can sink its claws into you and squeeze until there's no room for anything else. And I know how fucking good it feels when it retracts, even if temporarily.

Problem is, I can't seem to get enough of her. Can't stop thinking about the way her face flushed as she came, or that I could feel her pulse against me between her thighs, and how badly I wanted to tear the clothes from her body and bury myself inside of her.

Later, when she'd fallen asleep curled against my side, the inherent rightness of having her there began to wash away, replaced by guilt. An emotion I'm not used to feeling, and yet every time an illicit thought about my best friend's baby sister pops up, warning bells chime, signaling that our union might be apocalyptic.

I'm torn between the loyalty I have to him and his family, and the knowledge that if the situation were reversed, they wouldn't deny themselves something they're so desperate for.

So, I indulge, because I'm nothing if not a connoisseur of bad decisions.

Beating the side of my fist on the door one last time, I glance over my shoulder at where my bike's parked in the empty carport, wondering if it's possible LeeAnn took Riley somewhere. Then again, if she had, surely my aunt Dottie would've been notified since the Volkswagen LeeAnn drives is in her friend's name. Or one of the PIs I have occasionally tailing them would've texted me a heads-up.

My hand falls to my side, and I'm turning to move off the makeshift porch when the door finally swings open, revealing LeeAnn in a wrinkled beige pantsuit, pulling her dirty hair into a bun. She scans me from head to toe with a scoff, stepping back and walking into the kitchen, leaving the decision to engage up to me.

As fucking always. If she isn't in need, then LeeAnn doesn't make the first move.

Slamming the door shut behind me, I fold my arms over my chest and glance around the area. It's practically spotless, no evidence of the general filth she likes to live in or the mess from our fight last week. That, paired with the fact that she's awake and dressed before two in the afternoon, makes me wary.

"What'd you do, fuck a maid or something?" I grunt, watching as she pours a cup of coffee into a mug I recognize from my seventh-grade art class. It's black ceramic and has the words "WORLD'S BEST MOM" painted in white on the side—

something I'd asked my art teacher to assist with so I didn't mess up.

LeeAnn was always bad at receiving gifts, typically expecting money or jewelry, despite dating losers and me being a child. So, when I made her the mug, I wanted it to be perfect.

This is the first time I've ever seen her use it.

Spooning some sugar into the mug, she gives me a bland look. "Hilarious, Boyd. I've been cleaning my home since before you were born."

"Right, you're just usually too high to do it."

She rolls her eyes, taking a sip of her coffee and returning it to the counter. "Did you come here just to berate me again? Honestly, the constant bickering between us is getting exhausting. Do you think you can come here just once and not start a damn fight?"

My hands ball into fists and I bite down on my tongue, irritation swirling around at the suggestion that *I'm* to blame for the bad blood between us. Scrubbing my hand over the stubble on my jaw, I jerk my head toward the back of the trailer, not taking the bait. "Riley home?"

"No, she stayed the night at her father's. They were supposed to go to some lake this afternoon so she could get started on some kind of community service." Pausing, LeeAnn's head tilts to one side as she considers this. "What's she doing community service for, anyway? She in some kind of trouble?"

"Wouldn't you have heard about it, if she were?"

Her chapped lips curl around a short laugh. "Yeah, right. I'm not under any illusion that she doesn't go behind my back with things. Why should she be forthcoming to her mother when she knows her dad and brother are gonna bail her out, regardless?"

A sharp pain slices across my heart at the annoyance in her tone—not so much because I think she actually cares about Riley keeping secrets, but because I can tell she doesn't like not being in control. People like LeeAnn don't want to be caught off guard, and Riley's very existence poses a problem for her in that department.

Again, I ignore the implication that her rocky relationship with Riley is somehow related to me, choosing to change the subject. At least, at her dad's house, Riley's safe. He lives in Portland with his wife and owns a construction company that specializes in eco-friendly commercial building. A decent man, comparatively.

Gesturing toward the outfit she's wearing, I raise an eyebrow. "Got a hot date with your probation officer, then? What's with the suit?"

"I could ask you the same thing," she says, not missing a beat. Venom unleashes from her tongue, always a double meaning behind her words, and I can tell that beyond wanting my money, she's not impressed at all by the fact that I've made a name for myself.

The sinking feeling that accompanies the realization is unwelcome, and I shove it down before it can take root inside my soul. As if it's not been embedded there since I was a kid.

"I wear suits to work because that's the kind of attire my job requires."

"A job you *stole* from that poor Ivers boy. God, how can you even look at yourself in the mirror, knowing everything you touch is not rightfully yours?"

Clenching my jaw, I take a step back toward the door, the urge to flee surfacing. Flashes from the other night, blood and fists and ear-splitting screams float across my vision, reminding me what happened last time my temper snapped.

I've got to get out of here.

"Oh, what's the matter, dear? Not ready to face the facts?" She shrugs one bony shoulder, giving me a nasty grin. "You're a Kelly, no matter how hard you try to pretend otherwise. Not only would the Ivers never accept you, but you're destined for a life of being unworthy. Just the way the world works. People like us don't get what we want."

"Please don't lump us into the same category," I snap, my patience wearing thin. "We might share a last name, but we're not the fucking same."

"The way you attacked me and my date last week proves otherwise." Her smile turns sadistic, stretching thin across her hollow face.

154

My watch beeps, the alarm I set alerting me that my time here is up. "I don't have time for this."

"*Shocker*," she spits, taking a large drink of her coffee. The slurp that comes after grates on my nerves, violence coursing through my veins the longer I'm in her presence. "Running at the first sign of trouble. You really are my son."

"Yeah, remember how you used to hate that?" I say, the sudden flare of shock on her face satisfying; she buries it quickly, schooling her features into an innocuous mask. I huff, disgusted with the way she cowers after dragging the beast out in me, and turn for the door.

When I was a kid, I was starved for her attention. I let her serve it to me on a silver platter, and devoured any shred she'd give me, even if it was malicious in its intent. Even if she dipped it in poison first.

I was supposed to graduate from that need, from wanting her to treat me right. Should've realized she wasn't capable when she ditched me as a kid, and definitely shouldn't have welcomed her back years later, as if she's a person capable of changing.

But when you're spoon-fed malice your whole life, it mainlines into your bloodstream, becoming part of you. Until it's all you know, all you crave.

Hatred is addictive, and LeeAnn is my goddamn drug. One I choose over everything—over my sanity, over Riley. Despite the times she's begged me to let her stay at my place, despite knowing the environment here is toxic, I let my hatred cloud my judgment. Let resentment over Riley being the kid she kept bar me from taking care of her properly.

Fiona's words from the gala weeks ago play on repeat as I stare at the door, twisting the barbed wire around my heart so the organ pricks and bleeds.

People don't change.

Even though I'd challenged the sentiment at the time, wondered what made her so concrete in her convictions, I know she's right. If people changed, my life would be different.

I'd be different.

But here I am, the weak, violent bastard I've always been, wondering what it'll take for me to snap and not come back.

My hand grips the doorknob, the metal moaning as I squeeze, my thoughts racing. I hear her chuckle, and it pulls me from the introspection, launching me into a stratosphere of rage. Releasing the knob, I stalk over to where she's leaning against the kitchen counter, regarding me like she can't stand to be in the same room as me.

"One of these days, I will fucking end you," I snarl, my hand curling around her thin neck, fingernails sinking into her skin. Spittle sprays across her face, and she cringes, trying to move back out of my hold, but I tighten my grip and bend so we're eye level. "Because unlike you, *LeeAnn*, I don't bow to my demons. I become their worst fucking nightmare, and if you continue to push me, you will not enjoy the result."

"Are you threatening me?" she squeaks. "I could have you arrested for that."

"Like anyone would believe a thieving junkie over me. I have pull in town that you can't even fucking dream of, so my suggestion to you is to fuck off and leave me alone. And if I catch even a *whiff* of evidence that you've taken any of your frustration out on Riley, I'll slit your throat before you can even attempt to explain. Got it?"

Her eyes narrow, but she tries to nod, anyway. I release her, smacking her cheek roughly, before turning on my heel and getting the fuck out of there before my anger makes me do something I regret.

CHAPTER SEVENTEEN

Fiona

Staring down at my phone, I drag my eyes across the screen for the millionth time, my fingers poised over the car door handle, everything suspended in time as my heart thunders inside my chest.

Boyd: Go to dinner with me.

My father's voice snaps me from the cyclone of panic forming in my brain; I glance up, meeting his dark gaze in the rearview mirror. His forehead creases. "Did you hear anything I just said?"

"Um..." Stealing a quick look at my mother, whose chin rests on her hand as she stares out the window, I shake my head. "Sorry, I was reviewing midterm grades and calculating what I need to get on the finals to pass each class. Did you know that for the undergrad psych degree, you can get C's in all your courses except the core ones? It's like—"

"You're not getting C's though, right?" he cuts in, raising an eyebrow.

"Of course not," I say, swallowing. My stats class teeters on the threshold between a B and C, but he doesn't need to know that if I'm planning on acing the final.

"Atta girl." Nodding, he unlocks the doors, as if giving me some sort of signal. "Remember, we're on a strict curfew right now. Home by nine and no guests past then."

His jaw tics when he says this last part, and I wonder if it has more to do with Kieran sneaking Juliet Harrison into the house last week or the fact that my father's arm is in a sling as he recovers from a bullet wound. The day after Boyd stayed the night, my father had been mugged while changing his tire in the Ivers International parking lot, and even though he'd been discharged the same day, I can tell the incident has taken its toll on both my parents.

My mother slips farther from reality, sliding headfirst into one of her own making, and my father is cracking down on his rules while he otherwise pretends getting shot is a totally normal thing. Which, maybe for an ex-con it is, but I'm having a difficult time keeping up.

Still, I don't want to cause any ripples that might hinder his recovery, and I don't want to cause problems that might make my mother deteriorate faster.

So I nod, pushing open the door to his Aston Martin, and climb out, slinging my purse over my chest and starting up the front walk toward the community theater.

Tapping my thumbs absently over my keyboard, I contemplate my response to Boyd, truly afraid at this point that he only wants to hang out because he thinks I'm easy. Me writhing on top of him until I came last week like some sex-starved maniac certainly didn't help matters, and he's been pulling me into dark alcoves and away from prying eyes every chance he gets since.

I can't stop the anxiety from spiraling inside when I think he's only interested in young, virginal flesh.

Why else would the single most attractive, mysterious, terrifyingly stoic, and secretly violent man in town, possibly the world, want to kiss *me*?

"Maybe because he likes you?" Bea says when I pose the question to her, sucking on a red heart-shaped lollipop. We're situated down left onstage, the front corner, flipping through the script of Macbeth that Olga passed out a few moments ago.

"All of a sudden, though?" I say, smoothing the pages of my copy so they sit squarely on top of each other. "When I say

160

this went from zero to a hundred *real quick*, I'm not just referencing that Drake song."

Bea rolls her eyes, running a hand over the tightly coiled braids in her hair. "He's not, like, declaring his love for you, or anything, Fi. Cut the guy some slack."

"I don't know," Heidi chimes in, rolling her script into a cylinder. "You've never dated guys with any sexual experience. Men like Boyd take what they want; they don't ask first, and they certainly don't take their time getting there. Are you sure he's the one you want to be your first?"

My finger taps against the script in front of me, the urge to reach over and rip her blonde hair out almost overwhelming.

It's not even that I've never been with guys that have sexual experience—it's just that I never found myself interested in pursuing that route with them. If not for the way my body thrums with electricity when Boyd is around, I'd think I'm not attracted to men at all, but the truth is that's just a difficult place for me to venture to.

In high school, I went on dates with some of the guys in our inner circle other than Nico, even participated in some exploration of certain degrees of sex, but I could never lose myself in the act, always too preoccupied with *me* to relax fully and enjoy myself.

Eventually, I just stopped trying.

But with Boyd, from the very start, there's been no hesitation. No chance for my brain to falter and wonder what I'm doing, if I'm doing it right, or if it should be happening at all.

When we come together, it's an explosion of heat and passion that I find myself lost in, and that's what scares me.

My identity is already wrapped up so fully in the existence of other people. I can't help the fear accompanying the notion that whatever scraps I've got now might be erased in his presence.

Men like Boyd. Heidi's words play on a loop in my mind, twisting my stomach into knots.

Truth is, I don't *know* what kind of man Boyd is. Don't know how far his violence extends, don't know about the evils penetrating his soul beyond their obvious existence. The mystery lurking inside of him is part of the appeal, but it's part of the concern, too.

What do I do if I lose myself to a man not interested in finding me?

"Sorry not all of us were sucking dick behind the bleachers at every football game in high school," Bea says, pointing her lollipop at Heidi.

"No," Heidi says, flipping Bea off. "*You* definitely were. Remember? We didn't make the cheer squad, so we decided to show our school spirit by servicing the JV team?"

Bea laughs, tipping her head back. "Oh, right. Guess you're alone then, Fi."

I plaster a thin smile on my face, glancing down at the first page of the script. Olga doesn't believe in explicit stage directions, so the entire thing is just dialogue reprinted, with an occasional note about setting and involved characters.

"So, are you gonna go out with him?" Bea asks.

"I don't know." My finger taps a steady rhythm, a faint sensation washing over me as they stare, waiting for a concrete decision.

"Personally, I think it seems a little crazy," Heidi says. "You barely know him."

Nodding, Bea nudges me with her shoulder. "Maybe not *crazy*, but you've been drooling over this man for years and he finally wants to take you out. Don't you think you owe it to yourself to see what happens?"

"*Bea*," Heidi snaps, clearly unsupportive.

Resisting the urge to stab Heidi with the pen by my shoe, I just shrug noncommittally, promising to at least think about it.

And for the duration of rehearsal, it's all I *can* think about. Boyd's hands on my skin, how the contact burns and soothes somehow all at once.

How his kiss ignites flames inside me that otherwise lay dormant, and how he somehow pulls me from the spinning vortex I spend most of my free time in, how I can relax my hold on needing every aspect of my life to bend to my will and instead submit to his.

There's this nagging thought, though, about his friendship with my brother and the work he does for my father. If my father's words from a few weeks ago are true, and their employee roster is made up primarily of bad eggs, what does that make Boyd?

Is he darker than the wickedness inside of me?

After rehearsal, Bea and Heidi drop me off at home, and I continue staring at my phone screen, wondering what the hell I'm supposed to say to him. Torn between what I *want* to say and what I think I should.

'*Good girls should stay away from big, bad wolves,*' my mother used to tell me, even though at the time she was trying to keep me away from my brothers, who were much older and didn't want to play with their baby sister.

When I walk into the house, Kieran's lounging on the chaise by the main stairs, the white shirt he's wearing covered in reddish-brown stains, hair askew. He glances at me over the book he's reading, something thick with the spine nearly falling apart, and raises a dark brow. "You didn't go with Heidi and Bea to get milkshakes today?"

I shake my head, hanging my purse and keys on their wall hook in the foyer. "No, I wasn't feeling it."

Both of Kieran's eyebrows shoot into his hairline now, and he sits up, folding the book in his lap. "Are you sick? When have you ever not been in the mood for milkshakes?"

"Plenty of times, I'm sure." Blowing out a breath, I walk over to where he's sitting and flop down beside him, leaning my head on his shoulder. "Is that blood on your shirt?"

"Ah... no?" He pokes my cheek until I jerk away, and grins at me. "It's ketchup. I had a messy burger for lunch."

"That looks like a handprint," I point out, gesturing to the blurred spot resembling fingers near the hem. I'm not supposed to know what he does for a living, but you don't hear the rumors about your brother being the Devil incarnate without trying to discover why.

But he buys more into our mother's claim that perception is reality, so he believes I'm ignorant.

Innocent.

Comparatively, maybe I am. But the fire inside me that rages, hungry for something more, says otherwise.

He ruffles my hair, standing up and racing up the stairs two at a time, ignoring my observation altogether, and then it's just me alone in this part of the house. A chill passes through the air, making me shiver, and I wonder which ghost of our past is with me.

If they're the good kind or the bad, as if I believe they're really trapped inside these walls with us.

I head in the direction Kieran disappeared, passing his closed door and starting into my bedroom, pausing at the frame. Staring down the hall, I contemplate for a few beats whether or not I should go to the room at the end and check on my mother.

I didn't see my father's car outside, and her lack of hovering when Kieran was just downstairs makes me think she must not be aware that he's home.

Fear cuts through my chest as I tiptoe across the hardwood floor, my palm steady on the drywall to keep me upright. There's no telling what I might walk in on.

My joints lock up when I reach the closed bedroom door, terror seizing the planes of my body and holding them hostage. As I push the door open with my knuckles, my fist shakes, and I struggle to regulate my breathing.

Flipping on the ceiling light, I find my mother sprawled out beneath her silken sheets, mouth agape with drool pooling from it, and a gardening magazine open on my father's pillow. A harsh breath rips from my lungs, relief spilling like a waterfall from the depths it retreated to, and I cross the room to pull the comforter up over her bony shoulders.

She's so pale, I can easily trace the veins glowing blue beneath her skin and see the angle of each of her bones as they protrude almost violently, as if trying to break free from her body. Like a bird trapped in a shrinking cage, desperately trying to find a means of escape.

Glancing at the magazine as I reach to turn off her bedside lamp, I see a sticky note taped to the top of the open page, my eyes scanning her shaky chicken scratch quickly, recognizing what the note is before I've even gotten to the bottom.

To my darling family.

166

Unease filters back in, churning in my gut like hot magma, and I turn off the light and back out of the room, slapping my palm over my mouth to keep the broken sob from alerting my brother.

Sliding down the wall, I bury my face in my hands, tears slipping out past and down my fingers, the relief I felt at first nowhere to be found. It's replaced with that irrational, insatiable sensation—the one that tells me I need to *fix*. Conquer. Be the solution.

But as the crippling weight that accompanies that sensation takes root, I can't find the strength to search for a way out. Numbness clouds over me like early morning fog, hazy and debilitating, and for a while, I just sit in the hall, unsure of what to do.

The sticky note flashes over and over in my brain, pushing out every single other thought, and part of me wants to go back inside and rip it up. Maybe she'll forget she wrote it when she wakes up.

The other part of me wishes there wouldn't be a chance for her to remember.

Dread creeps up my spine, leaving chills in its wake, and I pull my phone out of my pants pocket. To do what, I'm not sure. I can't call my father, because I don't think he'd understand. I could grab Kieran, but the likelihood of him not blowing it out of proportion is slim.

My chest is heavy as I type 911, hoping the recipient knows the meaning and doesn't ask further questions. As I wait for a reply, I pick at my manicured fingernails, chipping the filed tips until they're jagged, sharp edges I could use as a weapon.

His response doesn't come for a long time, and I feel myself dissociating the longer I sit in the hallway. When my phone finally vibrates with his "here," I stand up on tingling legs and make my way downstairs, unlocking the door and pulling it aside.

Boyd stands almost flush with the doorway, worry creasing his brow, hands stuffed into the pockets of the jeans he has on. *Have I ever seen him in jeans?* I focus on the dark blue fabric, noting how neat and pressed they are, how polished he always seems.

I wonder what it must feel like to be able to truly bottle up your demons, how hard he has to try to keep them from breaking through.

If he's ever hurt someone else trying to keep them at bay.

My heart stalls in my chest as I hear a door upstairs open and close, then hear my brother's distinct footsteps, calculated and soft, as they start down the stairs. The fear of being found out takes hold inside me, immobilizing as I wait for Kieran's confusion behind me; Boyd's hand comes out and latches around my wrist, pulling me out onto the porch with him.

He pulls the door shut slowly, reaching into his pocket for a spare key I didn't realize he had, and locks it quickly.

168

I open my mouth to protest, but he just shakes his head, pressing the side of his index finger against my lips.

"Dinner," he says softly, and even though I'm still not sure what he wants from me — or why he's here right now — I don't have the energy to decline his offer.

CHAPTER EIGHTEEN

Boyd

Fiona stands awkwardly in my kitchen, arms wrapped tight around her midsection, like she's afraid that if she touches anything she'll be ruined.

I'm not entirely sure she'd be *worse* off, but it probably wouldn't help, either.

When I picked her up from her house, she was practically catatonic; her eyes were wide and distant, registering my presence but not really comprehending it. Her lips were dry, sweat-stained her forehead, and her finger tapped out that consistent fucking rhythm while she stood there waiting for me to come inside.

I don't think she even knew what she was doing.

When I heard someone coming down the stairs, I acted, not giving a second thought to the implications. I'd pulled her out onto the porch and shoved her into my waiting BMW, having ditched my bike when I stopped home to change from the gym.

Usually, I don't bring people back here—not because I'm embarrassed, although the little white bungalow Dottie gave me doesn't exactly scream *wealthy* bachelor—but because I don't like people in my space. Don't trust them not to snoop and try to get dirt on me.

But since Fiona knows what that's like, and considering who she is in general, that paranoia doesn't exist where she's concerned.

Now, I'm just worried she hates the place.

Insecurity rushes through me as I walk ahead of her, clearing clutter from the vinyl countertops in the kitchen and shoving things from the circular dining room table into random cabinets. I wince, glancing at the worn yellow wallpaper surrounding us, kicking myself for not fixing it last winter during the holiday break from work and hoping she doesn't notice.

She does.

Almost immediately, her eyes scan the area as I turn from the kitchen sink, zeroing in on one particularly bad spot where the paper is torn completely from the wall. Her doe eyes slide to mine, then back to the spot, and then meet mine again, and my skin prickles a little at the judgment.

Exhaling a harsh breath, I rub the back of my neck, trying to relieve some of the tension collecting there. "I don't, uh... get many visitors."

Smirking, she walks over and braces her palms on the edge of the counter, hoisting herself up and perching on the surface. "I can tell."

The urge to fit myself between her legging-clad thighs is strong, but I resist, knowing that if I go there, I'm not going to be able to stop myself from taking her.

And *fuck*, do I want to take her. Fold her body into a thousand different positions, devour her sweet, juicy little cunt until she bleeds and then shove my dick inside of her, see how deep I can go before she's choking on me.

The intensity of my want knows no bounds, blurring the lines between what's socially acceptable and what the beast inside of me craves.

Every day, she consumes a bit more of my soul, desire coursing through me that I feel slipping out of my fingertips with each thought I entertain of demolishing whatever innocence she has left.

I've never felt *anything* this fucking intense before, and I can't help wondering if it isn't the forbidden aspect that adds to the appeal.

After ignoring Fiona the last seven years, logically, I'm having a hard time catching up to where my dick suddenly wants to be, but thinking about getting caught and the trouble it may cause certainly makes the idea more appetizing.

Makes *her* more appetizing.

But that's not what I brought her here for. Frankly, I'm not a hundred percent *why* I brought her here, but now seems like as good a time as any to try and figure out why she texted me 911 and not someone else.

Opening a cabinet beside the white fridge, I pull out a box of spaghetti noodles and set it on the counter along with two jars of sauce, and some spices. Dottie usually grabs groceries for me when she leaves church on Sundays, keeping the place stocked even though I hardly ever eat in it.

"When you mentioned dinner, I didn't know you'd be cooking it," she says when I open the box, dumping the noodles into a large pot with water.

"Surprise." She winces as I set the stove temperature, and I raise an eyebrow. "Something wrong, princess?"

"It's just... are you supposed to put noodles in there like that before the water boils?" Scratching at her wrist, she tries to pose the question so it sounds nonchalant, but I can see the divots her nails make in her skin as she glares at the stove. "Don't they cook faster if it's already boiling?"

"They'll cook either way, though, right?" I shrug, popping open the lid on one jar of sauce and pouring it into a saucepan. I catch her cringe again from the corner of my eye, and set the jar down, turning to face her. I'm growing irritated, her criticism hitting a nerve too close to home. "If you don't like the way I'm doing it, feel free to help out. Most people know better than to bite the literal hand that's feeding them."

Sliding down from the counter, she walks around me and adjusts a few of the controls, adding some pepper, bay leaves, and rosemary to the sauce. "Sorry. Sometimes I can be a little crazy," she says with a breathless laugh. One that feels forced and practiced, like it's an insult she's been told before that she's trying to reclaim.

I don't like the way it makes my stomach twist, a violent storm on the precipice of destruction.

She scratches at her forearm again, stepping back to lean against the inside corner of the counter, just inches away from me in the tiny kitchen. I study the heavy circles beneath her eyes, wondering when the last time she slept was, and note the way she refuses to make eye contact with me.

The last time I was with her, she said I make her nervous, but this feels like something more. Like something she doesn't have any control over.

I'm not sure why she called me tonight, but when I remember how defeated she looked when I showed up at her house, how completely lost she seemed, I can't help but want to soothe that wound for her. Help her gain something from this night, something that puts the fire back in her eyes.

I pull out a few cloves of garlic, a knife, and a cutting board, gesturing for her to have at it. She tilts her head to one

174

side, then looks at the garlic and moves over to take my place, dicing with speed and precision I'm not capable of.

We stand in silence as she continues cooking, and when it's finished and plated we eat in silence, too, our mouths too full to do anything but chew. After setting our plates in the sink, I give her the grand tour, starting in the living room with its brown suede sofa bed and the flat screen television hanging above the fireplace, and ending with my bedroom and its king-size bed and single dresser.

I don't mention the detached garage or the studio apartment that sits above it, firm in my belief that no one but me steps in there. The things that follow you on the way out aren't demons I'd wish on anyone.

Not even LeeAnn.

Pulling an electric sherpa blanket from the linen closet, I plug it in and let it warm up while I unfold the sofa bed, stretching a sheet over the mattress and testing its strength. I don't take her to my bed upstairs because I'm afraid of how far I'll go with her in it, so the sofa is the next safest thing.

Fiona stands off to the side, looking at a picture hanging by the front window of me and Riley on her first day of kindergarten.

It's the only picture I have with her, period.

"Do... you have a kid?" Fiona asks.

A strangled laugh bubbles up out of my throat. "Jesus, no. That's Riley."

"And Riley is..."

Sighing, I spread the blanket out on the bed and sit down on the edge, facing her. She folds her arms over her chest, waiting. "Riley is my... biological sister."

Fiona's head jerks back in surprise. "You have a sister?"

"Siblings aren't that uncommon."

"Well, no, obviously." Her face turns the prettiest shade of pink, and she comes over, sitting on the bed beside me. Our knees brush, electricity flaring at the slightest touch, and the need to *claim* her rears its ugly head again. "But I don't think I've ever heard you mention anyone you're related to. Although, now that I'm thinking about it, you do fit the older sibling identity far better than the only child one."

I smirk. "Putting that psych major to use. Think you've got me pegged, huh?"

Her blush deepens, and she averts her gaze to the swirls in the hardwood floor. "I would never claim that. You're too much of a mystery, and we only just started doing... *this*."

"Hm," I hum, shifting so she has to scramble backward. She pulls her knees to her chest, leaning against the back of the couch, and narrows her eyes as I move closer, planting my palms on either side of her. "And what exactly is *this* we're doing?"

She licks her lips, wetting the pouty flesh like she knows I want a taste. "I don't know," she whispers, dropping her gaze to my mouth. Her pupils dilate, eyes darkening with lust I feel down to my fucking toes, and my fingers dig into the mattress as I continue resisting.

"Why'd you text me tonight?" I ask, reaching out and tracing my index finger over the curve of her knee. Tracking the movement with her molten gaze, she doesn't say anything, distracted. Hooking that same finger beneath her chin, I tip her head up and spread my palm along her jaw, keeping her trapped there. "What happened earlier?"

As I hold her in place, my grip harsher than it should be considering how new this all is, she never breaks from my gaze, staring straight back as if she can see into my soul. See the things hidden in the shadows.

"Why did you ask me to dinner?" she shoots back, raising a delicate brow.

"Because I wanted to." With my free hand, I tangle my fingers around the ends of her fiery hair, tugging slightly. She's deflecting, replacing one worry with another, but I figure I should take what I can get when it comes to her. "What're you really asking?"

"When I was out with Nico that one afternoon, you basically called me a whore."

"I'm an asshole. That's nothing new." I stroke her bottom lip with my thumb, reveling in the smoothness of it. "Did it piss you off when I called you that?"

Jerking her chin, she tries to escape my grasp, but I only increase the pressure. I feel my nails biting into her skin, but I don't stop or pull back. *I'm in control right now.*

Her eyes flare, jaw flexing beneath my grasp, and the raw fury radiating off her in waves makes me want to cover her mouth with my own and rob her of every breath she has.

"Let go of me," she snaps, her hand coming up to clamp down around my wrist.

"Tell me how me calling you a whore made you feel, and maybe I will," I say, dipping my head so we're only a whisper apart. So close, I can practically taste her fucking arousal.

Drawing her eyebrows inward, she glares at me, trying to wrench my hand away. "*Why?*"

"You're accusing me of... wanting to be with you because I think you're easy, right? Do you honestly think I'd be here right now, with you, if I didn't want to be?"

"I don't know —"

Shifting so our heads are side by side, my lips graze her ear when I speak next. "Besides… are you really going to tell me that me calling you a whore doesn't make you hot?"

"No, and it's —"

"Maybe you just don't understand the power of the word yet," I breathe, my tongue darting out to trace the outside of her earlobe. A shiver runs across her body, making her spasm against me. "If you knew how good it could feel... me, *deep* inside your tight little cunt, barely holding back my release as I fuck you so hard you see stars... maybe with my hand around your throat, your makeup ruined from your tears and my spit... whispering in your ear about what a *filthy little whore you are...* and not just any whore, but *my* whore... then maybe you wouldn't take such offense to the term."

My phone buzzes in my pocket as I finish my sentence, both our breaths labored as they wrangle their way from our lungs. Fiona's completely flushed when I rear my head back, and I press down hard when I run my thumb over her lips again, smearing the cherry red lipstick she wears like a fucking brand.

A brand.

Fuck, if she wouldn't look good with my words burned into her skin.

I smile devilishly as I get to my feet, admiring the way she squirms away, clambering under the blanket and turning on her side away from me.

As if that'd be enough to hold me off. She scrubs furiously at her mouth, probably trying to erase any evidence of me touching her, and I chuckle to myself at the dramatic display of defiance.

Like I don't know that if I shoved my hand between her thighs right now, I'd find her absolutely fucking soaked.

Heading toward the kitchen, I leave her in the house and slip out the back door, pulling my phone out as an unknown number flashes across the screen. Annoyed, I answer immediately, assuming it's LeeAnn trying to trick me again, but I'm greeted by a male voice instead.

"Boyd Kelly?"

I hesitate, squinting against the setting sun as I scan the back yard. "Speaking."

CHAPTER NINETEEN

Fiona

*E*motional whiplash.

Rubbing my thighs together beneath the warm blanket, that's the phrase that plays on repeat in my mind as I watch Boyd walk outside, leaving me frustrated in more ways than one. I'm a sticky disaster between my legs, the moisture pooling there cool against my skin, my entire body vibrating like I've been hooked up to a tens unit and left to fend for myself.

The stuff about my mom long forgotten, now all I can do is stare at the dormant fireplace and wonder how long it'll be before he comes back. If I have time to attempt some relief, or if he'd walk in before I finished.

More importantly, *why did the word whore stoke such a rapid, raging fire inside of me?*

As a feminist, the notion that I'd enjoy being called that should've offended me, but for some reason watching Boyd's lips curl around the single syllable turned my bones into melted butter.

Still, I don't think it's a kink, so much as the *way* he said it.

Like I belong to him already.

And even though I'm still not exactly sure what's going on here, I can't deny that the idea pleases me.

His switch flipped so suddenly, though, going from concerned and considerate, back to the raging asshole I grew up pining after. I'm not really sure how to reconcile the two, but maybe that's not the point.

Maybe everyone has two sides to them, and our job isn't to determine which is real, but to figure out how to coexist with them both. People create personas to wear as armor, as a means of protection, and it's dangerous to try and strip that away for our own personal benefit.

Besides, he didn't push me tonight, so maybe I should cut him some slack, just like Bea was saying. Anxiety bleeds into my thoughts, making me believe there's an ulterior motive to everything, and maybe that's the only real issue here.

Glancing at the back door, I settle down under the blanket again, basking in the warm cocoon as I wait for Boyd to return. There's an analog clock hanging on the wall above the dining room, reminding me of the spots in his wallpaper that need touched up and sending a wave of restlessness down my spine again; with each second that clicks by, I search the room for a new tear or worn area, counting thirty in total.

Three minutes pass with me counting the spots one-hundred-eighty times, wishing I knew if he keeps plaster or paste in the house somewhere. I take a mental inventory, recalling the closets from the short tour he'd taken me on, noting that if he doesn't return soon, I'll be forced to take measures into my own hands.

My arousal flees as the *itch* creeps in, and I kick my feet on top of the mattress as my body grows uncomfortable, trying to regain the control I just had over myself. But it's no use—my brain is looping on everything leading up to this moment, hyper-focusing on the wallpaper, and it's starting to pull me under.

Scratching at my scalp, I shift up against the back of the couch, the sofa suddenly lumpy and uncomfortable. The house is so quiet, a stillness present that I'm not used to, as if this place isn't haunted at all.

The ghosts must be haunting Boyd directly, instead.

As if I've conjured him, the back door squeaks open just as I think his name, his tall, muscular frame appearing against the backdrop of the cotton candy sky. He doesn't say anything as he walks to the stairs, shuffling up them and returning a few moments later with a long-sleeved Patriots T-shirt and a pair of gray sweats.

Tossing me the shirt, he starts to strip from his jeans, raising an eyebrow when he notices me not moving. "Are you planning on sleeping in leggings?"

I swallow, squeezing the soft material between my fingers. "I'm staying here?"

"Unless you're planning to walk home, yes." Yanking his shirt over his head, he lets it drop to the floor, then unbuttons his jeans and shimmies them down over his hips.

My core pulsates as my eyes explore the defined ridges of his chest, his tapered waist, abs so sharp and defined I could probably slit my wrist on them. The black boxer briefs he has on do little to hide how I affect him, and it makes my heart somersault realizing that he's as into all of this as I am.

Words are one thing, but the physical proof is hard to ignore.

And even though the words should mean more, there's something satisfying in the evidence.

There's a light bruise coloring one side of his ribs, and I think back to the black eye he showed up at my house with last week, wondering what it is he does that leaves him so battered.

184

Stepping into the sweatpants, he slides them up over his hips, marring my view, and crosses his arms.

His jaw clenches as he stares at me, something primal and angry lurking within him that wasn't there before he went outside. Something *dangerous.* I see it in the tic that forms, in how tight he holds his arms against his chest, in the frown that creases his forehead.

It feels directed at me, but I don't know what I did.

Shifting my gaze to the shirt, I sit up straight and let the blanket fall around me, lifting my arms and pulling my sweater over my head.

His eyes fall to the lacy pink bra I'm wearing, glazing over as they absorb the image, and I reach behind my back, using my thumb and index finger to undo the clasp. It falls off my arms into my lap, baring my breasts to him for the first time.

"Jesus." His throat bobs over a swallow, the tension in his arms relaxing slightly. Taking a few steps closer, he kneels on the mattress, extending his hand to gently roll his thumb over one nipple. His expression is subdued, almost reverent, and it sends sparks of excitement through my body.

He cups the underside of one, squeezing slightly. "Don't put that shirt on. I want you just like this."

My pussy tingles at his command, and I lean into his touch. "My dad would probably kill me for wearing a Patriots shirt, anyway. Or you, for giving it to me."

"I think," he says, scooting closer, pinching my nipple between two fingers. "He'd kill me for other things."

This time, when he moves in to kiss me, I don't hesitate or ask questions; I let his fire consume me as it grows brighter and faster with each stroke of his tongue, each caress of his hand, each murmured curse as he discovers something else on my body that he likes.

When this is over, I'm sure I'll be nothing but a pile of ash.

But the burn feels so fucking good, I can't justify extinguishing the flames.

Weeks pass slowly, things settling between Boyd and me while the rest of my life seems to be in constant upheaval.

Some nights, I fall asleep listening to Boyd's breathing, exhausted after a session of talking about nothing and distracting each other from our realities, and the dirty stuff that inevitably follows.

Other times, I toss and turn, random thoughts of malice and paranoia worming their way into my brain. Each time I entertain one, another pops up—it's a vicious loop of repetition, and once I lock onto one I can't stop thinking about it.

Despite my brain's attempt to get a grip on the control before it slips away completely, I've never felt less in charge of my life. I spend hours trying to fall asleep, plagued by the notion that the chaos is somehow my fault.

That the secrets I harbor are to blame for our misfortune.

The day I accuse my brother of keeping his girlfriend a secret during an early family dinner, Kieran's shot in the graveyard, making our father believe *someone* is targeting us, which means his rules get stricter than ever. I'm banned from drama club and only allowed to go to the grocery or pharmacy if someone else accompanies me.

Bea and Heidi drop by one day with chocolate milkshakes, and I take one up to Kieran, who's sitting in his room on his computer, sifting through some kind of security footage. I set the shake beside his mouse pad, watching over his shoulder as he pauses and makes a note in another browser.

"Whatcha doing?" I ask, poking his back with my pinky. The red shirt he's wearing covers most of his upper body, but I can see the gauze peeking out from where it's wrapped around his shoulder, evidence of something *else* I have no control over.

Kieran grunts, likely still annoyed from having the family accost him not long after he was shot, when he was entertaining Juliet in the privacy of his room. "I'm working."

"On what?"

"Trying to find the dick who shot me," he says, voice matter-of-fact, like I'm supposed to know that.

I nod, rocking back on my heels, and take a sip of my shake. "Where's your girlfriend?"

Swiveling in his desk chair, Kieran turns to face me, propping his chin in his hand and his elbow on his knee. "Not that it's any of your business after that stunt you pulled last week, but she's at a doctor's appointment."

"Did you give her crabs?"

A laugh bursts out of his chest, the first I've heard from him in a long time. "No, nothing like that. Just... personal shit, I guess."

"Oh." I stare at a spot on his wooden desk, considering that. "Therapy?"

"Fiona, it's really not my place to say."

"Okay, jeez, I was just trying to find out more about her. You've never had a girlfriend before, it's just so... shocking."

He grunts again, dropping his elbow and propping one knee over the other. "Well, the same could be said about you, right? Don't think I've forgotten about Dad saying he found you and Boyd in a *compromising* position."

Heat rises to my cheeks and wraps its fingers around my neck, pressing until it's difficult to breathe. When we'd accosted Juliet and Kieran while they lay in bed, my father tried to pass the torch of attention to the fact that apparently, that first night Boyd stayed the night, they ran into each other in the hall. A fact Boyd hadn't mentioned to me until after it was already out in the open, my embarrassment spilled all over the floor for everyone to witness.

It'd taken three orgasms before I'd forgiven him, but the sting of his secrecy still throbs inside of me, a wound that's scabbed but still not quite healed.

Kieran's eyebrows draw inward. "Oh, God, Fiona, are you fucking him?"

"No!" I say, the word rushed and overeager. His eyebrows raise, and I sip on my shake again, trying to use the icy slush to calm the heat ravaging my body. "I mean, seriously, no. I'm not... having sex with your best friend."

But God, do I want to.

Sighing, Kieran slumps in his chair, reaching out for his own Styrofoam cup, slurping down a big gulp. "There's a lot you don't know about Boyd Kelly."

"There's a lot I don't know about any of you," I say, shrugging, our mother's voice down the hall calling out to me.

"I'm just saying. Be careful." He salutes me as I back out of the bedroom, smoothing his hand over the bandage beneath his shirt. A pang flares up in my stomach as I drag the door closed on my way out, the realization that my family might be in actual danger hitting when I watch him wince from a flesh wound.

Ivers men aren't strangers to violence, but I've never before seen them so open about it. They've never felt the need to involve my mother or me in their issues, and I can't help wondering what the fuck is going on, and if I'm in trouble just by being here.

My brain is so preoccupied with the potential for danger that I don't even register Kieran's warning against Boyd, nor do I make a note to mention it to him later, hoping that's not the kind of thing that comes back to bite me in the ass.

CHAPTER TWENTY

Boyd

iley's knee bounces in the leather armchair, her anxiety almost contagious as we wait for the headmaster of King's Trace Prep to return to her office. She runs her hand over her blonde pigtails, twisting the ends between her fingers, and looks around the room silently for the fifth time since Dr. Yang excused herself.

"What's wrong with you? Why are you so jittery?"

She glances at me, turning her head as if just remembering I'm sitting right beside her. "Nothing's *wrong* with me, I just can't believe you're making me transfer schools at the end of the freaking year. It's *embarrassing*."

"You were *expelled*," I snap, thinking about the call I received from the police while pulling up the email from the county school principal.

After learning she'd only been fined for the underage drinking, I'd climbed back in bed beside Fiona and hoped that was the end of it.

I'd been overseeing an account acquisition between our security systems and a top-of-the-line company's newly-released encryption services when the email came through my computer, demanding my attention. Instead of finishing the meeting myself, doing my favorite part of the job and intimidating anyone into fucking with our business, I'd had to step out and let Craig close.

"Expelled for something fucking stupid," she mutters, huffing and slamming her back against the seat.

I don't respond, thumbing through the campus brochure I swipe from the table between our chairs; it's dated last spring, and immediately I'm drawn to a picture of a redheaded girl on the quad, surrounded by a sea of backpacks and people, yet still somehow standing out like the North Star itself.

Reality slams into me, a freight train running off the tracks. Fiona was in *high school* a year ago, and I haven't been in a decade. Most of the time I'm too busy wondering about how we'll look to her brother or father to consider there's another odd stacked against us — that she's so much *younger* than me.

If she were a few years older, maybe out of college even, it wouldn't be such an issue, but it's hard to justify her ruin at my hands when I realize she has so much of her life left ahead of her.

Me, I'm already half dead. My soul died long ago, withered away with my despair and the sins I indulge in, but my body's taking longer to catch up. King's Trace might think I'm morally superior to my fellow residents, but I'm much, much worse.

Violently irredeemable. Uninterested in changing.

Dragging Fiona down with me when she's almost the same age as my sister feels... wrong.

But even as my brain conjures that thought, it disappears, no concrete plans to extract myself from her forming in its place.

Truth is, I think I might be addicted to her—the sunshine that she works so hard at and the dark skies that lay beneath the golden surface, only shown when she's alone or in my presence. The connection is strong, heady, always leaving me *needing*.

"You agree that it was stupid, right?" Riley asks, pulling her feet up so they're in the chair with her, propping her scuffed red Converse up on the leather.

Dropping the brochure back in its slot on the wooden table, I reach out and shove her feet down, not wanting Dr. Yang to come back and think she's being disrespectful.

"Doesn't matter what I think, does it? Your school had an issue with it, and they terminated your enrollment. We're really fucking lucky that KTP even agreed to see us, all things considered."

She scoffs. "I'm sure they're only seeing us because they know you're a potential donor. A tattooed cash pinata for them to bleed dry."

"Actually, they agreed because of your grades and community service." I skim the email I got this morning from Dr. Yang's secretary, recalling how I'd been surprised when they didn't immediately ask for money, especially considering the private school's seedy reputation. "Said they believe in second chances and not letting one mistake ruin a kid's life."

Grumbling something under her breath, she slumps down farther in her chair, blowing a strand of hair from her face.

Sighing, I stuff my phone back into my suit pocket, folding my hands over my lap and stroking the skull tattoo on the back of my hand with the opposite thumb. "I have a lot riding on this, though, Riley. *Monetarily*. It'd be great if you didn't fuck it up, especially since I didn't get back the deposit on the New York trip."

Shooting upright, her mouth drops as if to protest, but I give her a long look and she settles back down, clamping her jaw closed.

It rolls as she grits her teeth, and I want to tell her to stop, to warn her that once you start clenching as a means of warding off your violent urges, to satisfy the thoughts of harming every person you care about, it never stops.

194

Not even if you give in, letting the barbarity consume you.

Instead, it adds to the repertoire of things you can't control, until your entire existence seems to boil down to the broken pieces of you.

"Don't worry, Boyd, I know how important your stupid reputation is." She turns away from me completely, opening an app on her phone and once again scrolling through the pictures of that musician with the curly dark hair she was drooling over a few weeks ago.

I watch as she pulls up photos she's already liked, double-tapping them as if out of habit, and then scrolls onto the next and repeats the process, and I can't help but wonder if this is some new generation gimmick, a nobody's attempt at garnering their idol's attention, or if we have more in common than I'd hoped.

If her obsession for someone unattainable rules her life the way mine is currently.

Dr. Yang returns, and we're saddled with an exorbitant amount of paperwork, an identification card that gives Riley access to the main buildings, and inexplicable shame.

It bears down on us as we leave the administration hall, passing the topiaries sculpted into the shapes of the school's initials and the massive fountain at the center of the campus.

How a town as poverty-stricken as ours even keeps a school like this afloat is beyond me; the Ivers are all alumnus, so I'm sure there's donor money with them, and the Montaltos and

Bianchis donate to any and all philanthropic efforts at the behest of the police, to make them look legitimate.

The rest must be coming in from tuition.

Riley's shoulders slump as we make our way to the parking lot; her blue eyes dart from one surface to the next, avoiding what's directly in front of her, and when we make it back to my black BMW, she gets in on the passenger side without a word, putting in headphones before I've even started the car.

My fingers flex against the steering wheel as I shift gears, reversing out of the spot, the shame from being outcasts compared to the students at KTP morphing into annoyance. Riley isn't my kid, and I shouldn't have to be the one trying to get her into a program so she graduates on time.

As usual, though, I'm the only one she seems able to depend on, despite the fact that I despise the responsibility.

But if I'm trying to distance myself from LeeAnn's narrative, trying to distance myself as her son, the most out of character thing she could ever do is care for one of the kids she brought into this world.

So I'll keep showing up for Riley, even though it kills a part of me every time I have to. Even though I wish she didn't exist in the first place so she wouldn't have to endure this life, and so I wouldn't be reminded constantly that LeeAnn didn't keep me.

When I drop her off at the trailer, I double check the living space for needles and alcohol, fully intending to take Dr. Yang's probationary period seriously—a kid that just got busted and expelled for underage drinking at a frat party definitely doesn't need the temptation, especially when she doesn't think she did anything wrong.

I raise my fist to knock on her bedroom door when I'm ready to leave but think better of it at the last second. She probably doesn't want to see me anyway.

Loading the dated dishwasher before I exit, I tuck a hundred dollar bill into Riley's raincoat hanging up beside the door and lock the doorknob behind me, an unsettling feeling washing over me as I walk to the car.

The feeling of being watched.

Sliding in behind the wheel, I sit there for a moment, scanning the trailer park for vehicles or people that seem out of place. Always on the lookout, since getting those flash drives and seeing Kieran and Craig get shot on two separate occasions.

I'm on high alert, hustling to get my affairs in order, refusing to wait helplessly while they come for us.

Now *I'm* coming for *them.*

"KTP is a good school," Fiona says, the sound of her chewing drowning out her words. They're mushed together, almost indecipherable, and I turn off the cylinder saw I borrowed from Kieran as she continues. "I didn't have any problems making friends while I was there."

"You didn't transfer at the end of your high school career, either. And you're an Ivers; people can't ignore you even if they want to."

"Yeah, but I'm *dramatic,* as my loved ones put it." I hear her pop a bubble against her lips and can imagine her pacing her bedroom right now, cooped up all day taking care of her mother and working on assignments for classes, fingers dying for something to sink into.

Something to distract.

If I wasn't busy and we were at that point, I'd be over there now with my face buried between her legs, feasting on her until she begged me to finish. But my appointment couldn't be moved, and she's stuck babysitting her mother.

It's only been a few days since I saw her last, but I can feel the need to be in her presence, to feel her skin against mine, to breathe in her floral, candied scent as it expands, pushing out room for anything else in my body until I'm a writhing, desperate shell of a man.

Settling for a phone call would typically be beneath me, but I'm not one to look a gift horse in the mouth.

Especially when that horse has no idea what I'm doing while she rambles. No idea how her voice sends waves of calm down my spine that typically I can only access through violence.

But I know it's her, because I haven't even begun the fun part of my evening, and I already feel somehow sated.

It feels dangerous, this attachment, but I don't let myself dwell on the potential for problems. Instead, I set my saw down and walk over to the knife on the metal table next to the exam bed, adjusting the blade in my palm.

Pressing the speaker button, I set the phone down on the table as Fiona talks about yearbook and the heavy presence of cliques at KTP—because when everyone comes from money, how else do you define yourself?—and slide the bandana up the man's sweaty, wrinkled forehead, revealing hollow sockets.

His eyeballs rest on his cheekbones, still attached to their nerves, but I sense the anesthesia I gave him earlier is wearing off as his hands start twitching.

"... think she'll do just fine," Fiona's saying now, splitting my focus as I lift the sharp edge of my knife to the optic nerve, slicing back and forth in a sawing motion.

It's somehow thin and thick at the same time, requiring a slight push in effort as I work to detach his eye completely; blood already coats my skin and the floors in the apartment above my garage since I slit his wrists an hour ago and let him bleed out for a few minutes, before bandaging the wounds and moving on to the more surgical manner of interrogation.

The man works for Romeo Bianchi, who, according to the intel and security footage I've gathered so far, has *some* part in the shit going on at Ivers International. In every bit of footage that exists, moments before Craig is shot and before Kieran leaves to go to the cemetery the day he's shot, Romeo passes by quickly, as if casing the places and preparing for a hit.

And since neither hit was successful, paired with the flash drives I received, I can't help wanting to get the drop on Romeo before he has another chance to strike.

This, however, isn't really an interrogation.

This is pure satisfaction.

With Fiona's voice in my ears, I work on detaching the other eye, unsure of how long I have before his body shuts down completely, since I didn't exactly contact Kieran or Kal before snatching the guy from the Crystal Knuckle. I just grabbed him and brought him back, acting on an impulse I so rarely allow.

Still, I work quickly, not wanting to perform on a corpse if I can help it. Reaching for the pliers beside my phone, I begin extracting molars, dropping them into a metal dish so I can wash them and put them with the others later.

Teeth are the best form of forensic evidence. You can match dental records to even the most charred bodies, so I always make sure to take them when I deal with people in the underground.

They're not so much souvenirs, like Kieran's bone collection, as they are insurance.

And tonight, when I drop the scalped, toothless, eyeless body of this random runner on Romeo's rumored doorstep, I'm gonna be the only one able to properly identify him.

CHAPTER TWENTY ONE

Fiona

A hand grips my shoulder, pulling me out of my spiral; I drag my stare from the laptop screen where my final grades are posted and try not to let the weight of crushing disappointment shine through.

Biting down on the inside of my cheek until the taste of copper spills onto my tongue, I glance up at Kal Anderson with a smile, my mind stuck on my stats professor's notes.

Student missed several big-point assignments and never reached out to make them up. Unfortunately, without an explanation on their part, I'm unable to allow them to pass.

My throat burns, a ball of fire lodged within that makes it hard to concentrate on anything but my mistakes, even with the epitome of tall, dark, and dangerous looming over me. Any other time, being in the presence of Doctor Death would chill me, but right now I'm too numb to care.

I don't even really care about the grade, except that I've never failed anything before. The thought lodges in my brain, trying to stake a claim on a new obsession before the one I'm really afraid of can edge its way in.

I didn't turn in my final paper because I was busy watching my mother, who'd fallen down the stairs and gotten a concussion. She needed to be watched for a full twenty-four hours in case signs of trauma outside the bruise on her forehead appeared, and I didn't have time to write a paper on the psychology of losing a parent when I'm living the fucking thing.

Sliding the laptop off where it's propped on my legs, I set it on the step beside me and stare out into the greenhouse, absently eyeballing the various potted tropical plants and bags of soil that line the rows of tables.

Kal exhales, bending to sit beside me, sprawling his legs out past the bottom step because they're too long to fit tucked against him.

Revered as one of the most attractive, unattainable bachelors in the country, Kal Anderson is the human embodiment of a solar eclipse; he's almost *too* perfect, the angles of his jaw and cheekbones so defined that they could be used as weapons, his irises so dark and terrifying that they look demonic.

He's tall, the tallest man I've ever seen, and intimidating in presence alone, and this is really the only time we've ever spent together alone.

Situation aside, it's unnerving sitting beside Death himself.

Carding a hand through his jet-black hair, Kal looks at me; I feel the implication of his stare in my soul, know what he's going to say before he even opens his mouth.

"How much longer does she have?"

He folds his hands together, balances them on his knees. His black trench coat fans beneath him, a staple despite the warm weather outside. "There's no real way to know for sure, but she's regressing rather quickly. She won't be in this stage much longer."

I know his matter-of-factness probably makes him a great doctor—and even better hitman—but right now, all it does is push down on the weight resting on my shoulders, making it impossible to carry.

Tears sting my eyes and my throat tightens, crumpling beneath the pressure. My hands spread along my thighs, my index finger tapping out a rhythm, but this time it doesn't do anything for me.

Isn't quite strong enough to deliver me from the pit of despair as its sinewy tentacles reach out and pull me under, drawing me toward an abyss I'm not sure I can come back from.

"So... what now?"

Kal's frown deepens, the crow's feet around his eyes expanding as he turns his head. "Did she ever get a chance to talk to you?"

"About what?"

"Getting her affairs in order."

My face grows clammy. *Why would she talk to Kal, of all people, about it? Was our conversation not good enough?*

"Yeah, she mentioned it a few weeks ago. Said she... didn't know if she wanted to wait for the disease to take her."

Reaching out, Kal plucks the petal of a nearby Gardenia, rubbing the soft yellow petals with his thumb and forefinger. It's such an innocent, calming gesture that my brain immediately locks in on the movement, enraptured by the rhythm of it contrasting against the darkness of the person behind the action.

Kal's more of a mystery than Boyd, having swept in one day years ago as an in-house doctor and occasional hitman for the Montaltos.

Supposedly, his particular brand of *hits* is unlike that of any others, in part due to his medical background — but even that's just a rumor.

Every once in a while, between jobs for Elia Montalto and his parent outfit in Boston, Kal will volunteer at clinics across the country, often offering his services in exchange for... well, nothing. He donates his time and knowledge, as if trying to recoup the morality lost each time he murders for hire.

If not for the relationship he'd already established with my brother and parents, I never would have agreed to let him become my mother's personal doctor, but she needed one who could be discreet—a great feat in a town as small as this one—and who wouldn't try to sabotage her condition because of the wealth behind her name.

"You know," he says after a long stretch of silence. There's a distinct lack of warmth in his words, something that almost feels practiced—like he's actively trying not to get involved. Maybe that's how he sleeps at night. "My mother passed when I was young."

"You mean you weren't hatched?"

His brow furrows. "What?"

A nervous tickle catches in my throat, and I shake my head, resuming the tapping on my leg. "Nothing, that's just a rumor people around town sometimes say. The joke is that you're not human, or something. The Devil's spawn or... some kind of reptile."

Clearing his throat, he crushes the petal in his fist and releases it. We watch it drift to the ground, ruined, and land with a silent thud.

"*Anyway*," he says, the word grating on my nerves like nails raking down a chalkboard. It feels dismissive, and even though my comment is worthy of brushing past, I can't shake the sense that I'm inconsequential.

To Kal, to everyone. A dramatic little princess whose only purpose for eighteen years was to be a companion to her mother. The child she *got right*. The one who'd take care of her when she needed it.

And now, like my entire life hasn't mattered at all, I'm supposed to just relinquish that. To be okay with her leaving.

My fingers curl into themselves, the thread holding my sanity together unspooling until it lies in a tangled pile at my feet, useless and unnecessary. Guilt washes over me, shredding any remnants of self-worth as I sit there, and I grit my teeth so hard trying to keep the tears from spilling over, that it makes my jaw ache.

"She had cancer on and off my whole life. When I turned thirteen, I'd lost track of the number of times we'd sent her to hospice and she'd been sent home with a clean bill of health. Went into remission four times before it ended up stealing her from me." He gets a distant look in his dark, almost black eyes, as if lost in his memories.

I study him from the edge of my vision, the tightness in my throat growing until I can't breathe.

Pain etches into the lines of his face, wounds from his past making themselves visible. My eyes get lost tracing the evidence of his hurt, soaking it in as a salve for my own, a vampire feasting on emotional vulnerability.

"I was a poor kid with too much time on my hands, so I spent every second I could taking care of her, and when the time came to just hold her hand while she passed from this life to the next... I didn't show up. Realized I didn't know what the fuck to do with myself if I wasn't taking care of her anymore, and I guess I thought that if I didn't go, that'd somehow make her less dead."

Fire ignites in my chest, flashing in a single spasm as he turns his head to meet my gaze. I don't like what he sees, how it feels like looking into a mirror—if that's the future awaiting me, one full of violence and death despite my attempts to avoid that fate, I'm not sure what to do with that information.

He seems to snap back into himself, as if just remembering who he's talking to. "That's not how this works, though. Death doesn't wait for you to get on board, it just collects." He raises an eyebrow. "You can't keep her here, Fiona."

My heart cracks wide open, the flames from my chest immediately filling the spaces in between, and I feel like I've been thrown down an elevator shaft and left for dead. "I'm not trying to."

"Then you need to tell her that. She told *you* what she wanted. No one else."

"What am I supposed to do?"

"Frankly, I don't really care. I'll still perform the procedure regardless, because that's what she asked me to do.

207

But I won't be sitting by her side, waiting for her to fall asleep and not wake up. I didn't do it for my mother, I'm sure as hell not doing it for someone else's."

Pushing to his feet, Kal brushes off the front of his black sweater, giving me a half shrug. "I coexist with my mistakes. I guess you should decide if you want to, too."

The door slams behind him as he exits the greenhouse, leaving me to rot inside of my thoughts.

Standing up, I glance around the enclosed space, my fingers trembling as I press them into my sides. Bile teases the back of my throat as unease slices through me, and I walk through the back of the house, letting the silence surround me.

It's not peaceful.

Not the way silence is supposed to be.

As I stand in the mudroom, staring down the hallway to the front door, the quiet waxes and wanes around me, scraping its fingers against my skin as it tries to push me over the edge.

My eyes flicker to the mess in the kitchen, a post-dinner disaster left for housekeeping in the morning. The aftermath of our first family meal without my mother, who always insists on cleaning right when we get up.

She says it helps the food digest quicker. Builds character.

Passing through the hall to the staircase, I take them slowly, trying to allow my brain the space to work through its quirks so when I enter the bedroom I can pretend to be normal.

Happy, even.

Kal didn't say it, but I know that's the kind of thing my mother needs right now.

I don't want her to feel guilty for wanting to leave us behind.

A lump forms in my throat as I push her door open and find my mother lying in bed, staring blankly at the muted television across the room. Her hair's pulled back into the rollers I put it in this morning, her pink robe stained with some kind of yellow substance, and she doesn't move a muscle when I walk in.

"Mom?" I say softly, edging my way to her bedside. Her frail hands are folded over her lap, her green gaze devoid of any of the fire it once held.

I climb on the bed beside her, careful not to jostle her too much, and slide my hand over hers, prepared to spend the rest of my afternoon watching *Family Ties* reruns. One of her thumbs hooks over mine, acknowledging me, and I turn to look at her.

"Murphy," she slurs, her lips barely moving with the word.

Freezing, my gaze darts to hers, searching for a joke hidden deep in her eyes. She blinks back, unperturbed, as my heart slams against my ribs so hard it moves the bed. Sadness flows through my veins, clogging my arteries, and making me shake.

We stare at each other for a few moments, the realization that she's mid-delusion settling in and providing a certain degree of comfort—until it doesn't anymore, because it's been months since she hallucinated like this.

My stomach heaves, disappointment weaving a tapestry of darkness that blots out any room for sunshine in this very moment.

She thinks I'm Murphy.

Digging deep, I try to shrug off the delusion, reasoning that she isn't in control of her thoughts right now. Knowing that denying my identity will only upset her, I swallow over the vomit threatening to spew and squeeze her fingers with a thin smile. "It's me, Ma. How're you feeling?"

"Oh, Murphy. I've missed you." One half of her mouth curves, as if she's trying to smile, too, but it doesn't quite work. "It's hard with you gone."

Her speech is so slurred I can barely make it out; I strain closer, listening for the ends of syllables and piecing them together myself. "I know, Ma. I'm sorry."

She pats my hand with her fingertips, shaking her head. "Don't be. You're here now."

Gritting my teeth, I bend down, resting my head in the crook of her shoulder and inhaling the rosy perfume she has on— the same kind I've been wearing lately, as if trying to memorize her scent.

Embed it under my skin so she never really leaves me.

"Don't leave," she murmurs, eyelids drifting closed. Her grip tightens around my hand as she squeezes with more strength than I'd think her capable of. "Stay with me awhile. You're never here anymore, and this house is a wasteland without you."

Driving the knife farther into my heart, I just nod against her and wait for her slurred speech to drop off completely; a few moments later, her snores fill the large white room, and I disentangle myself from her grasp, tucking the silk comforter around her and pressing a soft kiss to her forehead, discomfort a massive pit in my stomach as I sneak from the room and downstairs to my father's office.

I know what she wants, and I know what she asked from me.

I just don't think I can go through with it.

Some people in her condition live decades. They get extra time with their families, extra time to right their wrongs on this planet, extra time to miss the correct people. How can I help her when the possibility of *more* time is still technically an option?

Raising my fist to knock on the door so I can force my father into the foray and get his input, have him take charge where he should have been all along, I pause when I hear movement just inside. Stepping aside in case he's about to come out, I suck in a deep breath and hold it, listening. Waiting.

A moan comes from behind the closed door, startling in its volume. My eyebrows scrunch together, confusion lacing through the muscles in my brain, trying to make sense of the sound. It's too loud, too present, to be porn, and I know Kieran's not here tonight.

"Oh, *Craig*." A giggle and then another moan, this time throatier and deeper than the other, and I just *know* it's him. My father, inside his home office.

With another woman.

CHAPTER TWENTY TWO

Boyd

I glare at the thumbprint smudge on my computer monitor, contemplating setting fire to Finn Hanson's hand as he steps back out of range, as if sensing he's made a mistake. As the boss of the Stonemore gang, mistakes probably aren't something he's used to, but he doesn't make a fuss, regardless, which I like.

There's far too much emotional turmoil in my life as it is.

But Finn comes with no strings, which is why I reached out to him for this investigation while Kieran's teaming up with Elia Montalto on his end. Mine will be quick and clean, no evidence left behind to tie me to anything, unlike Kieran's initial investigation years ago, which is purportedly the motive behind everything going on now.

He got emotional. Sloppy. And now, we're all paying for it.

Finn crosses his tattooed arms over his chest, smoothing a wrinkle out from the front of the dark green T-shirt he has on. "*That* person, the one lurking in the shadows, is far more of a threat to you than Romeo Bianchi. If Romeo really wanted your people dead, they would be. He's an idiot, but he's got too many men on his crew that are just itching for a reason to kill."

I stare at the screen, studying the figure as it appears in every clip where Kieran, Craig, and I are concerned. Comparatively, the person is smaller in stature and seems less confident when they walk, perhaps the reason for not approaching us in the open.

They rely on sneak attacks to get the upper hand, which tells me they're not directly mafia-related for two reasons.

One, no made man would be afraid to approach someone else. The mafia trains the fear from your body, extracting it as though it's not there as an adaptive, evolutionary response in the first place.

It's why Finn stands here in my office now, helping me despite the fact that the audit I did for him weeks ago showed his organization is funneling cash in from something that has nothing to do with drugs.

He knows I know about the flesh sales, but he also expects I won't say anything. Knows that if I do, he'll just have me killed, anyway.

Two, while sneak attacks are certainly handy, the local mafias have a lot more leniency as far as what the police allow them to get away with—since the Montaltos bankroll half the state, the pigs are generally more willing to let certain things go—and don't usually resort to lurking. They come right out, put a bullet between your eyes, and then focus on the cleanup afterward.

"So, who would this be, then? Just a random vigilante citizen?"

Shrugging, he reaches up and runs a hand over the top of his hair. "Maybe someone who was affected by what Kieran's brother was doing with the trafficking? They weren't exactly discreet about it, you know."

"Not like you," I mutter.

He shoots me a warning look. "Could be a major donor to the former organization, mad about it all getting shut down. There's no scarcity of enemies when it comes to criminal activity. The cops aren't on your side, and even your sworn allies are potential patsies at best. I say keep looking at financial records, track them to the last place you know the organization was working from, and—"

A large crash in the lobby outside cuts him off; it sounds like a miniature explosion, glass shattering and screams echoing off the walls, even with my door closed.

Finn and I exchange a glance, and I reach into my top desk drawer for the pistol I keep there just as he reaches into his waistband for his Glock. We get up slowly, me taking the lead and swinging the door open, guns trained on the figure through the glass divider.

Fiona lets out a frustrated squeal as she bends down, scooping up dirt and trying to put it back inside a broken ceramic pot. A large flowering plant lays uprooted at her feet, and she swipes at her hair furiously, streaking the dark red with brown.

Dropping the mouth of my gun, I cock the safety and slide it into my suit jacket, walking around the reception desk and peering down at the beautiful little vixen, my body in her presence for mere seconds before it roars to life, begging me to join her on the floor. To take her into my arms and ravage her, the way it always wants to.

But I don't, if only because something doesn't seem quite right. Her hands shake as she tries to replant the flower, and I notice beneath the dirt that her fingernails are shredded, the manicured acrylics from before torn off completely while the natural nails have been chewed to the point they're bloody. Her arms are covered in bright red scratches, her doe eyes feral.

"Fiona?" I squat down beside her, my jaw clenching when I note her labored breathing. She ignores me, continuing to scoop at the dirt, and I glance up at Chelsea, who's watching us with an expression of apprehension. "What happened?"

Chelsea shrugs, brushing some lint off the red blazer she's wearing. "I don't know. She asked if Craig was in, and when I told her he was in Portland for an investor meeting, she freaked out and swiped the plant off my desk."

Tensing her shoulders, Fiona pauses, turning her chin up to meet Chelsea's gaze. Something flickers in her gaze, dark like recognition, and her face turns bright red.

"Your voice..." She trails off, eyes darting over a million different surfaces before finally coming back to Chelsea. They narrow into little slits, her hands balling into fists. "*You*. Oh, my God, you're sleeping with my father!"

A hush falls over the lobby, a few straggler employees gasping audibly, and I clench my jaw harder, the calm before the storm taking place right before my eyes. Chelsea's mouth drops, her tongue sliding over the front of her teeth, and she glances at me.

"Don't look at *him*, you whore!" Fiona screeches, scrambling to her feet and lunging at the desk; I shift to my knees as she moves, catching her around the waist and drawing her into my chest, locking her arms at her sides and holding her tight against me.

She thrashes, throaty growls tearing through her esophagus that I know she'll feel later, trying to wriggle free. "I fucking heard you last night, at *my* house! How dare you do that to my mother!"

I'm too preoccupied with the way her ass grinds into my crotch to notice her reach into her jeans and pull out a pocket knife, too turned the fuck on to react at first when she kicks the blade free and starts swinging it wildly. In fact, I barely register the knife at all until it's slicing against my forearm, a clean cut right through my dress shirt that splits my skin easily.

Hissing at the onslaught of sharp pain, I wrap my good arm around her neck and increase the pressure until she starts clawing at me, dropping the knife in her attempt to secure oxygen. "Finn," I bark, clenching my jaw so hard that my forehead starts to ache. "Go down to Kate in human resources and have her send everyone home. *Now.*"

I stand still, my hold tightening on Fiona as blood drips from my arm onto her pink ballet flats, staining the material and splashing against the exposed skin.

God, she looks good in red.

Pain splices up and down my arm as we wait for everyone on this floor to leave; when the elevator dings closed with the last person on it, I tangle my fist in Fiona's curls and drag her into my office, slamming the door shut with my foot and flipping the lock.

Her chest heaves when I shove her into the desk; she whirls on her heels, pressing her palms against the wooden surface, and glares at me. "Why did you do that?"

"Sit down and shut the fuck up, Fiona."

I ignore the shocked look that flashes across her face as I make my way to the private bathroom in the back. Pulling the first aid kid from the vanity, I inspect the cut, noting that it's merely a scrape since she didn't get a very good angle, and clean it up, strapping a large piece of gauze over the site, rolling my sleeves back down, and heading back into the office.

When I return, she's still standing, arms folded tight against her chest, making her tits press obscenely against the neckline of the light pink tank top she's wearing. I stop several feet away, putting my hands on my hips as I wait for her explanation.

I want to know what happened out there—what made her finally snap. I want her to *admit* that there's darkness inside of her, to give a name to the side of her I'm inexplicably drawn to, to form a concrete, coherent thought about what it is we're doing here.

Up to this point, I'll admit she's called a lot of the shots. It's all been new, exciting, and we've been lost in the passion of exploration. I wanted to ease her into what it's like to be with me, wanted her to come willingly, but there are some things that need to be forced.

Some cords that have to be severed before someone finally sets themselves free.

If I continue waiting for the paranoia that racks her every thought and drives her every action to subside, we'll never progress at all. I tried comfort, tried existing in her orbit, and it doesn't seem to have been enough.

She needs the decision to be taken away, for control to be out of reach so she isn't constantly grasping for it.

She needs me.

"So," I say, dragging my eyes over her curves, drinking in the sight of her gloriously untouched body. The slender slope of her neck, so rich and pale that a single bite would likely cause immediate bruising.

Her legs, long and smooth roads I want to spend my night driving between, and the gentle swell of her tits as they rise and fall with each stuttered breath. My mouth salivates, my tongue thick against the roof of my mouth, as I imagine all the things I want to do to her.

Hunger burns through me, an uncontrollable fire that can't be put out, and I know she sees it. The air crackles between us, hot and electric as I take a step forward, her eyes flaring with defiance and lust.

It's the lust I focus on as I rack my brain for the best way to proceed.

"Do you want to talk about it?"

"*No,*" she spits, her frown deepening when I smirk— that's what I'd expected her to say. "Unless you want me to stab you again."

"With what? Your knife's out in the lobby, and I've got a gun." Reaching around, I slip the pistol from my slacks and hold it up.

She doesn't even blink. "I'm adaptable. I'll find a way."

Chuckling, I walk to the other side of the desk and place the gun in the drawer, typing in the code so it locks back. I take a deep, cleansing breath and prowl back to the side she's on, gliding my finger along the wooden surface, not missing the way she tracks its movement.

"What were you planning to do, Fiona? Kill Chelsea? There were a half dozen witnesses out there, for Christ's sake."

Clicking my tongue, I round her body and stop directly behind her, less than a foot away. Her rosy perfume wafts from her skin in soft waves, and her broken fingernails tap silently against the desk.

Tap, tap, tap.

"I don't know," she says softly, turning her head to look at me over her shoulder.

My hand lashes out, gripping her jaw, forcing her to look at the wall across from us where my degree hangs. But the rest of me isn't touching her. Not yet.

"You don't know," I say. "That sounds like a great thing to get yourself thrown into jail over."

"She's *sleeping* with my *dad*!" she squeals, frustration bleeding into the coarseness of her words. They seem to tear from her throat, her jaw vibrating as she spews vitriol from the places inside of her she tries to keep hidden.

"So, she deserved to be attacked?"

As if sensing that I'm baiting her, Fiona clamps her mouth shut, jerking her head against my hold. Her arms dangle at her sides, fists curling into themselves, the internalized anger making her entire body shudder with the effort it takes to resist.

"What would you have done if it wasn't Chelsea fucking your father? If you'd succeeded in hurting her, and it turned out she's not even the one at fault?" I squeeze her jaw, but she doesn't answer me, nostrils flaring as she struggles.

"Cat got your tongue, princess? I asked a fucking question."

Shifting forward, I move into her body, letting them mold naturally together. My cock stiffens against the curve of her ass, its pulse so prominent I can feel it in my fucking throat, and I know she feels it when she sucks in a small breath of air, barely audible.

But I hear it.

"I wasn't... I just wanted to scare her."

"That it? Just wanted to see if you could make her piss herself?" Bending, I glide my nose along her bare shoulder, inhaling the scent of her perfume mixed with sweat.

Evidence of her own fear, her own arousal, fills my lungs, making my chest cramp with desire.

"Are you sure you weren't curious to see if you could actually go through with it? To see if the violence inside of you is the same kind present in your bloodline?"

"No," she says, voice firm. "That wasn't it at all."

Humming, I bring my lips to her ear, grazing the soft shell. "I don't believe you."

CHAPTER TWENTY THREE

Boyd

*H*er fingers flex against the air, itching for some kind of purchase that doesn't let me know I'm getting to her. But I can feel it. *Taste* it. The thin veil of control she has over her sanity slips further with each word I say, teetering on the precipice of complete loss, making her nervous.

She doesn't realize how good it can feel to give in.

Doesn't know what I'm up to.

"I didn't ask you to believe me," she growls, her body locking up in a way that just won't do.

Taking a step back, I release her from my hold and rake my gaze over her backside, trying to gauge if she'll bolt or wait to see what I do next. A long pause fills the air, silence settling like bricks around us, but she doesn't move a muscle.

I'm not even sure if she's breathing.

Arousal snakes down my spine as I consider the submission here, but I'm hesitant too, in case this is a ploy to attack me again. Unbuttoning my sleeves at their cuffs, I begin rolling them up my arms, swallowing over the knot in my throat she causes just by existing.

It's dangerous, what I'm about to do, considering her father could come back from his meeting any time or her brother could show up and come wondering why I sent everyone home early, but I don't even care.

My need for her is greater than the threat of the forbidden. Her brother could skin me alive after today and it'd have been worth every second.

She starts to turn around, but I tsk, making her pause. "Face forward, hands on the desk. Now."

A laugh tumbles from her lips, and she ignores me, continuing to turn anyway. Fury flashes across my vision at her defiance, and I move before she can finish spinning, yanking her arms from the sides of her body and pinning her hands down on the desk.

"Your impulsivity and inability to rationalize with yourself almost got you in a fuckton of trouble today, princess. I can't have shit like that going on in my office, not when there are people around. You need to blow off steam, need somewhere to funnel your violent little tendencies, you come to *me*. This will be the last public outburst you have."

I breathe into her ear, using one hand to unbuckle my belt and pull it free from its loops. Her bottom lip trembles, and I reach up to grab her face and wrench it backward so I can capture the pouty flesh with my mouth, plundering with teeth and tongue before shoving back.

She straightens, fear rolling off of her in tremors, as I slide the leather gently along her spine and down the seam of her jeans, a small hint of what's to come.

"*Off.*"

"Boyd, I'm not—"

Snapping my wrist forward, I let the tip of the belt lash against her ass. She jumps, her lungs clawing for air, but still doesn't move. My lips curve into a smirk as her fingernails dig into the desk, heat igniting in my chest at the realization that she's not asking me to stop.

"Stop talking, Fiona. You say far too much without actually saying anything at all. Now take your jeans off. I want to look at you."

She stands there for several beats, staring at the wall without moving. Impatience ebbs through me, and I smack the flat of the belt against my palm, making her flinch again before she springs into action, unbuttoning her jeans and tugging them down over her hips.

Once she reaches her knees, she stops, glancing up at me as if waiting for some kind of direction. As if she knows that's what *I* need.

I keep my face stoic, even as palpitations begin in my chest, giving her a slight nod. "All the way off. Panties too."

Swallowing, she reaches up and hooks her thumbs in the elastic waist of the lacy thong she has on, dragging it down her thighs and stepping out of the clothes entirely. My cock throbs painfully, hard as a fucking rock as I gaze over every inch of her glorious skin, zeroing in on the meaty swell of her peach-shaped ass.

Guiding my fingertips over the gentle curve, I revel in the notion that I'll be the first to mark her here. To show her how it feels to be branded with your lover's existence. Her lips are just barely visible in this position, glistening with the tell of why she stays in her spot, pretty and pink and waiting for me.

Moving back into position, she glances over her shoulder, fear lacing her features. "You know I'm not... I mean, I haven't..."

"Shh," I say, shaking my head and gripping the back of her neck to make her face forward. "Don't worry, princess."

She laughs, the sound forced and breathy. "Those two words have never, ever, cured anyone's anxiety, for the record."

Massaging her ass silently, I tilt my head to the side and pop my neck, loosening up. Trying to rein it in before I take things too far, too quickly. She leans into my touch just as I pull back, holding my fingers flush together as my palm cracks

227

against the fleshy underside of one cheek; she jolts forward with a grunt, elbows buckling.

"I said *stop talking*."

Punctuating each syllable with another smack, I cradle her hip in my other hand to keep from sending her into the desk, even though these are relatively soft, warm-up slaps.

Her toes curl against the tiled floor, her skin blooming pink where my hand connects, and I almost rip my dick from my slacks and plunge into her virgin cunt right then.

"In fact, if you utter a single sound or drop your elbows again over the next few minutes, your punishment will get progressively worse. Let go of your thoughts and just *feel*."

Her teeth sink into her bottom lip as she struggles not to keen against the next round of slaps I deliver, these slightly firmer than the last. My handprint starts to glow red on her ass, and I soothe the inflamed flesh as she tries to catch her breath, sweeping my fingers between her thighs and using some of her arousal to cool her skin.

"You're far too fucking perfect for me," I mutter, pushing her tank top higher up her back so I can see the dimples imprinted at the base of her spine and admire the way her taut stomach flares into her hips, wide and inviting. "So wet, without me even touching your sweet little cunt. Do you like being punished, princess?"

She doesn't respond at first, and fear snakes through me at the thought that I've gone too far. I tangle my fist in her hair, tilting her head back toward the ceiling.

"Answer me when I ask you a question, Fiona. That will be the only time you may speak or think about anything other than me pleasuring you."

"I-I don't know," she whispers, licking her lips.

"*I* know," I say, dipping my index finger between her slick folds before slipping the tip inside of her tight channel; not far enough to shatter the innocence I want bleeding on my dick, but enough to make her squirm.

I pump in and out in careful, shallow strokes, the sounds of her sopping arousal a symphony I want to die listening to. "Hear that? That tells me you fucking love it."

A whimper falls from her mouth as I pull my hand away and straighten to my full height. Wrapping the belt in my fist, I tease her with soft strokes against her abused flesh, every muscle in my body pulled tight like the strings on a guitar.

"If at any point this gets to be too much, yell red. Otherwise, the only sound I want to hear coming from those perfect little lips of yours is you choking on how good this feels." My hand collides with her ass one last time, prompting her. "Tell me you understand."

"I do."

"Good girl."

The moment my belt slaps against her, painting a rippling pink and red sunset along the expanse of the creamy flesh, I'm fucking gone. Lost to the sensation of the tiny cries spilling out from her pinched lips, the way her shoulders tense with each smack and release when I rear back for more, how she seems to buckle under the weight of the discipline.

But not the bad kind of buckling.

This is the kind that accompanies freedom. Vulnerability.

The shedding of masks in favor of revelations.

I belt her until I'm close to passing out from how engorged my dick is, tiny welts sprouting along her skin in my wake — not enough to keep her from sitting, but enough that she won't forget this encounter soon.

And since I know I can't *cure* her, can't be the solution to the need for control that she latches onto so tightly, I'll have to settle for the reminder and hope it makes a difference.

The belt falls to the floor, and I move against her, collecting spit at the front of my mouth and letting it drizzle down the crack of her ass, smoothing the saliva with my palm over the areas that look particularly painful.

I worked up to the harder hits, but if you work at the same spot over and over, no matter how gentle you handle it, eventually even that will split and bleed.

She starts to push up off the desk, but I push her chest down so her tits are flush with the wood, then grab her hips and drop to my knees, once again holding her in place.

230

"Don't move," I say, her soft groan making my cock pulse behind my zipper.

Gliding my hands down over her hips, I push her thighs farther apart, revealing the dripping crescent shape of her plump cunt. My fingers stroke through her folds in painstakingly slow sweeps, her arousal sticky and alluring as I coat myself in it.

Using my index finger to spread her, I bare her throbbing clit and flick my tongue over the angry bundle of nerves, my first taste of her sending a sharp spark down my spine. It collects at the base, making my balls tighten as she writhes forward, a gasp ripping from her throat.

"What are you doing?" she breathes, pressing her forehead into my desk as her back arches.

"Well, before your little outburst, I was about to eat lunch. I'm famished." I lick her from top to bottom, moving to suck on the inside of her thigh before diving back in. "And you, princess... well, you're about to meet God."

Burying my face between her legs, I alternate between laving and sucking, swirling my tongue in fast, circular motions around her clit while holding her hips in place. She bucks against me, swiveling like she can't get close enough but also isn't sure she wants to, and I lose myself in the rhythm.

She tastes like the candy you're denied as a child, sweet and sugary, yet completely off-limits because it's no good for you.

The kind of candy that, when you finally sneak a piece, ruins you for all other vices, a sticky obsession that overtakes your entire mind for all of eternity.

She tastes like she could save me.

Redeem my soul.

I lap at her juices like a man who's been thirsty his whole life and didn't know what he's been missing, capturing her clit between my lips and reveling in the way she cries out, beating her fist against the desk, one hand coming around to force me deeper into her.

My entire face disappears between her legs, my nose and chin as involved as my tongue and lips, and when I pull back just enough to rim her entrance with my pinky, she's already coming, her clit spasming on my tongue as I slip my pinky inside, my dick about to explode with the way she clamps down around me.

Giving her one final lick, I extract myself and get to my feet, adjusting the lapels of my suit jacket as she slumps against the desk. I wipe my face with the handkerchief in my pocket, and then gently clean up between her legs as best I can.

"Stay still," I say, running to the bathroom to grab a wet wipe and some aloe vera lotion; I drag the wipe over my face again, then pour the lotion in my palm and smear it over the raised flesh on her ass, smirking when she hisses at my touch.

"I can't believe that just happened," she says, pushing into a standing position when I'm done. Her legs almost buckle, and I slide my arms around her waist, holding her up. She glances up at me through long lashes, her face flushed the same color as her hair.

"Was it... okay?"

Blinking, like she hadn't considered any other possibility, she shrugs. "It's new to me, the whole... *dominant* thing, but I liked it. Liked... giving up control, for once."

"Did it live up to the fantasies you've had of me?" I tease, pushing sweat-slicked hair back from her forehead, pleased with her answer.

She sighs, leaning her head against my chest, the altercation from earlier and the troubles happening with the rest of the world long forgotten. "The fantasy doesn't compare to the real thing."

Later, when she's pulled her clothes back on and lounges in the leather chair across from my desk, reading on her iPad while I finish up a few software audits, I glance up and watch her for a few beats.

She hasn't mentioned her father's affair again, although I suspect it's not far off in her mind—apparently, she hasn't put together that I was aware of its existence.

But I can tell something else is bothering her; pink bubblegum smacks against her lips every few moments, the pop somewhat deafening in the space between us. I want to ask what else is going on, and that's when it hits me.

Guilt slams into my chest like an asteroid crashing to Earth as I realize what I've just done, tongue-fucking my only friend's baby sister. A girl he expects me to care for as a sister, to watch out for while the investigation is going on and they're being targeted, not to devour any chance I get.

And that's not even where the guilt really stems from.

Sitting behind my desk, studying her delicate face and the forty-seven freckles spread across the bridge of her nose and cheeks, I realize something worse than me just fucking around with my best friend's sister.

I really fucking like her.

CHAPTER TWENTY FOUR

Fiona

My father never returns to the office the day I almost attack Chelsea, and part of me is glad on the one hand, because I don't want what happened between Boyd and me to be tainted by the fury I feel toward my father over his affair.

I spend the rest of the afternoon curled up in the armchair in Boyd's office, alternating between stealing glances at him while he pours over his work and scrolling through Stonemore

Community's online course catalog, trying to figure out what to take in conjunction with repeating stats.

Easy classes are probably my best bet, ones that won't challenge the workload in statistics, but I'm also afraid of falling farther behind than I am now. I don't want to get to a point where I can't catch up at all, and trying to fit the next semester into a world of uncertainty has anxiety spiraling again in my gut, renewed even after the pleasure Boyd managed to wring from my body.

The high was nice while it lasted, my mind flattened like roadkill at the touch of his hand, his belt, his tongue on my skin — but now it's over, and since I can't very well live with his mouth attached to my pussy, I need to move on and get back to coping.

Chewing my gum, I hold it between my teeth and wrap it around the tip of my index finger, lost in thought. Lost in the sensations from hours before, Boyd's harsh and demanding tone, the way he played me like a fucking instrument designed just for him.

I've never felt any of that before — the vulnerability that came with trusting him not to hurt me, the euphoric waves that erupted in my core when he forced me to relax.

To let go, completely.

It's like this unspoken essence tethering me to him, one that makes me trust blindly and without question, just as I hope he trusts me, considering I seem to already know more about him than the average person.

236

More than my brother even knows.

Still, the longer I sit and stew, the quicker my insecurities come flooding back in, a massive tidal wave taking me under. I can't concentrate on my iPad, switching from one app to the next before stuffing it between the seat and my leg and pulling my knees up to my chest, wrapping my arms around them.

I watch Boyd work in silence, his lips curling around a joint as his tattooed hand moves the black computer mouse in different directions, concentration etched into his brows.

His jaw flexes as he inhales, his cheeks hollowing out, a muscle beneath the skulls inked on his neck jumping as he sucks smoke into his lungs. My stomach clenches in jealousy, though it's hard to tell if it's of the joint or of him.

Glancing around his office, I note the minimalistic vibes that seem to echo his home decor; aside from the chair I'm in and the desk, there's a single wall of filing cabinets back by the bathroom, a table with his joint tin and a decanter of amber-colored alcohol, and a lonely black rug just large enough for the desk to sit on.

His master's degree hangs on the wall, but there isn't a single other shred of memorabilia, and I realize that other than the time he mentioned his sister, he's really never talked about his life before he worked at Ivers International.

What do I really know about him?

What do I really know about anyone?

Shifting in my seat, I pull my knees tighter against me, my thoughts spiraling as I swing my gaze back around, meeting his. Hazel eyes bore into me, seeing straight into my soul and stealing the feeling from my body, the implication terrifying.

"What are you thinking about?" he asks, pointing at me with the butt of his joint. "You've got that weird look on your face that says you're about three seconds from launching yourself off the cliff of sanity. Do you need me to make you come again?"

Scrunching my face up, I roll my eyes. "I was just wondering how many girls you've been with."

"Three."

I blink, my head jerking back in surprise. "*Three*? That's it?"

"Yep." He licks the tip of one finger and pinches the end of the joint, setting it on the little glass tray next to his computer. The gesture makes my core clench, wanton even though it hasn't been that long since he had me.

Boyd pushes back from the desk and walks over, perching on the arm of my chair.

"Is that surprising?"

"Yeah, kind of. I mean, *look* at you."

He smirks. "What about me?"

"You're two degrees short of being disgustingly perfect. It's insulting, honestly."

Threading his fingers through my hair, brushing some leftover dirt out of the strands, he shakes his head. "I am far from

238

perfect, Fiona. Far from having it together. Don't start idolizing me."

I lean into his touch, letting his fingertips soothe the looping thoughts. "Is *that* why you've only had sex with three people?"

"No, I just like monogamy." He holds his hand out, and I slip mine into it, the inked canvas of his skin a massive contrast against me. Yanking me up, he wraps his arms around me and pulls my hips into his, pinching my chin. "Which reminds me. If we're doing this, I'm all in. I expect the same courtesy back."

"But what exactly *is* it that we're doing?"

"Whatever we damn well please," he rasps, bending to fuse our mouths together, an explosion of heat and passion as our tongues tangle, warring for dominance. His flicks against mine, the taste of expensive weed, mint, and *me* creating a potent combination.

Growling into him, I grab the back of his head and pull him in deeper, twisting my head for better access. His hands slip down my back and cup my ass, hooking beneath in an effort to get me to wrap my legs around him.

Pulling back, I hold his gaze, wiping some of his saliva from the corner of my lips.

He groans, squeezing my ass in his large palms. "Come home with me. I don't care what we do, as long as you're naked in my bed in an hour."

My stomach flips, the thought of spending the night away from my mother when I know what's going on with my father making me hesitate. She was slightly more cognizant earlier today, but still not totally with it, and I can't help the guilt that presses down on my chest like an avalanche, setting my nerve endings on high alert.

"What happened? What did I say?"

I sigh, pressing my forehead into the base of his throat, knowing that if I ditch him to stay home, I'm abandoning my mission to figure out what his *deal* is.

Instead of wondering about all the ways I might fix him, I'll be up rearranging my bedroom or reorganizing the books in our home library, trying to distract myself from the world around me as it crumbles.

Plus, there's no telling what I'll do to my father when he comes home.

So instead, I relent, following him out of the office building and down to his bike in the parking lot, thanking the gods that I wore jeans today and not a skirt. And when I climb on and let him take me home, I try my best not to think that the roles have already reversed.

That I've failed in my initial mission to be the thing that heals Boyd Kelly.

Because I think he's trying to fix me, instead.

And I'm afraid that will only make things worse.

Boyd's soft snores pull me from my slumber; I turn in his arms, running my fingers along his pecs in the dark, amazed by the sheer fact that he's here at all right now.

That he wants *me*.

This is the fourth night in a row he's come by and fallen asleep after faking to Kieran like he's heading home and slipping up the back staircase instead.

I'm starting to think my brother is suspicious, especially given his recent habit of strolling into my room unannounced, but I can't find it in me to care when Boyd's mouth is between my legs, showing me what spirituality feels like.

My stomach is in a constant state of unrest, unsure of what will happen if Kieran does find out — will he even care? Will his relationship with Boyd crumble, or will mine break before it's really even begun?

Rolling out of bed, I reach down and grope around for my pajama shorts, pulling them up over my legs and yanking Boyd's white T-shirt over my head. I grab the empty rotisserie chicken container from my dresser where we left it, having eaten with our fingers once I'd gotten my mother settled for the night, and tiptoe from the room.

Padding down the hall, I peek inside the master bedroom first, ensuring I can still hear my mother's breathing, then double back around and head for the stairs, flipping on dimming lights as I pass through.

Tossing the chicken container into the kitchen trash, I'm rinsing my hands in the sink when the light above the island counter flickers on, illuminating the space.

"Fiona. Nice to see you come out of your room."

I jump at the sound of my father's voice, so used to the silence that lives in the walls here. Whirling around, I see him seated at the island, watching me with an unreadable expression, his phone and a bowl of cereal in front of him.

"Are you eating in the dark?"

He smiles, the gesture pulling at one corner of his mouth, making him look significantly younger. The hairline fractures crisscrossing his skin and the hollow circles beneath his eyes somehow age him at the same time, creating this frozen effect that almost makes him hard to look at.

It's like having one foot in the past and one in the future, and not being able to see either well enough to matter.

The sound of his moans the other night filter through my perusal, the look on Chelsea's smug little face when she said he was out of town becoming the only thing I can focus on as they flash across my vision.

"Got into the habit as a kid," he answers, penetrating the chaotic prism of memory wreaking havoc on my brain. "There's something peaceful about it, knowing no one can see you or judge your taste in food."

"Judge you?" I step forward, crossing my arms to keep some sort of barrier between us. "What for?"

"I'm a middle-aged man eating Lucky Charms at one in the morning," he replies, moving his phone toward me. "Not to mention, scrolling through Sci-Fi Twitter, as if the first half of my situation wasn't bad enough."

A grin cracks my lips, splitting them apart for a moment. "Well, everyone already knows you're a nerd."

"That's true, but when you do things in the dark, there's less chance for evidence."

It's an admission slipping off his tongue, but he doesn't even realize the double meaning.

As he glances back down at his phone, scrolling past different posts and liking the occasional one, anger builds like floodwaters inside me, a hurricane crashing along the coast and destroying everything in sight.

My stomach cramps, invisible knots forming as all my anxiety morphs into rage, my hands balling at my sides. Like a volcanic eruption, the accusation tumbles out of me, hot lava coating him where he sits.

"I know you're sleeping with your receptionist."

Blinking, his finger freezes mid-scroll, and he lifts his chin. "Excuse me?"

"I said, I know you're sleeping with—"

"Jesus, wait. I heard what you said." He holds up one hand, then scrubs it over his face, fingers disappearing into his dark hairline. Dropping his arm on an exasperated sigh, he shakes his head. "But how did you... ah. Boyd told you."

"No, I *heard* you in your office," I snap, my nerves firing on all cylinders now, churning at accelerated speeds. He exhales, tipping his head back to stare at the ceiling, and his words finally catch up with me. "Wait. Boyd knew?"

"Yeah, he saw me a few weeks ago with her. I figured he'd have told you immediately."

Disappointment settles in my gut like dead weight, my mind trying its best to keep track of the secrets unraveling. "You've been sleeping with her for *weeks*?"

"Fiona, what I do in my spare time isn't—"

"Do *not* finish that fucking sentence."

My body springs into action before my mind can tell it not to, reaching into the wooden block at the center of the island and pulling a filet knife from its slot.

I hold it up, trying not to read too much into the fact that this is the second time I've threatened someone with a knife this week—maybe I'm far more like my family than I thought.

"What you do in your spare time is *exactly* my business, Daddy, because do you know what I do in mine?" I raise my eyebrows, pointing the tip of the knife at his chest. "I take care of your fucking *wife*. You know, the one who gets a little closer to death every single day. Who *literally did not know who I was* this week and mistook me for her dead son. The woman you've supposedly loved for the last thirty years? That ring any bells?"

"Fiona, put the knife down and we can talk about this like adults."

Tears spring to my eyes, a sob catching in my chest. My grip on sanity slips as his words set my world ablaze, razing the beacons of control I've erected to the ground. "Why, am I being too dramatic for you? Scared I might pull a Kieran and make you pay for hurting our family?"

"It's not like that—"

"It's always like that! I've put my entire life on hold to make sure Mom lives out the rest of her life as comfortable and well-taken care of as possible, and you're out here *cheating* on her. Wrecking the only foundation I've ever known like none of it fucking matters at all."

The words spill from my lips, unbidden, taking us both by surprise. Silence stretches between us, a tether pulled to the breaking point, and he gets up from his stool, reaching out to pry the knife from my hand without so much as a wince, as if he knows I'm not actually going to hurt him.

Part of me really wants to. Wants him to suffer.

But the anger inside me dissipates as I try to make some sense of what's going on, racking my brain for some logical explanation.

I know I didn't make up the love my parents have for each other. Even if the foundation was sometimes rocky, I know it was poured from a good, genuine place. That's not the kind of relationship that can be forced or faked.

I know my father once changed himself for love. Altered his state of being and became the man my mother needed.

But I don't know the man standing in front of me now, with his panic-stricken gaze and the stiffness in his shoulders. Don't know how someone can cheat on their wife in the same house she's dying in and go to sleep next to her every night.

"It doesn't make sense, I know." His voice is soft, strained, as he puts the knife back in the block. "If you... want to stop by the office this week, we can discuss it further. After you've had some time to cool down. I promise things are not as they seem."

"I don't think there's any way you can justify cheating on her," I whisper, not daring to look at him.

"I'm not trying to justify it, I just... need to explain. Stop by for lunch, okay?" Backing from the room, he walks toward the greenhouse, and a moment later I hear a door slide open and then closed, then the hollow thud of his footsteps on the hidden stairs.

I stand in the same spot for half an hour, staring at the clock on the stove as the minutes tick by, replaying the entire reaction in my head like I can change the outcome.

Like there's a universe where he'll deny my accusations instead of promising to explain them, and all of this will just be some giant fucking nightmare I can't figure out how to wake up from.

Breaking out of the spell of despair, I stomp my way up the main stairs, bursting into my bedroom with a vengeance reserved for one man at this point. If I can't take it out on my father, Boyd will just have to do.

I climb on top of him and rear my arm back, my mouth practically watering as the limb flies through the air, connecting with his cheek in a satisfying, gruesome smack that seems to echo off the walls.

It reverberates in my eardrums even as his eyes snap open, malice seeping through the pores of his groggy body.

CHAPTER TWENTY FIVE

Boyd

Fiona straddling my lap is enough to make my cock hard all on its own, but the unadulterated fire burning behind her big brown eyes and the sting rippling across my skin from where she slapped me is what really does the trick.

My eyes take a second to adjust to the darkness, her gorgeous body barely illuminated by the sliver of light spilling in from the cracked door. She's glaring down at me, her chest heaving beneath the T-shirt of mine she's wearing, that sweet little cunt flush with my hips.

I can feel its heat through the thin material of her shorts, can feel her pulse as it kicks up between her legs. My hands wrap around her hips, fingers bunching up the cotton material there.

"Did you just fucking slap me?" I ask, still trying to catch up to what just happened. One second, I was dreaming about fucking my girl on my desk, and the next her hand was connecting with my face, yanking me from the best sleep I've ever had.

"We slap liars around here," she hisses, seething.

"What the hell did I lie about? I've been unconscious."

"Don't try to play innocent with me, Boyd Kelly. I might be young and inexperienced and *dramatic*, but I'm not stupid."

"Princess, I'm not calling you stupid." Reaching up, I rub my eyes with the back of my thumbs, wiping the disorientation from my vision. "But you've just assaulted me out of a very deep, *sensual* sleep and I'm still trying to catch up to where you're at."

If her face flushes from the implication of my words, I don't see it, nor does she falter. Her legs tighten around my hips, bringing her core even closer, and she pulls her arm up in the air, poising for a second attack.

As she brings her hand down, I capture her wrist in mine, using the momentum from taking her off guard to buck her off of me and onto the mattress. Before she has a chance to recover, I cover her body with mine, wedge myself between her thighs, and take both of her wrists, yanking them up above her head.

"What the hell happened since you fell asleep in my arms a few hours ago?" I ask, trying to regain control of my breath.

Having her spread out beneath me, like some kind of all-you-can-eat buffet, doesn't exactly help, though.

Through the thin veil of hall light, I see her nipples puckering against the material of my shirt, the fabric so thin I can make out their dusty pink peaks. And even though she's glaring at me like she wants me to swallow a bullet, I know she's aroused, too.

We haven't done much since that day in the office, just me going down on her once and some light petting; I've been trying to take things slow because I know that once I have her, once I break her, I'm not going to want to let go.

She's a drug I willingly inject into my veins, making me wonder if I'm more like LeeAnn than I ever wanted to be.

So fucking weak for the women in my life.

Wriggling her hips to try and get away, she lets out a frustrated growl. I grin, shifting so my dick presses firmly into her center, blood rushing to my erection the more she struggles.

"I suggest you stop moving, or I won't be held accountable for what happens next."

"You probably won't be held accountable, anyway," she huffs, returning the pressure by canting her hips upward. "You'll just boss me around and make me come again, like that solves all of our problems."

"The purpose of what happened the other day wasn't to *solve* anything," I say, tightening my grip on her wrists. "It was to give you a sense of fucking direction when your brain was melting."

"My brain was *fine*, thank you."

Fisting the material of her T-shirt, I begin sliding it up, revealing her flat stomach, pausing at the underside of her full tits. "What's gotten into you?"

"Nothing, now get *off*. I need to scrub you from my body."

Grappling for even the slightest hint at what she could be so pissed over, I aim instead for the approach she was just complaining about. Bending down, I push the T-shirt over her breasts, baring the swollen flesh to my hungry gaze.

Dipping my head, I lave my tongue up to her nipple, circling around the protruding peak without actually touching it. I hold her gaze as I blow gently, relishing in the goose bumps that sprout across her as she inhales sharply.

She tugs her wrists, trying to twist free, but I crush them against the pillows, clicking my tongue in disapproval. "Are you done being pissy?"

Glaring at me, she tries to kick, pulling her ankle free and ramming it into my back. I sit up and haul myself up enough so I'm hovering over her lower half, then pin her leg to the mattress with my knee and start working her sleep shorts down over her hips with my free hand.

"Stop! I'm mad at you and you don't even care!"

251

"I don't care because you haven't given me a fucking reason to." I fit myself between her legs again, leaving her shorts around her ankles so she has to work harder to kick them free, and then I dive back down to her chest, sucking one pert little nipple into my mouth.

Curving my lips, I bite down gently, pulling on the distended nub as I release her and repeat the process on her other breast, this time sucking and biting hard enough that her skin blooms the color of wildflowers under my touch.

Her back arches, a strangled sound emanating from the base of her throat, driving me wild. Making me move faster and harder until she's panting and gasping for air.

Sitting back on my knees, I pop her tit from my mouth and run my thumb over the marks, dizzy from the painting I've begun.

"So responsive," I praise, knowing she needs to hear it. "Now, if only you'd stop being a spoiled little princess for a moment and just tell me what's wrong, I could let you up."

As if relaxed into submission, Fiona's chest rises and falls as she continues glaring, though she no longer tries to escape. Her eyes grow wide, sadness pooling there that replaces her defiance and rage entirely.

Something inside of my chest aches, a chasm cracking open like a scab that's been picked off and never allowed to heal.

"You knew about my dad and Chelsea."

My stomach drops, my heart lurching into my throat and catching, regret radiating like a thousand little pinpricks down my back.

Her voice is impossibly soft, so thick with emotion that *I* almost choke on it. "You knew all this time what he was doing, and you never told me."

"Fiona," I sigh, scrubbing a hand over my stubble. "It wasn't my secret to tell."

"Maybe not, but I deserved to know."

Now, she does move, rolling her hips as she tries to wrangle her legs away, but I grab her thigh and hold her in place, desperation coursing through me at the heartbreak lacing her features.

It's sewn into the knit of her delicate brows, the tension tugging her lips down at the corners, and it sends shock waves of apprehension down my spine when I realize what this is a precursor for.

Goodbye.

Panic swells inside me like the sails on a shipwrecked boat attempting to catch a gust of wind and return to its course, inflating but unable to move anything else. I'm frozen, the thought of her leaving pushing me off the edge of a fence I've been teetering on my whole life.

"Boyd, I don't want to play. Stop."

"We're not *playing*, princess."

Paranoia is what's driving her actions, convincing her brain that she hates me.

That she can't trust me.

That she shouldn't be with me.

Reaching down to the floor, I rip my belt from the dress pants I discarded earlier, shifting so I'm straddling her chest. She lets out a gush of air when I pin her down, legs thrashing behind me as I fold the belt into its buckle, hooking the loops over her hands and yanking tight. Her elbows stay kinked, hands above her head, as she opens her mouth to protest.

Not giving her a chance, I suck on the inside of my cheeks and let spit drizzle from my lips directly into her mouth; she gags, tossing her head back and forth on the pillow, an irritated gurgle coming from the back of her throat as I cover her with my lips, sweeping my tongue over hers and ensuring she keeps as much of my DNA inside of her as possible.

"You want to scrub me off your body, huh?" I ask, pulling back and pressing a kiss to her sweaty forehead. Hopping off the bed, I jog to the door, easing it shut and flipping on the ceiling light, not wanting Kieran or anyone else coming in and ruining this.

When I come back, her legs are propped up as she tries to maneuver into an upright position; I rip the shorts from her ankles and throw them over my shoulder, pushing my boxers down my hips as I spread her legs wide and nestle between them again.

My cock bobs up against my abs, and I spread the bead of precum over the tip, reveling in the way she averts her gaze. So innocent, so completely fucking *pure.*

As I stare down at her, my shirt bunched around her neck, my belt binding her in place, a sharp realization cuts through me, pushing beyond the notion of liking her from the other night.

It's so much fucking more than that, something heady and fiery and all-encompassing that simultaneously sets me on fire and douses me in icy water at the same time.

Fuck, am I in love?

I'll admit, I haven't even considered the notion since college, but now, staring down the barrel of losing this girl who's become a benign tumor on my brain, growing until all I do is think about her, it's the only thought consuming me.

Thoughts of being with her, helping her.

Of her helping me.

Maybe it's not totally healthy, the speed with which this attachment has erupted, but I can't seem to stop myself from catapulting over the edge and trying to make things right.

To keep her from leaving.

My control slips out of reach, tumbling off the mountainside until it's nothing but a blip on my radar, and I lean fully into the madness I try so hard to keep at bay.

"How about I crawl so deep, you can't ever get me back out?" I draw my thumb through her silken flesh and bring it to her mouth, rubbing over her lips. "What if I stain your tight little body with my cum? Would my girl like that?"

She jerks her head away, straining against the belt around her hands. "I'd *like* to be left alone."

Ah, but she didn't deny being mine.

"No, you wouldn't. If I walked out right now, you'd fall into a compulsion and probably spiral." Her eyes flare, shock igniting her irises, and I smirk, gliding the head of my cock between her glistening folds. Happy to have caught her off guard, and that my suspicion was correct.

Mouth parting on a soft gasp, Fiona's hips buck up, searching for extra friction, and I know that despite the anger radiating from her body, this is what she wants.

What she needs.

"Didn't realize I'd picked up on that, did you? You don't think I notice you, Fiona, but ever since that night at the gala, I haven't been able to see *anything* else."

"Then you should've known I'd want to know what my father was doing."

I consider her words as they cut through the haze of hysteria bubbling inside me where she's concerned. "So you could spend your free time agonizing over his decisions, wondering if there was anything you could've done to keep him happy in his marriage? Newsflash, princess, his affair has nothing to do with you. And I refused to add to your burdens."

"Keeping secrets doesn't help me. How am I supposed to believe anything you ever say to me?"

"You want my secrets, Fiona? There are *plenty.*"

"Is that—what is that?" she stutters, lifting her head to try and see where my cock drives between the pouty lips of her cunt.

I grasp the base of my length, red against the ink that covers every inch of the rest of my body, and smack her clit with the tip, the frenum piercing on the underside of me cool against her wicked flesh.

"Never seen a dick piercing before? There's secret number one."

The balls of the silver barbell slide against her folds while the bar beneath my skin grinds into her clit, and I pump my hips, making her squirm.

"Secret number two: you're *mine,*" I say, stroking my shaft quickly, arousal at having her completely at my mercy shuddering through me as I move against her.

It collects at the base, drawing my balls up until they ache with resistance, and she watches in rapture, breaths tumbling quickly from her pretty little mouth. "I'm not letting you go after this."

Her lips part in surprise, and I shake my head with a short, strained laugh.

"I don't generally take kindly to being slapped, but I did tell you that when you needed an outlet for your violence to come to me. So, I won't punish you for that." Craning my head so our breaths mingle, I plant my free hand beside her head and stare into her soul. "Now, I need an outlet for mine. One that'll pull you from the brink along with me."

"Boyd, I'm not—"

"Ah, ah. What did we say about talking? If you're talking, you're thinking, and that's not a good thing. Your brain plays tricks on you, Fiona, and you fall for them every time. Let me take care of you."

Sitting back up, I spread her thighs even farther apart, beating my dick so fast I feel my desire unspool and slither along my spine, down to my extremities.

She's staring, eyes blazing, like she can't possibly look away.

"You like this, princess? Watching me jerk myself to you?"

A soft moan escapes her as she moves her hips, responding even though I can see in her eyes that she wants to fight. I press the crown of my dick against her clit and grind it down in circular motions, absorbing the spasms as they rack her body.

"God, you're so fucking perfect. Bet your tight little cunt is hungry, hm? Should I give her something to swallow?"

Fiona whimpers, pressing her wrists into the pillow above her. The image spurs me on, release tingling in my balls as I fight it back. "Fuck," I rasp, flattening my palm between her breasts, pinning her. "I have to come."

258

Need drowns out reason, and I'm sliding down the seam of her sweet little cunt, my fist tugging so hard I start to see stars, before I can stop to think about what I'm doing. My head bumps against her entrance, and for a moment, neither of us makes a move.

I'm not even sure if we're breathing.

This is a big step. It requires trust, beyond letting me tie her up or spank her or give her orders. It means placing her vulnerability in my hands and expecting me not to take advantage.

At the same time, I'm ripping out a piece of my dead soul and handing it over, praying like hell she doesn't leave anyway.

Release draws near, a raucous fire exploding in my veins and incinerating every rational thought on sight. I press into her entrance, feeling her thighs tense up as it stretches, waxing and waning against my shaft. Trying to suck me in.

Nothing has ever felt so fucking warm and inviting in my entire life.

I meet her gaze, holding steady; her teeth sink into her bottom lip, and I wait.

"Boyd..." she whispers, her arms shaking with the effort it takes to stay held above her head. "I don't think we should."

"*Trust. Me.*" I don't ask, I command, upping the speed of my palm thrusting as I keep myself wedged just inside of her, my orgasm barreling through me like an unstoppable tsunami.

"But I'm not—"

"I don't *care*. Keep your eyes on me, princess, or you don't get to come."

My thumb finds her clit once more, swirling over the pulsating nub until she can't possibly say anything else, her body convulsing beneath mine.

Stroking my cock furiously, spitting on her cunt and letting it collect around me for extra lubricant, I crest over the edge of oblivion, euphoria splicing through me as my nerves spin out of control, spilling my hot, sticky seed right inside of her as she spasms through her own release.

CHAPTER TWENTY SIX

Fiona

I try to shrink into myself, try to get my mind to shut off as Boyd slides from the bed, retreating to the bathroom to, presumably, get something to clean up with.

I swear, I try.

But the second I feel him leaking from my center, my clit still throbbing with aftershocks of my orgasm, tears spring to my eyes; I move my arms down to fold my hands over my eyes and realize I'm still trapped by his belt.

A hot wave of embarrassment washes over me, and the rest of my thoughts take root, cycles of irrationality that spin freely in my gut.

It's not the sexual exploration that unsettles me, it's the realization behind the kink; the need to be dominated, controlled, in order for my mind to put its intrusiveness on hold and just *exist*, for however brief a moment in time.

It's the possibility that my obsessive-compulsive disorder maybe isn't as in-check as I once thought, especially if Boyd could *guess* that I have it. It's supposed to be hard to distinguish, when you're managing it correctly, and I'm afraid mine's been spiraling out of control for so long that it might be past the point of return.

When the bathroom door opens, I pinch my eyes closed, not wanting him to see the despair that's crept back in. Afraid that he'll get tired of trying to wring it out of me.

I don't know how to tell him this is probably as good as it's going to get.

He drags a warm washcloth over my center, the act of cleaning me up after what just transpired so wholly intimate that it sends a sharp, stabbing pain across my stomach. His lips leave hot, open-mouthed kisses on the inside of my thighs as he works, soothing after everything.

He gets up again, leaving me exposed to the elements, and I snap.

A sob contracts in my throat, burning as it pushes through, tears spilling over even as my body works to reabsorb them.

"Shit, are you crying?" The overhead light flips off, and Boyd comes back over to the bed, undoing the belt and tossing it onto the floor, then scoops me into his muscular arms.

He wrangles me out of his shirt, and I press my head against his chest even though I'm still angry, too drained to fight off the soft warmth he provides. "Did I hurt you?"

I shake my head, afraid to speak, and he hooks his chin in my hair, settling back against the headboard and pulling the covers up over us. Stretching my legs out, I let myself melt against the sturdiness of his body, his legs cocooning me in place.

"You need an electric blanket," he says after a beat, running his fingers through my hair.

"Bring yours over," I whisper, wiping at the tears staining my face.

"Talk to me."

I stare into the darkness of my room, shapes forming and disappearing in front of my eyes, trying to figure out where to even begin. "When's your birthday?"

"December fifth."

"Favorite color?"

"Um... gold?"

"Do you have any tattoos you regret?"

Chuckling, he pinches my side. "I'm covered in them, so there are bound to be a few. Like the crowns on my knuckles — those were done in a friend's basement back in college. Got infected and almost lost my entire hand. Or the one-eyed mermaid on the back of my calf. That one's bad, too."

I blink, considering this, and then double back around to one of the matters at hand, settling on the most relevant. Anything to keep my mind from settling. "You shouldn't have done that."

"Done *what*?"

"I'm not on birth control. Well, I get the shot, but I missed my appointment for the booster last time because I had to take my mom to the doctor, so..."

He exhales, and I hear him scrub a hand down his face. "I won't apologize for being the first man to claim you, Fiona. Won't apologize for wanting to be the only one who ever does. You bring out this primal need in me that I've never felt before. It's... *deranged*, but I can't help it."

Sucking in a deep breath, he pinches my chin. "If something happens, we'll figure it out."

I think about his sister, the one I've never heard him mention outside of the one time I asked about her, my heart squeezing inside of my chest. "Do you want kids, Boyd?"

The air between us charges, electricity desperate to be funneled somewhere — but it doesn't feel like the good kind. It feels lost and lonely and dangerously destructive.

264

"I've never really thought about it, to be honest. But I wouldn't... leave you to deal with it on your own. I take responsibility for my mistakes."

Pain throbs through my stomach, making my chest tight, and I don't even know why.

I don't want kids right now. *Definitely* can't afford to get pregnant. So, why does hearing him refer to a potential child as a mistake make something ache deep within me?

Is that how he views me? He once said kissing me was a mistake. Does that mean that what he's doing now is just atonement for his sins?

Anxiety unravels in my stomach, making me nauseous, so I change the subject. "How did you know?"

"Know what?"

"About... me. The obsessive-compulsiveness. Most people don't notice; I don't think Kieran even really knows."

He stays quiet for so long, I'm sure he's not going to answer, moving on from the conversation because he's no longer interested in it. No longer interested in me.

My finger starts its tapping, three consecutive points followed by a three-second break, and then starting all over again, the movement light against his bare chest. *No longer interested. Probably wants someone with more experience, someone not crazy. Someone who—*

Fingers slip beneath mine, not holding or restricting; his hand rests under my fingers, absorbing the soft vibrations from the tapping. Providing support, not demanding control.

Not this time.

"I was in and out of therapy a lot as a teenager," he says finally, voice low, as if he thinks someone might overhear. As much as he doesn't want Kieran to find out about us, I suspect he wants my brother to know about his past even less. "The waiting area at one of the clinics lumped everyone together—the alcoholics, the kids with behavioral issues—like me—and the people with your run of the mill psychological issues."

Swallowing, my heart aches, slamming against my rib cage. The desire to interrupt, to talk about my own experience in counseling and distract him from what I suspect are painful memories, expands into an overwhelming need, prickling inside my mouth like I'm jonesing for a cigarette or some gum.

Biting down on my tongue, I force the urge away.

"I fucking hated that place. Hated waiting with the people who seemed more obviously sick than me. At the time, this was the only place my..."

For a moment, he trails off, and my mind scrambles trying to fill in the blank, wondering where it could be headed.

"My *mother*, LeeAnn, couldn't afford a place any better, and she didn't bother signing up for insurance because she was too busy getting high. Always too busy getting high."

His voice grows thick as he trudges through his words. "But therapy was court-mandated after too many incidents at school made my principal suspicious, and alas, this was the clinic

I got. The kind of place where the irreparably damaged go when there's nowhere else to turn. An absolute last resort."

"Anyway," he continues. "The place itself sucked, but the counselor I ended up getting paired with, Dr. Schriver, was amazing. She suffered from pretty severe obsessive-compulsive disorder and I think borderline personality disorder, but she never let them hinder her. She was always working to heal—everything you'd hope for in someone getting paid to fix you."

"I don't—"

Boyd raises his index finger and holds it against my lips, shushing me. "I know that's not what it's for, but when I was a kid, I didn't know any better. I was looking for a fix, and it never made any sense as to why I couldn't find it, until I was older and realized some things just stay broken."

Pushing up, I move his finger and turn my head, trying to make out the contours of his face in the dark.

I can tell he believes it about himself, that he's destined to keep bleeding from invisible wounds until he dies, and I think back to my words to him at the gala about how people don't change.

Maybe they don't—there's no real way to tell. Maybe who we are isn't ever set in stone, anyway, and it changes constantly, the way our skin regenerates every seven years.

Maybe it's circumstance that rewires our DNA, makes us delve from our character norms.

I think circumstances changed my father. I think falling in love is changing my brother — can see it every day that his fears ease, his soul becoming more content with the way life has panned out.

Everyone may still be on edge with my mother's declining health and the unknown family assailant still lurking around town, but I still see the subtleties.

Maybe the best we can do is evolve our temporary parts and hope that's good enough.

"You're not broken," I say, reaching up to cup his stubbly jaw.

"I'm not whole, either."

"So, what? You're just gonna forgive him for not telling you?" Heidi asks, bending the paper straw in her peach boba tea. Nico's back for the summer, so the four of us met for brunch, grabbing croissants and drinks from the bakery inside the Green Apple Grocery, and we're sitting on the patio outside Starbucks, watching downtown prepare for Memorial Day.

"I didn't say I forgave him. Just... I don't know, I guess I can see his point. My dad should've been the one to tell me about his affair, I shouldn't have had to hear it from someone else."

"Yeah, but that didn't even have anything to do with him and he kept it a secret." Bea shoots Heidi a dirty look, and Heidi shrugs, holding her hands up in mock innocence. "*What?* I'm just saying. How is she supposed to trust him?"

Nico sighs, running a hand over his dark hair. "Everyone in King's Trace has secrets. I think you have to decide which ones are worth knowing, and which you can live without."

Furrowing her eyebrows, Bea frowns. "How is she supposed to do that if she doesn't know what they are?"

"It's a gut thing," Nico says, shrugging. He points to his stomach, then takes a sip of his coffee. "If your gut is saying Boyd's secrets are worth it, then I say go for it."

"Enabler," Heidi mutters, sweeping hair from her shoulders.

I roll my eyes, irritation spiking in my chest like a pot left to boil over.

Heidi's always been the most outspoken of us, and it's never really been an issue until now. Partly because I can't shake the feeling that she's acting out of spite and envy, and partly because I'm afraid, deep down, that she's right.

Still, I'm getting sick of hearing about my bad decisions.

Yanking my straw from its plastic cup, I point it in her direction, flinging foam everywhere. "You haven't exactly been keen on this relationship from the start, you know. From the second I said he was interested, you've been rude about me and Boyd. If you're jealous, come out and say it and stop hiding behind your dirty remarks, because frankly, I'm over your bullshit."

Silence falls over the table, each of their heads rearing back like I've slapped them. While not necessarily strangers to hearing me say what's on my mind, the tone seems to throw them off, my voice sharper and thicker than ever before.

Clogged with emotion, everything bubbling to the surface as I struggle to maintain control.

My fingers grip the underside of the table, my index finger tapping lightly, the rhythm lulling my racing heart.

Tap, tap, tap.

Three sets of three, and then I suck in a deep breath and take another sip of my iced coffee, watching my friends slowly regain themselves.

Heidi's face slumps, her mouth curving into a vicious frown I've only ever seen reserved for enemies. "Friends are supposed to *help* you, Fiona. I'm not fucking jealous of Boyd, or you getting to be with him. I'm worried about you and the fact that it looks like you're jumping into something headfirst, the way you always do. I'm sorry for being the only one with the balls to tell you I don't like it, but I refuse to be responsible for this kind of mistake."

That word, again. It punctures my internal organs, searing straight through them and smearing them along the concrete sidewalk, my insecurities on display for everyone to see.

I wince as she pushes out from the table, pulling on the drawstrings of her Unity hoodie, and takes off down the street, not sparing us a second glance as she disappears.

"We're your friends, not your parents," Bea says after a moment, still staring off in the direction Heidi left. "They're your mistakes to make."

"What's your gut telling you?" Nico asks, arching an eyebrow.

The problem is — I have no clue. My gut and I don't seem to speak the same language, because while my brain is saying I can't trust Boyd, my gut is churning with the feelings developing in my heart.

Sure, he told me about therapy, but since he cherry picks the parts of himself that he shows to the rest of the world, anyway, I don't see how I'm really any different.

And the possibility that I'm not, that he sees me as he sees everyone else, is enough to make me question everything.

CHAPTER TWENTY SEVEN

My hands shake as I sit in the plastic chair across from my father's desk, staring at the large family portrait hanging between the built-in bookshelves on the wall.

It's the five of us on an Easter Sunday years ago; my mother and I are wearing matching pink hats with a white tulle bow while the guys have pink ties, because it'd been my year to pick the color.

There are dozens of the same photos buried in albums in our attic, photos no one's touched since Murphy's death. It's easier to ignore your ghosts when you're not constantly being reminded that they exist in the first place.

Checking my phone, I clear the group messages from Heidi and Bea, not really in the mood to talk, and watch the clock as it inches another minute forward, apprehension spiking along with it. I've been waiting fifteen minutes now, and I'm starting to wonder if I should've come here at all.

I don't know what excuses my father might have for cheating on my mother, but I'm also not sure they'll matter.

A betrayal is a betrayal, even when it's dressed in good intentions.

I'm two seconds from getting up to leave when the door swings open and my father strolls in, a paper bag from Opulence and two Styrofoam cups in hand. He sets them on his desk and drops into his chair, not meeting my gaze as he begins pulling out individually wrapped items.

Sliding one across the desk to me, he nods. "Portobello burger with Swiss and pickles."

"My favorite," I mutter, stomach growling as the savory scent hits me. When he places a carton of curly fries next to the burger, my eyes narrow. "Are you trying to buy my silence with good food?"

He pauses, setting his burger down in front of his keyboard. "No, I just thought we could eat lunch. Typically, it's

273

your mother and I up here while you sit in the corner or run off to fraternize with my best employee."

Mortification sears my cheeks, and I tuck a strand of hair behind my ear. "I don't know what you're talking about."

"Fiona, our walls are not soundproof." Unwrapping his burger, he tucks a paper napkin into his collar and sinks his fingers into the bun, taking a bite. "Not to mention, I've caught him sneaking in and out on the security cameras on numerous occasions over the last few weeks."

The comment reminds me why I'm here in the first place, bursting the bubble created by the food. "Well, I'm not here to talk about that."

Sighing, he chews another bite, glancing around the room with a thoughtful expression. "No, I suppose you're not. As your father, I do want to ask, though... how serious is it between you two?"

"Really, Dad? How serious is it between you and your little office slut?"

"Not at all, which is why I need to know. Is this a fling for you, or something more?"

Gritting my teeth, I bite into my burger, chewing slowly to buy myself some time, because I'm not exactly sure how to answer him.

Part of me wants it to be serious. Wants something concrete to form between Boyd and me, something that changes us for the better.

But the other, more prominent part is terrified of what he's hiding. Afraid that whatever haunts Boyd Kelly would ruin any relationship. Outside of the lust, I can feel my heart being drawn toward him more and more each day, but there's also something holding me back.

Maybe it's the way he claimed me the other night, the intensity behind his dominance, veiled as a way to help me out of my problems.

The sense that he's only using me to ignore his own is something I just can't shake.

"I don't know," I say around bits of burger and mushroom, swallowing. "What do you mean your affair isn't serious? You're cheating on Mom with someone who doesn't even mean something to you?"

"Yes."

Blinking at his unabashed response, I set my burger down as he slides a Styrofoam cup my way. Gripping the sides, I bring the straw to my mouth, practically melting as the sweet, chocolatey frozen dessert hits my tongue, cooling me down. "I just feel like that makes everything worse."

He finishes his food before continuing, disposing of his wrappers in the trash can below his desk, sipping on his shake as he leans back in his chair, studying me. My face grows warm the longer he stares, the realization at how long it's been since I had a real conversation with him settling like wet cement over me.

I guess when you're trying to prove your worth beyond what everyone expects because of your last name, certain relationships suffer.

"I fell in love with your mother the moment I saw her. It was this... immediate, visceral reaction that happened when I turned around in my advanced world history class, a measly freshman in college, and saw her smiling at a note her friend handed to her. It was the first time I realized what it felt like to have your heart beat outside your body.

"She didn't want anything to do with me, romantically, at first. Had a boyfriend, but was one of those people who collected friendships like they were special coins. So, I became her friend, and the rest... well, that's sort of history now. Besides, you know the story of how we got together."

Nodding, I suck on my shake, waiting.

"The problem is, you don't earn back the pieces of you that mold or go missing when you give your heart to someone else. And I didn't think I wanted those pieces back, didn't think I needed them. Being with your mom gave me an immeasurably happy life, three kids I couldn't be more proud of, illegal activity and other issues aside — and yes, I was proud of Murphy most of his life. Even a little at the end."

Clearing his throat, he adjusts the tie around his neck with one hand, shifting in his seat. "When I was twenty, I could've easily dealt with her loss. I'd already been orphaned and to federal prison, so I was rough around the edges, anyway. This

276

kind of thing wouldn't have fazed me. But now... I don't know what to do with myself. I don't remember how to exist without your mother."

Sadness burns my esophagus, hot and discomforting. Pushing my shake onto the desk, I fold my hands in my lap, considering his words.

Like me, he's afraid his identity is fractured. Maybe absent altogether, outside of the relationships he's forged and the people he takes care of.

But *unlike* my father, my fear isn't hurting other people.

My mother's tired face flashes before my eyes, followed quickly by Boyd's stoic, impassive one, the truth a stick of dynamite with a slow-burning fuse.

Or am I?

"You're cheating because you're a coward," I accuse, pushing to my feet. "And that is *undeniably* worse than if you were cheating because you fell out of love with her. When you love someone, you don't ever, *ever*, give up on them, even when it means sitting on the sidelines waiting for them to get better, or if it means you might be uncomfortable, because I can guarantee she has it worse."

As he swallows my words, I turn, starting to make my exit and pausing at the last second, pointing at him.

"And while you've been *struggling*, I've been watching my fucking mother disappear and dealing with it completely by myself. And I can't *do* it anymore, Daddy. I just can't. She absolutely refuses to let anyone but me help her, and I'm drowning in schoolwork trying to take care of her. I'm a kid, I'm not equipped to handle this shit."

He drags a hand down his worn face. "Sweetheart, I know it's hard."

"It's not hard, it's *impossible*. She loses more and more control over her body every single day and refuses to acknowledge it. Half the time, she can't even remember her own name, or she's off in dreamland with Murphy, acting like he wasn't practically burned at Kieran's stake."

"Stress can have a great toll on our memories —"

Leaning forward, I smack my palms against his desk in frustration, another downward spiral hitting as I replay the conversation my mother and I had where she hinted she wanted me to help her kill herself.

That's not the kind of service *I* can provide.

"Mom needs *help*. And not the kind I can give her." I gulp, each word a hot knife to my throat, slitting me wide open just so I can bleed out.

Voices in the lobby draw my attention, and I clear my throat, wrapping up our lunch. "Twenty-four-hour care, Dad, or she's gonna be gone before you even have time to feel bad about fucking someone behind her back."

Sweeping the garbage from his desk into the trash can below, he sighs as I reach the door. "I'm... I don't want to be alone, Fiona."

"Who does?" I ask softly, my heart shattering for a million different reasons — for him, our family, my mother. It cracks wide, fractures that can't be repaired, only haphazardly glued and replaced. A stronger vessel, maybe, but a makeup of separation that doesn't ever quite look the same. "You wouldn't be alone, though, you know. You'd have Kieran and me."

As if I've conjured the Devil just by speaking his name, he and Boyd are half crouched with their ears pressed against the door when I throw it open. I spare one single glance at Boyd, dozens of thoughts filtering through my mind when I meet his heady gaze, but I swing my head toward my brother, tilting my chin up.

"Mom's moving into a home and we're selling the house." I tack the last bit on for good measure, sure I don't want to keep living in the mansion where my father is fucking some bimbo. Don't want to continue being trapped by the ghosts stuck in its walls.

Kieran blinks, raising his eyebrows. "Excuse me?"

Rolling my shoulders, I shrug. "You heard me. All of us need out of that haunted mansion, and she needs twenty-four-hour care that I can't give her. Talk to Dad about the specifics, I'm going to drama club."

Flipping my hair over my shoulders, I keep my stare straight ahead and march from the lobby to the elevator, climbing on and darting to the back. My hands curl over the railing in desperation, anxiety clawing through my stomach like a caged

279

animal, but I don't drop my head until the doors close and it begins to move.

When it does, I collapse.

CHAPTER TWENTY EIGHT
Boyd

Kieran watches me with a curious expression, leaning back in the leather chair I tongue-fucked his sister in not long ago, unaware of the air of depravity he's surrounded by.

I wonder if he'd still try to give me his blessing if he knew.

He'd attempted to reassure me that he was fine with whatever is going on between Fiona and me while we stood outside her father's office, eavesdropping on their heated conversation.

Still stuck in the phase of denial, still afraid of ruining this before it really solidifies itself. I'd refused that anything was happening with her, saying her lifelong infatuation was one-sided and noting that I'm not destined for a happily ever after.

The last part's true, at least. Regardless of the feelings sprouting within me, my brain knows what my heart doesn't want to acknowledge; that, in the end, Fiona doesn't end up with a man like me. One drowning in secrets and childhood trauma, locked in a cycle of abuse with a woman who abandoned him as a child and still doesn't want him.

Even if Riley weren't in the picture, I know I'd still be checking up on LeeAnn, ensuring she's still alive. Because no matter how many fucking mistakes she makes or how many times she lets me know I mean nothing to her, I can't seem to cut the cord.

Wanting to saddle Fiona to a life of brokenness hardly seems fair, but I can't let *her* go, either. Don't even want to, selfish as it is.

I want to pour every ounce of my love into her and watch it seep from her pores.

Watch it heal her.

Not because love is the be-all and end-all, but because I think I could be the exact kind of support she needs.

And if I don't get to keep her, I want to extend my stay as long as possible—and that means keeping her a secret from the people I don't think truly want us together.

Especially her brother.

"Are you ready for this mission?" Kieran asks, resting his chin on his fist. "It's been awhile since we didn't just grab a guy from the back of a club or his bedroom in the middle of the night. You sure you're up for it?"

"Kieran, if you're concerned for my well-being, just ask. Don't fake concern over my capabilities."

He laughs, twisting the little black flash drive in his hand. It's supposed to be collateral for the person stalking us, but the weight of its contents sits heavy on my chest.

These aren't just Kieran's secrets, or the assailant's secrets. They're the secrets of our entire town — tales of embezzlement, affairs, murders, and espionage. Crimes against humanity and against our neighbors.

I'm not sure how King's Trace will recover if the files are leaked.

Not sure how *I'll* recover once people find out I do more than launder money and make sure business looks legitimate for the mob.

But I suppose that's the price you pay when you get in bed with evil. Eventually, everything under the sun comes out.

Some secrets are just too powerful to be kept.

"I'm just saying, shit could go wrong." Kieran crosses his leg over his knee and grips his ankle with his free hand, green eyes glittering in the fluorescent overhead lighting. He looks almost sad, although I can't imagine why. This is the kind of thing his devilish soul lives for.

Action, suspense, and *death*.

"Shit could go wrong at any time," I say, shrugging. An email pops up on my computer, the notification pulling me from the money transfer I was watching.

It's from Riley, saying she's been grounded and that email is the only way she can contact me, and only while LeeAnn's working.

Pinching the bridge of my nose, I sigh and pull a joint from the tin on my desk, offering one to Kieran as I light up.

He shakes his head. "No, thanks. Never did like that shit. Fiona was always the one sneaking off to smoke whatever she could get her hands on — although, now that I think about it, she hasn't been doing that lately."

"Maybe she's cured," I say. *Or maybe she's been too busy to even think about it.*

Kieran's lips curve up in a devious grin. "Nah, that can't be it. Once you're addicted to something, you never really get over the craving. Just learn how to manage it."

His words ring between my ears, loud and cumbersome as I try to focus. Then he changes the subject to how things are going down at the christening Sunday — with the entire town out to greet the newest Montalto child, it's the prime time for our assailant to strike.

While he goes over the game plan once again, I lose myself in thought, wondering how you manage an addiction that's clawed its way into your heart.

That seems like the kind of damage you don't come back from.

When I leave the office for the day, I stop by the trailer out of fucking habit, and because I don't like Riley not being able to contact me directly—especially given I'm the one paying her goddamn phone bill.

I haven't heard from LeeAnn since the day I got Riley enrolled at King's Trace Prep, and the silence has been deafening.

If not for the distraction of the redhead I spend my nights with and the shit going on at work, I'd have already tracked the bitch down and figured out what her problem is, but I'd just be playing right into her hands.

She ignores me to punish me, and I fucking hate that it stings, even after all this time.

Propping my bike against the Volkswagen parked outside, I sling my helmet off and bound up the makeshift steps, not even bothering to knock before I rear my foot back and drive the heel of my Oxford shoe into the door just below the knob.

It swings open, popping off the top hinge with the force, and I'm met with a pungent stench that has me covering my nose as I stalk inside.

I'm nowhere near fucking prepared for what I walk in on.

Romeo Bianchi curses in Italian as he scrambles to his feet, his beady little demon eyes locking on me instantly. The zebra-print dress shirt he has on hangs open off his chest, his hair damp with sweat, his left palm curled around a giant shard of glass.

285

Blood drips from his palm and streaks down his face and chest, and it takes me a few beats before I realize that it isn't *his*.

My chest tightens to the point that I can't fucking breathe when I glance at Riley lying prone on the floor, drenched in blood to the point that she'd be unrecognizable if I didn't know what I was looking at.

Bile rises in my throat, eliminating any passage of oxygen as I begin choking on the effort it takes not to puke, my hands shaking so violently at my sides that my shoulders ache.

Clenching my jaw, I remind myself that I need to remain calm. I'm no use to Riley if I lose my cool, even though murder pumps clean through my veins at the moment, expanding until it's damn near the only thing I can imagine.

Romeo keeps repeating something in Italian, and the sound grates on my shot nerves. "Speak English, you fucking piece of shit."

He bares his teeth like a feral animal, running a bloody hand through his brown hair. It slicks back, sticking up in places, making me boil; I launch myself at him, limbs flailing as adrenaline and pure malice course through me, driving my movements.

The glass falls from his hand, and his head smashes against the wall as I slam him into it, the resounding crack satisfying for the briefest moment. I grip his chin in my hand and repeat the motion, slamming his skull into the plaster until it splinters under the force, a hole breaking open behind him.

He spits in my face and it lands on my tongue as I shift for better access to his windpipe; when I taste the tangy copper of my sister's fucking blood, I see crimson. My hand shifts from his chin to his throat, squeezing until I feel his tendons struggling and his esophagus crumpling under my fingertips.

He claws at my hand, scraping his nails against my skin and trying to kick at me, but I'm taller and stronger and lift him just far enough off the ground that he can't gain any purchase.

Gasping for air, his chest heaves and his face turns a reddish-purple, a fucking sunset I'd be content to watch for the rest of my life. I'm reveling too much in the way his eyes bulge in fear to notice he's dropped his hands and reached behind him, wriggling a gun free from the waistband of his pants.

The butt of the pistol cracks against my forehead, sending a sharp pain across my skull as the skin splits under the impact. I release him with a curse, and he hits me with it again, this time in the back of the head, sending me to my knees.

Not because he hits particularly hard, but because I've been beaten there too many times at this point for the surface not to be tender, and it catches me completely off guard.

Sprinting toward the door, Romeo keeps the gun trained on me as he disappears, leaving me cradling my head and hoping my sister isn't fucking dead.

I've never been a spiritual man, but as I crawl to my feet and wrench my phone from my pocket, I ask the universe for a second chance with her. To not let *this* be the end.

My nostrils flare with anger as I get up and search the rest of the trailer, my beast craving LeeAnn's flesh as I send Kieran a text saying what kind of assistance I need right now.

Unsurprisingly, she's not here — typical, having someone else do her dirty work and not even being around to ensure the job's taken care of.

Big fucking mistake, Mother.

I don't approach Riley yet, not sure I can handle seeing her broken up close, but my eyes never leave her when I come back into the living room.

Surveying the damage, I note the broken television against the wall, the end table with its legs ripped off, and the shattered mirror lying a few feet away, likely where the glass came from.

My phone rings a few seconds later, an unknown number flashing on the screen, and I answer immediately, putting it on speaker.

"What can I do for you, Boyd?"

Kal's cool, unaffected voice is what I try to focus on as I kneel at Riley's side, my heart in my throat.

There's too much blood outside of her body, but when I press my fingertips to her forearm, her pulse beats faintly beneath, sparking tentative hope in my chest.

"Romeo Bianchi... got to my sister," I say, swallowing over the nausea.

"What do you mean, he *got* to her?"

"I mean she's laying in front of me bleeding to death," I snap, tears springing to my eyes for the first time since I was a kid, fear making me shake. "She's... she's just a fucking kid, Kal."

"What interest does Romeo have in your sister?" He pauses, but I'm not exactly sure what he's asking. "Does this look like a general assault, or is it possible she was abused sexually, as well?"

"How the fuck should I know?" She's wearing what looks like a sundress, but I can't tell if it's hiked up her legs on purpose or just from her position.

"Calm down, Kelly. I only ask as a precaution, so I know what equipment to bring. Is she still breathing?"

"Yes."

"Good, good. Don't move her, text me the address and I'll come to you."

Pacing outside my guest room, I try to find a way to occupy my thoughts. To keep from leaving the house and tracking down both LeeAnn and Romeo and making them atone for their sins with blood. I pick up a book—*The King's Stepdaughter*—from the table in the hall, flipping through the pages as I try to calm down, but it doesn't work.

The only thing I can think about is Riley.

When Kal arrived at the trailer, he'd wrapped her up in white sheets and carried her carefully to his vehicle, checking her vitals inside the massive SUV in case someone returned. He said she looked *bad*, but didn't elaborate when I asked what that meant, exactly, given the things he's supposedly seen and done.

He transported her to my house while I rode my bike behind them, had me carry her to the guest room and has been locked in there with his equipment, washcloths from my linen closet, and two buckets filled with lukewarm water ever since.

Tossing the book to the floor in frustration, I run my hand through my hair, pulling hard at the ends. It was one thing when it was LeeAnn hurting me, but for some reason, the idea of her abusing Riley never fully crossed my mind.

She was the one LeeAnn kept, so why would she hurt her?

Truth is, I probably just didn't care enough to see the signs. Let my resentment color my vision in their presence, determined to come out of the relationship with both of them somehow unscathed, not realizing that the original wounds never bothered to fully close in the first place.

Violence flashes across my eyes when I close them, red splattering against the dark backdrop, pulling me back in time to when I was the one fending LeeAnn's friends and boyfriends off.

To the times I stepped in, trying to help her, and she let them abuse me instead.

I lost my virginity when I was twelve. Unwillingly.

Killed a man for the first time when I was fourteen.

Riley wasn't supposed to have the same fate, but the fact that I didn't do anything to change it, too blinded by my hatred, is what makes the violence take root, coagulating in my gut like a cement brick, sending searing pain down my spine.

A knock at my front door draws my attention, and I head down the stairs cautiously, positive in my convictions that LeeAnn wouldn't be stupid enough to turn up here.

As I pass the kitchen table, I swipe my gun from its surface, just in case.

Peeking out through the little window, I spot a splash of red hair, my body heaving a sigh of relief even as it locks back up, guarding itself.

Considering the danger just being here is putting her in, I have to think of a way to make Fiona leave.

I crack the door, raking my gaze over the leggings and off-shoulder sweatshirt she has on, a lump forming in my throat for entirely different reasons.

"Hi," she says, a shy smile spreading across her red lips. "Are you—didn't we have a dinner date scheduled? Are you ready?"

Fuck. "Fi, now's not a good time."

"Fi?" Her smile fades, and she takes a step back. "What's with the formality? You haven't called me that in months."

I shake my head, unable to concentrate fully on her standing here when I hear the door upstairs creak open. "I can't do dinner right now, is all. Go home, I'll call you later."

Her eyes narrow. "Why can't you do dinner, Boyd? Do you have someone in there with you?"

"I—" Snapping my mouth closed, I bite the inside of my cheek, realization dawning on me. The fact that this is her first conclusion is telling, but more so, leaning into it is probably my best chance at getting her to safety.

I swallow over the vomit teasing my throat, ignoring the ache in my heart. "Why is that your first assumption, Fiona? Do you really think so little of me that you think I'd be fucking someone else while I'm messing around with you?"

"No, I just... we aren't official, or anything, so I wasn't sure—"

"You're right, we're not. I'm not your fucking boyfriend, so you can't just show up on my doorstep whenever you please and demand I give you my time. I'm an adult, and I've got responsibilities. I can't just let you distract me every chance you get."

She blinks, eyes widening under the dim porch light, and takes another step back. Crossing her arms over her chest, her index finger starts that little ritual against her stomach. A chasm rips open inside of my chest at being the cause of a spiral, but I can't back down right now.

Can't focus on anything except getting her the fuck away from me, hoping I can fix things later.

Swallowing, Fiona scratches at her neck, dropping her eyes. "You're right. Sorry for the *distraction*. Have a nice night, Boyd."

I stay rooted in place while she descends the porch steps, heading to where her Jeep is parked at the end of my driveway. And I don't stop staring, don't stop hurting, even after she's long gone.

CHAPTER TWENTY NINE

Fiona

Dragging the brush through my mother's hair, I adjust her head in my lap as her skull digs into my thigh; she stirs from the nap she'd been taking, giving me a deflated smile.

The new medication she's been switched to helps with her cognitive function, but her muscular capabilities have significantly decreased, which means right now she can't even hold her head up long enough for me to do her hair before I leave for the church.

Part of me can't help wondering if the recent spell she went through was a side effect of the stress caused by everything going on at Ivers International, but that's the thing about Lewy Body—it's entirely unpredictable, attacking and retracting whenever it pleases.

At least, that's how Kal described it to me. Said the disease has a mind of its own, and that's why there's no definitive answer for how long she has left with us until she enters the later stages. When that happens, he said, the body is pretty much giving up.

With no set timeline, though, we're stuck waiting, and I know it's killing her slowly inside, possibly more than the disease itself.

The fear of what's to come, of not knowing when to expect it, is probably taking much more of a toll than it would if we could see the future.

My father relented when I left the office the other day, surrendering to one of my demands—the twenty-four-hour private nursing staff he hired starts tomorrow, and I can't even begin to express my relief.

It's short-lived, of course, when I remember the *why* behind my father caving.

Reaching up slowly, my mother smooths her fingertips over the crease between my eyebrows, giving the slightest shake of her head. "You worry far too much, darling."

"Wonder where I got that from," I mutter, setting the brush beside my leg. She's stretched out on her bed, the television playing an episode of *House Hunters* on mute, the air around us still and calm in spite of the calamity within.

"You're not supposed to worry about the things you can't control," she says, the ends of her words curling a bit as she tries to keep the slur from them. "Isn't that what I always tell you?"

"You say to *find* something I *can* control and let go of what I can't."

"And?"

I blink. "And what?"

"Are you searching for the things you can control, or are you letting the things you can't control *you*?"

Sighing, I gently lift her head, sliding a pillow beneath her neck and rolling onto my side. I smooth my hand over the silk comforter, admiring the texture beneath my hand, and remember Boyd's words from the other night.

'I can't just let you distract me every chance you get.'

It'd been such a stark contrast to the man I've come to know that my heart is still reeling, doing its best to piece together why he'd say that, given the show he'd made recently claiming me as his. Was it all a lie, or some sick little joke?

Or is the thing I wanted to distract him from in the first place finally bearing down with its full weight, crushing him to the point of exhaustion? Have I been too much of a distraction, barring him from any sense of healing on his part?

When I chose to keep seeing him behind my family's back, the point was to *help*. I thought he needed me, and I liked having him around.

But if that isn't the case anymore, and if I can't even trust him, then... what am I doing with him?

When help turns to hurt, it's time to let go.

So, that's what I did the night I walked away. I haven't contacted him since, nor has he reached out to me.

Both of us controlling the things we can and letting everything else figure itself out.

If only my heart would stop bleeding, aching for him to come back.

If only everything was different.

"You'll be careful today, right?" my mother asks, penetrating my swirling thoughts.

Rolling my eyes, I nod. "Kieran's not letting me do anything dangerous. We're just scoping the perimeter, keeping an eye on things in case something suspicious goes down."

She exhales, pinching her eyes closed. "I know, but still. This is... well, family work has a history of getting messy, and I just want to make sure you're prepared for anything."

"What happened to controlling only what we can?"

"You can control your safety, Fiona. You're the only one who really can." Bringing her hand to her chest, she presses down over her heart, her breathing growing ragged as she gets sleepy. It's time for her late morning nap, and her body just knows. "I won't be around much longer, Fiona. I just want to make sure you can take care of yourself."

My nose burns, fire cascading down my throat at her words. "I'm not ready to stop taking care of you."

She squeezes my knee. "I know, my sweet girl. You've been such a ray of sunshine for me the last few years, and I don't think there's anything I could ever do to repay you. But I can't keep on like this. My body is tired of fighting."

I take her hand and bring it to my cheek, letting her palm cool my heated flesh. The question is unspoken between us, my presence at her demise a coin toss. One where you lose either way it lands.

An itch forms behind my left ear, and I scratch at it furiously, achieving no relief.

I don't want to say yes. Don't want to acquiesce my mother's existence on this planet. My heart is selfish and wants her to stay, but as I watch her grow more exhausted and incapable with each passing day, I can't find it in me to ask her to try.

To hold on, just for me, when I'm not the one in pain.

So, even though the second my mouth opens, tears well up behind my eyes and spill over onto her bed, I nod slightly.

She reaches out, pulling me into her chest; I curl up under her chin and hold her cold hand, the anxiety in my body lessening as our hearts beat in a syncopated rhythm, relaxation settling in despite the chilled air settling around us.

Later, I pull into the church parking lot, scanning the area for my brother's girlfriend Juliet—a friendly face, even if we haven't actually spent *that* much time together.

Frankly, she's usually too busy hopping on Kieran's dick when she's around, so I don't even see much of her.

But I'd recognize her signature golden hair anywhere; as I step out and start walking toward the St. Francis Cathedral, I spot her near the tall doors at the front of the stone church, talking to a brunette who keeps stealing sips from a tiny flask.

Straightening my shoulders, I head their way, deterred only when a hand clamps down around my wrist, halting me. I whip around, my fist raised to fend off the attacker, and the breath whooshes from my lungs.

Boyd stands there, so close I can taste the alluring cologne he has on, a navy suit stretched across his tattooed body. He looks downright delicious, a tall glass of water that any other time I'd be excited to gulp down, but irritation spikes instead, reminding me of how he dismissed me at his house.

How I'm supposed to be done with him.

There's a purple spot above his eyebrow, half bruise and half gash, the skin sewn together with little red stitches, and I struggle to remember if he had it the other night.

What demons are you fighting, Boyd Kelly?

My core pulses at the sight of him, at our proximity, but I clench my thighs to make it go away. "What are you doing here?"

He shrugs. "Same as you, I assume. Didn't know you were gonna be here, though."

"Would it have kept you away if you did?"

"Why would I ever want to be somewhere you're not?"

Knots form in my stomach at his words, waves of conflict rippling through them. Gritting my teeth, I yank my hand from his and cut the sound on the comms unit in my ear, wishing mine had a microphone so I could tell my brother what I think about him right now.

"You have a hilarious way of showing you want to be around me," I snap, turning away.

Catching up easily, his long legs eating twice the distance mine do, Boyd nudges me with his shoulder. "I'm sorry about the other night, Fiona. It's just, there's a lot going on—"

"That I don't know about, yeah. I *get* it. Really. And it's fine. If you don't want to tell me, you don't have to, but don't come around here pretending you give a shit about me if that's the case."

Gripping my bicep, he stops me again, glaring. There's heat in his eyes—anger and arousal intertwining until I can't separate the two, and it makes my core clench around nothing, aching for him.

"I *do* want to tell you," he rasps.

"Then do it! Prove that to me. You told me I'm yours, make me fucking believe it." I swallow, licking my lips; his hazel gaze latches onto the movement, jaw flexing as he stares.

300

"Tell me about your sister, Boyd. Or your real mother. Give me something more than a slightly embarrassing hobby and the fact that you went to therapy as a kid—newsflash, *everyone* tries therapy at least once."

Folding his lips together, he glances over my head, a mask of stoicism falling over his features. All business.

He reaches to his ear, touching a finger to his earpiece, and spouts off some kind of code. The device in my ear crackles, my brother's instructions to get closer and figure out who's just approached Juliet clear over the line.

Shaking my head, I give Boyd a sad smile. "Duty calls."

"Fiona—"

But I don't stop to listen, trudging up to where Juliet and her friend have been joined by a familiar-looking middle-aged woman with a bad dye job and bright eyes.

Manic eyes.

I notice the facial resemblances between her and Juliet before I register their conversation, and it adds to the fire already searing my skin.

"...you're crazier than I remember," Juliet says, gesturing at the crowd surrounding them.

The woman's face hardens, something evil lurking there. "Ah, but the apple doesn't fall far from the tree, does it? I heard you started therapy. Good for you, darling, considering how your mental health has stupendously stunted your growth."

Fury takes flight in my chest, scorching a path right down to my toes, propelling me forward. I'm butting in where I don't belong, but my anger spurs me on, has me latching on to the first thing it might be able to fix.

"That's fucking *rude*." Crossing my arms over my chest, I glare daggers at the woman, trying my best to accurately place her in my head.

They all turn to face me, Juliet's friend shifting closer to her as they take in my appearance—diamond stilettos, a pink crushed velvet dress, red hair pulled into an elaborate updo.

I know what I probably look like outside of the outfit, can feel the crazy in my eyes exploding like a thousand individual supernovas. My shoulders square, and I feel Boyd take a step forward, but I refuse to look at him.

Recognition seems to dawn on the older woman as she takes me in, and I watch her clutch at the necklace dangling around her throat, as if she's prepared to make this a *thing*.

She doesn't know how close I am to snapping for real.

"Fiona..." Boyd says in his warning voice, low and throaty. Normally, it'd make my pussy flutter, but right now it just makes me angrier.

I just want to know what he's hiding.

"What?" I snap, narrowing my eyes at the woman. "You want me to sit and be quiet when an old hag insults my friend? I think the fuck not."

Friend might be a liberal use of the word, considering I really only barely know Juliet, but I notice the flash of surprise that flickers in the woman's eyes at the thought of Juliet having support in me, and it sends satisfaction to my very soul that I've caught her off guard.

As I step forward, I'm yanked backward when Boyd wraps his hand around mine. I whip my head around to fix him with a nasty look, almost getting lost in the sternness on his face; the downturn of his plush mouth, the hard set of his jaw, the flare in his eyes that says he wants to flog me again, maybe this time with something more powerful than his belt.

The look is mesmerizing. Captivating. I feel myself falling for it, succumbing to his domination, but then I remember him kicking me off his property two nights ago and it refuels my anger, sending it flying in different directions, difficult to get a hold of.

"Let go of me," I growl, jerking my hand in his.

His grip tightens. "Stop trying to make a fucking scene."

"You're not allowed to tell me what to do, dick. You're not my father, or my brother, *or* my boyfriend. *Remember?*"

I'm vaguely aware of the fact that the pitch of my voice is reaching dangerous heights, but I'm too far gone to make it stop.

I feel dozens of pairs of eyes on us, the intensity of their perusal sweltering; Boyd notices, too, dropping my hand like I've burned him, his lips pulling back in a snarl.

He adjusts the collar of his suit with a shrug, releasing me, seeming to force his face to relax. "Have it your way, *princess.*"

Venom laces the word as it spits from his mouth, making my stomach cramp as he turns and stalks off, leaving me to rot in the mess of my own making.

I watch his back as he makes his way back to the parking lot, feeling incredibly stupid, then offer Juliet a soft smile and take off after him, my heels sinking into the grass as I sprint.

'The apple doesn't fall far from the tree.'

Recognition fogs my vision.

Oh, Jesus. That's Juliet's *mother.*

Boyd's mouth moves furiously as he stops at the edge of the parking lot. I call out after him, guilt pressing down into my skull like being buried in an avalanche.

Just as I reach him, he freezes, and I turn my comms unit back on as Kieran asks if we recognized the woman.

"No, I didn't stick around long enough. Didn't want her to recognize me in case she can make a connection." Boyd sends me a sidelong glance, his mouth pressed into a firm line, and I reach forward, yanking the unit from his ear and tossing mine to the ground, adrenaline coursing through my veins.

"*I* saw her," I say into Boyd's piece, my breathing staggered from running to get here. "That's their mom. Lynn Harrison, or something? Don't you remember she fled town right after all that stuff with the senator went down?"

Boyd's eyes widen, a flurry of activity happening as he pulls his phone from his pocket and dials a number, barking orders that don't make any sense to me, because I'm still not totally filled in on what we're even doing here. I just know I was on lookout duty, but I don't know *why*.

I had to beg Kieran to even let me do that.

Waiting by a random car for Boyd to finish up, he hooks his phone back into his suit pocket and walks over to me, snatching the comms unit from my ear, wrapping his hand around my wrist *again*, and pulling me into his hard body.

"Come with me, right fucking now," he breathes, chest heaving beneath the soft material of his shirt.

He doesn't wait for me to answer, just starts dragging me toward the side of the church, far from the crowd. I think he's about to take me to confession when he passes the side doors, heading for a little storage building at the edge of the property.

It's white and looks deserted, but he kicks the door in anyway, the sudden onslaught of violence sending a shiver down my spine.

Shoving me inside before I have a chance to protest, he slams the door closed, shrouding us in stuffy darkness. I trip over something and my body buckles, my nails scraping against nothing as I fall.

Boyd catches me around the waist and stands me up straight, pushing me into the wall, wrapping his hand around my mouth as if he thinks I might scream.

I relax into his hold, my words from earlier not even on my radar as I sink into the feeling of him against me. His erection digs into my back, long and thick, and I have a hard time catching my breath as he shifts his hips, grinding into me.

"What did I fucking tell you about public tantrums?" he rasps against my ear, his free hand gliding down my body; he squeezes my left breast through the thin material of my dress, pinching the nipple as it beads perfectly for him, then ghosts over my stomach, making the muscles ripple beneath his touch.

Mumbling against his hand, I try to answer, but it's clear he doesn't want me to. My heart races inside my chest, beating on my rib cage as it tries to escape, and my throat is thick with arousal, even though I know all of this is wrong.

His anger is being redirected instead of dealt with, and while it might be a good cooldown method, I know too well that everything just comes right back when the high of the orgasm wears off.

But I don't stop him.

Don't fucking want to.

When his fingertips skim the hem of my dress, hefting it up over my butt cheeks, I bite my tongue and shift backward, pressing more fully into him. He gulps, hand shaking as it comes back around and dips between my legs, breath hot against the side of my neck.

"I said there'd be no more public outbursts," he growls. "Said you were to come to *me* when you needed a violent release. You know what happens when princesses disobey?"

I shake my head, even though his grip around my mouth leaves little room for the movement.

His fingers delve between my folds, the sound of my arousal embarrassingly loud as he strokes and swirls, making my legs tremble.

Pulling out of my panties quickly, he spins me around, not bothering to fix where my dress is hiked up, and places his hands on my shoulders, pressing down. I drop to my knees with a hard thud against the dirty floor and hear the distinct sound of a zipper releasing.

"Their crowns get revoked."

My mouth waters, desperate for the taste I know is coming, my stomach wrought with butterflies in spite of itself. I'm nervous, but for a completely different reason, and the combination of anxiety and desire is a potent one, making me abandon my morals and thoughts of letting him go.

If I can't keep him, I at least want this.

CHAPTER THIRTY

Fiona

"*E*ver sucked a cock before, princess?"

Boyd's question echoes in my mind, bouncing off the walls of my brain, but I'm not really sure how to answer.

The simple way would be to lie, because the taunt in his voice tells me he isn't expecting me to be experienced in this department. Or that he doesn't want me to be.

But the deviant part of me is curious to see what he'll do if I say yes.

My hands grip my thighs above the knees, my core throbbing in anticipation. Excitement twists around my DNA, coating each double helix in liquid heat as electricity zings through my veins. I can't see him because of how dark it is, but I can *feel* him — his heat, his anger, his complete and utter rapture.

It washes over me in fiery waves, the appreciation that comes with being wanted, and I grab onto it before it slips past, letting it blot out the nerves fluttering inside me.

I want this. No matter how he tries to punish me, I won't let him leave thinking this was all his doing.

I'll take the sexual domination, revel in the way he coaxes my insecurities from my body for a brief time, but when the gloss of sweat and cum dries up and all I'm left with is me, I'm not going to let him think that he won.

Because that's what this is — a power play. As anger, hurt, and secrets crackle between us, this dance we're about to begin is a contest to see who breaks first. Who gives in.

And I'm so damn tired of being the first to shatter.

Fingers hook under my chin, yanking my face up. I can just barely make out the contours of his nose and lips and can see the slightest glow in his irises from where a single sliver of light spills through a crack in the door.

"When I ask a question, I expect a fucking answer."

My mouth dries up at the command in his tone, the authority in it making my body temperature spike. One of his fingers curls into my bottom lip, rubbing roughly with the flat pad, probably smearing my lipstick just the way he likes.

"Yes," I whisper, nerves flooding my system, making me dizzy.

He tsks, tapping his finger against me. "Good. Then this should be no problem for you."

I wait for more instruction, my clit pulsing erratically, the darkness providing an extra element of danger to what we're doing here. Anyone could waltz in and find us, especially given Kieran's probably on his way and will wonder why we ditched our posts, but neither of us seems to mind the risk.

Maybe it's because deep down, we know this is it.

"Take me out," he says, pinching my bottom lip until it stings, a bruise likely forming where he touches. I move my arms up and take his undone jeans in my hands, but he bats me away with a dissatisfied grunt. "No hands. Take me out with your mouth."

"I don't think I can—"

"Did I ask what you *thought*? No. In fact, the time for chatting is long over. Take my cock out with your mouth or I'll add to your punishment."

For a moment, I stare at the dark blob of him, confused as to how I'm supposed to maneuver this. I consider the times I've wrangled a maraschino cherry out of a milkshake with just my tongue and resolve to approach it similarly.

"Hands behind your back, so I know you're not cheating."

My chest feels tight as I lock my arms behind me, leaning forward to brush against his pants with my nose, trying to find an opening. The zipper slides against me as I move, and I bump up against his bulge, gasping slightly at the contact.

He's not wearing underwear.

Even though technically, Boyd's dick has been inside of me, and I've seen it, stroked it once or twice, this is entirely new territory. The other times with us seemed to have been focused on me and my pleasure, and now — it's all about him.

A sense of power surges through me, the desire to do a good job — nay, to *blow him out of the fucking water* — rising like a high tide inside me, and I bite down on the zipper, pulling with my teeth until I feel the pants give way and slip to his knees.

Still, I can't see him, so I flatten my tongue and lean forward, licking up the front of his thigh and inching inward. The shudder that racks his body covers me in goose bumps, and I can't stop the smile that spreads across my face at how hard up he is already.

"Make it sloppy, princess." One hand comes up, petting my hair and cupping the back of my head while the other guides me to him, bumping the crown of his cock against my upper lip and stroking the pierced underside over my tongue. "This is all the lube you're gonna get."

My mouth opens to ask what exactly he means, but then he's shoving himself to the back of my throat, cutting me off; I retch instantly, bile burning the base of my throat as his piercing scrapes against me, and he lets out a strangled groan.

"*Christ*," he grits out, his other hand cradling the side of my face as he pulls me off him. I sputter, coughing on my saliva, and glare up at him through the dark. "Thought you said you'd done this before, or am I just bigger than the other dicks you've put your little whore mouth on?"

He's *far* bigger than anyone else I've ever gone down on, but I don't take the bait, even as his dirty pet name makes me shiver.

The challenge in his question is clear, renewing my determination to make him buckle first. Wiping some of the snot from my nose, I dip my head, searching for his tip, and take it between my lips, flicking against the piercing on the underside.

His breath hitches as I swirl my tongue around his slit, lapping at the pearly beads of precum leaking from him. Focusing on keeping my breathing steady, I edge forward, bobbing slowly as I envelop more of him.

"That's right, work me in. I fucking love feeling your mouth stretched around me. Can't wait for it to be your tight little cunt."

An involuntary moan rips from my throat, making my lips hum against his silky skin; he jerks inside me, tangling his fingers in my hair.

"Deeper," he snaps, starting to cant his hips, taking charge of what's supposed to be me proving him wrong. Annoyed, I disobey him for the first time and wrap my palm around his shaft, my fingers just barely touching each other.

His fingers tighten in my hair, and he starts to drag me off again, but I begin pumping my hand in time with his hips, matching him thrust for thrust, and he seems to get lost in the sensation.

I suck him in as deep as I possibly can, gagging and letting the drool spill out from my lips, coating him with it when I resume the messy motions, my fingers sticky and warm against him.

"Oh, fuck, *yes*." His throaty sounds make my body feel lighter than air, carrying me off on a cloud of ecstasy as his hands grip the sides of my head, pumping faster and faster. "Goddamn, Fiona. *Goddamn*. That... *Christ*, that feels so good. Just like that, baby."

I feel him twitch inside me, and I'm mentally preparing myself to swallow him whole, working my hand and forming a tight seal around his crown, his piercing clattering against my teeth, when he tears me away.

His cock bobs against my cheek, covered in my spit and snot.

Still holding him at the base, I dart my tongue out and run the tip over the purple vein on the underside of him up to the barbell, kissing his crown and searching for his gaze in the dark.

I find it, just barely, that familiar magnetism coursing powerfully between us, an electric charge that's impossible to ignore.

"Why didn't you finish?"

If he realizes I've spoken without permission, he doesn't admonish me, only chuckles darkly. "Not where I want to come."

Something animalistic wrenches from deep inside his chest, the sound feral and *sinful*, and I hear the swooshing of clothes being removed before he speaks again.

"I'd hoped to see your face the first time you came on my cock, but I suppose this will have to do."

There's some shuffling, and then he's grabbing my hips and hauling me up; I grasp at him blindly, trying to find some kind of purchase as he moves, and he settles me over his naked hips as he lays flat on the ground, fingernails digging into my skin.

He tugs my dress up, pulling it off over my head, then works my panties down over my hips, shifting to pull them off my legs and toss them away.

"Sit on my cock, princess."

My mouth falls open, half shocked and half turned the fuck on, desire pooling in my core. I feel myself leaking, adding to how soaked I got while I was sucking him, and the dampness between us makes me squirm.

I press my fingers into his chest, wishing I could see the tattoos inked into his skin, so I'd have something to concentrate on besides the heat ebbing between us.

"I can't," I say, my embarrassment scorching a path up my sternum, obliterating everything in its wake. Shifting, I try to slide off of him, but he holds my hips in place, propping his legs up for added restraint.

He leans up, brushing his nose along my jaw and inhaling deeply.

"I said," he breathes, moving so our lips brush. "Sit on my fucking cock, *whore*. Take your punishment like a good little girl."

Punishment feels like an understatement—as I grapple with how to proceed, flames rain down my body in the form of every insecurity and evil thought I've ever had, the reminder that I'm supposed to be letting him go stuck on a loop in my head, sucking me out of the moment completely.

My chest caves in on itself, fear filling the cracks where arousal should be, and my throat constricts, making it impossible to swallow. Sitting up, I pull my hands from him, trembling uncontrollably.

"Fiona." He cups my cheeks in his palms, holding my face straight. I find the slope of his nose in the dark, just the sharp outline, and focus on it, tapping my finger against my thigh. "Come back to me."

Heart pounding, I reach up and cover his hands with mine, letting him absorb my anxiety the way you might suck venom from a snake bite.

"Kiss me," I whisper, not even done with the sentence before he's capturing my mouth with his, nipping and sucking until I feel like I might faint from the shared oxygen.

His tongue pushes inside, entwining with mine as he kisses me with so much passion, it's almost easy to forget how he kicked me out of his life a few days ago.

Almost easy to forget he has secrets, that we don't work, as he pours himself into the gesture, pulling his hands from my face and sliding them down my body.

Reaching around, he grasps my ass in both hands, using the position to slowly start grinding me on top of his cock; it glides between my slick folds, his piercing bumping my clit and making me moan.

Sliding one hand farther down my crack, he teases my entrance with the tip of his finger, pushing in each time my hips swivel back and the pressure leaves my clit.

The dueling sensations, one penetrating, one massaging, have my thighs quivering on either side of his hips, and I feel the apprehension drain from my body, replaced with a better tension coiling inside my belly and expanding to my core.

Boyd pulls back, dropping his mouth to my throat and peppering kisses along the expanse, moaning into my skin. "God, you feel *so good*."

316

Wrapping my arms around his neck, I claw at his shoulders as euphoria washes over me, threatening to push me over the edge. A whimper drags from my mouth, unbidden, and he speeds up his movements, his breaths harsh against me.

"Tell me it feels good, baby." His voice breaks, its sharp edges slicing through me. "Tell me you need to come."

"I need it," I gasp. He pushes two fingers fully inside me as the thin band holding my control snaps, and I come apart on top of him, a convulsing mess crying out with pleasure.

Taking a second to catch my breath, I sit up and press down on his chest, making him lie back on the floor. My clit throbs against him, distracting as I lift my hips.

Getting to my knees, I fist his shaft, paying particular attention to the piercing and loving how me rolling my thumb over it makes him shudder. Pumping firmly, I hold him erect below me, my heart racing.

"You hurt me," I say, trying to find his eyes in the dark. "I bared my soul to you, told you my secrets, and two days ago you told me to leave you alone, like I was nothing."

"I know."

Licking my lips, I wait. "Is that it?"

"Fiona, I told you I don't apologize."

"You're a liar, Boyd Kelly. A liar and a coward. I don't know what's going on with you, but I know I can't keep doing this. You shut me out when it's convenient, don't tell me about the things that matter, but still expect me to trust you?"

"What do you want from me? I never said I was perfect."

"I'm not looking for *perfect*," I say, rising up and lining his tip with my entrance. It bumps against me, pulling a shocked gasp from us both, but I don't move further. Not yet. "I wasn't looking for anything. *You* started all of this."

Finding my hips again, he squeezes, nails breaking through the skin. "I couldn't stop it if I fucking wanted to. Don't you get that? You're mad I threw you out, mad I keep secrets — have you ever fucking considered how I feel? What I'm going through?"

"That's all I've tried to do!" I sink lower, and he bats my hand off of him, replacing it to hold himself steady. My hands claw at his pecs as he stretches me, the slow slide down unable to stop the burn of expansion.

My breath catches in my throat at the excruciating pain of having him enter me, and I choke on my saliva, freezing in place. I don't think the entire crown of his cock is inside me yet, but it hurts too much to move any more.

"Keep going, Fiona," he groans, one hand coming up to play with my breast. He kneads the flesh and rolls my nipple between his fingers, making my body relax ever-so-slowly.

Biting down on my lip, I try to obey, lifting up and sinking back down again; he slips in another inch, and I swear I can feel him in my stomach already.

"It hurts," I whimper, pinching my eyes closed against the pain.

"Relax, princess," he whispers, sealing his mouth around my other breast, flicking his tongue over the puckered nipple. My head falls back, my hair brushing against my ass, as another wave of ecstasy tumbles through me, and I feel his hands on my hips again, rocking me slowly up and down as he laves over my flesh.

Without warning, he lifts his hips at the same time his hands pull mine down, fully seating himself inside of me in one singular, blinding flash of pain. I cry out, my pussy wet but still not used to the intrusion, and he covers my mouth with his, consuming my pain.

Claiming me.

We stay still for a while, him kissing me while I struggle to adjust and release the vise grip I've got on him.

"You're choking my dick," he says, a nervous laugh brushing against my lips.

My nostrils flare, my fingernails digging into the back of his neck. "Maybe I should just choke *you* instead."

"Kinky." He massages the top of my ass, licking my lips. "Do you think you can move?"

"I don't know." Shame floods me, heating my skin, making me forget the fire between my legs. "I might be bad at this."

"Not possible."

Slowly, I swivel my hips, unsure of what else to really do. Each stroke still burns, but the flames die away the more I move,

319

an intense pressure building in my belly that I've never felt before. It spirals like a tornado, growing until I feel myself getting lost in the sensation.

Boyd's hands guide my hips into a figure-eight pattern, his soft coaching in my ear making me dizzy. "Bounce on it, like the little whore you are. My whore. *Mine.* Fuck, you're gonna make me come so hard."

I listen, raising my hips and doing my best to keep rhythm, knowing I don't want this to be something I regret, no matter what happens after.

It takes a few minutes to get the hang of the motions, but when I do, there's no stopping me.

Something ethereal shatters inside of me, the pressure mounting until it's on the cusp of exploding; a spasm shoots through me, and Boyd lets out a moan, reaching between my legs to circle his thumb over my clit.

"You feel so goddamn good riding me, princess. *Too* fucking good." He chokes on the last syllable, and I can feel his release as it unravels, his control slipping with each thrust of my hips.

Clutching my hip, he drives me faster, bringing the hint of pain back as he rubs my clit and fucks me hard, and everything in my mind whips past so quickly, I don't have a chance to latch onto anything.

"I'm gonna come, baby," he grits, trying to move me off of him, but I clamp down, pressing my pussy flush against him and grinding.

His tip feels like it's in my throat, sending shocks of pleasurable pain down my spine, and then he pulses inside me, releasing with a low moan as he holds me to him.

"Fiona, princess, *fuck*. I fucking love you."

CHAPTER THIRTY ONE

Boyd

I know the second I say it that it's a mistake, but the words tumble out of me before I can stop them, desperate to make her understand. To show I *am* trying and that I *do* care, but that I'm a giant fucking mess who will never deserve her.

She freezes as I spill, thick ropes of my seed painting the inside of her glorious cunt, her clit spasming against my thumb as she shatters with her orgasm. I can tell she doesn't come from the penetration, her pussy clenching but not spasming, and it makes me feel like an asshole for taking her virginity like this

Problem is, I *am* an asshole. And I don't know how to be gentle with her, not like this—not when she's spiraling, teetering on the edge of sanity and needing someone to help her regain control.

She scrambles off of me in an instant, the loss of her warmth sudden and startling; I smell the faint scent of her blood mixed with our sweat and cum, and I already know that's going to be difficult to explain when we go back outside.

I hear her run to the door, and she props it open just enough to see inside; her naked body glows in the glittering sunlight, even as she holds her breasts in one arm and covers her cunt with the other, as if I haven't seen everything she has to offer.

Her hands scrape along the floor, searching for her clothes, and I clear my throat as I reach for mine, stepping back into the suit I had on before. She yanks her pink dress over her head and runs a hand through her hair, exhaling a shaky breath as she gets to her feet, her heels still somehow intact after all that.

"So," I say after a long stretch of silence, an awkward feeling settling in the pit of my stomach. "Are we gonna talk about what just happened, or..."

Getting to her feet, Fiona scrubs her hands over her freckled face, turning her brown eyes my way. She reaches behind her head, pulling her red locks into a low bun, and shakes her head. "I'd rather we didn't."

My eyebrows knit together in confusion, and I slide my slacks up over my half-flaccid dick, tucking my dress shirt inside and zipping them up. "You don't want to talk about me telling you I—"

"You don't love me, Boyd."

Her words take me by surprise, making my head jerk back. Not exactly the warm reception I'd expected. "Now you're an expert on what I'm feeling?"

"Since we started sneaking around, how many times have you *dealt* with the demons harassing you? And don't say there aren't any, because I know. Maybe not the specifics, but I see you're struggling. Sometimes it feels like looking into a mirror," she says.

"Just because you don't see me doing it, doesn't mean—"

"Who was at your house this weekend?" she asks, interrupting me the way I used to her when she'd run off on a tangent, nerves getting the best of her. "*Why* were you in therapy as a kid? Why did you stop going?"

My hands clench at my sides, the invasive questions causing a chasm of discomfort to open up in my chest. "That's not really any of your business."

Mouth slackening, her face falls with the motion, disappointment seeming to etch itself into her soul as she stares at me, half shrouded in the darkness.

Meanwhile, she stands in the sunshine, basking in its warmth, and it feels like we're worlds away.

"If you loved me, you'd want to confide in me. You'd share your problems with me, and we'd work through them together." Taking a few steps closer, she stops just in front of me, reaching out and placing her hand over my heart. "You don't *love* me, you love what I do for you. I'm a distraction, and it feels good to focus on me instead of everything else that's going on in your life. Everything that's going wrong."

I cover her hand with mine, squeezing—trying to keep her tethered to me. But even as we connect, that magnetism weakens, as if sex was a catalyst and we've suddenly burned up the pieces that make up the two of us together.

"I won't lie and say I wasn't doing it, too. All of this. But... I think we've just got too much going on in our lives right now. Too many secrets between us. I don't think I can handle the added anxiety that comes from wondering why you can't open up to me." She tilts her head, smiling sadly. "I'd never be able to stop thinking that you're hiding something."

An electric spark contracts the muscles in my chest, pulling them tight. Alarm worms its way into my soul. "I'm *sorry* about the other night. Christ, I... I was trying to protect you, I didn't really want you to fucking go."

"Protect me from what?"

I hesitate, still not ready to reveal the attack on Riley when she hasn't woken from the drug-induced coma Kal ended up putting her in.

He'd said her injuries were extensive, though not life-threatening, and that the coma would ensure she rested and allow her body to heal on its own.

Otherwise, if she resumed physical activities or stressed herself too much, she could cause more internal damage that could end up requiring surgery or being permanent.

And with LeeAnn and Romeo still lurking around town, I especially don't want Fiona involved. Don't want to be the reason she gets hurt.

"The what doesn't matter." I reach for her, sliding my hands around her hips, but she steps back out of the way. "Christ, Fiona. What am I supposed to do here? Do you want me to grovel? Get on my knees and say I'm fucking sorry for being a dick, for sometimes using you, for chasing you away instead of inviting you to help?"

"Do you mean any of that?"

I stay silent, my pride raging inside as she calls me out on my bullshit. It makes my heart ache, like she's driving a dull knife right into the organ, baring my soul for all to see. I'm bleeding out in front of her, and she continues turning the blade, wringing out as much from me as she can possibly get.

Truth is, I mean all of it. Everything I should be sorry for, I am — but the martyr in me, the darkness inside, refuses to let me admit it. Because if she saw what was *really* lurking in my depths, it'd probably terrify her. Disgust her.

I'm fucking disgusted with *myself*.

For spending my entire life chasing something unattainable, something toxic that almost took away one of the most important people I know.

For letting anger and resentment keep me from saving Riley when she initially needed it, for not being brave enough to take the leap and bridge the gap between us.

For not being good enough for Fiona, as much as I pretend to be.

For using her, even as I tried to justify it by helping her.

Clearly, none of that was good enough, because here I fucking am—the rest of my world in complete shambles while the woman I want to be with looks at me with goodbye on the tip of her tongue.

And this time, there's nothing I can do to stop her.

I have to let her go.

She sighs, giving me a slight nod. "I think you should be honest with yourself, Boyd. Figure out what demons are worth living with, and which ones are worth slaying."

Clearing her throat, she takes a step back from me, her voice growing thick. It makes my chest burn, and I drop my gaze to the ground before she says anything else, not wanting to see the look on her face when she gives up on me. "And I think... we shouldn't see each other again. I'm sorry. For all of this."

Lifting my chin, I just stare at her, trying to memorize what her face looks like clouded with shadows. I think about her chocolate milkshake addiction, her bubblegum bedroom, the sunshine she tries her best to show to the world.

I could ask her to stay. Beg her not to leave me.

But if the result remains the same, I suppose there's no point drawing things out.

Gritting my teeth, I push past her, my heart plummeting to my stomach like a lead balloon, lodging in the tissue there. I don't look back, don't pause one last time to say goodbye.

I just leave.

Kieran arrives as I'm jogging back to the front of the church, Juliet apparently having been taken hostage by her mother while I was away.

I ignore the dirty looks he shoots me as he and Elia Montalto leave to scour the premises, and when I see Fiona making a beeline for her Jeep in the parking lot, I take that as my cue to duck out, trusting that my best friend can handle himself.

I stop by a McDonald's on the way back to my house and pick up some fries and chocolate shakes, noting the array of text messages from Craig that range from claiming Kieran's been killed to Kieran's alive and being admitted to the hospital in a matter of a few hours.

Because the Devil can't be killed.

Pulling up in front of my house, I park my BMW in the garage, double check that the door to the apartment upstairs is still locked with its security code, and head into the kitchen from the side entrance.

The house is quiet, something I'd normally welcome, but when waiting for someone to wake up from a coma, that only equals disappointment.

Kal's been checking on Riley several times a day since the night of the attack, the only person I'm willing to let know what happened to her at this point other than her father, who thinks she was mauled by a bear while doing her community service and has plans to come visit during the week.

Otherwise, I'm keeping her close to my chest, where she should've been all along.

I hear canned laughter coming from the inside of the guest bedroom and wonder if Kal left the television on again— his suggestion, a way to entice her to wake up—but when I push the door open and scan the room, I notice she's rolled onto her side, eyes open and glued to the screen mounted across the room.

"Riley," I breathe, relief breaking the dam holding all of my emotions back, making my voice catch on the last half of her name.

Crossing the room, I bend down and study her face; without all the blood, she looks more like herself, although she's missing a large chunk of her cheek, the area hidden beneath gauze.

Her left eye is swollen, bruised, and has several busted capillaries that make her look like a demon spawn, and there's a deep gash at the corner of her mouth, stitched together like the spot above my eyebrow.

I know what's hidden beneath the covers tells a much worse story — one of internal damage that has to try and heal on its own, a sexual assault I hope she never remembers, and more emotional trauma than any sixteen-year-old deserves to experience.

"Don't... touch me," she croaks, and I freeze, realizing my hand is outstretched. I drop it to my side, perch on the edge of the mattress, and she watches me with glassy eyes. "Sorry, I'm just... hurting."

She's hooked up to a portable IV machine that also tracks her vitals, and I glance up, noting the spike in her heart rate.

"Was the doctor here? Maybe I need to ask him to up your morphine dosage."

"No," she replies quickly, the word shooting from her mouth like a hockey puck launched across an ice rink. "It's not... I can manage, I think."

I study her battered face, a sinister sensation gripping the chambers of my heart and squeezing tight, refusing to let go.

Her eyes dart to a plastic cup on the nightstand, and I reach over, bending the straw and holding it so she can take a drink. She raises up slightly, wincing, and swallows with what looks like a massive effort before dropping back onto the pillow with a harsh exhale.

"My... throat hurts."

Nodding, I replace the cup and fold my hands in my lap. "Dr. Anderson said it likely would. You'll need to rest and drink clear fluids as it heals."

She blinks, sadness and pain washing over her features, though her eyes remain dry and unfeeling. "What... happened to me?"

Scratching at the back of my neck, wincing when I scrape my nails across the cuts Fiona left on me a few hours ago, I hesitate. "I don't know if we should—"

"It was Mom... wasn't it?" When I don't say anything, she scoffs, pinching her eyes closed. "I knew it."

A twinge of grief rattles my chest, the feeling of betrayal all too relatable. Somehow, it's the disappointments you expect that hurt the worst, like your worst nightmares coming to fruition.

Riley's eyelids begin to droop, the conversation appearing to take its toll on her traumatized body; she sighs, pulling the white covers up to her chin, and closes her eyes.

"Are... you gonna... send me back?" she whispers, not daring to look at me.

The twinge expands into a full-blown throb, the muscles inside shriveling beneath the pain as it lances straight to my heart, prodding the spoiled organ.

Fear makes a home in my gut, pinching my nerves as tight as it can, and I let out a sigh, struggling to maintain a grip on my control as it withers into nothing.

"No," I whisper, swallowing over the lump in my throat.

This time, I mean it.

CHAPTER THIRTY TWO

Fiona

Medicine bottles clatter into the sink as I sweep my hand over the vanity, checking labels, panic settling in when I get to the end of the stash and don't find what I'm looking for.

My fingers clutch at the porcelain, chest heaving as I glare at myself in the mirror, a hatred bubbling up inside me that I haven't felt in a long time.

It lends itself to the violent tendencies, that hatred. A self-loathing that lashes out at others, makes me say and do stupid things. Convinces me I'm unworthy of love, that I'm toxic, that I'm better off alone. It's my greatest obsession, and today I let it run rampant as I ruined my entire relationship with Boyd Kelly.

While part of me still stands by the decision, knowing that we're not ready for anything more, I also can't shake the feeling that I gave up on him. On us. And it eats away at my insides, a cannibalistic tumor devouring me, because I'm no quitter.

I'm an Ivers. We persevere.

But today, I crumbled.

Today, I was weak.

And while I can try to pass it off on my uncertainties about Boyd's sense of self and his real feelings, or the fact that my life is imploding all around me, the truth is I was just scared.

Maybe I don't face my demons as much as I like to claim.

Maybe I'm more like my father than I ever realized.

My chest pulls taut the longer I stare at myself in the vanity, the lines and colors of my face reminding me of my mother's when she was young. The similarities remind me of everything I've lost, everything I'm losing, and I can feel myself spiraling.

Sweat beads along my hairline and my throat constricts; I clutch at the neckline of my shirt, yanking it away from my skin to give myself room to breathe, but it's no use.

Grunting, I push off from the sink and stomp back into the bedroom, my eyes darting around the room, trying to remember where I might have put the Zoloft I took once upon a time.

I'm not even sure if it'd work at this point, but the way my heart thumps inside of my chest, so hard and heavy against my ribs that my entire body feels each aching pulse, has me desperate.

My fingers tremble as they scour every surface, toppling perfume bottles and searching my jewelry boxes, throat growing tighter with each passing second, anxiety wrapping around my heart like a coiled snake, waiting for a chance to strike.

Turning around after knocking my textbooks and school papers to the ground, resisting the urge I get to immediately pick up the mess, I dive for my bed, ripping the sheets from where they're tucked in at the corners and throwing them off the mattress.

I'm frantic now, my sanity slowly unraveling, panic mounting inside of me until it's all I can focus on. All I can think about, looping brokenly in my head, and I push the mattress off the box spring, heaving it so it flips over, hooking on my nightstand and dragging the table lamp down with it.

Gently trailing my fingernails along the fabric of the box spring, I press down between the wooden slats; the fabric tears easily, withering under me, and satisfaction washes over me in waves as I start to shred the rest of it from the wooden frame.

When my mother first got sick and had a bad habit of forgetting when she'd already taken her medicine, we'd stuffed it in the box springs beneath her bed, knowing she wouldn't have the strength to search for it.

Maybe that's what happened to mine.

A few minutes later, though, and my nails are jagged and bleeding from scraping against the wood and ripping into the fabric, fragile from when I chewed them down to nubs after finding out about my father's affair.

I need a cigarette.

Giving up on finding the prescription, I leave my bedroom in its disarray, my mind hopping right over to its next obsession. Heading downstairs, I scurry down the hall, ducking out past the greenhouse to the back yard overlooking the hedge gardens and the acres of unnecessary land the house sits on.

I'm not expecting someone to already be in my old smoking spot, seated on an old rubber tire that's been there for so long, it's part of the patio surface now. But when I round the corner of the house, there my father sits, a cigarette poised between his lips, staring up at the night sky.

I start to retreat, not wanting him to know I come out here — especially given how well I've been doing at resisting even the thought to smoke — but when I move my foot backward, he turns his head, spotting me.

Smoke billows up above his head, disappearing into the stars. "I was hoping you'd join me one of these days."

Confused, I get closer, crossing my arms over my chest. "You were hoping your daughter would join you for a cigarette?"

"I wouldn't want to shame-smoke with anyone else by my side." He shakes a menthol from the green pack in his shirt pocket, offering it to me along with a Bic lighter. I take it, dropping down onto the tire beside him, and turn the cigarette in my hand, studying the smooth surface and inhaling the sweet tobacco scent.

It took me months to get the smell out from under my fingernails, and even though I so very badly want to, I'm not exactly sure I should indulge.

My stomach cramps, my brain hyper-focused on what I shouldn't do, thoughts of inhaling the sweet smoke taking over until I forcibly shove it from my mind, trying to find something else to give my attention to.

"What're you doing out here?" I ask, curling my fingers around the white stick.

"Same thing as you. Trying to relieve myself of my regrets."

"How's that working out?"

He laughs. "I don't know, ask me again three cigarettes from now."

A comfortable silence falls around us, the calm after the chaos of today—thinking we'd lost Kieran, my secret breakup with Boyd, my mother starting her day out well and progressively getting worse as the hours dragged by, like they were sucking the remainder of her life out along with it.

It's the kind of calm you only get before everything goes bad again—a serene blip in time, before the universe chucks more hurdles at you.

"I broke things off with Chelsea," he notes after a while, flicking ash to the ground. "Switched her to a different department, too."

Nodding, I mull this over. "Are you gonna tell Mom?"

"I don't know, Fi. I'm not sure I want to risk the last memory she has of me being a bad one. You know what she always says about that."

"Those are the ghosts that come back to haunt you," I mutter, a soft smile splaying across my lips as I recite one of her many mantras. My stomach twists painfully, my mind flickering to how Boyd's last thought of me will forever be of him taking my virginity and me telling him he needs to get his life together.

"You're just like her, you know?" I raise an eyebrow, and he nods, taking another drag. "So similar that sometimes I wonder if we didn't accidentally clone you."

Scoffing, I stay silent, pinching the end of the cigarette in my hand so I'm no longer tempted. *Controlling what I can.* "That what caused the rift between us?"

"No." Glancing at me from the corner of his eye, he shrugs. "I was drawn to your mother because she didn't want anything to do with me. She was strong and self-sufficient, and it... relaxed me, because I knew she'd never need me to take care of her. Would never want me to. And then we had you after your

338

monstrous brothers, and all you wanted to do was take charge, just like her. You were always so much braver than the rest of us."

"I don't know about that," I mutter after a moment. "Most of the time I wallow in my fears."

He shakes his head, pointing at me. "People who are *afraid* don't spend their lives taking care of others. They cower and let other people take the reins, hoping that if they're quiet, disappointment will forget about them."

A knot lodges in my throat at his comparison, because right now I don't feel particularly brave. I feel defeated.

"I shouldn't have let you take care of her all this time by yourself," he says, sighing, and something inside of my chest pinches tight at the weight of his words, a boulder shoving farther in place, because I can't deny it. "I should've been there for both of you. That's not the kind of thing a kid should have to go through alone. But *I* let fear rule, and it fractured us and stole what little time I had left with your mother. I have to live with that."

Wiping beneath his eyes, emotion hanging thick on the edges of his eyelashes, he takes another drag, shaking his head as he gazes up at the stars.

"When you fall in love, you never think about what your life will be like if they're suddenly taken from you one day," he says. "I still don't know if I'm ready to face that day. What's the point of existing when the part of you that matters is gone?"

I open my mouth to tell him about my mother's wishes, about how she wants things to be forcefully ended before she gets to a point where she can't ever recover, but the words don't come.

I don't tell him how we've planned the date for her birthday in September, or that I can't stop feeling like my heart is being torn to shreds when I think about losing her.

I don't mention the anxiety it gives me, how it drove me into the arms of his employee. My brother's best friend, who I might have damaged irrevocably, when all I wanted to do was fix him.

Fix myself.

I don't mention that I wish he would tell my mom about his affair, that I think he deserves to be haunted — honestly, I think he knows that anyway. It's probably why he's sitting out here chain-smoking after being clean for decades.

'I have to live with that.'

Guilt eats away at your strengths, breaking down each wall you've erected, and necrotizing things from the inside. It's evil, worming its way into your bloodstream and making a home in your veins, manifesting in a million different ways.

Maybe it's a bad habit. Maybe it's a tic. Maybe it's your secrets.

Whatever the case, it exists inside all of us, a tidal wave crashing against the shore of sanity, robbing us of the beauty of life.

And as angry as I might be at my father for what he did, I don't want to add to his pain.

So instead of saying any of that, knowing it won't do any good to make him feel worse and that a little sunshine is probably what he needs right now, I lean my head on his shoulder and try to find comfort in the fact that he's here at all.

God knows it's so much easier to give up and walk away than it is to fight for something.

Later that night, when I'm lying in bed, staring at the ceiling, I roll over onto my side and inhale, hating that my sheets still smell like Boyd.

My mind loops over the scent until I can't stand it anymore, and I get up, stripping the mattress at three in the morning and replacing everything with fresh linens.

When I sink under the covers, I roll over to his side and curse.

"How does it *still* smell like him?"

My earlier thoughts about not giving up on people swirl in my mind, deafening as I toss and turn, trying to extract him from my nostrils. But it's no use; the guilt wreaks havoc, seeks to steal my comfort and drive me crazy.

I can't shake the feeling that I gave up too soon—that whatever is going on with Boyd was just too large of a burden for him to shoulder, and maybe being crushed under its weight is what made him keep it a secret.

No one wants to advertise their weaknesses.

Maybe I shouldn't have pushed him or tried to wring a confession I didn't really deserve.

Pulling out my phone, I dial his number with shaky fingers, wondering how I might fix this.

Needing to fix it.

Because even though I'm worried about him, about us, I don't really want to face a reality that doesn't have him in it.

The phone rings and rings, going straight to voicemail twice.

Eventually, the calls stop going through at all.

CHAPTER THIRTY THREE

Fiona

Four Months Later

After a quiet summer that eventually turns into a beautiful fall in Maine, my mother passes away on her birthday without any assistance. I'm coming back from my morning adjustment and personal growth class on Stonemore's campus when I get the text from my father, asking me to hurry home.

Professor Garrett, a wiry woman who wears Bohemian style dresses and an opaque quartz crystal on a cord around her neck, stops me as I rush past. "Everything okay, Fiona? You almost left without turning in your exam."

Biting my lip, I clutch my backpack tighter against my shoulder, not realizing until this second that I'd crumpled the packet against my chest in my escape. "Oh, right. Sorry."

She takes the paper when I hold it out, then offers me a soft smile, the wrinkles around her lips disappearing with the gesture. "Is it your mother?"

Nodding, I ignore the pang that shoots across my stomach—the curse of small-town living. Someone's always watching, waiting, especially when you're one of us.

I've lost track of how many times the local papers have compared my mother's declining health to that of Murphy's descension into insanity, posing questions about our family's karma and wondering if our reign in town is coming to an end.

Professor Garrett lets me pass, and I bolt from the classroom and out of the building, doing my best to keep some of her mantras in mind as I make my way to the parking lot.

Climbing behind the wheel of my Jeep, I push down the flare of guilt that attempts to crawl up my throat—that I've somehow failed my mom by not getting to her before this point, even though this was the date we had planned all along.

The feeling that I've prolonged her suffering in exchange for a little extra time prods at the back of my skull, a white-hot brand I can't erase as I leave campus.

I don't stop for a chocolate shake this time, shucking the ritual as I bypass the little cafe that popped up on the border between King's Trace and Stonemore, speeding my way down the cobblestone streets to make sure I'm exactly where I should be.

I might miss the ritual later, might have to come back for a shake all the same, but that doesn't matter at this moment.

Pulling up outside of the Ivers mansion, a place I haven't lived in since the beginning of the summer, I park just outside the front steps and bound up them, throwing the front doors open; they crash into the walls, the sound echoing through the empty, haunted house.

Kieran moved out around the same time I did, shacking up with his girlfriend-recently-turned-fiancée, leaving our parents to spend the remainder of their marriage in this house, alone.

My father's hope was to spend as much time with my mother as possible while he still could, but as she fell into the late stages of her disease and became a hollow husk of the woman she once was, I think it forced him to face reality.

We don't talk about Chelsea, but I can see in the slump of his shoulders and the anguish on his tired, aging face that he's never regretted anything more in his life. And I guess I just have to make my peace with that, even if I'm still not quite over it.

I hadn't been expecting anyone else to be here when I showed up, half planning on once again being the only one my mother can count on. But when I push into her bedroom and find her lying in the hospital bed that hospice moved in a week ago, my father and brother flank her on both sides, holding her hands.

She's barely recognizable after all this time — her sallow skin hangs from her bones like a haphazard sheet that's been draped over her body. In the last few weeks, she'd opted to stop eating, refusing everything — and since she'd signed a form early-on declining to be tube-fed if that time ever came, we'd been forced to just watch her wither away deliberately.

When she stopped taking the medication, though, that's when things went downhill, and they progressed quickly.

My father noted that she'd been sleeping more and more, her cognitive function dwindling as the days dragged on. She'd occasionally fill the silence with a sentence or two, but the rest of the time she'd succumbed to making simple noises, unintelligible sounds that really only let us know when she was in pain.

A knot lodges in my throat when I cross the threshold into the bedroom; the air shifts immediately, turning cold against me even though the heat's on high to keep her comfortable.

Anxiety scratches beneath the surface of my skin, desperate to break free as I approach the bed, keeping my gaze trained on her unconscious form. My hands shake as I reach for

346

her foot through the quilt stretched over her—an ancient number with floral patterns and frayed edges, made by her mother when mine was a kid.

Surrounded by the things that give her comfort, as if that makes the transition easier.

I suck in a deep breath, trying to remember the breathing exercises we learned from Professor Garrett. Grounding myself in the moment, pushing through the unease before it can take root.

Sitting on the edge of the bed, I reach out, running my fingers over the wooden rosary tucked beneath the hand my father's holding. My face grows hot as we sit in silence, listening to the sounds of her labored, sporadic breathing, holding our own while we wait for hers to stop.

Eventually, like everything else in this life, hers comes to an end.

It's nearly twelve hours after I arrive home, and it's not particularly peaceful; she vacillates between shaking, her body seizing up, and occasional gasps that rip from her lungs, each time giving us false hope that it's really the end.

My chest is tight, emotion clogging the cavity and making it hard to exist in the room, when she finally slips from sleep to permanence.

We let out a collective sigh—of relief, sadness, I can't really be sure.

My throat burns as I gaze down at her lifeless form, trying to etch the pieces of her that matter beyond the scars of her disease — the red hair we share, the freckles on her nose, the soft curve of her lips that suggest a life full of kindness and contentment.

Kieran clears his throat as a hospice nurse comes in, stepping back away from the bed. His eyes are red, his features taut as he struggles to remain stoic — trying to protect me from seeing his pain, I suppose, but it's there in the way he curls his fists and swipes under his nose, increasing the pressure of the emotion caught in my throat.

He disappears from the room after a few beats, leaving just my father and me and the nurse; eventually, my father squeezes my shoulder and leaves, too. I don't look at him, afraid that if I do I won't be able to contain the visceral sadness welling up inside me, threatening to spew like a volcanic eruption.

And it's not that I care if they see me bleed out, because even the sun hides behind clouds from time to time.

I just want my grief to be confined between my mother and me.

Selfishly, I don't want to share it right now.

When the door closes and I'm left completely alone, I crumble, burying my face in her lap and letting the tears burning my throat spill, soaking the blankets beneath me. Sobs rack my body, shaking me with their raw intensity, and I cry for all the things I don't get to have her here for, all the things I'll never be able to tell her.

I mourn my best friend, cursing a universe that'd take the purest soul out of its rotation but leave the evil here to dwell.

My heart splinters into a million little pieces in that bedroom, broken and bloodied and aching like never before. I lose track of time as I lay there, but eventually I sit up and collect myself, sniffling, and press a kiss to her forehead, the emptiness in my chest throbbing as I walk to the door, leaving her there.

The hospice nurse is sitting in the hall when I come out, and she takes my place, preparing my mother's body to be transported to the funeral home.

Heading downstairs, I leave the lights off, the moonlight filtering in through the windows the only guiding presence as I make my way to the greenhouse.

Kieran and my father are already sitting out there, having pulled up lawn chairs in front of the first row of plants. My brother holds up a Styrofoam cup, pointing to the pink chair between them.

I walk over and take the cup silently, plopping down in my designated spot.

"She loved chocolate shakes," Kieran murmurs after a moment, breaking the spell of quiet that'd settled around us, shattering the darkness.

My father reaches over with his free hand, squeezing my knee, and I tip my head back, admiring the stars through the glass roof as I suck on my straw, swishing the dessert around my teeth.

Tears prick my eyes again, blurring the sky until it becomes a kaleidoscope of color and souls, strangely comforting in their ambiguity.

Closing my eyes, I blink the tears away, focusing on the way my breathing comes and goes from my lungs without fail, without conscious thought, noting the things I can control and releasing the ones I can't.

CHAPTER THIRTY FOUR

Boyd

Ripping the plastic smock from around my neck, I walk to the apartment bathroom and rinse the stains from my hands, glancing at myself in the vanity. Aside from some of the splatter, everything else looks normal. There's no blood on my collar, no evidence of the brain matter smeared on the walls just outside, which is good since I don't exactly have time for a second shower.

Riley hogs all the hot water, anyway.

Drying my hands on a paper towel, I adjust the lapels of my suit and exit the bathroom, scanning the studio in all its horrible glory. LeeAnn's ex-boyfriend, a skinhead who made the mistake of staying at the house she was supposed to be at, lays on a gurney with his intestines half hanging out of his abdomen, his blood painting the tarp spread out on the floor.

His refusal to tell me where my darling mother is was not met with mercy — that word doesn't exist in my vocabulary anymore where she's concerned.

Since the night I found Romeo trying to gut Riley like a fucking fish, LeeAnn's been in hiding, skipping her usual drop spots and bouncing from house to house, somehow evading even my top private investigators.

Considering the things she has to atone for, she's playing her cards right. But the time on her freedom dwindles with each passing day, my anger for the woman mounting every time I don't find her.

Turns out, the person who'd attacked Kieran and Craig earlier this year and sent me the blackmail on the flash drive had been Juliet Harrison's mom, who had ties to the human trafficking ring Murphy Ivers was involved in that Kieran got shut down. Hurting financially, she'd been seeking revenge and only ended up saddled with felony charges.

But she hadn't acted alone — we tracked the operation back to the Bianchis and had been watching them closely ever since, waiting for a slipup. I didn't mention this to the team at Ivers International, but my hunch was that Riley was meant to be sold to Romeo the night he assaulted her and that my mom was somehow more involved with the mob than ever before.

So, I've been scouring the ends of the earth ever since, destroying anyone who gets in my way.

Today, though, all of that gets pushed to the back burner as I close up the apartment and head back into the house for a pair of sleek, black oxfords to match my suit. I'm lacing them up when Riley hobbles down the stairs wearing a pair of black jeans and an oversized sweater — funeral attire, but also the norm for her these days.

Her blonde hair is cropped in a short bob, sticking out by her ears in different angles; it'd been matted with so much blood and skin after the attack that she decided to chop it all off, and she looked slightly freer because of it.

The shadows follow her, though, same as they do me. Demons lurking everywhere she looks, waiting to consume her and drag her to Hell. Her blue eyes aren't as bright as they used to be, replaced with a guarded ambivalence that sometimes chills me to my core. The mangled skin on her cheek where they grafted part of her thigh and the scar at the corner of her mouth are the only visible reminders, but neither of us need the proof.

She's safe, though, and for now, that's what I'm focusing on. Becoming a sudden parent to a teenager is hard enough without the added pressure of trying to fix her.

At least, that's what the online parenting forums say. I check them before bed each night, searching for reassurance from strangers on the internet that I'm not completely fucking this up.

Hard to beat the job LeeAnn did, though.

"We aren't going to the wake, right?" Riley asks, leaning on the stair railing. "I don't think I can look at a dead body right now."

I grunt, lifting my other foot and tying that shoe.

"You know, I was legally dead for two minutes back in May," she continues, sending a pang of guilt scorching down my sternum.

"I'm aware, yes."

"I just don't want someone to mistake me as a corpse and add me to the collection of bodies beneath the St. Killarney Cathedral."

"Riley," I snap, irritation spiking. "Stop joking about that. You don't look like a fucking corpse."

She shrugs—at one time, my tone would have bothered her, as if she directly correlated the way I spoke with the way I felt about her. Which, I suppose, I did before.

The resentment is still there, a dull ache I'm not quite sure what to do with, but it's buried beneath fear now. The expectation of loss, something I've become too familiar with in my life.

The only thing that truly terrifies me.

Now, though, Riley doesn't appear to be affected by or interested in anything, and I'm not exactly sure how to handle that, either. So far since we began our living arrangement, we've just been coexisting in the same house, not bonding and certainly not healing.

Part of the reason is because I'm so hellbent on finding LeeAnn and Romeo, but the other is because I just don't know what the hell I'm doing.

Too many parenting books and articles say that the most important thing is to *show up* for your kid, but that's all I do and it doesn't seem to be working. Riley slips farther from my grasp every single day, farther into a pit of despair, and I don't think I'm equipped to pull her from it.

Can't even figure out how to pull *myself* out.

"If you keep joking like that, they're going to try to make you go to therapy again," I tell her, getting to my feet and swiping my keys off the counter. "Remember how well that went?"

"Well, if they didn't keep trying to get me to talk about the night I *literally died* over and over, maybe I wouldn't have *accidentally* set fire to the bathroom."

"They ruled it arson, which means it wasn't accidental."

"Doesn't really matter, since you got them to drop the charges." She smiles sweetly, but it's the fake kind of sweet—the kind that still sours in my mouth, even five months after my last taste of it.

We drive to the cemetery in silence, her fiddling with the vents on the dash of my car, me popping sunflower seeds because I gave up joints in an effort to be a better influence on her.

It fucking sucks.

Although, it certainly doesn't suck worse than burying the woman who'd been like a mother to you the last seven years, accepting you as part of her family when you never fully felt like you had one. And as we park and head to the burial site, the morning sun far too bright for such a depressing occasion, the realization that we're *burying* Mona Ivers is a sucker punch to my gut, winding me before we've even approached the crowd.

What's left of the Ivers family stands at the open plot, a hole in the ground in front of a massive stone monument, talking to Father O'Shea — if grief could be embodied, it'd be the three of them standing together, pale and dressed in all black, as if Death itself split into three souls and made its home in them.

I approach Kieran and Craig, offering them a handshake; Craig pulls me in for one of those half hugs, patting my back, but my best friend hangs back, his arm wrapped around the shoulders of his fiancée, more sullen than I've ever seen him.

Juliet gives me a little smile. I haven't seen much of the two of them since they moved in together — family dinners at the mansion stopped that day at the church, and with Riley needing constant supervision, I just haven't been around much. I go to work, I go home, and that's about it.

"Boyd, we're really glad you came," Craig says, clamping down on my shoulder. He smells like scotch and sorrow, and I pull back to keep the scent from bleeding into me.

Nodding slightly in return, I stare straight ahead at the hole in the ground where Mona's casket sits, desperately trying not to look at the redhead to my left. My heart kicks at my chest, trying to break free and launch itself at her, but my head knows better.

Knows all too well the damage that Fiona Ivers can wreak on a man.

"You gonna stop by for the reception?" Kieran asks, glancing at Riley behind me. "We're having it back at the church."

"Still surprised you're able to step inside one," Juliet says to him, rubbing her hand over his chest with a soft giggle. He grins, the gesture lighting up his entire face, and kisses the crown of her head, pinching her bicep.

"Who's the kid?" Kieran asks, before I can answer his first question. He squints at her, as if trying to figure out how he recognizes her face.

"That's Riley," I say, hooking my thumb in her direction.

She crosses her arms over her chest, turning to stare at a commotion coming from another plot across the cemetery. Silence is something she's adopted, too, especially around strangers and especially in public, and the reminder prickles in my stomach, churning like acid.

"Well," Kieran says after a beat, raising an eyebrow at me. "Riley, see if you can't get Boyd to bring you by the church, okay? The Montaltos catered, and we all know there's nothing better than home-cooked Italian comfort food. Except maybe garlic salmon."

They walk past, clapping me on the shoulder as they go, and I glance at Fiona for the first time since arriving. She's watching me, her big brown eyes somehow full of warmth despite the misery hidden in them, a thoughtful expression plastered on her perfect face.

My heart stutters, desire and pain coming together to form a ball of fire that lodges in my throat, choking me at the same time it burns. Her fingers flex at her sides, temptation making them shake, but she doesn't start tapping, just sucks in a deep breath and meets my gaze head-on.

"Boyd."

The lilt in her voice cracks open the chasm of longing that I sealed inside a vault months ago, just like that—one fucking word and I melt for her all over again, stuck with the painful reality that so much time has passed and nothing at all has really changed.

I bite the inside of my cheek until I taste the coppery tang of my blood, and give her a polite nod. "Fiona."

Riley steps forward, glancing between us with her eyebrows raised. "I'm Riley," she says, surprising me with the voluntary information. My eyes snap to her as she studies Fiona, a curiosity lighting her blue eyes. "Boyd's—"

"Sister," Fiona finishes, giving us a thin smile. "I remember your picture."

At my sides, my hands tremble so bad I have to stuff them in my pockets to hide it—anger, embarrassment, so much *lust* all directed toward this one woman melds together inside of me, making it hard to concentrate on anything.

"You've seen my picture?" Riley asks, and I don't miss the slight sense of awe in her tone.

"Just one." Fiona tucks her hair behind her ears, and Father O'Shea calls out to her from his makeshift podium twenty feet away.

She glances at him, then back at us. "It was nice to meet you, Riley. And Boyd..." She hesitates, chewing on her bottom lip. "You look good. Mom would've been glad to see you here."

And with that, she walks off, leaving the chasm inside me unattended, bleeding profusely just like it was five months ago.

Like it never stopped in the first place.

CHAPTER THIRTY FIVE

Fiona

Pushing the tortellini around on my plate, I scan the reception hall for the fiftieth time since arriving—not that I'm keeping track, or anything. It's just that every time I look up from the table, my gaze is drawn to the front doors, waiting to see if he shows up.

Ignoring the despair clotting my arteries, I let out a sigh and study the shrine to my mother at the center of the table—votive candles and various sizes of her high school graduation photo and a photo from a family vacation when she was still pregnant with me sit around a small hibiscus plant from the greenhouse.

It wasn't easy getting ready to come here, but I've been prepping for this day for weeks. If nothing else, I owe it to her to make an effort, even if some days I miss her more than I can bear.

People bustle in and out all around us, coming from all exits — the bathroom, the kitchen where the buffet is set up, the offices upstairs where some of the men keep slinking off for business liaisons and brandy, leaving the women to grieve amongst themselves.

Fewer people turned out for the funeral than I'd thought, maybe afraid our curse would extend to them if they showed any support, or maybe giving us privacy. We'd had a closed casket at the wake, and the interment had been quick, none of us wanting to drag out putting our matriarch to rest any more than we already had.

I hadn't expected Boyd to show up at all, although maybe I wasn't giving him enough credit. Or perhaps giving myself too much.

To say I was shocked he brought his sister to the cemetery would be an understatement, although the shock turned to fascination when I took in her punk-rock appearance, punctuated with facial scars and a chip on her shoulder.

The way she ignored my brother but spoke to me made a root of hope sprout inside my chest, waiting for the sunshine and rain to help it bloom. Makes me think that maybe Boyd talks about me, and if he still talks about me, maybe there's still a chance I didn't ruin us permanently.

Juliet catches me looking around and takes a sip of her wine, the solitaire diamond on her finger glittering beneath the overhead lighting. "Are you ever gonna tell anyone what happened between you and Boyd?"

My saliva gets caught in my windpipe as I turn toward her, coughing in surprise. "What are you talking about?"

She rolls her eyes, brushing hair off her shoulder. Since that day at the church, the day my brother sacrificed himself for her, we've been spending a lot more time together, working on friendship—there's an otherworldly sadness that exists in her soul, something murky and unclear, that I find refreshing.

Not that it's there, but because she doesn't try to hide it. Since moving in with Kieran, she seems a lot happier, but I can still sense it just under the surface, a constant burden that she chooses to embrace rather than smother.

Controlling what you can and releasing what you can't.

"I know a secret relationship when I see one. It's obvious *something* was going on with you two," she says, quirking a blonde brow. "Then all of the sudden, nothing. Kieran says Boyd went from being slightly tolerable for a time in the spring to completely unbearable, with no outside factors seeming to have contributed. Sounds a lot like heartbreak, to me."

"Maybe you should leave the armchair psychology to the psych major," I say, tossing a piece of garlic bread in her direction.

Mrs. Alessi, the owner of Opulence, and Mrs. Thomas, a city commissioner, stop by our table and offer their condolences, pinching my cheeks and leaving behind stale perfume and bad breath.

Leaning in, Juliet lowers her voice. "Maybe you should swallow your pride and go talk to him."

"He'd have to *be* here for me to do that."

"Lucky for you, he just walked in." Her blue eyes sparkle as she glances over my shoulder, giving me a wry smile. "And found you immediately."

Turning my head, I cast a quick look around the room and spot him standing under the archway leading into the hall, as if undecided if he should come in or not. His sister's at his side, eyeing the crowd like she'd rather die than step foot in the same room as these people, but he's watching *me*.

His hazel gaze burns a path straight to my core, igniting my skin in a way that feels wholly inappropriate given the situation.

But that's what happens when you deny yourself the things you want most in life — when given the chance, the longing comes back in full force, the taste of the forbidden, the broken, the irreparably damaged too great to resist.

Snapping my head back around, I press my thighs together, trying to relieve myself of the ache he awakens in me. *Filthy sex in a custom suit,* Bea calls him, even though she knows I despise the reference to the one and only time we ever fucked.

Unfortunately, I hate the reference because she's not wrong.

"How are you in awkward situations?" Juliet asks, playing with the heart-shaped locket around her neck.

I glare. "*Not good,* Juliet. Not good at all."

"Well, you'd better get good."

"That's not even proper English."

"Whatever, your lover is on his way over, and if looks could kill, you'd probably be on fire right now."

Somehow, I feel like I am.

My fingers shake beneath the table, and I clamp them around my thighs, resisting the urge to fall into old tics. The bite of my nails against my skin makes me wince, but I focus on the pain and try to regulate my breathing against it.

"Boyd and Riley!" Juliet greets, their presence large and looming behind me. "Glad you two could make it after all. Have a seat, my sister's around here somewhere. I'll tell her you guys haven't eaten yet."

There's a flash of panic behind Riley's eyes that I don't quite understand, and she glances to her brother, who stands in my blind spot.

"Oh, no," Boyd says quickly, a hand coming to rest on the back of my chair, making my spine go rigid. His thumb grazes the buttons on the back of my dress, his heat seeping into me like spilled coffee, incinerating my resolve in an instant. "We already ate. Just stopped by to say hi to Craig and Kieran before we head home."

"I'll show you where they're at," Juliet offers, pushing her chair back and rounding the table. Riley plops down beside me, reaching to fiddle with one of the votive candles in the middle of the table.

Boyd clears his throat, removing his hand from my chair. "Riley, let's go."

"Sounds boring," she says, shrugging. "I'll catch up with you later."

I feel him hesitate, and when I finally raise my eyes, I'm met with his intense stare, losing myself in the longing and hatred raging in his depths. "I can stay with her," I mutter, unable to break away.

His nostrils flare, and he glances at his sister once more, the hard set of his jaw stern and intimidating and completely hot.

Jesus, what is wrong with me? Where's the evidence that he's any different from the guy I couldn't be with a few months ago?

"You know what?" Juliet says, clasping her hands together. "Why don't I show Riley the dessert table? Surely you have room for carrot cake. My sister makes the cream cheese frosting from scratch. And Fiona can show you where the guys went, Boyd—she knows this place better than I do."

I can tell he *really* doesn't want to take his sights off his sister, but he doesn't protest when she willingly puts her hand in Juliet's and lets her tug her away. He stands there staring at the spot they disappear through, shoulders more tense than I've ever seen them.

"It's really good cake, for what it's worth," I say. He turns, eyebrows raised as if surprised I'm speaking to him. "I think, with carrot cake especially, the icing can really make or break it, and Caroline's is perfect. Plus, the cake itself has this moist quality—"

"*Fiona.*" The curt way he interrupts, like I'm an annoyance and not something he finds the least bit entertaining, cuts deeper than it should, given we aren't anything to each other. "Can you show me where your brother and father are, or do I need to just find them myself?"

Heat sears my cheeks, and I just know my face is as red as my hair. Pushing my chair back, I get to my feet and smooth out my dress, swallowing over the embarrassment coating my throat. "I'll show you."

We walk upstairs in silence, passing paneled walls with the various paintings of patron saints and portraits of the Pope over the years hanging up. My nerves are needle pricks beneath my skin, making me dizzy even as I try to get them under control.

Guilt floods me, warring with the desire funneling into my veins, leaving me feeling completely powerless against the pull Boyd Kelly has on me.

The door to the admin office is locked when we get to it, and even though I knock as hard as I can, no one comes to open it.

He leans against the wall, turning his head toward the crown molding on the ceiling, and I take a moment to drink him in after all this time. The ink on his skin, the honey-colored hair that's a little longer than it once was, swooping down just right over his forehead, the sharp angle of his jawline.

All the things that fueled my lust for him in the first place, culminating together now to remind me of how badly I messed up.

How badly I miss him.

How, when I went to bed the night my mother died, all I wanted to do was call him. Have him comfort me like he used to, distract me until I wasn't spiraling and couldn't feel anything but the pleasure he was giving me.

But that's not coping, that's codependency—at least, according to Professor Garrett, who, in lieu of therapy, has become something of a mentor for me. Even if she doesn't realize it.

Boyd clears his throat, shifting as if he's uncomfortable. "I'm really sorry about your mom. She was an amazing lady."

When I swallow, it feels like I'm eating gravel, and I force a smile as I nod toward the door. I don't want his condolences, or his pity. *I want him.*

"I'm sure they'll be out in a minute," I say, turning back toward the stairs, eager to put some distance between us. To clear myself of the dirty thoughts I'm having while I'm supposed to be in mourning.

His hand lashes out, encircling my wrist, keeping me in place. "Fiona."

Pinching my eyes closed, I fold my lips together with a devastated sigh.

"Fiona," he repeats, this time with more force, like he can't believe he's saying it in the first place. I can feel the restraint in his hold, can sense the fear holding him back, reminding him that he's supposed to hate me.

I shake my head. "Please stop saying my name like that."

"Like what?"

"Like you wish you'd never stopped."

Tilting my head up, I see his eyes darken with lust, liquid heat spilling into the caramel swirls. His jaw tics, the muscle jumping beneath the stubble, and he tugs me into him, the clean yet crisp scent of his expensive cologne invading my senses and making me lightheaded.

"I wish we'd never started," he rasps, roving his gaze over my face as my body temperature spikes. "You are without a doubt my biggest regret, Fiona Ivers."

My mouth parts, my stomach dropping at the admission. I gulp, noting how the way he looks at me, how he clutches me closer with each harsh breath escaping his nostrils, seems at odds with the venom spewing from his lips.

It feels like a lie, like he's trying to convince himself that what he says is true, but the words ring hollow, rattling in my ears. It's pride and pain mixing together, a way to punish me for hurting him.

Licking my lips, something strange comes over me—a sense of defiance I haven't felt in ages, the need to prove him wrong flaring deep inside me, blazing through my veins as we stand off in the hallway.

Anyone could pass us or come out of the office at any given moment. Anyone could stroll up here and see me defiling my mother's funeral. But that doesn't stop me from leaning in and accepting his challenge.

Reaching down, I run my palm over the zipper of his dress pants, my mouth watering at the distinct bulge waiting just beneath. Raising up onto my tiptoes, I press my lips to his ear and squeeze. "Might want to tell that to your cock."

"My cock and I aren't exactly on speaking terms," he replies.

"Is that because he remembers what it feels like to be inside of me?" Batting my eyelashes, I pull back to look into his eyes. They burn bright with molten lust as he hardens under my fingertips, making my core spasm.

A feral sound tears from his throat, and his hand slips from my hand to grip my elbow as he pushes me up against a closed door; it falls open with the force of my back hitting it, flinging us into darkness, and I get déjà vu as my ass connects with what feels like a sink.

Before I have a chance to collect my bearings, his mouth descends on mine, all of our pent-up tension pouring into the kiss. His hands are everywhere, scraping and pinching and tugging, as his lips steal the breath from my body and simultaneously replace it.

He pushes the cardigan off my shoulders and rips it from my arms, tossing it behind him, then pushes the straps of my short black dress down, sliding my arms from them one by one. My chest flushes even though he can't see me, a gasp falling from my mouth as he dips his head, yanks the cups of my lacy bra down, and sucks one of my nipples into his mouth.

His tongue flicks against the puckered peak, making me squirm and pull his head flush against me, and he switches to the opposite breast, sucking so hard I can feel my skin breaking under the suction.

Our hearts beat in time against each other as he hauls me into his arms, pushing my dress up around my waist and shoving me against the sink. I hear rustling, his hand fumbling, and then the vanity lights come on, revealing our dirty passion.

We're in a private bathroom, a toilet and sink and a Jesus calendar the only objects inside, letting lust block out everything else in the world. Letting ourselves succumb to it once again, like this worked well the last time.

But right now, I can't find it in myself to care.

CHAPTER THIRTY SIX

Fiona

Deep purple bruises dot both of my breasts, lesions I barely even registered as they were happening. Boyd's eyes glow as he runs his thumb over the spots, and he slides his hand up, smoothing over my throat, before gripping below my chin and tilting my head back.

My ass sits on the edge of the sink while he licks his free thumb and slips it between my legs, pushing the elastic of my plain cotton panties aside and finding my clit immediately.

He swirls in tight, rhythmic circles that have me panting within seconds, grasping at the dress shirt he has on, trying to ground myself into the moment.

"Gonna fuck you in the light this time," he rasps in my ear, drawing me nearer to the edge of euphoria with each stroke of my pussy, each puff of breath that rolls over my skin. "Make sure you can't hide your shame in the dark."

"Wait!" I squeal, feeling the head of his cock bump against my entrance; my core expands, desperate to suck him in, but my brain is running a million miles a minute. "I'm seeing someone."

He pauses, lifting his chin to raise his eyebrows. "*What?*"

"Well, we've been on one date."

"Did you let him fuck you?"

I shake my head, my cheeks so hot I feel faint.

He scoffs, pressing against me again. "Doesn't fucking count, then."

"*Wait.*" Huffing, I press my hand to his chest. "Have you been with anyone else?"

"I don't even *dream* about anyone else, princess."

It all happens with lightning speed; my orgasm crests as he finishes his sentence, my pussy apparently starved for his attention, and then he's unbuckling his slacks and letting them fall to his knees, fisting his angry dark pink cock, rolling the silver barbell on its underside over my sensitive clit, and pushing into me before I've even recovered from my haze of explosive desire.

373

The pinch of pain snaps me out of it, though, and when Boyd drops his hands to my legs, tightening their grip on his waist, I wrap my arms around his neck and hold on.

He fucks me hard against the sink, a punishment all its own—like each manic thrust in is his way of releasing the anger and hurt I've caused him, and each time he pulls out to the tip, I feel empty and wanton, before he slams back in again.

Part of the sink pulls away from the wall with the force of his fucking, and I let out a string of incoherent sounds as pressure coils tight in my stomach, his piercing seeming to rub against a spot inside of me, creating unimaginable ecstasy.

"Touch yourself for me, princess," he rasps, the strain in his voice indicating that he's close. "Work your clit and come on my dick so I can fill you up."

Reaching my hand between us, I obey his command, my fingers rubbing, the friction making my pussy spasm around him. He groans, long and low, his pumps growing erratic as he pulls back just enough to watch me.

"Look at me," he snaps, catching his bottom lip between his teeth. The fact that he's still completely dressed while I'm in a state of disarray makes it a thousand times more erotic, and I lock my gaze with his as I combust, shocks of electricity zinging through each of my nerve endings.

He comes at the same time, seating himself as deep inside of me as he can get, groaning against my neck as he pulses his release. We're slicked with sweat and reek of sex, but for a second, it's easy to pretend like nothing went wrong with us in the first place.

Until he rips himself from me and stalks to the other side of the room, glaring like I've done something wrong.

"You're seeing someone?"

Sliding off the sink with my jelly legs, I adjust my dress and pick my cardigan off the floor, tying it around my waist. I feel him leak down my thigh, but he's standing in front of the toilet paper looking like someone two seconds from a psychotic break, so I ignore it, anxiety sliding over me like a second skin.

"Was I supposed to just sit around and wait for you to get your shit together, Boyd? Supposed to die hoping you'd come back to me?"

"Goddamnit. *Goddamnit.* I am such a fucking weak bastard." He laughs, but the sound is short and startled. Chaotic. Lifting his hand, he points a finger in my direction, wagging it like I'm in trouble. "*You* dumped *me*, Fiona. Stop trying to make it seem like I had any say in the matter."

"I didn't *want* to dump you. I just wanted to be able to trust you." I swallow, my eyes burning. "I wanted you to choose me over the facade the rest of the world gets. I *still* want you to choose me."

His mouth opens, a response poised on his tongue, but then it clamps closed like he thinks better of saying it.

Reaching up, he scrubs his hands down his face, exhaling throatily. "You wanted my secrets. The biggest one is waiting for me downstairs."

I take that as my cue to leave, thinking he's saying he needs to get back to her, but when my hand touches the doorknob, he continues.

"That night you showed up on my doorstep, wanting to get dinner, Riley was in my guest bedroom upstairs, *dead*. She'd been attacked earlier that night, and I brought home a bloodied, battered body that I couldn't even fucking recognize. For a full two minutes, I lost her — and she doesn't fucking let me forget it."

My heart stalls in my chest, pain lancing the organ at his confession. I search his face for signs of deceit, feeling my stomach revolt against his words — against the pain of the truth.

"What's worse," he says with a dark, hollow chuckle. "Is that it was our biological mother's doing. The woman who gave me up as a teenager after abusing me my entire life, emotionally and physically, letting her drug buddies do whatever they pleased, and still somehow controlling me even after I was out of her custody."

As he speaks, violence vibrates off his body in waves, making tension coil so tight in my stomach that it cramps, tectonic plates shifting to make room for an earthquake.

Is this what I wanted?

"You asked me why I went to therapy as a kid — how does being gang-raped before you even really know what sex is,
376

because your mother decided a quick fix was important enough to warrant that against her own kid sound? How about beating the fuck out of any man that stepped into our shitty little trailer, because I knew I'd need to establish dominance early on, or else I'd get fucked up again? Killing when I became a teenager to avoid the same fate? That a good enough fucking reason for you, *princess*?"

Tears sting my eyes, my throat tight as he bleeds himself dry, tearing his heart from his chest and tossing it at my feet. "Boyd, I'm —"

He holds up his hands, barring me from coming closer. "The *worst* part is, that I could've spared my sister if I wasn't such a chickenshit. If I'd gotten over myself and just taken her in any of the dozens of times she asked, I could've saved her from a lifetime of trauma. But I didn't, because I let my pride get in the way, like I always do. Because I was scared, and hurt, and trying to reconcile how LeeAnn could keep my sister but not want me and couldn't shake the hold she had over me. I'm *weak*, Fiona. That's my big fucking secret."

Covering my mouth with my hands to keep the sobs at bay, I swallow over the knot in my throat, nausea burning a hole in my stomach.

My mind reels from each of his revelations, trying to piece together that kind of trauma and fit it into the cracks of the broken man I've come to know.

How could I ever have thought he was something I could fix?

Guilt settles on my chest like a cement block, crushing me beneath its weight, when I realize how much worse I must have made things. I meet his furious gaze, trying to think of something to say, but the words never come.

Misery ebbs inside the chambers of my heart, pumping through my bloodstream, and eventually Boyd just sighs, his body sagging against the wall.

"I'm sorry, Fiona, that I didn't want to expose you to all of that. Sorry I couldn't find it in me to fight for you, when I can barely find it in me to fight for myself, sometimes." He pushes off the wall and steps toward me, reaching out and cradling my jaw in one hand. "This isn't me telling you so you can feel sorry for me. It's me saying... I think you were right to end things. Not a day has passed by that I've stopped being in love with you, despite what you think about that, but four months ago I wasn't the man you deserved, hard as I tried to be. I'm probably not even the one you deserve now. To be honest, I don't know what the fuck I'm doing ninety percent of the time."

I lean into his palm, absorbing the soft feel of it against my cheek.

"You broke me, Fiona. Decided that what I was giving you wasn't enough. And while I agreed, because I thought that's what was best for *you*, I'm not over it. " He swallows, releasing me, taking half of my heart with him. "It's nothing personal, it's just..." Trailing off, he shrugs, and I clench my jaw to steel against the tears threatening, all of my emotions waging a battle inside me that I'm not sure can really be won.

"Just… leave me alone, okay?" he says, and I scoff when he pulls away, heading for the door just as someone knocks on it. Throwing it open, we're met with the piercing green gaze of my brother, whose fist is raised as if he was about to knock a second time.

His eyes widen, darting between the two of us inside the bathroom and taking in the state of our disarray, and I curse under my breath, knowing this might make things worse.

Boyd clears his throat, adjusting the collar of his suit, and slides past Kieran without a word, leaving the place ten times more awkward than it was before.

"So…" Kieran says, leaning against the doorframe. "That just happened."

Letting out a low groan, I bury my face in my hands, wishing now more than ever that my mom was around to talk to. Grief spirals inside my chest, a fire searing through my muscles, suffocating as it works over me.

I glance at my brother. "*Please*, can we not talk about this?"

Pursing his lips, he studies me. "Depends. How embarrassed are you right now, on a scale from one to ten?"

"A million."

He snorts, walking in and closing the door as I lean against the wall, sliding my back down until my butt hits the floor, letting the waves of a spiral wash over me.

Control what you can and release what you can't.

Kieran sits on the floor beside me, stretching his legs out in front of him, and sighs. "I miss her."

Sniffling and grateful for the change of subject, I nod, resting my head on his shoulder. "Me too."

Sucking in a deep breath, I exorcise the bad emotions from my body, tears spilling silently until I'm dried out, and then I close my eyes and try to focus on what comes next, not on what already is, absorbing the comfort my brother is offering.

Focus on what I can fix.

CHAPTER THIRTY SEVEN

Boyd

I slam my office phone down on its receiver just as Craig walks inside, holding a small cardboard box in his hands. It's been a week since I tried to torture information out of LeeAnn's ex, but he ended up dying before I actually got anything out of him.

According to Kal, the expert, I'm too emotional when it comes to my approach, and it makes me sloppy. He also thinks I should invest in therapy or stress balls, and I'm starting to wonder if he isn't right.

It's not just the fact that I can't find LeeAnn, though, that has me wired—it's the phone calls, the texts, the emails I continue to get from the only girl to ever shatter my heart into a million pieces.

It's the fact that since I fucked Fiona in that church bathroom at her mother's funeral, I haven't been able to think about anything else since. I can't concentrate on my work, can't concentrate on Riley, can't even focus when I'm scouring the Crystal Knuckle, getting my ribs kicked in just to see if anyone's talking about Romeo Bianchi.

The pity that shone in her eyes was exactly what I've been trying to avoid this entire time.

Pity changes the way you see a person. You don't pity the strong, or the warriors, or the survivors. You pity victims, martyrs, and the weak. Pity isn't love — it's an emotional barrier, something you erect that keeps you from having to feel someone else's pain.

It's selfish and insulting, and her constant attempts to contact me after I asked her to leave me alone don't necessarily bode well. I can't tell if she's genuinely sorry, or if she's only trying to absolve herself of guilt.

And I don't know which I want less.

Not to mention, Kieran hasn't spoken a single word to me since that afternoon, and though I know he's busy with work and renovating his cabin, I can't help the impending sense of doom that his silence casts over me.

"Special delivery from a secret admirer," Craig says, tossing the box onto my desk and leaning against the leather chair. We'd all been expecting him to take a leave of absence after Mona's passing, but two days after the funeral he'd been holed up in his office, working on securing new international accounts, throwing himself into the work like he needs the distraction.

Like father, like daughter.

I push the box back, annoyance stretching thin across my skull, a dull ache that Fiona keeps prodding at. "Why are you encouraging her?"

"I'm her father, and you've been like a third son to me." He shrugs, running his tie through his fingers. "Am I crazy to want you kids to work things out and be happy?"

"Nothing to work out," I say, sitting back in my chair. "Nothing going on between us in the first place."

He rolls his eyes and scratches at his chin, his five o'clock shadow making him look decades older than he really is. Or perhaps that's the grief. "Are you forgetting who you're talking to, boy? I have plenty of footage I can show of you coming and going from my house during the wee hours of the night. If I hadn't seen you with my own eyes going into Fiona's room that one night, I'd be questioning your relationship with Kieran, but alas. Here we are."

Here we are. As if existence is that simple and can be explained away so easily.

Tapping my fingers on the edge of my desk, I sigh as another email comes through, the pop-up window automatically expanding on my screen.

From: chaoticprincess@iversinternational.net

RE: Forgiveness

I have to assume at this point that you're just not getting my messages. Maybe they go to spam because I use too many emojis? I don't know, but I had Dad set me up a company mailbox just in case.

I'm sorry about the other day. I'm sorry about a lot of things.

I'd like to try and make things up to you.

Sincerely,

The most sorry girl in the world.

PS: Am I still your emergency medical contact? Just wondering, no reason related to the box I had Dad bring.

Snorting, I steal a glance at Craig as he watches me, and raise an eyebrow. "What, did you guys time this?"

He shrugs, pushing to his feet. "Surely, I have no idea what you're talking about." As he walks toward the door, he pauses. "Word of advice? If you want to be with her, *be* with her. Life's way too damn short to play games. Whatever problems you two have can be sorted out, but every day you spend apart is a day you risk losing her before you get her back. Kieran will get over it."

As the door closes behind him, I pull my keyboard forward, shoving a handful of sunflower seeds into my mouth as I type out my reply. Glancing at the little plastic window on top of the box she sent, I see the label says ONE DOZEN

CHOCOLATE CHIP COOKIES from the bakery that Juliet's sister owns downtown, Care's Crazy Cakes.

Despite myself, a smile spreads over my lips as my fingers move.

From: bkelly93@iversinternational.net

RE: Forgiveness RE: Space

If you want forgiveness, maybe don't send me death threats in the shape of cookies.

Fitting email, by the way.

Sincerely,

This is fucking ridiculous.

PS: Yes.

PS, PS: How does your boyfriend feel about you stalking me?

Her reply comes moments later, and I can't help wondering what it is she's doing right now — if she's in a campus library or the Starbucks downtown, if she's thinking about getting fucked in the bathroom at St. Killarney's the way I am as she types her responses, or if she's just happy I've finally responded.

Are you really sure you want to go back down this road, Kelly?

My computer pings, her newest email showing up at the top of the thread.

From: chaoticprincess@iversinternational.net

RE: Forgiveness RE: Space RE: Friendship

Thought you'd enjoy the cookies, honestly. I know how you like things that you think are bad for you.

I'm not one of them, you know.

Bad for you, I mean.

I mean, I *can* be, if that's something you're into. But, you know, health-wise I'm really kind of perfect.

Sincerely,

Answer my phone call next time.

PS: Good to know.

PS, PS: Not my boyfriend.

PS, PS, PS: Would it be inappropriate to tell you I got myself off to thoughts of you fucking me in the church last night? Probably, but I'm not above coercing you into a cup of coffee.

Cursing under my breath, I pinch the bridge of my nose and spit my sunflower seeds into the trash can beside my desk, the image of Fiona playing with her sweet little cunt almost enough to make me crack. It's ridiculous that she knows how to play me.

Ridiculous that I'm tempted to take her up on her offer, all things considered.

So much for willpower.

Shutting down my computer, I grab my coat off the back of my chair and sling it over my shoulders, locking up my office as I exit the room. Craig's light in his office is still burning bright, and for a second, I think about checking in and seeing if he's pulling another late night, but I choose not to, not wanting to pry where it's none of my business.

The man can deal with the loss of the love of his life however he wants, I suppose.

I know I am.

Riley's splayed out on the couch when I get home, Dottie having picked her up from KTP and dropped her off with a stockpot full of soup, as is the Monday tradition. She flips through the categories on Netflix aimlessly, not stopping long enough to actually note what any titles are.

"Clam chowder again," she deadpans as I close the front door and secure the deadbolts and security system for the night, kicking my loafers off as I punch in the code that alerts the police the second someone steps on my property.

Installing it was the only way to get Riley to sleep at night.

"Did you eat?" I ask, hanging my coat on the rack in the foyer, glancing at her as I walk to where the pot sits on the stove, removing the lid.

"Yep," she calls, but as I stare at the soup, seemingly untouched with no dirty bowls or spoons in sight, I find it hard to believe.

She never eats. And I pretend I don't notice, because I'm not sure what to do about it. Not sure how you coax someone who went through what she did back to the brink of sanity.

It's not like it was with Fiona, who could be drawn off the ledge when I made her submit, made her let go of her thoughts. Riley isn't the submissive type, probably from having grown up needing to intimidate the people LeeAnn hangs around, and so if I push her too far, she might just break.

And I have no clue how I'd even begin to glue those pieces back together.

I eat quickly, downing two bowls at the sink before heading into the living room, lifting her legs so I can flop down on the couch beside her, letting out a groan as my muscles relax for the first time today.

Her blue eyes flicker toward mine, one eyebrow raising. "Rough day?"

"Rough life."

She smirks. "I don't think that's how the saying is supposed to go."

Sighing, I tip my head back and rest it on the back of the couch, staring up at the chipped paint on the ceiling, my body exhausted. I feel her toe poke my stomach and turn to look at her.

"Are you okay?"

"I'm supposed to ask you that."

"Well, you already know my answer." She flexes her feet, pulling them off my lap and curling her knees to her chest. "But
388

you seem off. Since the funeral, actually, you've been more surly than usual."

"*Surly*? Jesus, how old am I to you?"

"Ancient." She smirks, the closest I can get to a smile these days. "Does your mood have anything to do with Fiona Ivers?"

Heat creeps up my neck, and I roll my head back, eyes dancing across the ceiling. "No."

"Oh, okay liar." Pushing into a sitting position, she pulls up the sleeve of the oversized black sweatshirt she has on with some rock star logo on the front of it, and blinks at me expectantly. "Tell me about her."

"No."

"Fine, then I won't tell you about the black SUV I saw following me and Aunt Dottie home from school today."

My blood freezes at her words, the pump in my heart stalling out as they register. I sit up, eyes wide, apprehension slithering over my skin in the form of goose bumps. "The *what*?"

Shrugging like it's no big deal, she runs her fingers through her hair in an attempt at nonchalance, although I can tell by the way her bottom lip curls inward that she knows she could be in danger. It's why she fought to stay here with me in the first place over going to her dad's, and since I'm the one funding her KTP tuition, guardianship was easily granted when it became clear LeeAnn wasn't coming back for her.

I don't know who that hurt worse.

"Tell me about Fiona first, and then I'll tell you."

"Riley, this isn't a fucking game—"

"I *know*, Boyd. I'm freaking terrified, okay? But I didn't know how else to tell you without you immediately flying off the handle and going out to try and avenge me." Her voice shakes as she speaks, the only indication that she's feeling anything right now. "So, just... tell me about Fiona, just for a second, so I can think about something other than the fact that Mom might be coming to find me and finish the job as we speak."

"She's not—" Riley swallows, and I cut myself off, inhaling deeply even as violence spreads like ivy through my body, curling around my DNA and embedding itself there. "I'm in love with Fiona Ivers, okay? I have been since May, approximately two and a half months after I started pursuing her. But we aren't good for each other, so that's the end of that."

"What does that even mean?"

"Fuck if I know." I drag a hand through my hair, trying to control the thoughts running through my mind. "It means we have issues."

"Hm." Riley nods, thinking this over. "Well, I like her."

"You don't know her."

"I'm an excellent judge of character. Whatever it is, I'm sure you two will work things out."

Truth is, I selfishly still want to work things out, even though I shouldn't. Even though I know I should cut my ties to Fiona and let her live unencumbered by my existence.

Rolling my eyes at the second attempt of the day to get me to forgive Fiona, I sit up and pull my phone from my pocket, sending Finn Hanson and one of the private investigators I keep on retainer a text that says to procure any and all security footage of black SUVs driving near King's Trace Prep around four-thirty this afternoon. Turning to Riley, I raise an eyebrow.

"Enough about Fiona. Tell me whatever you can about this fucking SUV."

CHAPTER THIRTY EIGHT

Boyd

"You know," Kieran says as I hop out of the moving truck I rented, pulling a pair of leather gloves on. "If you wanted to apologize for fucking my sister behind my back, you didn't need to go to such theatrical measures. A simple sorry would probably work."

Ignoring him, I unlock the truck door and slide it upward, revealing the two bodies, bound and gagged, laying on the truck floor. He glances inside, raising his eyebrows, then gives me a nod.

"Angelo Bianchi and Francisco Moretti." He whistles, putting his hands on his hips. "What the fuck have you gotten yourself into, Kelly?"

With a grunt, I pull Angelo's body from the truck first, letting him drop to the ground with a thud, reveling in the crack that sounds when his face connects with the ground. I should feel bad about picking him up, but frankly, I'm running out of time to track down Romeo and LeeAnn, if my intel is any indication.

An offshore account in the Cayman Islands popped up around one in the morning last night, with the account holder's name being an alias Romeo used back when he was peddling kids. If he's planning on fleeing, then odds are LeeAnn is too, and once they're off the grid and out of the country, my resources dwindle significantly.

It's not like I can leave Riley to scour the earth for them. So, I need to catch them before they leave the state. The fact that they haven't already tells me there's something keeping them here, I just haven't figured out what.

The SUV that followed Riley home didn't have a license plate and was abandoned by the time we tracked it down, but I still think it's safe to assume it was one of the two trying to finish their job. Possibly why they're still around in the first place.

I'm hoping I can lure them to me somehow and act then.

Kieran drags Francisco's larger body out over the tailgate, letting gravity take over once he's halfway out of the truck. My best friend nods at the bodies, then looks at me.

"This is still a very Fiona-style apology, you know."

I roll my eyes, bending and gripping beneath Angelo's armpits, hauling him up and starting toward the house. "If you're fishing for information, you're in the wrong pond, Ivers."

"It's just, back in May, I asked if you were fucking my sister, and you said no." He mimics my movements with Francisco, and I shove open the front door, glancing around the inside of the gray stone house. The inside is completely protected with tarp, and I raise a questioning brow once we've gotten both bodies inside. He notices the look on my face and smirks, shaking his head. "Easy cleanup, and easy to replace before the construction workers come back."

Nodding, I walk over to the sawhorse where his bag of tools sits, digging around until I find a pair of pliers and a cat-o'-nine-tails, running my thumb over one of its metal claws.

"Anyway," Kieran says as I return, rolling Francisco's body because he likes to see people when they scream. "You said you weren't fucking her, and yet what I walked in on at my mother's funeral seemed a lot like a post-fuck argument. Am I wrong?"

"No," I grit out, wishing he'd drop it.

"So, what the fuck? You lied?"

Dropping to my knees, I set the tools on the floor and adjust the gag around Angelo's mouth. "Yeah, Kieran, I lied, because I was falling in love with your sister and couldn't shake the feeling that she didn't feel the same. That I wasn't good

394

enough for her to love. And surprise, I was right, because she dumped me not long after."

Tearing through Francisco's shirt, Kieran purses his lips, and I exhale, annoyance slithering down my spine — why does everyone feel entitled to knowledge about my relationship? Why the fuck can't I grieve in peace?

"We don't do *feelings*," I say, gesturing to the men in front of us. "This is our thing. How we bond. Not with me spilling my guts and hoping you don't kill me for being into your much younger sister."

He rolls his eyes, yanking the gag from around Francisco's mouth and holding open the man's jaw; he's unconscious now, but when he wakes, the pain from the tooth extraction will be all he thinks about.

"Whatever, I told you I didn't care about that. Sounds like you were insecure and so you kept her a secret." He watches while I position the pliers in my hand, and shrugs. "For what it's worth, Fiona doesn't waste time on people she doesn't love. So, I think you're wrong about her."

Hooking the metal tool around a back molar, I mutter a "gee thanks," and he laughs. "I also think you're a dick, but that's nothing new."

And that's the last of our conversation.

As I stare through the glass window of Opulence, a string of violent thoughts plague me, the effort to keep from waltzing in and making a scene almost overwhelming.

Fiona's inside, sipping water at a booth in the back corner of the restaurant, on a fucking date.

She's been harassing me for weeks, begging for forgiveness, and yet here she is going out with someone else. Someone who is definitely not me.

Not that I even want it to be me. I don't think.

But it's the fucking *principle.*

Pulling my phone from my pocket, I pull up the most recent missed call and press down on the number, holding it to my ear as it rings. I watch her glance at the screen, then check the dining area as if she's afraid of someone hearing her conversation, and then she picks up.

"Hello?" Her voice is soft, breathy, and it makes my dick jump behind the zipper of my jeans, remembering how she'd flush and her throat would grow raspy when I was making her come.

"What the fuck is your game here, Fiona?" I snap, skipping all formalities as my blood boils. "You fuck me, get me to spill my secrets, then spend the next few weeks practically stalking me, and now you're on a *date*?"

Furrowing her eyebrows, she scans the dining area once more, confusion lacing her delicate features. "Where are you right now?"

"The better question is, where is your date? I'd love to stop by your table and meet the fucker."

"If you don't want to be with me, what does it matter who I see in my spare time?"

My lips part around words I shouldn't say — that the *only* thing I want is to *be* with her — but they die in my throat, wilting away with the reminder of how she ended things. How she looked at me after I put my secrets on display, how she let me walk away *again*, just to come back and try to act like things are okay.

Inhaling a deep breath, I will the thoughts away, reminding myself that I need to get home to Riley. "You're right, Fiona. It doesn't matter. Have a nice dinner."

I hang up before she replies, anger still ebbing through me, an electric current not so easily shaken, and I slide to the side out of view, watching and wishing I could go back to the spring. Be honest about her father's affair and Riley's attack, and maybe she wouldn't have given up so quickly.

With a sigh, I start to turn away from the window, feeling like a creep standing outside and just staring at her, when a flash of color catches my eye, moving into my frame of vision.

A sinking feeling settles deep in my gut as I press my nose against the glass, trying to figure out if my eyes are playing tricks on me, or if I really do recognize the figure as he bends down, kissing her cheek.

My blood boils, so hot I can feel it percolating beneath my skin, every muscle in my body tensing and coiling.

I'm shaking as I scrape my fingernails down the glass, the screeching sound piercing my ears, flashes of blood and sobs and death marring my vision.

Standing there, watching them, I die and go straight to Hell.

CHAPTER THIRTY NINE

Fiona

My heart's racing as I hang up the phone, stealing another quick look around the restaurant, searching for Boyd. Since I started trying to edge my way back into his life, trying to convince him to meet with me so I could explain things, he's never been the one to initiate contact.

He barely returns it as it is, and I'm usually soaking up whatever breadcrumbs of conversation he allows, wondering how I got to this point.

It doesn't feel degrading, necessarily, because I don't think he's toying with my feelings, but the struggle to keep in contact with a man who truly isn't interested is exhausting.

I did an extra set of yoga with Heidi last night in the apartment I share with Bea just because I've been so on edge, trying to figure out how to make things right between us.

Heidi stops by most evenings when she's in town from Unity, joining me for nighttime yoga and milkshakes after.

After apologizing for not being able to get on board with my relationship over the summer, relenting that she had been a little jealous but was working on it, I'd admitted to working on my own things, like keeping up with my prescriptions and trying hard to follow through with the mindfulness exercises I practice regularly now.

It's a start, anyway.

Our friendship isn't perfect. Maybe it never was. But we're trying, and I'm learning that sometimes that has to be enough.

"He could probably file a restraining order against you, at this point," she said last night as we cooled down, Bea watching from the couch as she flipped through the script for a modern retelling of *The Canterbury Tales*. Heidi and I quit drama over the summer, but Bea is still at it, working harder than community theater really requires.

"If he wanted to, he would've done it by now," I replied, shrugging. "It's been weeks since the funeral, and it's not like we've had any sexual contact since. So, what could he possibly be gaining from this?"

"An ego boost?" Bea asked, raising an eyebrow.

I shook my head, saying he's not like that, but now as his harsh voice rings in my ear after our call, I wonder if maybe I was wrong about him altogether.

Maybe he is stringing me along, and maybe I'm stupid for playing into his hand.

Anxiety claws up my neck as I take another sip of water, resisting the urge to fall into compulsions I've worked so hard to rid myself of.

Rewiring your brain isn't easy — it requires constant, daily effort, and even with the refilled prescription on my dresser at home and the guided meditations I do each night before bed, I still have to actively keep from practicing avoidance.

Leaning into the nerves instead of away, I try to position them toward things that are okay to be worried about. Like the waiter across the restaurant trying to balance six drinks on a tray clearly built for two.

Or the couple in a corner booth diagonal from me that looks to be in the middle of a heated argument, their faces growing more and more red under the dim Opulence lighting as the seconds pass.

A hand grips my shoulder, making my nerves spike, and Romeo's face appears close to mine; he dips, kissing my cheek, and slides into the booth across from me.

"Sorry about that," he says, the hint of his Italian accent curling at the ends of his words. "Long line for the bathroom."

I nod, wrapping my fingers around a breadstick from the basket at the center of our table just for something to do. Truth is, I only agreed to go out with Romeo when Nico suggested he was interested, and only because I knew Boyd had problems with the Bianchi boys. Kieran too, for that matter, although no one ever gave a concrete reason why, and since I know the rumors about Nico being a manwhore are untrue, I figured maybe they are about Romeo, as well.

We'd gone on one date back in June, and I hadn't heard from him until last night, when he called asking if I could meet him at Opulence. And since Boyd isn't exactly trying to wine and dine me, I figured what was the harm in free food and decent company?

A waitress drops by to take our orders, and Romeo answers for me, rattling off menu items in their native Italian language. When she disappears to place them, he folds his hands on the table and rakes his gaze over my face, smiling.

"Who were you on the phone with a moment ago?"

I blink, taken aback. "Excuse me?"

"You heard me, slut." He leans forward, his smile turning malicious, and fists his fork, pointing it toward me. I jerk back in my seat, startled at the sudden shift in atmosphere as something sinister clouds around us. "Are you fucking Boyd Kelly again?"

"*What?*" I ask, confused as to how he could even know I had in the first place. With the exception of Nico, who is in California and barely speaks to his brother as it is, no one that knows about Boyd and me is also friendly with Romeo.

Something is very, very wrong here.

Dread creeps into my fingertips, and I pull my hand from the breadstick, settling it in my lap. "I don't know what you're talking about."

His dark eyes narrow into evil little slits, menacing and a complete flip from the guy I went on the other date with. "Call him back, tell him to come meet us. I'd love for him to watch me fuck you on this table and then slit your throat. Bet your pussy tastes better than that bratty little sister of his."

Nausea spreads through my chest, teasing the back of my throat, and I dig my fingernails into my thighs at his words, trying to keep the fear from overtaking me. *Panic is of no use to you right now,* I tell myself, steeling my breaths from the way they wrap around my sternum like vines, constricting until I feel lightheaded.

Focus on what you can control.

His words press down on my skull, making it ache as I struggle to comprehend what he's saying.

My throat burns as they process, and I begin to slide out from the booth, glancing around the restaurant to see if I can attract any attention. The place is too dark for me to make out anyone, and the angry couple from before has disappeared, leaving a full table across the room and us.

Oh, God, this is where I die.

Swallowing, I keep my gaze trained on Romeo, inching my way out of the seat. He's seething, although I still don't fully understand why it's directed at me all of a sudden, he doesn't seem to register my movements. Slipping my phone out from beneath my thigh, I use muscle memory to unlock the screen and open my call log, hitting the most recent number and praying he answers.

I can just barely hear the din of a voicemail beep, and my insides deflate, fear building like a threatening storm inside me. My body is so tense, so prepared for the slightest move from Romeo, that it starts to ache; my knees throb, my shoulders pulse, and a tremor racks over me, the first visible motion either of us has made in minutes.

"Where do you think you're going?" Romeo asks, scooting to the edge of the table along with me. "I asked you to come here hoping you'd bring your little boy toy. He hasn't shown up yet, so you don't get to go. I have unfinished business with him."

"He's not going to show up," I croak, surprised I'm able to talk at all. "You're using the wrong person as leverage. He hates me."

"That's not what it sounded like on the phone. I think he was jealous, and I think it's because he saw you. He's close by."

When he glances around the restaurant, I take my chance, hold my purse tight against me, and bolt from the seat; his hand lashes out, grasping the ends of my hair as it billows behind me, but my momentum carries me before he has a chance to really latch on.

I feel hair as it's plucked from my scalp, but I don't stop to mourn its loss. Knowing he can't chase after me inside a restaurant without raising suspicion, I head for the back alley, hoping I have enough time before he comes around to get to where my Jeep is parked.

Pushing open the emergency exit, ignoring the beep it makes while it swings open, I look left and right; one way is a dead end, cut off by a barbed wire fence, and the other is the street near the entrance of the restaurant. Panting, I make the decision to duck behind the dumpster and hide, hoping Romeo will assume I've fled and go looking after me.

I'm shaking uncontrollably as I crouch down, the smell of rotted food not even registering as I cover my mouth to quiet my breathing. A drainpipe drips in the distance, the sound echoing off the brick walls around me, and I scratch at my skin as panic swirls in my gut, cursing myself for being so fucking stupid.

Boyd said his mother attacked Riley, but Romeo claimed to have done it.

He raped her.

Is it possible they'd been working together? I don't exactly know much about his mother outside of the fact that she's

405

a drug addict who apparently hates her kids, and in a town like King's Trace, there have been crazier notions.

Footsteps draw me from my thoughts, and I suck in a deep breath, holding it as I try to sink into the shadows, my heart beating so hard and fast I'm afraid it might give me away.

"Come out, come out, Princess Fiona," Romeo taunts, his voice growing louder as he advances down the alleyway. "I promise I'll play nice, long as Boyd gives me what he owes me."

Rolling my eyes, I move my purse to the ground and tip my foot back so my heel sticks out, watching his shadow loom larger as he comes toward me. His steps are slow, calculated, indicating he doesn't know where I'm hiding, which means I have the element of surprise on my side.

Placing my palms against the cold pavement, I anchor myself and position my foot—this is why my mother always insists—insisted, fuck. The adrenaline is warping my sense of time—I wear stilettos on dates, because they are easily weaponized.

I send a silent prayer, thanking her, and grit my teeth just as Romeo's pant leg comes into view.

He's got a handgun clasped between his hands, pointed right toward my head, but I can tell he isn't exactly sure if he has a good shot because of the darkness. He hesitates, and it's his downfall.

Kicking with all my strength, my heel connects with his shin, startling him to the point that the gun falls away. He yelps, bending down to clutch at his leg, and I spring to my knees, glad I wore jeans, my hands searching the ground for his gun.

My fingers brush the cool metal just as he wraps a fist in my hair, yanking so hard I black out for a second, and then he's pulling me backward and up off the ground, grabbing my throat and shoving me against the wall.

He squeezes until I can't breathe, and I kick at his waist, trying to gain purchase as the life drains from my eyes; finally, I connect with his balls and he releases me, howling to himself. Throwing my shoulders back, I channel every ounce of my bloodline that I can, raising the gun in my hands, and shoot as fireworks erupt in the night sky, celebrating Halloween King's Trace style.

CHAPTER FORTY
Boyd

Riley groans, tipping her head back to glare at the ceiling from where she's seated at the dining room table, a piece of Dottie's lasagna on a plate in front of her.

She's not supposed to leave until the entire thing is finished.

Bad parenting, according to the forums, but right now I'm too fucking wired to give a shit, still fuming over the fact that Fiona was out with that bastard and waiting to hear back from Kieran on when we can find him.

SAV R MILLER

"I don't want to hear any sounds from you unless they're 'oh, this is delicious,'" I call from my spot on the sofa bed. I've been sleeping on it recently because I want to be the first thing someone sees if they break in, and because the mattress is somehow more comfortable than the one on my bed.

Maybe it also makes me nostalgic for the first time Fiona stayed the night, but I won't admit that.

"This is stupid," Riley says, poking her fork into the lasagna.

"You know what else is stupid? Starving yourself."

She snorts. "Who'd you take parenting advice from this time, Casey Anthony?"

"You're not even old enough to know who that is."

"I listen to a lot of true crime podcasts, remember?"

"Just eat the fucking lasagna, Riley."

"*I can't!*" she screams, the sound so loud it reverberates off the glass windows. When I sit up and glance over at her through the foyer, there are tears streaming down her face as she glares at the food, the fork in her hand shaking violently. She releases it, and it clatters to the table, a sob wrenching from deep inside her chest as she drops her head into her hands.

Getting up slowly, I grit my teeth, really out of my fucking element now. My hands ball into fists at my sides, anger reigniting in my bones when I think about how normal she was just a few months ago. How bright and sunny, genuinely happy to be alive.

There aren't a lot of people like that in the world, and maybe that's part of the reason the human condition sucks so bad.

Guilt stabs at my chest as I approach her, watching the way her shoulders shake as she cries, the first real emotion I've seen from her in longer than I care to recount.

She's rail-thin beneath her baggy clothing, her cheeks so thin that they're almost translucent, revealing the bone underneath. There's a knit cap pulled down over her hair, probably to hide the fact that it's been falling out in droves recently. She always tries to wash the evidence down the drain, but when I snake it out on the weekends, inordinate amounts clog her shower.

My stomach flips violently as I grab the back of my neck, weighing my options. Deciding I don't want to incite another outburst or make things worse, I grab the plate and dump the lasagna in the trash, a lump lodging at the base of my throat as I set the plate in the sink and walk back over, dropping into the chair beside her.

"Riley," I say softly, once her wailing has subsided enough that she can hear me.

She moves her hands, wiping her nose, raising her bloodshot eyes to mine. "I'm sorry," she sniffles, the words causing a black hole of misery to open up inside my chest, sucking in everything until I can't breathe. "I don't know what's wrong with me, I just..."

410

Cutting off on a hiccup, she sits up, pulling at her sleeves. I don't press for more information, afraid that if I do, she'll spiral.

Or worse, tell me what else she's been doing to cope.

Swallowing, I tap my finger against the table; she watches it with rapt attention, sucking on her lower lip. "I think you should try talking to someone again."

"I'm talking to *you* right now."

"Okay, let me rephrase." I inhale, releasing the tension from my shoulders with the exhale. "I think *we* should talk to someone. Together."

"You want to go to therapy?" She raises an eyebrow. "I thought you didn't believe in it."

"It's not that, I just… haven't been in a long time." Sitting back in the chair, I nod to myself, relief flooding through me that I don't think I've ever felt before. It rolls over me in waves, calming and soothing, like the taste of hope.

And as I glance at Riley, who's watching me closely, studying my every move, I realize she's waiting for a cue from me. That she needs me to make the first step, to show her it's okay and that things can get better.

That's what the both of us need. *Hope.*

Something to latch onto instead of our pain.

The possibility of tomorrow.

"Okay," she relents eventually, pulling her sleeves down over her dry, cracked fingers. "If you go, I'll go. But if they bring up the arson incident, I'm out."

I smirk. "Thought that was an accident."

"There's a little intention behind every accident."

Halloween fireworks are by far the worst tradition in King's Trace, but tonight, it's not their excessive explosion keeping me awake.

The incessant buzzing coming from the end table draws me from the sleep I've just fallen into. A vacuum of sound envelops me, my heart launching into my throat at the possibility of who the fuck might be calling this late.

Tearing myself from my pillow, I drag the back of my hand across my mouth and sit up, yanking the phone off its charger.

My stomach plummets, my heart stuttering at the name flashing across the screen for the fifth time tonight.

Gritting my teeth, I hold the lock button down until the phone powers off and toss it back on the end table, ignoring the stab of guilt lancing my chest. I already know I'm not interested in anything she has to say.

Fiona could be bleeding out on the side of the street and I wouldn't go to her fucking aid. Not after tonight.

"Who was that?" Riley asks, appearing at the bottom of the staircase with a glass of water.

Apprehension flares inside my stomach, twisting like a sharp blade as I climb back up the mattress. "Nobody important."

Even as the words leave my lips, I know they still aren't true.

The problem is that Fiona Ivers is *too* important, and she knows it. Uses it to her advantage, like with all the calls, texts, and emails she's bombarded me with since the funeral.

So, even though it's possible she's gotten into some kind of trouble with her date, especially since I still haven't heard back from Kieran, it's not my fucking problem. There are plenty of people around who'd kill for the chance to help the little princess out.

I gave up that role long ago.

Besides, deep in my heart, I know the truth. Fiona Ivers isn't in danger.

She *is* the danger.

Riley goes to a window in the dining room, peeling back a dark curtain and peering outside. "Do people usually trespass on your property at night?"

"Sometimes, yeah. We live in a shit part of town, if you hadn't noticed." Shrugging, I flip through categories on Netflix, trying to find something I can fall asleep to. "They usually leave when they realize they're barking up the wrong tree."

"Oh. Well, someone's coming our way right now."

Furrowing my brows, I push back the covers, anxiety flooding the chambers of my heart as the image pops up in my mind of the one woman who makes busting into my life unwarranted one of her annoying habits. Slipping into a pair of slippers, I clamber over to where Riley's standing, peering through the sliver of moonlight as it illuminates the street.

A figure staggers up the sidewalk, pausing and staring at the house for several beats. Contemplating a decision, I assume, wringing her hands together. She releases her hold, dropping one hand to tap on her thigh in quick successions of three, a gesture my traitorous body recognizes immediately.

Fury ignites my blood, a wildfire spreading unencumbered. "Stay here," I tell Riley, clenching my jaw as I sprint from the room, bounding down my narrow hallway and out the back door in record time.

Swinging around the house, I watch her creep up the porch steps, holding her side. Her tiny hand grips the railing for balance, and she winces once before planting her foot on the next step.

She's mumbling, talking about her father needing to spend time with her mother and not wanting to bother him, and for a second, I'm genuinely concerned she might be having a stroke.

I launch forward without thinking, my body colliding with hers before I have a chance to fully comprehend what the
414

fuck I'm doing. My hand flattens over her pretty red lips, hating how soft they feel against my skin, while my free arm wraps around her waist, pushing us up onto the porch so I can force her against the white siding of my house.

She squeaks in protest, trying to wriggle out from my hold, rubbing her ass against my crotch in a way that has blinding light flashing across my vision, despite the fact that I'm angry with her.

Bending down to the shell of her ear, I press against her skin, keeping my hand over her mouth. "I fucking told you not to come here anymore."

Not in so many words, but I'd thought the implication was there, anyway.

She mutters something against me, the vibrations shooting straight to my balls. My cock stiffens against her as her rosy scent invades my nostrils, the swell of her ass a perfect cocoon to bury myself in.

When I feel her thighs clench, seeking some sort of purchase against me, it yanks me from the spell and I spin her in my arms, shove her back against the wall, delighting in the way her eyes widen to the size of gaseous planets.

Gripping her wrists in one hand, I pull them up and pin them above her head against the wall, watching her bite down on the inside of her cheek—her tell. As she sucks skin inward, I can tell the control she keeps wrapped so tight around her fingertips is slipping, dissolving into a puddle between us. Inhaling a deep breath, she steels her gaze against mine.

"I need your help."

CHAPTER FORTY ONE

Fiona

B oyd releases me almost immediately, and I sag against the side of his house, my skin clammy, my mind floating through a swampy fog of memories and present-day, struggling to discern which are which. I twitch under his perusal, aware that just a few hours ago he hung up on me.

"You need my help," he says, narrowing his eyes. "I'm not giving you advice on how to fuck another guy, if that's why you're here."

Fatigue surges through my veins, making me dizzy as I let out a short laugh. "Unless you have tips on fucking dead bodies, then I don't need the advice, anyway."

The air around us freezes, growing static as he absorbs what I've just said.

"What?" he hisses, reaching out to grasp my biceps. He hauls me up the wall, holding tight but not in a way that hurts, almost as if he's using me to prop himself up. Joke's on him, because the wobble in my knees says I could drop any second.

"He-he told me what he did to your sister," I hiccup, regret and shame bubbling inside my chest, making it hard to breathe. "Boyd, I'm s-so *sorry*. I s-swear to you, I h-had no idea."

Covering my mouth gently with his palm, he nods, shushing me. "Fiona, baby, I think you're going into shock."

My body trembles like a leaf as he stares into my eyes; I try to ground myself in him, try to imprint the feel of his body against mine just in case this is the last time I ever get to experience it, because it feels like my organs are shutting down with each labored breath that rattles from my lungs.

For a few moments, he just holds me in silence, trying to get me to settle even as I feel my nerves spiraling out of control, gearing toward an explosion.

And then, we hear the crackle of sticks breaking beneath the weight of someone's footsteps. The air shifts again, this time to something sinister, something *vile*, and Boyd tenses, tilting his head to listen.

418

Snap. Some more shuffling. The wind picks up, carrying the sound toward us, along with the smell of bleach and tobacco.

Boyd's voice drops to a whisper against the crown of my head. "You killed Romeo?"

I nod.

"Did he say anything to you tonight? Other than about Riley?"

Racking my brain, I nod again. "He said he was using me to lure you out, and that you owed him." I glance up, my eyes searching his. "What do you owe him?"

"Nothing, baby. But my piece of shit mother probably promised him a body, and he was trying to collect on the one he didn't get." He presses a kiss to my temple, cursing under his breath as the steps get closer. "They're working together, that's why I couldn't find him. *Shit.* I shouldn't have left you with him."

Pulling my head into his chest, he yanks me to the front door and bangs on it until it swings open, Riley's tiny form appearing at the threshold. He tips my head up, plants a firm kiss to my mouth, and passes me off to her like I'm a rag doll or an injured animal.

"Lock yourselves inside, call her brother, and take her upstairs to get cleaned up. Do not come out of the bedroom until me or Kieran come to get you." He pauses, gripping my chin. "Do you understand?"

"What's going on?" Riley asks, wrapping one bony arm around my waist.

419

"*Do you understand*?" he snaps, making both of us flinch. "Christ, I'm sorry. I don't know what's going on, but I just... I need you to do what I say and not ask questions. I'll be up to get you soon."

She nods, and there's another brief pause in which Boyd hesitates, seemingly unable to tear his gaze from my face. I open my mouth, three words on the tip of my tongue that I should've said months ago or any of the dozens of times I thought them in-between, but he shakes his head with a wry smile.

"We'll talk later," he promises, breaking the spell and reaching to pull the door shut.

Riley and I stand there, stunned, for a minute before we hear his weight leave the porch, and then she springs into action. There are six deadbolts and a keypad that secure the front door, and I can't remember if there were that many there the last time I was here, but I don't have a chance to dwell on the added protection, because then she's grabbing my hand and dragging me up the stairs.

Pushing me into the guest bedroom, Riley stalks into the attached bathroom and switches on the shower, her movements panicked but her face serene, as if this is a moment she's been preparing for for ages, and she's finally comfortable in this element.

"Take off your clothes and get in the shower," she barks, bossy, just like her brother. I just stare at her for a moment, confused, and she gestures at my soaked clothing. "You're covered in blood and guts, dude."

If she's surprised or grossed out, she doesn't show it, just waits for me to disrobe. I pull my shirt over my head, kick off the sneakers that I'd had in my purse and slipped on before running here, then shimmy out of my jeans, stepping into the spray.

I close my eyes, letting the water wash over me, trying to will it to take my panic with it. Unfortunately, that's written into my DNA, so it sticks to me like bubblegum, stretching out across my skin until I'm shaking all over again.

Pulling the curtain aside, I see Riley walk back into the room, some ginger ale, pretzels, and a thick book in her arms. She walks to the wicker dresser across from the queen-size bed with its leopard print sheets, grabs some pajamas from the top drawer, and comes back to the bathroom as I'm wrapping myself in a towel.

"Feel better?" she asks, and I shake my head no, my fingers trembling as I take the clothes she holds out. "Yeah. Been there."

Leaving me in the bathroom to get dressed, when I re-emerge, she's sitting on the floor with her back propped against the side of the bed, sipping on one of the cans of ginger ale. Her door is shut, bolted with a padlock, the thick black curtains pulled shut over her window.

She looks completely at ease, even though her brother's outside right now, dealing with an unknown assailant. A random trespasser, maybe, but the ease with which both of them handled the situation tells me there's something else going on.

I walk over and sit down beside her, running my fingers over the silk cow-print pajama set she gave me. "These are cute."

Nodding, she scrolls through her phone without looking at me. "You can have them. I don't really wear pajamas anymore."

Blowing out a breath, I stretch my legs out, trying to get a grip on my sense of control before it spirals and I can't get it back. There's a thin thread that runs the line between sanity and lunacy, and even though I normally toe it in general, I can feel myself falling.

Backsliding.

All because of a little danger. A little violence. A little blood.

Okay, a lot of blood, but still.

After the initial shock of *murder* wore off in the shower, I realized I wasn't even upset about the fact that I'd killed.

More so about the fact that I'm not upset at all.

There'd been a brief flash of relief when I pulled the trigger, buried by nerves and adrenaline, a euphoric rush from catering to the violence that's been trying to hatch inside of me all along.

It's not a craving, but I can't deny there was a rush when I finally went through with it, as if I finally have something to connect me to the Ivers' namesake.

422

Only now, it feels like Boyd's paying penance for my deeds, since we have no idea what the hell is going on outside.

Tapping my fingers on my thigh, I scan the room, looking for something in need of fixing.

Anything.

I note a puzzle tucked beneath her dresser, and reach out to slide it my way — it's a thousand-piece cottagecore scene, the box so old I have to imagine it belonged to the house's previous owners, but it'll have to do.

"What are you doing?" she asks as I take off the lid and dump out the pieces, immediately searching for edges.

My nerves are shot, so my fingers still shake as I comb through the colors, separating the edges from the others. "If I don't do *something*, I'll go crazy just sitting up here waiting. Doesn't it bother you at all that we have no idea what your brother's doing outside?"

"No." She shrugs, still scrolling. "He's a big boy, he can take care of himself."

I huff, shaking my head. "Well, that's not how my mind works."

"How is worrying about him gonna help the situation?"

"It's *not*, but it's — it's not something I can just turn off. Most of the time, anyway." I gesture toward the puzzle. "Hence, the distraction."

She hums, finally setting her phone on the floor. "I see why my brother likes you. You're as crazy as he is."

Pursing my lips, I don't reply, and she slides closer, helping me separate the pieces. We work in silence for a while, until the sound of a gunshot rings through the air and a loud banging reverberates off the walls, making us jump. Riley gets to her feet and turns off the bedroom light, shrouding us in the dark, and slides the other can of ginger ale my way.

"Drink," she says. "I don't want you passing out."

I take the can and crack the tab, thinking to myself that it's weird being bossed around by someone my age, and then lean against the bed.

"What happened tonight?" she asks finally, her voice small and unsure, cracking on the last syllable. Something tells me she already knows — that this is a night she's been anticipating for a long time. I think about the baggy clothes I see her in, the cropped cut of her hair, the scars lining her otherwise perfect face, and wonder how much she's struggled over the last few months.

Boyd probably wouldn't want me to tell her, but if it were me and a demon of mine had been slain, I'd want to know. I think it's the only way I'd be able to sleep at night.

"I killed Romeo Bianchi."

Neither of us moves, even the moonlight outside seeming to still at my confession. Then she nods, the movement barely visible. "Good."

And then, we wait.

CHAPTER FORTY TWO

Boyd

Sweat slicks down my back as I step slowly off the
porch, my eyes darting around the shadowy
yard, searching for the source of the footsteps.

I know you're here, Mommy.

Because she's a coward, though, she stays hooded in the
darkness, where she's lived her entire life, just barely getting by.
A succubus feeding on the souls of her children, only ever
concerned with herself.

Rage ignites beneath my skin, a slow burning chemical
fire that has me winding the trees dotting my front yard, using
them as a cover as I search for her.

"Come on, LeeAnn, I don't have all fucking night to play your games." My breath is visible against the night sky, a foggy contrast against the stars. I glance up at the window to Riley's bedroom and see the light is still on; gritting my teeth, I make a note to remind Riley of the safety protocols after I've gutted our mother on my front lawn.

I also make a note to fuck Fiona in my bed once this is all over, because I know she'll be needing that part of me.

All of my anger and apprehension melted away when I saw the look in her eyes before I shut them inside the house—the look that said she wanted to tell me *something.* To open up to me, once and for all, and spill her heart out into the open for me to pick up the pieces.

But I didn't want it to be adrenaline-fueled, or one of those things you spout out when you think you're in danger.

I want her to mean it.

I'm kicking myself for leaving her with Romeo, for letting my jealousy get the best of me and not immediately dragging her from the restaurant where I could keep her safe, but my first thought at seeing him out was to go home and check on Riley, knowing he'd be looking for her.

She was in a public place, and Riley was home alone. It doesn't necessarily lessen the guilt I have, but I'm latching on to it anyway.

My fingernails scrape against the trunk of another tree as I pass it, the smell of cleanser filling my nostrils. A sound to my left draws my attention, and I step out from behind one tree, spinning with my arms spread wide.

"Hiding is a coward's game, LeeAnn," I say, recalling the way she'd taunt me as a kid for hiding inside cabinets during her benders. "Come out so I can shove my fist down your throat and watch you choke on it."

For a moment, I'm met with more silence, and I start turning again, trying to keep track of any movement in my peripheral vision. A twig snaps to my left, and then she steps out from the shadows right in front of me, holding a gun in my direction.

It's the first time I've seen her in months, the first time I've ever gone this long *without* seeing her, but this time I'm not met with the usual wave of guilt or remorse. Like the hold she's had over me broke the second she put Riley's life in danger, and it never recovered.

An age-old curse being broken over bloodshed, and now I'm putting it to bed for good.

Riley won't spend her life stuck under this bitch's spell.

"I don't think you're really prepared enough to be making such predictions, dear." She tilts her head, studying me, and laughs. "Then again, idle threats were the only thing you were ever good at."

Rolling my eyes, I cross my arms over my chest, refusing the bait. "I've followed through on plenty of threats, LeeAnn. My only regret is that I didn't kill you sooner."

427

"Yes, well, you always were rather soft." She circles me, keeping the gun trained on my chest, edging around so she's closer to the house than I am. "Surprising, really, given who your father is."

"There's no record of me actually having a father," I say, trying to keep her talking while I work out a plan. I don't have a weapon, and I'm not sure when Kieran will get here—or if the girls even actually called him. I could ambush her, I suppose, bank on the surprise of my attack throwing her off enough that she doesn't shoot me.

But in the event she does, then I'm probably not of very much use.

"Just because I never put him on your birth certificate doesn't mean I don't know who he is. Just means I didn't want him coming around and bothering us or trying to get custody."

My eyebrows shoot up, a pang rippling through my stomach. "*You* didn't even want custody of me. Why the fuck would you care if someone else had gotten me?"

"I needed you, Boyd. Needed you around all this time, even if you couldn't actually *be* with me." She laughs maniacally, tilting her head back. "Every time I let them beat on you or take you to the back bedroom in our trailer, they paid me. *Handsomely*, too, and not with cash. You think I was just too high to notice when they hurt you, but the truth is I just didn't care. Little boys went for a lot of premium blow back then."

Bile churns in my gut, pressing up against my esophagus, threatening to spew.

"The man you killed because you thought he was raping me when you were a teenager? He was behind on payments, and I set him up. Knew you'd try to be a hero, and gave his dead body to the Bianchis—back then, the Esposito family—because he'd turned their don in to the feds, and they paid me back in spades. You've been playing into my hand your entire life, baby boy. It's embarrassing that you ever thought otherwise, but damn, was it easy to keep you coming back. Every dealer, every ex you ever killed for me was someone I wanted dead, anyway."

She's a drug dealer.

Kicking myself internally, I try to figure out how I didn't see any of this sooner. The biggest dealers in King's Trace, besides the Montaltos and Bianchis, are the no-names—the ones who lurk in the shadows, turn souls into addicts and trade freedom for money.

"That's fantastic, LeeAnn," I deadpan, shrugging my shoulders, even though the weight in my chest intensifies, expanding like a toxic supernova, explosions of light morphing to blinding pain. "I already knew you were a piece of shit, nice to see it solidified. What were you planning on doing with Riley?"

"I'm pretty sure you've already figured that out. Since your friend had our glorious operation shut down, we've been having to grab girls on a case-by-case basis, pretty much snatching them whenever we can and getting them sold as soon as possible. I knew Riley would be a fighter, but I didn't realize Romeo wasn't equipped to handle her. Honestly, when I didn't get word of her transport, I'd assumed she was dead. Until I got a report card in the mail, detailing her work at summer school."

LeeAnn smiles, her yellowed teeth just barely visible in the moonlight, sending another hot wave of fury over me. I'm growing impatient, listening to her fucking monologue, my hands itching to wrap around her throat.

"A shame I missed out on the last few months, but better late than never," she says, and I hear the click of her turning off the safety, followed by the magazine loading into its chamber. My chest pulls tight as I wait, wanting to see if she makes the first move. "Romeo might be dumb, but he did follow through with his side of the deal. Didn't think he'd be able to, given his temperament."

"Romeo's dead." *Soon to be buried in a watery grave with his father.*

"I figured he would be. I wasn't interested in him, anyway—just wanted him to give me access to the Ivers girl, so I could track her here and have you play the hero once again. Still so terribly soft. So *weak*."

She seems to get lost in the revelation of her plan, her hand drooping slightly, and that's when I strike. Her hesitancy is what drives me forward.

Before she has a chance to pull the trigger, I dive for her waist, tackling her to the ground. The gun falls from her hand,

430

and I kick it away as she slaps me in the face, one fingernail slicing the skin open.

Groaning, I climb on top of her and pin her arms by her sides with my knees, squeezing her torso until she coughs, struggling to reach oxygen.

My fists ball and surge forward as if they're separate from the rest of my body, pummeling her face until she's sputtering, blood and saliva caking her lips. The moonlight shines where a tooth used to be, and she spits it in my direction, nearly hitting me in the face.

When I pause, she's a moaning mass of muscle and tissue, and there's adrenaline and the bare bones of evil cravings pumping through my veins, making me lightheaded.

Scrambling to my feet before she reorients herself, I sweep my arms along the grass, searching for her gun several feet away, then train it on her left thigh and pull the trigger, reveling in the bloodcurdling scream that tears from her throat.

"Too bad you didn't have one of your sick clients put me out of my misery, like they always tried to do," I sneer, walking to her, adding a bullet in the other leg just for good measure, salivating at the way she convulses in pain, her body spasming through her screams. "Maybe this would've ended differently for you."

Bending down as I hear another set of footsteps approach, I take my thumb and drive it into the bullet wound in her thigh, pressing down as hard as I can; the blood pulses, gushing out around me in waves, and I reach up, smearing it across her face as her gargled screams turn to begging.

"Where was my mercy, *Mother*? Or Riley's? How the fuck could you do that shit to your own kids?"

But I don't wait for an answer — don't fucking want one. At this point, there's no explanation, no reason she could give that would absolve her of her sins.

Tonight, she atones for them.

She gasps as I shove my hand down into her mouth, pushing my knuckles to the back of her throat until I feel it throb; when she vomits, I yank free and clamp my dirty hand down over her mouth and nose, reveling in the way she thrashes, trying to claw herself free.

Choking on her own filth.

With my free hand, I stick my middle finger into her wound, pressing through the skin and muscle until I feel bone. Her movements slow as the fight leaves her body, and I pull my hand away just before she passes out completely, not wanting her to miss this next bit.

Limp but still alive and breathing, she rolls to her side, spitting out the vomit she didn't swallow. She sucks in gulps of air as Kieran *finally* approaches, a red gallon of gasoline in hand.

That was always the plan for her.

Trial by fire.

"'Bout time you showed up," I say, yanking the gas from his hand. "I thought she was going to shoot me for a while there."

432

He rolls his eyes, pulling out a matchbook. "Had to fucking clean up Fiona's disaster. She'd put a tarp over him and just left him by the dumpster like this is amateur hour or something. Can you imagine what Kal or Finn would say if they saw that and knew a relative of mine had done that? My reputation would be ruined."

LeeAnn rolls back onto her back, her screams subsiding to chest-rattling sobs. "*Please...*" she croaks, her voice ruined, broken the way she tried to make Riley and me.

But this is only the end of her story, not ours.

Ours is just beginning.

Kieran groans, stuffing his hands in his pockets as he tosses me the matches. "Jesus, don't *beg*. It never changes the outcome. Have some fucking dignity."

Swallowing, I take a step forward and uncap the gasoline, tipping it forward and pouring it directly onto her face. She screams, raising her hands to try and block the liquid, but it leaks through her fingers and into her mouth and nose, making her sputter.

I'm almost sad that I can't see her bruised, bloodied face right now, but the sounds — the choking, the gagging, the crying. All of that's enough.

Her clothes are soaked through when the gallon runs out, and Kieran looks at me, shrugging. "Any last words?"

I glare down at her, removing a match from the box and striking it on the side; the flame glows bright orange, angry and ethereal, the symbol of the end of all my suffering. Of Riley's path to healing.

Of happiness. Warmth. Love.

All things I've never considered myself worthy of, because of this woman.

Shaking my head, I flick the match from my finger, watching it descend and land, engulfing her body in flames almost instantly. "Nope."

And as I head into the house with her vomit and blood on my skin, the weight of her sins seem to lift from my shoulders, a lightness taking their place that I've never known, even as her screams bleed into the night sky, deafeningly satisfying until they cease completely.

CHAPTER FORTY THREE

Kieran cleans up the yard while I head inside; Fiona and Riley are huddled together on the floor by Riley's bed when I kick in the door, not feeling patient enough to wait to see either of them.

They're scrolling through that rock star's social media *again*, Riley explaining the importance of his bad-boy brand while Fiona stuffs pretzels in her mouth, and I fall in love with her a little bit more in that moment.

She's the embodiment of true sunshine — starlight and chaos combined, a raging ball of fire that my entire fucking universe has revolved around for months. The kind of sun I wouldn't mind orbiting for the rest of my life.

I still feel like a dick for how I've treated her over the last few weeks, especially earlier today, leaving her at the restaurant while I ran home to check on my sister, but I'll deal with that later if she lets me. I'll spend forever trying to make it up to her.

Getting to their feet, Fiona raises an eyebrow, raking her gaze down over my form. "You look... interesting."

Nodding at her cow pajamas, I chuckle. "So do you."

"Touché." Glancing at Riley, she clears her throat and clasps her hands together. "Well, I believe my brother's outside? I'll just go see if he needs any help."

As she passes, she pauses like she wants to reach out and touch me, but seems to think better of it, giving me a curt nod and darting from the room.

Riley sits on the bed, her eyes glued to my hands. I start toward her, and she holds hers up, palms facing me. "Dude, you cannot sit down in here."

"Fair enough." I stick my hands in my pockets, rocking back on my heels, trying to figure out a way to best approach the subject.

We'd talked about what would happen if either LeeAnn or Romeo ever came to the house looking for her, ran drills where she could lock up everything and hide out in her room in under three minutes, but we never talked about what it'd mean for the two of us if the nightmares ended.

If we were no longer bound to a sense of loyalty or addiction. If the object of our insanity, the people we feared most, were eliminated, no longer pawns in our little game of chess. I open my mouth, prepared to ask how she's feeling, when she speaks first.

"Romeo's dead," she says, completely devoid of any emotion. "Told you I liked Fiona."

A smile tugs at the corners of my mouth. "She's not so bad, I suppose."

She rolls her eyes. "I'm gonna tell her you said that at your wedding."

Uncomfortable silence ebbs between us, the grim reality of what happened just outside descending its ugly head, demanding discussion. My chest pulls tight, part worry and part relief—worry that Riley *won't* be relieved, and relief that I'm free, regardless of how she ends up feeling.

I'm fucking free.

"So..." Riley says, swinging her legs over the side of the bed. "That was some noise outside. You're lucky the neighbors are scared of you." Rubbing her hands on her sweatpants, she swallows, glancing up at me through hooded lashes. "Who... who was out there?"

Chewing on the inside of my lip, I exhale sharply through my nose, wanting to get this over with despite the apprehension growing inside my stomach like a tornado, wild and imposing. "LeeAnn."

Her fingers curl into fists, knuckles blooming white with the pressure, and she pinches her eyes closed, dropping her chin to her chest. Nodding over and over, I think she's broken for a moment, but then she's inhaling deeply and straightening her shoulders.

When she looks up, her baby blues are glassy but not leaking, and she huffs out a humorless laugh. "I don't know why I'm crying."

I shrug, discomfort wedging into the cracks in my heart. "It's okay to be sad. She was still your mom."

"Are *you* sad?"

There's the tiniest sliver of a pinprick that shoots down my spine at her question—it's quick, just a flash of grief, but it's gone before I have a chance to latch onto it and dissect its meaning. Deep down, part of me is sad, but it's mostly when I think about all the time I lost out on trying to be what my mother needed, not realizing that it wasn't attainable.

Selfish people are just selfish, and they don't give out pieces of their hearts like the rest of us. They hoard them close to their chests, doling love out when it's convenient. Sometimes, like with LeeAnn, not even then.

Sometimes it's all pain, all the time.

Her anguish echoes in my head, a reminder of everything she did to the two of us—people whose only crimes were existing.

So, no. I'm not sad.

Not even a little bit.

But I know that it'll haunt me for the rest of my life. Her memory will never leave, even if she's not physically here to torment me. And I think that's enough to keep the guilt at bay, at least for now.

"Me neither," Riley whispers, taking my silence as an answer. Yawning, she climbs under her covers and rests her head on the pillows, staring up at the ceiling, signaling the end of our conversation. I walk to the door and am pulling it closed behind me when she calls my name.

"Yeah?"

I hear her swallow. "I'm glad you're okay."

Not exactly sure what she's getting at—or that it's even true—I smile as I leave, closing the door on my way out. "I'm glad you're okay too, Riley."

Crossing the hall into my bedroom, I shuck off my soiled clothes and toss them into the hamper in the corner of my room, then get into the shower in my en suite, letting the scalding spray soothe and massage my aching muscles.

'Just because I never put him on your birth certificate doesn't mean I don't know who he is.'

LeeAnn's words replay over and over in my head, fogging up the free space with interest. Do I even want to know who he is? Would it really matter, after all this time?

No, I resolve, shaking my head. *I don't think it would.*

Pressing my hand against the wall, I feel the dirt and blood and vomit roll off my body, and then the curtain is pulled back and Fiona's standing there, completely naked, her dark hair pulled into a bun, eyes roving over my chest.

Just the sight of her standing there is enough to rob me of all the air in my lungs.

She swallows, looking nervous, white-knuckling the curtain. "I thought you could use some company."

Moving more directly beneath the spray to give her room, I gesture at the empty space. "All yours, princess."

Hiking her leg over the lip of the tub, she steps inside, immediately reaching for a bottle of citrus body wash, squirting some into her palm and edging closer. I suck in a sharp breath when she presses the soap into my chest, the chill a stark contrast to my skin.

Working the soap in circles over my pecs, she presses down on spots that are particularly sensitive, making me jerk forward from the soreness. I almost topple over when she swirls the pad of her finger around my nipple, looking up at me through hooded lashes.

Hooking my arm around her waist, I yank her body into mine, reveling in the perfect fit. She continues massaging up my neck, digging her fingers into my muscles, eliciting a low groan from deep within me, the pain wrapping around the soothing sensation of having her hands on me, making me dizzy with desire.

"How're you feeling?" she asks in a low voice, stopping the massage and instead just flattening her palms against my chest.

"Better now that you're here."

Worrying her bottom lip, she sighs. "I swear, I didn't know about Romeo. If I had—"

Cradling her jaw in my hands, I tip her head back and cut her off with a deep kiss, my tongue tangling with hers with such ferocity, you'd think it'd been more than just a few weeks since I last tasted her.

Dropping my head to her throat, I glide my lips along the smooth expanse, biting down gently on her pulse, making her jolt.

"I don't want to talk about anything that happened tonight," I breathe, alternating between sucking and catching her flesh between my teeth, fire spilling down my spine as she arches into each movement.

"What do you want to talk about, then?"

"No talking, period." My fingers tingle as they skim down her shoulders, pressing along the divots in her spine, and settle on the firm swell of her ass.

Gripping hard, I haul her into my arms, bringing her wet little cunt flush with my pelvis, and press her back into the shower wall.

She gasps as she collides with the cool tile, her tits bouncing as she tries to escape the feel of it on her skin; I dip my head, laving the flat of my tongue over one pebbled nipple before sucking her into my mouth, relishing the way her moans echo above us.

"Boyd," she sighs, her head bumping against the wall. "We should really talk. I want to apologize."

Dragging my tongue up between her breasts to the dip in the middle of her collarbone, I shake my head. "I don't accept."

Scoffing, she fists the hair at the nape of my neck, drawing me up so my forehead is level with her chin. "You can't just 'not accept' an apology."

"Wrong, my little manipulator. I don't *have* to do anything."

Reaching beside me, I wrench the hot water off, the sudden loss of the stream causing goose bumps to pop up along our wet skin. Shoving the curtain aside, I step out gingerly, keeping my arm wedged tight beneath her butt to avoid slippage.

Without stopping to towel off, I toss her into the middle of my bed, drinking in the sight of her luscious body — my cock hardens, bobbing up against my abs as I stand over her. Pink floods her cheeks and chest, her breathing growing ragged the longer I stare, the effect I have on her sending wisps of arousal down my spine, hot and heady and completely desperate for her.

"Remember, I said I don't care for apologies," I say, kneeling on the mattress by her feet. Crawling over her, I palm the tops of her thighs and spread them as far as they'll go, the crescent shape of her glistening cunt making my heart race, my cock throbbing painfully. "I like an exchange."

Gulping, she nods. "Sex will be enough to make you forgive me?"

"Well, not *one* night, no." My fingers slide down her taut stomach, over her hips, and settle between her legs, swiping through her slick heat.

She bucks against the friction, and I quickly remove my hand, bringing my fingers to my lips and wrapping my tongue around the tips, almost coming from her taste alone.

Meeting her hungry brown gaze, I drop my hand again, this time slipping lower and rimming her entrance, my thumb swirling over her clit as one finger pushes in.

She clamps down around the intrusion, thighs already quaking as I start to move, stroking up against her inner walls in sync with the way my thumb massages her bundle of nerves.

"A lifetime of sex," I muse, gripping her throat with my free hand. "That'd probably do the trick."

She wraps her hand around my wrist, increasing the pressure against her neck, eyes flaring with a fire I have no intention of putting out. "An entire lifetime, hm?"

I nod, adding a second finger; she flutters around me, the seedlings of an impending orgasm. "I think that's a punishment that fits the crime."

"I think you're crazy."

Releasing her throat, I slide down her body and replace my thumb with the tip of my tongue, flicking against and suckling her clit until she can't form a coherent sentence, my fingers continuing their assault inside her tight heat.

Her juices coat my chin and fingers, soaking me with her need and making precum leak from my tip.

"Jesus, *Boyd*." Her hips lift off the bed, searching for release, and I press the flat of my palm against her stomach, pinning her in place, redoubling my efforts.

"If you can still talk, I must not be doing a good enough job." Pulling back an inch, I blow cool air over her pulsing clit, aching at the way she arches into everything I do to her, like she can't get enough.

Forming a seal around the top of her cunt, I add a third finger and drag out the motions, curling and sucking with a slow fervor that has her head whipping back and forth on the mattress.

When she spasms around my fingers, her inner muscles waxing and waning against me in warm waves, I hold my tongue flat against her clit, absorbing each pulse and feeling it shoot straight down to my balls.

They seize up as I withdraw from her angry, swollen sex, and she whimpers at the loss.

"Don't worry, princess, I'm gonna fill you right up." Jerking her hips down, I bend for a quick kiss, licking her tongue so she tastes herself, groaning when she laps it up.

Gripping her ankles, I drape them over my shoulders, teasing her lips with the head of my cock, before slowly sliding in.

Her warmth envelops me with every passing inch, and I bite my lip to keep from coming immediately. Bottoming out, the tops of my thighs slap against her ass, and she lets out a surprised squeak.

"Oh, fuck." Her words are a gasp, followed by a wiggle of her hips as she adjusts to having me inside of her again. "You're so *deep*."

"Christ," I mutter, my fingers digging into her thighs as she reaches up to cup her breasts, pinching and rolling her nipples as I start to move my hips against her, thrusting in and out in long, slow strokes, my piercing colliding with a spot that has her panting and canting upward.

"So fucking tight, princess. I love knowing I'm the only man who's been inside this perfect, juicy little cunt. You like me fucking it? Like me fucking you?"

She nods, frantic, her eyes drifting closed as I piston faster, harder, electricity shooting across my veins and collecting at the base of my spine.

"Want it for the rest of your life?"

Her eyes pop open, annoyance sparkling in her irises. "*Boyd.* Talk about manipulation."

Shrugging, I keep fucking her, the sound of our skin slapping together and her arousal fueling me on, making me catatonic. "I'll ask you again after I've filled you with my cum, if it helps. But my sentiment remains the same. All in or nothing, baby."

An animalistic groan tears from her throat as she clamps down around me, my words apparently her undoing—and all the answer I really need.

She works her clit with feverish fingers, stretching her orgasm out, and I feel myself starting to spill, losing my grip on control as she throws her head back in rapture.

Grasping her ankles in one hand, I shift so they rest together on one shoulder, seating myself so deep with each stroke that I feel like I'm inside her stomach.

"*Come,* princess. Fall apart for me."

Not that she needs the encouragement, but the sounds scraping up through her esophagus send a shock of white hot heat through my thighs, drawing my balls up for a split second before *I'm* coming, pumping myself dry inside of her, her cunt sucking up every ounce of my sticky seed like the greedy little bitch she is.

Collapsing beside her on the mattress, I reach over and pull Fiona into me, nuzzling the top of her head with my nose, inhaling that fucking rosy scent that I never seemed able to forget in the first place.

She wraps one leg over my hip, wincing slightly, and shifts until I can feel myself leaking out of her. "We're terrible at remembering condoms," she whispers against my throat, licking a bead of sweat from the base.

"The worst thing in the world would not be making a baby with you," I say, slinging my arm over her shoulders.

"We're kind of a mess."

"Messes can be cleaned up," I say, shrugging.

"You really want a lifetime with me?" She pushes up on her elbow, studying my face. "I have obsessive-compulsive disorder, you know. I can be a real nag. And I'm still mourning my mom's death, so you'll have to deal with random bouts of sadness and drives at two in the morning to get chocolate shakes in her honor."

"I see your issues, and raise you: a severely dysfunctional relationship with my depressed sister, who is now my ward until she graduates, not to mention the trauma from my childhood makes me kind of a dick, because I didn't really learn how to open up to people correctly. And I killed my mother tonight and have no remorse, so I'm sure that's something I'll have to talk about in therapy."

Her eyes light up. "Therapy?"

"Yeah. Riley only agreed to go if I did, so..." I trail off, reaching up to rub my thumb over her lips, mesmerized by the fact that I get to touch her like this again. The hurt from before doesn't magically disappear, but that isn't the point, anyway.

Hurts remain so you can remember the good shit. The laughter and the happiness, the fucking sunshine on a cloudy day. They're not there to dwell on, but to enhance everything else.

"I'm, ah… on medication." Her eyes drop to my chest, her teeth kneading her bottom lip. "For my issues. I used to take it when I was younger but stopped because I thought I could handle the anxiety and the obsessions. Turns out, I was wrong."

"Sounds like you're getting back on track, though," I breathe, gliding my lips along the crown of her head. In truth, I'm not surprised, given the change in tone from a few months ago to now.

"It'll probably be a struggle," Fiona says, tapping my shoulder with her index finger. "You and me."

Tap, tap, tap.

"I'm not afraid of the work."

I press a kiss to her nose, then pinch her nostrils closed for a second, throwing her off.

She giggles, pushing me away, and I cup her cheek, my heart beating in my throat as I cut myself open again for her, hoping this time she doesn't want to watch me bleed freely.

"Christ, you lit a match inside me that grew into this uncontainable fire, and I haven't been able to put it out since. I never stopped being in love with you, even when I wanted to hate you. I'm willing to work on my shit, but I don't want to do it without you by my side, in my bed at night, sitting on my face each morning. I just want to do life with you, and I'm sorry that I couldn't admit that months ago."

448

She bites her bottom lip, fluttering her lashes. "I love you, too. And before you stop me, I'm sorry, too. For walking away, and hurting you, and also for going out with Romeo. Sometimes I can be a real bitch."

"Sometimes it's hot," I breathe, making her laugh.

This time, when I lean in to kiss her, fireworks explode behind my vision, and when I bury myself between her legs for the second and third time tonight, euphoria washing over me with each release, I'm pretty fucking positive I've never been happier.

We curl up under the covers a little while later, talking about everything and nothing, trying to make up for the time we lost in the dark, as if the daytime might shatter the illusion of peace and contentment that's settled over us, erasing the sting of everything bad that's happened recently.

It doesn't. When I wake up the next morning, the sunshine glittering off of Fiona's perfect skin, my arms wrapped around her naked body, I know this isn't an illusion.

This is the real fucking deal, warts and all.

EPILOGUE

Fiona

Four Years Later

H *ow do people do this without peeing on themselves?*
Wiping my hand on a piece of toilet paper, I pull the plastic stick from between my legs, place the cap on the end, and set it on the counter, staring at the little window.

Anxiety grips my heart in its claws, although I can't quite pinpoint why. It's my college graduation party signifying the start of my life and career, so technically I should be praying silently for a negative result.

And yet, when the single line fills the screen, disappointment is what floods my chest cavity, rooting deep in my soul as I step back into my black gown and readjust my hat, washing my hands in the porcelain sink.

Wrapping the test in several rounds of toilet paper, I swing open the door and find Juliet standing right outside, a wide smile plastered on her face and a toddler who looks just like my brother propped on her hip, sucking on her little ravioli-sized fist.

Eden was something of an oopsie-baby, the product of a tropical honeymoon in the Caribbean and the stress of Juliet being hired as an ecology instructor at Stonemore Community, although I still wonder if Juliet wasn't feeling a bit competitive with her sister and the capo, who were working on their fifth kid at the time.

And I can't even make one.

"Well?" Juliet prompts, excitement dancing in her blue eyes. She bounces Eden in the air, waggling her eyebrows at me. "Are you giving E a cousin or what?"

"Jesus, why don't you announce it to the entire house?" I hiss, the disappointment festering into a sour wound and picking away at my insecurities.

To be honest, I'm a little worried, considering I stopped taking the shot for good back when Boyd and I officially started dating, and we don't use *anything* during our rigorous, spontaneous sex marathons. No foams, no pulling out, no post-romp abortifacients.

Sometimes, I think he's subconsciously trying to knock me up, but he won't admit it, and I wonder if it has to do with letting his sister down so much when she was a kid than anything else. If he's trying to atone for his past mistakes.

But there are nights he wraps me in his arms and just cradles my stomach until he falls asleep, like he's trying to imagine what it'd be like with a baby inside.

And on those nights, I want nothing more than to give him that. Seeing him step up and be a guardian to Riley, a real big brother, shows me he'd be an amazing dad.

Unfortunately, the universe seems to have other plans.

Juliet's face falls when she realizes where my hostility is coming from, and she frowns, pity curving the corners of her eyes downward. "Oh, Fi. I'm sorry." She squeezes my arm, offering me a half smile that only makes me feel worse. "Getting pregnant is a lot harder than the teenagers on TLC make it seem, you know. There's plenty of time to keep trying."

"I know," I say, swiping at a stray tear that spills from my eye. "I don't even know why I'm upset, it's not like I need to be pregnant right now, anyway. I *just* graduated."

"Who's pregnant?"

My brother's voice flits through the air behind me, and I close my eyes, wishing he didn't have ridiculously good hearing.

He comes over and grabs Juliet's cheeks, pulling her in for a sloppy kiss, before reaching for his daughter, tucking a dark brown curl behind her ear.

I feel Boyd's presence before he's even anywhere near me — it's this dark, heady essence that has me pulsing at the apex of my thighs when he's across a room, not even paying me any mind.

Except, that's the thing with him. Even when he's not looking, he's got an eye on me, and the knowledge of it is enough to keep me hot during public functions.

But right now, I can't muster up the same enthusiasm, sadness weighing down on my chest like a two-ton brick.

His large, inked hands cover my shoulders, and his lips graze my ear as he bends to greet me. "Princess," he rasps, the baritone of his voice sending liquid heat down my spine, making me tingle in spite of myself.

It's one of my favorite things about him — this uncanny ability to pull me, at least a little bit, from any episode, his body so finely tuned to mine that he can almost sense them before I do.

Therapy really does work wonders when you let it.

Kieran glances at his wife and then me, narrowing his eyes. "If one of you is pregnant, I demand to know this instant. I'm already up to my fucking balls in house renovations for this one, please tell me now if I need to add a third bedroom instead of a study."

"Pregnant?" Boyd repeats, hooking his chin over my head and pulling me back against his body.

Juliet ignores Boyd and smacks her husband in the stomach. "Stop fucking swearing around her, Kieran. Jesus. You know she's starting to copy us."

"*You* just swore," he points out.

"I don't do it when she's around."

"She's *right here!*"

Her nostrils flare, heat pulsating between the two of them that makes me uncomfortable, as Kieran's little sister.

Clearing his throat, Boyd excuses us, pulling me down the hall to one of the back decks off the cabin my father rented for the weekend in the Smoky Mountains.

I don't know why he decided to come all the way down here just to celebrate me for a weekend, but I'm not complaining about the vacation, even if it has been slightly ruined.

To be honest, I think my father's just been trying to get away from our toxic little town, and I can't even blame him. When I moved in with Boyd three years ago, staying in King's Trace wasn't something we were sure we wanted.

Too many ghosts exist for us there, haunting just by nature, and I'm not sure I want to spend my adult life bound to my demons the way everyone else I know is.

I want to be free.

Boyd leans against the warped wooden railing, the backdrop of the bluish-green mountains making him look more stunning than usual.

At thirty-one, the man looks a full decade younger, the sharp angles of his jaw, his honey-blond hair, and his tattooed body combining into one disgustingly hot specimen.

If looks could kill, Boyd Kelly would be a serial offender.

Most of the time, I try not to think about the fact that he actually is.

Not that my hands are clean themselves, though.

There was no funeral for LeeAnn Kelly four years ago, no obituary, no headstone erected in her honor. It was almost as if, when my brother disposed of her bones and ashes, he erased the evidence of her entire existence, which seemed to be a good catalyst for Boyd and Riley.

It wasn't closure, exactly, but it still gave them peace of mind, and I never questioned their feelings or lack thereof, because I knew I didn't really get it.

For all our evil doings, my family was still pretty normal, and while we barely mourned the loss of Murphy because of the way he acted toward the end of his life, losing my mother was still the single most devastating thing we'd had to go through.

So while Boyd relishes in the fact that his mother is gone, I miss mine every single day and drink chocolate shakes every weekend with Riley, who's become a good friend in the years

455

since we were forced to sit together and wait to see if her brother came back for us.

But I got lucky with my mother, and they didn't, so I reserve judgment, refusing to take on the responsibility of helping them cope in a healthy manner, when I work at my own mental health on a daily basis, sometimes still struggling with it.

That's what therapy and medication is for.

Besides, healing isn't linear. It's chaotic and subjective and completely up to the individual.

Clearing his throat, Boyd grabs my hand and pulls me to his chest, wrapping his arms around my waist. "Something to tell me?"

Sighing, I shake my head, dropping my chin to his chest. "No."

"You're not pregnant?"

Another tear slips out, and he catches it with his thumb, one eyebrow raising in concern. I groan, frustrated with my body's inability to control itself. "No, I'm not pregnant."

"And does that... upset you?"

I lift my face, searching his bright hazel gaze. "I... don't know. It's just, I'd been moody and nauseous for the last week, and thought maybe... and then I took a test a few minutes ago and it said I'm not. So. Sorry to disappoint."

Chuckling, he spreads his legs and fits me between them, cradling my jaw in his hands. "You could never disappoint me, princess."

A sob slips from my lips, and I press my forehead into the base of his throat, letting him soak up my tears and my insecurities. "Why do I feel like I've disappointed myself?"

He strokes up and down my back as I cry, feeling stupid for even being upset but also not being able to stop. When the tears have subsided, he lifts my chin and kisses me, licking along the seam of my lips. "This is a weekend for celebrating, baby. You're a freaking college graduate as of two days ago. Don't let something you aren't even sure you want ruin all that for you."

Sniffling, I nod, but can't find it in me to fully agree. "What if I *do* want it, though?"

The air charges between us, electric heat tethering me to him as his eyes darken and his grip tightens around my chin. "You want me to put a baby in you?"

Biting my lip, I don't break his stare as I nod, my heart racing at the thought of rejection. The presence of the unknown.

But unlike before, I don't run from it this time. I look it straight in the face, even though sometimes it hurts, and I push through.

"Well," he breathes, bringing my hand up to stroke his erection through his dress pants, already hard for me. "What princess wants, princess gets. But I'm gonna make you work for it."

With us, I'd expect nothing less.

We're a work in progress, but that's kind of true for everything, anyway. The whole point of life isn't to attain

457

perfection, but to keep improving. Perfection is madness, a concept contrived to bring out our fear of failure.

There's no way to know what the future holds, and I'm learning to be okay with that. It's scary, that uncertainty, but there's also a kind of excitement within.

The promise of *potential*.

Boyd pushes me to my knees, and I start to glance behind me to see if we're visible inside the cabin, but he fists my hair, keeping my mouth level with his prominent bulge. "What if someone comes—"

"*Someone's* going to come, all right."

He rubs his thumb over my lips, and I take that as my cue to undo his zipper, pulling his length from the confines of his pants and licking the bead of precum that's already leaking from the tip.

"And then someone else will come, and we'll come together, until we're a panting, sweaty mess of cum and depravity. I'm not leaving the mountains until I've knocked you up, Fiona Ivers, so I hope you're ready."

Grinning, I wrap my lips around the crown of his dick, eager to get started. "I love you," I moan around him, reveling in the way it makes his entire body tense.

"I love you too, princess." He strokes my cheek, then applies pressure to the back of my head, guiding me farther onto his shaft. "Now, no more talking."

The End

ALSO BY SAV R. MILLER

King's Trace Antiheroes Series

Sweet Surrender (Caroline & Elia)

Sweet Solitude (Kieran & Juliet)

Sweet Sacrifice (Boyd & Fiona)

Monsters and Muses Series

Promises and Pomegranates – Releasing 2021

Standalones

PFR – Releasing 2021

Secrets and Silk (Twisted Tales Collection) – Releasing Winter
2021

ACKNOWLEDGEMENTS

The fact that I'm writing these at all, given that I very nearly abandoned this story and my entire writing career multiple times while writing it, is a freaking miracle. Seriously. Writing is my single greatest passion in this life, and I can't imagine wanting to do anything else, and yet there were more than a few times during this one that I almost gave up.

But, as we can see… I didn't.

I finished the damn thing, and now the King's Trace Antiheroes series is complete.

Long live the kings and their queens.

Anyway, I just wanted to acknowledge myself first. I don't usually give myself any credit, which is weird, because I'm the one writing. And I'm a badass bitch who does not quit.

More importantly, I want to give an obvious special shoutout to my very best friend, my soul sister, my life guru. Emily, once again I could not have written this book without you. Thank you for your *constant* support, for not giving up on me even when I'm ready to, for being the best person in the entire world, and every single laugh in between. I love you the most.

For those of you who don't have an Emily McIntire in your lives, you need one. But not mine. Get your own.

To my man and my four-legged son: without you two I'd probably be wasting away, having forgotten to eat or get some exercise when on strict deadlines. Thank you for everything.

To the friends and family who stick around even when I ghost them for weeks because I'm truly the worst at replying: thank you for loving me enough not to ditch my sorry ass. Let's make more plans and not go through with them, yeah? Love you guys.

To Clarise, cover designer aficionado: thank you for making my vision for this bad boy come to life. Your talent astounds me.

To Ellie and Rosa, editor and proofreader extraordinaire: thank you for existing. You make my manuscripts gorgeous. Thank you for being amazing and not making fun of the amount of times you changed "further" to "farther."

To AJ, my multi-talented friend: you rock. Thank you for being you.

To the girls, Kayleigh, Greer, Emily, and Christina: y'all are a constant source of happiness and light in this world, and I'm lucky you put up with me.

To Savannah Richey with Peachy Keen Author Services and the best PA in the world: thank you for making this release (and the last!) so stress-free for me, and for taking some of the stress out of my life. You're the best.

To my betas, Zoe, Ariel, and Michelle: thank you for taking me on even though it was crazy last minute, and thank you for your support and dedication. This book wouldn't be what it is without you three. You guys are incredible.

To my ARC team: I love you guys. There's such a special place in my heart for those of you who've decided you want to permanently read/review my stuff, and I can't thank you enough. Thanks for hitching your wagon to mine.

To every reader and promoter in between: thank you, from the very bottom of my heart. King's Trace may be over, but these books live on through you. There's no point to any of this without you. You literally make the world go round. Thank you for loving the King's Trace series and making my dreams come true.

And to anyone I'm forgetting, this is also for you.

Sav R. Miller writes dark, contemporary romance with morally gray characters and steam that'll make you blush. She prefers the villains in most stories and thinks everyone deserves happily-ever-after. Currently, Sav lives in central Kentucky with her fiancé and a Labrador/Great Pyrenees mix named Lord Byron. She loves sitcoms, silence, and sardonic humor.

Visit savrmiller.com for more!

Made in the USA
Monee, IL
25 June 2021